BRENDA NOVAK

Take Me Home for Christmas

D0037034

H HARLEQUIN® MIRA®

PLEASE RECYCLE · THIS PRODUCT IS RECYCLABLE

Recycling programs
for this product may
not exist in your area.

ISBN-13: 978-0-7783-1546-9

TAKE ME HOME FOR CHRISTMAS

HARLEQUIN®
www.Harlequin.com

Printed in U.S.A.

To Sandra Standley and her mother, Diane.
I think you two have read every book I've ever written.
Thanks for your tremendous enthusiasm and support!

Dear Reader,

I've had many of you request Ted and Sophia's story—so I'm excited to see it published, especially at Christmas because Christmas is such a perfect time for forgiveness, and that's what Sophia longs for. If you've read the rest of the books in this series, you already know that she needed to learn a few lessons. Fortunately, they were nothing that the school of hard knocks couldn't teach her. By the time I finished this story I admired her as much as (or even more than) all the other characters in Whiskey Creek, even the ones who've lived exemplary lives. I hope you'll agree as you come to know her and her situation better.

I am often asked if my Whiskey Creek books can be read as stand-alone stories or if they need to be read in order. The answer to that question is, yes, they can be read alone and should be just as enjoyable. So dive in and meet the group of friends who've made Whiskey Creek "The Heart of Gold Country."

Please visit my website at www.brendanovak.com for more information about this book and all the others I've written (I think I'm getting close to forty-five, although it's been a while since I've counted). If you're all caught up on Whiskey Creek, you might be interested in trying my other small-town series (with a total of eight books) set in the fictional town of Dundee, Idaho, until *Come Home to Me* (Aaron and Presley's story) is released in April 2014.

At my website you can also drop me an email, enter my many giveaways and participate in my annual online auction for diabetes research. So far, we've managed to raise nearly $2 million to help those (like my son) who have diabetes.

Enjoy!

Brenda

WHISKEY CREEK Cast of Characters

Major Characters

Cheyenne Christensen: Helps Eve Harmon run Little Mary's B and B (formerly the Gold Nugget). Married to **Dylan Amos,** who owns Amos Auto Body.

Gail DeMarco: Owns a public relations firm in L.A. Married to movie star **Simon O'Neal.**

Ted Dixon: Bestselling thriller writer.

Eve Harmon: Manages Little Mary's B and B, which is owned by her family.

Kyle Houseman: Owns a solar panel business. Formerly married to **Noelle Arnold.**

Baxter North: Stockbroker in San Francisco.

Noah Rackham: Professional cyclist. Owns Crank It Up bike shop. Married to **Adelaide Davies,** chef and manager of Just Like Mom's restaurant, owned by her grandmother.

Riley Stinson: Contractor.

Callie Vanetta: Photographer. Married to **Levi McCloud/Pendleton,** veteran of Afghanistan.

Other Recurring Characters

The Amos Brothers: Dylan, Aaron (who was in a relationship with Presley), **Rodney, Grady** and **Mack.**

Olivia Arnold: Kyle Houseman's true love but married to **Brandon Lucero,** Kyle's stepbrother.

Presley Christensen: Cheyenne's sister.

Sophia DeBussi: Jilted Ted Dixon to marry **Skip DeBussi,** investment guru and richest man in town.

Joe DeMarco: Gail DeMarco's older brother, owns the Whiskey Creek Gas-n-Go.

Phoenix Fuller: In prison. Mother of **Jacob Stinson,** who is being raised by his father, Riley.

1

Sophia DeBussi's husband was gone. As in...*disappeared*. Nowhere to be found. At ninety feet, the *Legacy* was a sizable yacht—Skip never bought anything except the very best—but not so sizable that a full-grown man could easily be overlooked. The six-member crew had just helped Sophia and her thirteen-year-old daughter scour every inch of the boat.

Other than his cell phone, which he wasn't answering, Skip's things were where they should be, but he was not.

Holding back her long hair, Sophia squinted against the sunshine glinting off the water, trying to see the coast of Brazil a few miles to starboard. Could her husband have gone for an early-morning swim and somehow reached land?

That was a possibility, but it was a remote one. Why would he go off on his own? It was too windy to enjoy the beach today. And although he traveled all over the world for business, she'd never heard of him meeting anyone in Rio de Janeiro.

Besides, he'd planned this trip for their thirteenth

anniversary because he wanted to spend quality time as a family. She couldn't imagine he was working, not when this vacation was supposed to be about starting over, about saving their troubled marriage. He'd said he wouldn't take *one* call. If he'd made that promise just to her, maybe she wouldn't have relied on it. He'd said such things before and hadn't followed through. But he'd also promised their daughter, and he and Alexa were very close.

So...where was he?

Sophia gazed down at the water itself. Had he fallen overboard and drowned in the choppy Atlantic?

That thought led to a surge of relief. It was macabre to wish anyone dead, but only if Skip was gone for good would she ever escape him. She'd lived with him long enough to know he'd never willingly let her go. He'd said as much.

The moment Alexa came to the railing to stand beside her, guilt replaced the relief she'd been feeling. Her poor daughter might have lost her father. How could she be *happy* about that?

"What happened, Mom?" Lexi asked, her big blue eyes filling with tears.

Sophia put an arm around her child's thin shoulders. "I don't know, sweetheart." She kept going over the past twenty-four hours in her mind, but could point to nothing out of the ordinary. Skip had gone to bed with her last night at eleven, as usual. He'd demanded sex, as usual. If he was around, he insisted on some sexual favor at least once a day. She was pretty sure he slept with other women when he was traveling, especially since he was often gone for a week or longer. But she never tried to check up on him. She just did what she had to when he was home to keep the peace, to survive. She knew how he'd act if she refused him. Even if he didn't strike her, he'd sulk for days.

Except for the embarrassment of having to tell everyone, including their daughter, that she'd tripped and fallen into a door or slammed on her brakes and hit the steering wheel, she would've hated the sulking even more. Sometimes it lasted far longer than the bruises.

Alexa wiped her wet cheeks. "You *really* don't remember when he got up this morning?"

They'd already been over this. Sophia *didn't* remember. She didn't rise as early as he did. It wasn't as if he'd allow her to have a job. On a school day, she typically went back to bed after Alexa left, staying there until ten or so. Then she'd get up slowly, work on maintaining her beauty, which was all-important to Skip, and drink away the rest of the afternoon. Alcohol was the one thing that seemed capable of dulling the disappointment, not to mention the boredom, she lived with on a constant basis.

But it also gave him a club to use when he needed it. *I thought I was getting something special when I married you. You were someone, remember? The mayor's only child. The most popular girl in school. Now look at you. You're nothing but a lazy drunk.*

She tried to shove those hateful words into the back of her mind, where they resided. They made her crave a gin and tonic, but it was too early for that. She couldn't have one, anyway, she reminded herself. Not only had she just spent thirty days in rehab, she'd promised Skip, as part of their "starting over," that she'd really quit the booze this time. He'd threatened to have her committed to a mental institution like her mother if she didn't.

She wasn't sure what he'd use to make her seem crazy, but he'd figure it out. Her mother's condition, the fact that there was mental illness in the family, definitely wouldn't work in her favor.

"Mom?" Lexi said.

Sophia pulled herself out of the whirlpool of her thoughts. "He didn't wake me, honey. I'm sorry. He didn't tell me he was leaving, either. I would've remembered."

"Are you *sure?* He says you forget a lot. That you'd live in a bottle if you could."

He often criticized her to Lexi. He was the dazzling father who swooped in bearing outlandish gifts. The parent who'd promised her a Porsche for her sixteenth birthday. He never had to raise his voice to insist she do chores, finish her dinner or improve her grades, because he wasn't around long enough. "I've quit drinking," Sophia said softly. "That's why I went away, remember? Why you had to stay with Grandma and Grandpa."

Alexa didn't pursue the old argument. She was too bewildered by her father's disappearance. "This is just so...*weird.*"

"It *is* weird." Sophia could tell that the captain and his mates agreed. She'd heard them asking each other if anyone had seen Mr. DeBussi on deck in the wee hours. No one had. No one had heard him, either. But with the engine chugging away and the waves splashing against the sides of the boat, would anyone notice if he fell overboard?

"I keep thinking he has to be here *somewhere.*" Dressed in cut-offs and a white tank, Alexa leaned on the railing as her troubled eyes ran over the deck, the bar, the stairs going below. "I'm *so* worried."

Sophia didn't want her to have to accept the worst quite yet. She didn't want her to suffer at all. Alexa was the only reason she'd remained in her loveless marriage. Skip had told her she'd never see her daughter again if she left, and she believed him. *He* had the support of a rich and powerful family who lived in the same small town they did. With her own mother diagnosed with schizophrenia and her father dead, *she* had no one. "He might turn up."

A fresh tear rolled down Lexi's cheek. "But you heard the captain. He said there's no way Dad could've reached shore. *No one* could swim that far."

The captain would've been right had he been talking about anyone else. But he didn't know Skip, not like she did. Skip could do anything he set his mind to. Sophia had never met such a strong-willed individual. Or such a controlling one.

She pulled her daughter into a hug. "We've contacted the U.S. Consulate, and they've called the police. We'll be docking at Rio to wait while they check the city and the beaches. We won't leave without him. Let's not give up hope too soon."

Alexa's head bumped against Sophia's chest as she nodded, but she was obviously struggling to believe those measures would do any good. She couldn't picture her father jumping over the side in the middle of the night and swimming for shore—and neither could Sophia.

The captain approached. "I've secured a slip at Marina de Gloria, Mrs. DeBussi," he said. "We should be in port in less than thirty minutes."

"Thank you, Captain Armstrong."

His nod had the same effect as a salute. He turned away, but then he paused.

"Is there anything else?" she asked.

"I just—" he faced her again "—I wanted to warn you."

A sense of foreboding chilled her despite the ninety-degree weather. "About…"

"The police. When I spoke to them on the radio, they…they asked me if…" He cleared his throat as his eyes flicked to Alexa, and she nudged her daughter toward the stairs.

"Lexi, why don't you go below and check our bedroom one more time, okay? Make sure everything of Daddy's is there, even his shaving kit."

"We *know* it's there," she protested.

Sophia gave her another little push. "Check again, will you?"

Reluctantly, her daughter headed to the stairs, casting a frown over one shoulder before she disappeared from view.

"What is it, Captain Armstrong?" Sophia asked.

"They had questions about your marriage, Mrs. De-Bussi. If I've ever seen the two of you fight, that sort of thing."

He *hadn't* seen them fight. No one had. Skip kept up appearances at all costs. His reputation as the man who had everything meant more to him than something as malleable as the truth. He never grew violent when someone else was around, and that included Lexi. If he got upset, he simply punished Sophia later.

But anyone who was astute could no doubt feel the tension. Sophia was terrified of him. Even when he wasn't overtly abusive, she endured many small but vicious reprisals.

"And you told them...what?" Her heart thumped so loudly she was afraid he could hear it. Skip wouldn't like this intrusion into their personal lives, so why had he left her vulnerable to it?

"That I don't know anything about your private life. But...I want to reassure you that even if I did, I wouldn't speak of it."

She found his loyalty comforting, especially because she would never have taken it for granted. She barely knew him, had hardly ever spoken to him. It didn't matter that he was old enough to be her father, or that he was married himself. Her husband was too jealous. Any interaction would've risked the captain's job. "Thank you, Captain Armstrong."

"You're welcome. I have the utmost respect for you, Mrs. DeBussi. But..."

She pulled the gauzy white scarf she'd paired with her summer sheath dress tighter. "Yes?"

He lowered his voice. "You should be prepared. They will ask you the same thing."

Suddenly she grasped why he was telling her this. "You don't mean... They don't think *I* might've harmed Mr. DeBussi?" The irony of anyone suspecting *her* of hurting *him* almost made her laugh.

"They have to rule out that possibility."

She could understand why, of course. But how would she convince them? Although the U.S. Consulate was acting as a liaison, she'd be dealing with foreign police; she couldn't even speak their language. What if they arrested her?

Her face must've betrayed her panic because the captain took her elbow and led her to a chaise. It was nothing he'd risk doing in her husband's presence, but she was grateful for his kindness.

"They won't be able to prove anything, Mrs. De-Bussi," he said. "You just need to remain strong and insistent."

They won't be able to prove anything? What did that mean? That he suspected her—but didn't blame her? She dared not ask him to clarify. Forcing a smile, she said, "Of course."

If only "strong" felt like a possibility. She'd been strong once, even willful and rebellious. She regretted a great many things about those days, had been paying for her sins ever since. She considered living with Skip to be part of her penance. But the one attribute she'd lost that she wished she'd retained was her fighting spirit.

Maybe it was there, somewhere. But having a child had completely disarmed her.

2

Sophia slipped out of Alexa's room. She was finally asleep, and Sophia was grateful. It had been a long, hard day. Although she could scarcely believe it, there'd been no word from Skip. As promised, the police had met them at noon, when they docked at the marina. While a handful of crime-scene techs went through the boat, searching for blood or any other clue, an investigator had spoken to her. In a heavy Portuguese accent, he'd asked all the questions one might expect under the circumstances.

And Sophia had lied in response to almost every one of them.

What made you decide to take a trip to Rio?

Where better to celebrate our anniversary? We've been meaning to get away for months.

Do you consider you and your husband to be a happy couple?

Oh, yes. We've never been more in love.

Is there anyone, maybe a member of the crew, who might've been angry with your husband?

Of course not. Skip is wonderful, well-liked by everyone.

Her muscles had ached with tension, but she dared not tell the truth, especially when she was asked who might want him dead. She was pretty sure she was the only one. Mr. Armstrong's three mates were new hires. They'd met Skip at the beginning of the voyage so they'd had very little time to get acquainted. And although it was possible the captain, the cook and the maid found him as egotistical and overbearing as she did, without him they wouldn't have a job. None of them had any reason to push him into the ocean.

So where had he gone? They had no more answers now than before they'd docked. But, thank God, the day was over and she had the night to try to recover.

Taking a deep breath to calm her nerves, she went up on deck and gazed out at the city. Rio was lit up like an amusement park, but it was a lonely sight as she sat on the *Legacy* so far from California, wondering what had happened to her husband.

Her cell phone lay on the table nearby. Today, Carlotta, the maid who cleaned up after them and saw to their personal needs, had helped her make arrangements with her carrier so she'd have service while she was out of the States. No doubt Skip's phone had had international calling from the beginning but, until now, there'd been no need for Sophia to have it. She rarely spoke to anyone outside Whiskey Creek.

After eyeing it for several minutes—as though it was a snake ready to strike—she picked it up and dialed. She'd tried calling Skip earlier, on the captain's phone. Then, when the police were here, they'd called together. Skip hadn't answered, of course, but that didn't mean he wouldn't.

"This is Skip DeBussi of DeBussi Worldwide Investments. I'll be unavailable until October 23rd. My assistant, Kelly Pctruzzi, will handle any work-related matters in my absence—"

She hung up before he could recite Kelly's contact information. She'd checked in with Skip's assistant several times today. He hadn't heard from her husband, either, which made no sense. Kelly always knew where to reach him in case there was an emergency.

If Skip was alive, he had to pick up at some point. He never went anywhere without his phone, and it certainly hadn't been left on the boat.

Determined to put an end to what felt like a bizarre dream, Sophia tried him again. And again and again. If the police checked his phone records, it'd look like she was frantic to speak to him. But, in her heart of her hearts, she knew she was merely trying to confirm that he wasn't going to answer.

The calls went directly to voice mail. Although she listened to his greeting every time, she left only one message. "Skip? Where are you?"

"Mrs. DeBussi?"

The voice didn't belong to her husband. Startled in spite of that, she jumped and hit the end button. "Yes, Captain Armstrong?"

The *Legacy*'s captain came closer, his tall body momentarily blocking the lights of the city behind him. "You didn't eat much dinner. Can I bring you a plate of cheese and crackers? Or a glass of wine?"

She *definitely* wanted a drink. Some chardonnay would relax her, help her get through what promised to be a rough night of wondering and waiting. But she knew she wouldn't be able to stop at one glass. And she needed a clear head. Her daughter was depending on her for emotional strength and direction. The last thing she wanted to do was let Alexa down or prove Skip right—that she was nothing but a lazy drunk.

"I'm fine. Thank you."

He seemed disappointed that she'd refused. He didn't know she'd recently come out of rehab, or he would never have offered her wine. Skip, embarrassed by her addiction, had kept her stint at New Beginnings in Los Angeles a secret from everyone except his parents, who'd watched Alexa so he could work while she was gone.

"You should have some food to keep up your strength," the captain coaxed.

Sophia wanted to eat for that reason but couldn't swallow a bite. "I'm okay, really."

With a nod, he moved toward the stairs. "I'm going to turn in, then."

It was only nine o'clock, but why shouldn't he enjoy some private time? There wasn't much anyone could do to change the situation, except wait and see if Skip returned. Although the police had tried to find him by tracking his cell phone, there'd been no signal. According to them, he hadn't placed a single call since early last night, when he'd talked to his office.

"Good night, Mr. Armstrong," she said, "and rest easy. There's nothing a ship's captain needs to worry about while we're docked at the marina."

"This ship's captain is worried about *you*," he told her.

She glanced up. The light of the moon let her see the sympathy on his ruddy face.

"I'm sorry, you remind me of my daughter," he said. "I can't help feeling protective of you."

Sophia might've been surprised, except she had that effect on most men, not just the fatherly types. Her mother used to laugh about it. *You're like a china doll,* she'd say. *Flawless but fragile. There isn't a more potent combination for attracting the opposite sex.*

Skip, of course, had put a darker spin on it. *You're like Marilyn Monroe. You have the kind of sex appeal that drives men crazy. You've constantly got them sniffing around, like dogs after a bitch in heat.*

The first time Skip had ever hit her was following a chili cook-off sponsored by his wealthy parents. His own cousin, visiting from Denver, had pulled out a chair for her, and that was all it had taken to set him off— once they got home, of course. He'd accused her of flirting, of making his cousin believe she found him attractive.

"I appreciate your concern," she said to Armstrong, "but...I—I'll get through this somehow."

"And if your husband doesn't come back? Will you be able to get through *that?*"

Her life would be far easier than if he did. But she couldn't admit it. "I'll do my best for my daughter's sake."

"I hope it won't come to that."

She didn't say anything, merely smiled as he left. Then she called Kelly to see if there'd been any news.

"Mrs. DeBussi?"

Her husband's thirtysomething assistant sounded impatient, upset. At first, Sophia felt guilty, assuming she'd bothered him after hours. It was dark where she was—but then she remembered that Rio was five hours *ahead* of California. Back home, it was three in the afternoon.

"I'm sorry to interrupt you again," she began, slightly put off, but he broke in before she could go any further.

"No, I'm glad to hear from you. *Relieved.* As a matter of fact, I was about to call."

A tight ball of nerves formed in her belly. He'd never been excited to hear from her before. During their brief encounters, even the ones earlier today, he'd treated her with professional courtesy but that was it. Skip kept his business completely separate from his personal life. He hardly ever talked about what he worked on from day to day, or the places he went—unless it was to brag about some multi-million-dollar deal he'd closed.

"You've heard from my husband," she said.

"Not a peep. But I *really* need to talk to him. He's not back yet?"

She might've been glad there was still no sign of the man she'd grown to hate, but the anxiety in Kelly's voice kept her on edge. "No. What's going on?"

"The FBI is here. They're looking for him."

So soon? She'd had no idea the Brazilian police were going to contact *the FBI.* They hadn't mentioned it. Did the FBI get involved in every case involving a missing American? Maybe if that American disappeared while out of the country. "That was fast. He's only been gone fifteen hours or so."

The tension in his voice rose a notch. "They're not here for the reason you think. They have a search warrant."

Sophia got to her feet. "What does that mean?"

"They're demanding access to the offices, the files, everything." Kelly's emotions were obviously escalating toward panic. But other than an occasional speeding ticket—usually when he was driving his Ferrari since he had a chauffeur take him to and from the company offices in San Francisco—Skip had *never* been in trouble with the law.

"Why?"

He seemed to make an effort to keep his voice down. "I guess…I guess he's the target of a probe. They plan to bring him up on criminal charges."

Sophia was so stunned she couldn't speak.

"Mrs. DeBussi?"

After clearing her throat, she managed to find her voice. "I'm here. What—what kind of criminal charges?"

"There's a whole list. Just a sec, they gave me something—" She heard a flustered sigh, then sheets of paper rattling in the background before he came back on the line. "Here it is. He's looking at several counts of conspiracy to commit mail and wire fraud, securities fraud and engaging in monetary transactions in property derived from specified unlawful activity."

After such a windy day, the night was, by contrast, calm. But Sophia hardly felt calm inside. Conspiracy. Fraud. Unlawful…whatever that was. Those charges sounded like a jumble of very bad words. "And that adds up to…"

"From what I understand, he could go to prison for the rest of his life."

Knees weak, Sophia felt behind her for a chair and sank into it. "It *can't* be as bad as that."

"They claim to have proof," he said, "and they think they're going to uncover more in their search."

"They *claim?*" she echoed. "Is it true? *Could* it be

true? Wouldn't you know if he was doing something that…terrible?"

"How would I? He only tells me what he wants me to hear, and he's never said anything about fraud. But—" he lowered his voice "—he *has* been acting strange lately."

Somehow she'd missed every sign of that. But she'd been in rehab for a month, during which he could've done almost anything. During the first two weeks, she wasn't even allowed to talk to him. And she'd been absolutely focused on maintaining her sobriety ever since. "In what way?"

"Distracted. Worried."

"Why didn't you say so earlier?" she asked, appalled. "When we called, you claimed everything was fine." Kelly hadn't seemed concerned in the least. He'd said that maybe Skip had arranged for a boat to pick him up and take him to Rio or somewhere else in Brazil.

"I was trying to keep the business running here and I wanted to handle the call the way he'd expect me to. What if I'd gotten everyone worked up and then he returned by nightfall? I never thought…I mean, I guessed a particular deal might not be going well, but there are always ups and downs when you're managing investments. I had no idea his problems were *this* serious."

Kelly had referred to *prison.* In a town the size of Whiskey Creek, the humiliation of criminal prosecution would be devastating—not just for her and Skip and his parents, who were so proud of him, but for Alexa, who'd had everything money could buy and was used to feeling important and admired.

"Those charges you mentioned—mail fraud and… and securities fraud. They're not murder. They're not anything...*violent.* If he gets a good attorney, he'll be able to stay out of prison, won't he?"

"It's white-collar crime, but those are serious charges."

She rubbed her temples. She had *such* a headache. She needed a drink but refused to succumb to the pressure. How could she handle all this if she was drunk? *Lexi needs me.*

"They're not coming after you, too...."

"They haven't said, but I can't imagine they are. All they have to do is follow the money to know *I* haven't been involved." But his job was in jeopardy. That couldn't be easy to hear, especially out of the blue.

"I'm still not clear on what he's done," she said. "Or what they *say* he's done."

"He's stolen money, Mrs. DeBussi."

But he always had so much. Why would he need to steal? "From who?"

"From his investors."

Oh, God... "Then what's the mail fraud?"

"I can't say how that figures in, exactly. It's one of the charges. According to a special agent by the name of Freeman, your husband's been taking investors' funds and funneling them into private accounts and privately held companies instead of putting them into the SLD Growth Fund. Maybe they mailed him the payments. The FBI is asking a lot of questions but they're not giving a lot of answers."

Funneling money into personal accounts? Why would Skip be so dishonest? "He wouldn't cheat anyone. He must've been borrowing the money. He'll pay it back."

"Impossible."

"Excuse me?"

Kelly's whisper grew louder. "Do you have any idea how much we're talking about?"

Her eyes burned with unshed tears. She wanted to be home where she could find solace in the familiar. "No. How much?"

"Sixty million dollars."

Sophia felt faint. "That's a huge amount of money." Even to her, and she was used to hearing Skip talk in big figures.

"More than he'll ever be able to come up with."

"So...who's been hurt? Which investors?"

"Anyone who gave him money for the SLD Fund."

"And the SLD Fund is..."

"The money that was supposed to be invested in a diverse array of assets and publicly traded equities."

Wait. The "publicly traded equities" reference jogged her memory. She'd heard Skip talking about the SLD Fund with various people around town. That was the big moneymaking opportunity he'd been pushing for the past year. "You're saying these investors have lost their money? There's no way to get it back?"

"Now you're catching on," Kelly retorted. "I'm guessing he wouldn't have taken it if he didn't need it, but that doesn't make this right. He's been struggling to cover our overhead here for months. I thought he'd get the finances straightened out when he closed the next deal. That's what he told me. He said he had a big one coming down the pike. But now...I'm wondering if he's been saying that just to buy time, so I'd stick around until the end and help him keep up appearances."

"You're making it sound like...like DeBussi Invest-ments is defunct. Broke!"

"It *should* sound that way. Because unless he's sitting on a secret stash somewhere, it's true."

"That can't be possible." Skip always had money. Although he'd entered the business world right out of high school and hadn't attended a day of college, he'd been independently wealthy by the time she married him, when they were twenty-two. And he'd grown richer as the years passed. Not long ago, *California Business,* a respected magazine, had touted him the best investment consultant in the state.

"But if there's no money in DeBussi Investments, what about our *personal* finances?" she asked. "Maybe *I* can pay some of it back." At least to the people she knew.

"I have no idea how things stand on the personal side," Kelly said.

That gave Sophia *some* hope, but she found out soon enough that she wouldn't be able to right Skip's wrongs. When she tried to buy fuel for the *Legacy* the next morning, she learned that the FBI had frozen *all* of their bank and credit accounts.

3

Sophia squinted against the bright afternoon sun. She'd never been fond of her in-laws, especially Skip's mother. Generally, they treated her with a sort of mild neglect, and she pretended not to notice, but occasionally she detected real disdain. She could only assume that her husband had complained about her to them the way he did to Lexi. She'd never said or done anything that should put her out of favor—but there *was* her drinking problem. Their disapproval and their coolness toward her made it difficult to turn to them, even in her hour of need. She'd called them today because they deserved to know that their son was missing. He was fairly close to them, as close as he was to anybody, and she needed money to fly Alexa and her home. It wasn't as if she could go to *her* parents for help. It'd been twelve years since her father had died of prostate cancer, fourteen since her mother had been hospitalized for good.

"What are you talking about?" Sharon snapped. "This can't be true."

Sophia had just told her that Skip hadn't been on the boat when she woke up yesterday and she hadn't seen him since. She'd decided not to mention the FBI. She figured hearing that their son had disappeared and was likely dead would be hard enough; they could deal with the rest once she got home and had more information. Despite the harsh reality of her current financial situation, or perhaps because of it, Sophia kept hoping that there was a logical explanation—other than what the facts seemed to suggest.

"Sharon, it's true," she said. "I have no idea where he could be. I contacted the Brazilian police, of course, and they've been searching ever since. But it's been thirty-two hours and there's no sign of him."

"Have you called his cell?"

"Over and over."

"He must've had business in Rio," his mother said in her usual brusque manner. She always acted as if she had all the answers. "You know how he is. He works nonstop."

"Are you saying he *swam* to his appointment? Because that's the only way he could've gotten there—unless we all missed the fact that a boat came alongside us in the night."

Silence met this response. Sharon had heard the sarcasm, but at this particular moment Sophia couldn't tolerate her mother-in-law's supercilious attitude. She was having trouble holding herself together. Although she'd made it through the entire night without a drop of alcohol, she hadn't slept. Her eyes felt like sandpaper, her head and her stomach ached, and she had some terrible truths to face—truths that would change her whole life. If Skip didn't come back, if he didn't straighten out the mess he'd made, she'd have no way to survive, let alone take care of their daughter.

She stared at her naked ring finger. On their tenth anniversary, Skip had replaced her wedding ring with a five-carat diamond that was worth over two hundred thousand dollars. But when she entered rehab, he'd taken it back, saying he wanted to have it appraised for insurance purposes....

In light of what she'd been told during the past two days, she suspected it hadn't gone to an appraiser.

"I'm sorry." She hid her hand from view, so she wouldn't have to be reminded of the ring, and struggled to gain control of her emotions. "I—I'm upset, as you can imagine. Like I said, I have no idea what happened, why Skip isn't here or where he might be. I hope he's okay, that everything will end well. But I desperately want to come home. I *have* to come home. I can wait for him there."

"It's been a day—*one* day. Surely you wouldn't give up hope and leave your husband so quickly."

Flinching, she grappled for an explanation that wouldn't include admitting that the FBI had accused Skip of being a criminal. She knew what that would do to his parents. They thought he walked on water. They'd always preferred him to his brother, who worked as a plumber and had five kids with four different women. "I *can't* stay here. There's been a...a mix-up with our accounts, and I'm not able to cover food and supplies or pay the crew."

"Good Lord, now you're talking about *money*? What's that got to do with finding Skip before it's too late?"

"If you could just wire enough for me to get Alexa home... Then I'll explain everything, or as much as I know, anyway."

There was talking on the other end.

"Sophia?" The phone had switched hands. This was Dale, Skip's father.

She gripped her cell tighter. "Yes?"

"What the hell's going on?"

As a rule, men treated her better than women. That was why she typically preferred them. But her father-in-law was a notable exception. "It…it's unbelievable," she said and told him what she'd told Sharon.

"My son would *never* leave his family high and dry," he said when she'd finished. "It must be foul play, a—a kidnapping."

"There's been no ransom note."

"Then something else happened. He wouldn't abandon you and Alexa on that damn boat if he'd had a choice."

A tear dripped down her cheek because she was pretty sure Skip had done exactly that, and she felt terrible for their daughter. How could he promise Alexa a wonderful two weeks at sea as a family—and then disappear?

"You—you're probably right," she said but only to get through this phone call without an argument. The more she considered the timing of Skip's disappearance, the more she believed he'd gone on the run. He *had* to have known the FBI was closing in on him. Or maybe some of his investors had been pressing him for the fabulous return he'd promised, and he'd run out of excuses.

"Did he have problems with the crew?" his father asked.

Was he talking murder? "No, none. The crew is great. No one would hurt him."

"Someone must've done *something*, by God! And

now you want to leave, to come home without him? When he's probably in trouble—maybe even stranded in the ocean? He could need your help!"

The lump in Sophia's throat made speaking an effort. "I told you, I don't have the money to stay. I—I can't even provide the necessities for Lex. Think of your granddaughter, please. I need to get her home."

"*Why* don't you have money? This whole thing stinks, Sophia. What is it? What aren't you telling us?"

She dropped her head, resting it in her free hand. She realized that this conversation couldn't wait, after all. "The FBI has frozen our bank accounts, Dale."

"Let go of the phone," he told his wife. Then he spoke into the receiver again. "Did you say *FBI?*"

She sighed. "I'm afraid so."

"Why would the FBI freeze your accounts? The FBI doesn't do that unless…unless—"

"Unless they have reason," she finished for him. "They claim Skip's been defrauding his investors."

"What?"

"It's true. They've frozen all the money so they can return as much as possible. But Kelly tells me that'll be a nominal amount, if any at all."

"This is bullshit!" he exploded. "My boy would never cheat a soul. He doesn't need to cheat. Everything he touches turns to gold. You've seen what he's done, what he's provided for you."

Had he been breaking the law all along? Or just recently? "I hope he's innocent, like you say. And I hope we can prove it."

"You do? Really? Because you sound beaten." His voice grated. "Don't you have *any* confidence in him?"

"I only know what Kelly told me, Dale, and he said

the FBI plans to bring Skip up on fraud charges for mishandling the SLD Fund."

There was a brief silence. "No way. Not the SLD Fund. That fund's making great money. I saw a report last month."

A wave of unease swept through Sophia. "Why would *you* see a report? *You* didn't invest in it…" Skip wouldn't defraud his own parents, would he?

"I sure did," his father said proudly. "I put my life savings into that fund. So did almost everyone else in Whiskey Creek. And when they see how fast my boy will double their money, they're going to be damn glad they did."

Sophia started laughing. And once she started, she couldn't stop, not until she was crying instead.

"Sophia? Sophia, stop it!" Dale barked. "Are you *drunk?*"

That got her attention. "No," she said. "I haven't had a drop."

"Then what's wrong with you?"

Sniffing, she wiped her eyes. "Whether you want to believe it or not, your boy is gone," she said. "And so is the money you and everyone else invested."

4

Two days later, on Sunday, which was as soon as they could make the arrangements, Sharon and Dale met Sophia and Alexa at the airport. Her in-laws were drawn and pale, and Sophia knew she looked no better. She wheeled her luggage out to the car, while her daughter did the same, her hair smashed on one side from when she'd leaned against the wall of the plane, trying to get some sleep.

"Thank you for helping us get home," Sophia said. "And for sending enough money for the crew to return with the *Legacy*." She had no doubt the FBI would confiscate the yacht once it was safely docked. The agent who'd been dealing with Kelly, Special Agent Freeman, had contacted her when she was about to board the plane. She'd told him she couldn't help find Skip. And he'd told her the government had seized everything of any value except the house. Since there was no equity in it, 910 Wonderland Drive wouldn't be worth their time.

Thank God for small favors. At least she and Alexa would be able to stay in familiar surroundings until the bank kicked them out. How long that would be, Sophia couldn't even guess. She had more pressing matters to worry about before she got to that. The way Agent Freeman had questioned her made Sophia believe he suspected *her* of being a party to Skip's fraudulent activities—and when they'd hung up, he'd seemed far from convinced that she wasn't. He kept asking her how much she knew about her husband's business, implying that Skip couldn't have done everything he'd done without her knowledge. Because California was a community property state, the law held her accountable for any debts he'd incurred, so her credit was going to be ruined, too.

The DeBussis hugged Alexa, then turned immediately to helping with the luggage.

"Of course we were going to make sure you got home. We would never strand our granddaughter," Dale said tightly.

Sophia tried not to be hurt by the fact that they hadn't greeted her quite as warmly. Maybe she hadn't been the perfect wife. No one admired an alcoholic. But she *had* been part of the DeBussi family for thirteen years, since shortly after she'd found out she was pregnant with Lex. She felt she deserved a *little* kindness. "Since I love Alexa, too, I appreciate it," she said.

Other than a few comments about the weather and the length of the trip, they drove the hundred and thirty miles to "The Heart of Gold Country" in silence. Sophia knew her in-laws didn't want to discuss Skip's situation in Lexi's presence; neither did she. She hadn't told her daughter that he was wanted by the police. She'd simply said there'd been a mix-up at work and perhaps he'd gone somewhere to take care of the problem.

"Do you think Alexa should come home with us?" Sharon asked when they reached the top of "DeBussi Hill" and pulled into the circular drive.

Judging by the look her daughter shot her, Alexa didn't want to go. She was probably as eager to sleep in her own bed as Sophia was. Besides, Sophia didn't want to be alone. All the sudden changes had left her reeling. "Not tonight."

Sharon twisted around in her seat. "Why not?"

That her mother-in-law would challenge her answer made Sophia grit her teeth for a second. Sharon didn't show her the proper respect because Skip had always discounted Sophia's opinion. But she managed to respond in a normal voice. "The trip's been hard on both of us. We're worried about Skip and feel we should be here in case he calls."

"Okay, but you won't drink tonight, will you? With all the stress you're under—" she narrowed her eyes "—I wouldn't want you to resort to your old tricks."

Tricks? Sophia glanced at her daughter. She hated having Alexa hear that. "I haven't had a drink since I went into New Beginnings."

"Or so she says," Dale muttered under his breath. "If that was true, maybe she'd have a clearer memory of…certain details."

Like where their son had gone or what had happened to him. She understood that. But she didn't dignify the remark with a response for fear he'd try to make her look worse. She didn't want Alexa to blame her, to believe alcohol was the reason she had no idea when Skip had gotten up or where he might've gone. "Thanks again."

When they drove away, Sophia stared after them. If Skip didn't come back, she'd have to continue dealing with his parents on her own, and she could tell that wouldn't be any easier than dealing with the FBI.

"You coming?" Alexa spoke as she climbed the steps to the elaborately carved front doors Skip had purchased abroad.

"Right behind you." Normally, she would've stopped to admire the Halloween decorations she'd put up before they left. She loved the holidays, from Halloween to Christmas. But tonight none of that seemed important.

She bumped her suitcase up the steps because she was too tired to carry it, and let them in. The house smelled of grapefruit and mango from the expensive candles Sophia liked to burn.

"Home at last," she breathed.

"If only Dad was home with us," Lexi mumbled and, head bowed, started for her room.

"No kiss good-night?" Sophia called after her.

Dropping her suitcase onto the marble floor with a resounding bang, she came hurrying back. "I'm sorry, Momma. I'm just… It hurts. I'm afraid I'll never see him again."

"I know." She held her daughter tight, wishing *she* loved Skip as much as Lexi did. At least now she wanted him back—for their daughter's sake and because living with him, difficult as it was, would probably be easier than solving the problems he'd left behind. "Let's get some sleep," she said as she straightened.

After Alexa had settled in, Sophia went to bed telling herself that it would all get better in the morning.

But the call that woke her in the middle of the night told her it was only going to get worse.

Ted Dixon almost didn't attend Friday morning coffee with his friends. It was a ritual, something he looked forward to all week. As a novelist, he sat in front of his computer for hours every day, didn't get out of the house very often. And he'd known most of the people he met at Black Gold since he was in grade school. He always enjoyed seeing them. But after the shocking news that had swept through town the past week, he could easily guess what the topic of conversation would be, and he wasn't sure he wanted to participate. Everyone would be studying him, trying to ascertain his reaction—and although he'd had plenty of practice at pretending he wasn't interested in anything to do with his old flame, he felt that some of his friends could see through him.

On the other hand, if he didn't go, they'd likely figure out why. Not showing up might give away more than joining the group as if this Friday was no different from any other.

"Hey, you made it." Callie Pendleton, a photographer by trade, was the first to greet him. She'd had a liver transplant a year and a half ago, but no one would've been able to tell. She looked as healthy and robust as any other woman. Levi, her husband, was in line to order, along with Riley Stinson, a building contractor who had a fourteen-year-old son but had never married.

"Why wouldn't I make it?" he asked, pretending to be unaware of the added interest he was about to face.

"You haven't heard?" This came from Noah Rackham, who was nursing a cappuccino while sitting next

to Adelaide, his pregnant wife. Noah had recently re-
tired from professional cycling, which had taken him to
Europe for half of every year. But he still owned Crank
It Up, the bike shop in town. To help her aging grandmother, Adelaide ran the diner, Just Like Mom's—an
institution in Whiskey Creek.

Ted hadn't known Levi or Adelaide very well until
they'd started coming to coffee. The same could be said
for Brandon Lucero and his wife, Olivia. They were
younger, had been behind them in school. Callie, Riley,
Kyle, Eve and Noah were the people Ted had grown up
with, as well as several others who normally came but
weren't here today.

"Heard what?" Ted strolled over to the table and
slouched into his usual seat. "Don't tell me Baxter's
not coming back for the Halloween party." Baxter was
one of their closest friends, someone who used to have
coffee with them every week, but he'd moved to San
Francisco a few months ago.

"This year the party's at Cheyenne and Dylan's, isn't
it?" Adelaide asked.

"Last I heard," Callie said. "I don't know why they're
not here today." She glanced at the entrance as if she
expected them to walk in any second.

"Chey went to visit her sister this morning," Eve
informed them. Eve and Chey both worked at the
B and B owned by Eve's parents, so they stayed in
close touch. "But she and Dylan will be at the Halloween party and so will Baxter. I called him last night.
He said he's coming."

"How does he like his new digs?" Ted asked.

Noah broke in before Eve could answer. "Whoa,

whoa, whoa. Don't charge down that path. You know I wasn't referring to Bax when I asked if you'd heard the news."

Ted eyed the crowd at the register. He wasn't a man with a lot of patience. He preferred to sit and talk until he saw an opening and wouldn't have to wait, but today he should've gotten in line. That might have provided him with a buffer. Maybe they would have covered Sophia's situation and gotten embroiled in some other gossip before he returned with his usual—a cup of Black Gold's finest fresh-roasted coffee. "If you're talking about Skip DeBussi, of course I heard."

"That his body washed up on the shore of *Brazil?*" Noah asked.

"It's in all the papers, isn't it?" Ted said. "AOL even had something about it online."

"And?" Noah prompted. "Don't you have any reaction?"

"I'm sorry for his parents and his daughter, if that's what you're after."

Riley came back from the counter with a giant muffin, a fruit-and-yogurt parfait and an apple. Apparently, he planned to eat it all himself; his son was in school so he wouldn't be sharing it as he did during the summer. "You're sorry for everyone but his wife?" he asked, quickly picking up on the conversation.

Ted tried not to picture Sophia's face. He'd never seen a more beautiful woman. She turned heads, including his, wherever she went. He hated that she still had the power to affect him and often reminded himself that her beauty was only skin-deep. "I'm sure she'll manage. She always seems to land on her feet."

Callie frowned. "You're so hard on her. I won't argue that Sophia was a…a difficult personality in high school, but—"

"A difficult personality?" he echoed. "She was the meanest girl Eureka High has ever seen. She stole other girls' boyfriends, toyed with the guys she collected, manipulated anyone who'd let her and used her power and popularity to lord it over the less fortunate. You can feel bad for her all you want, but let's not forget the facts." He left out that she also had a slew of *good* qualities. That she'd been sexy and funny and determined and just mysterious enough to keep him guessing. At one time she was all he'd ever wanted. He expected someone to call him on that, but no one did.

"People grow up," Riley said. "She seemed nice when she was coming to coffee."

Because they hadn't given her the chance to be anything else. Ted was glad she'd changed her mind about trying to be part of their group. He didn't think she should have the right to hang out with them after behaving so badly, and he'd made sure she knew it. "Don't let those big blue eyes fool you."

Callie shot him a quelling look. "Ted, she just lost her husband. Can't you have *some* sympathy?"

No. He couldn't. He needed to keep up his defenses, because he knew where any softening would lead. He'd tried to rescue her once before. It'd been years since then, but he'd learned his lesson. "Like I said, I feel bad for her daughter and Skip's parents. Losing a son or father would be hard, but finding out he cheated almost everyone in town and then died trying to fake his own death so he could start a new life somewhere else…"

He'd never liked Skip, but he hadn't expected him to do anything quite *that* bad.

"Skip died trying to fake his own death?" Levi sat down with some coffee and a yogurt he slid in front of Callie. "Last I knew, they were assuming it might've been an accident—that he fell off the boat and drowned."

"It was no accident," Ted responded. "No one 'falls' off a yacht with a waterproof bag containing a disposable, non-traceable cell phone, a change of clothes and a hundred thousand dollars in cash strapped to his back. What you saw must've been before news of the FBI probe broke. I doubt anyone would've been leaning toward 'accident' if they'd possessed that little detail. Maybe *suicide*," he added.

Brandon poured a packet of sugar into his coffee. "So he meant to go overboard, was prepared for it. Why didn't he survive?"

Ted shrugged. "No one knows. They're speculating he had some sort of flotation device that he lost for whatever reason. Maybe he encountered a shark or some rocks or fell asleep and slipped out of it. Or he might have given it up, thinking he could move faster without it. Maybe he underestimated the distance to shore or his ability to fight the currents."

Noah finished his cappuccino. "I could see him doing that. He's always been over-confident."

"What he's done, to everyone, is terrible." Olivia wiped the condensation from her orange juice. "Especially little Alexa. How will Sophia ever explain that he died trying to skate out on them?"

Ted shifted to one side so he could cross his ankles

without getting in anyone's way. "I'm just glad *I* didn't invest, and I hope none of you guys did, either."

He'd said it flippantly. He hadn't really believed any of *his* friends would be victims, but when Kyle and Noah exchanged a glance, Ted sat up straight. "Tell me you didn't."

"He talked a good talk," Noah said, his face turning red. "I mean, look at his house. Look at the cars he drives and all the trips he takes—or used to take. I thought he knew what the hell he was doing."

"He did!" Ted said with a laugh. "He got you to invest, didn't he?"

Kyle's expression was just as chagrined as Noah's but he came out fighting. "Don't be so damn smug, Ted. The only reason you kept your distance was because you didn't want to give Skip the pleasure of thinking he had anything you appreciated or admired."

That was true. Like almost everyone else, he'd been tempted by the promise of easy money, especially when so many people he respected seemed to be jumping at the opportunity. It was Skip's connection to Sophia that had stopped him.

For once his history with her was actually in his favor. "Doesn't matter what saved me, *I* didn't invest." He leaned his elbows on the table. "So how much did you two lose?"

"I don't want to talk about it," Noah said. Kyle didn't answer.

"You didn't give him a lot, did you?"

Obviously defensive of the man she loved, Adelaide put an arm around her husband. "You didn't do anything wrong, honey. *He* did. I bet lots of people in Whiskey Creek lost more than you."

"I hope not," Noah said, aghast. "What hurts the most is that I turned him down the first couple of times he called. Addie and I have had a rough year, as you guys know. But once our personal problems cleared up, the oily bastard offered me 'the opportunity' again. And he made it sound so…safe and lucrative." He pushed the table, which was crowding him, a few inches away. "I had every reason to believe him. He's been the richest man in town for years. None of *us* drive a Ferrari or have our asses chauffeured to work."

"You want a chauffeur to drive you ten feet from your door to your bike shop?" Levi teased.

"No, but I'll take one of the Ferraris."

"Too bad he's not alive so I could punch him out," Kyle grumbled.

"Come on, how much did you guys lose?" Ted eyed Noah, since he'd had him in his sights first.

Noah flipped him off, but then relented. "What the hell. I admit I was a stupid sucker. Fifty thousand. I lost fifty grand."

The way he said it showed how humiliated he was.

Brandon whistled; Callie dropped her spoon. "That's a lot!" she exclaimed. "Maybe Levi and I should be glad for my medical bills. We didn't have enough money for him to bother with us."

Ted turned to Kyle. "And you? How much did *you* lose?"

"Kiss my ass," Kyle replied, his nose in his cup.

"Noah just gave us a figure," Brandon said.

Kyle scowled at him. "So? I'm not telling."

Ted couldn't help smiling at his petulant response. That meant he'd lost even more than Noah. "I'm sure there'll be a list of victims in the paper at some point."

"Then you can just wait and read about what a damn fool I was," he said flatly.

Riley leaned forward so he could catch Kyle's eye. "Your business has been doing great. Why would *you* invest with DeBussi?"

"The demand for solar panels is going up. I wanted to expand the factory, but I guess I'll be putting that off for a while."

Ted tapped Brandon's calf with one foot to get his attention. "I'm surprised he didn't come to you, too, Mr. Extreme Skier. I'm sure he knows you made some money in your heyday."

Brandon's mouth curved in a self-satisfied grin.

"What?" Kyle said, cluing in.

"He *did* come to me," Brandon told him. "Last time he was in town. I passed on the offer."

"Shit!" Kyle smacked the table, rattling the silverware. "Are you kidding me?"

Brandon rocked back at this unhappy response, but he was chuckling when he did. "What? You wish I'd gotten ripped off, too?"

"Pretty much," Kyle mumbled.

"Misery loves company, huh?"

Everybody laughed except Kyle. It was always interesting to watch him interact with his stepbrother, to see how they got along, particularly since Brandon married the woman Kyle had wanted. Every once in a while, Ted saw Kyle look at Olivia with a touch of longing. It made him sad because he knew he did the same thing with Sophia, even though he professed to hate her.

Brandon polished off his second doughnut, which he must've bought on the way in, because Black Gold didn't sell doughnuts. "Yeah, well, thanks for that, big brother."

Kyle didn't have a chance to respond. Olivia spoke up. "Do you think…"

When she paused, everyone waited expectantly. "What?" Riley asked.

She winced as if she hated saying what she was about to suggest. "Do you think Sophia could've known what Skip was doing?"

"No." Callie shook her head, adamant. "Sophia wouldn't go along with him cheating anyone, especially the people here in town."

"I don't think so, either," Riley said. "It was all Skip. The guy had no shame. I heard he scammed his own parents. Took them for their retirement, their savings, everything."

Olivia shoved the tinfoil lid of her orange juice into the plastic cup. "That's tragic, but I've never been a fan of the DeBussis."

"Who could be a fan of his brother?" Brandon asked. "That dude's a mess."

"I wasn't talking about Colby," she told him. "At least Colby doesn't act as if he's better than everyone else. It's Skip's parents who swagger around this town like they own it. You've seen them—in the Fourth of July parade, showing off their fancy cars." She took a bite of the coffee cake she'd been sharing with Brandon. "Still, I would never have wished anything like *this* on them."

"What's Sophia going to do?" Callie asked, her voice filled with concern. "From what I've heard, Skip took all the money they had left, and now that the feds have his cash, they won't give her a cent of it. How will she get by?"

Ted got the impression she was asking him—maybe because she glanced in his direction. "How would I know?"

"She'll have to go to work to support her daughter," Kyle said.

Riley disagreed. "No, her in-laws will help."

"I don't think they can," Eve said. "Not after this."

Levi set his cup down. "He ripped them off *that* badly?"

Eve gave him a helpless look. "From what I've heard. I doubt Sophia has many options. That's why I encouraged her to apply for Ted's housekeeper position."

Ted nearly fell off his chair. "You *what?*"

"Well, I didn't actually speak to her," Eve said with a sheepish expression. "I just…left a message telling her that might be an option."

"Well, it's not an option," Ted snapped. "That position's not open to her."

"Why not?" Callie asked, immediately taking Eve's side.

"Forget it." He waved her off. "She's been a kept woman her whole life. She probably doesn't know the first thing about scrubbing toilets and making dinner."

"I don't think she's ever had a housekeeper," Callie pointed out.

She'd had the money to hire an army of domestic servants. "I bet she's had one all along," he argued.

"Besides, I'm offering $2,500 a month. That wouldn't even cover her spa treatments."

"You wouldn't give her a chance if she applied?" Eve asked.

"I don't have to answer that because she'll never apply. I'm sure she'll find another sugar daddy before life gets too grim, even if it means moving away." He hoped she *would* leave town. Then there'd be no more risk of bumping into her when he went out. He'd spent years trying to avoid her.

Thankfully, Olivia shifted the focus of the conversation. It was a slight shift but at least his friends were no longer suggesting he employ his ex-girlfriend. "Does anyone know when the funeral will be?"

"Skip only washed up a couple of days ago," Ted replied. "I doubt they've set a date, considering it'll take some time to get the body home from Brazil."

Kyle hooked an arm around the back of his chair. "If anyone's interested, the funeral should be announced in the *Gold Country Gazette*."

"That's a weekly," Noah said. "It wouldn't be the place to go for information if they decide to have it soon."

"Word spreads like wildfire in this town," Brandon told them. "I'm sure we'll hear about it."

Riley gazed around at the group. "Who's planning to go? Kyle and I aren't. That's for damn sure. I bet Noah won't, either."

Noah confirmed that with a muttered, "Hell, no."

"What about the rest of you?" Riley asked.

Ted raised both hands. "Don't look at me."

"I'll go, to support Sophia." Callie wiped her mouth with a napkin.

"Me, too. It's not like any of this is *her* fault." Eve sent Ted an accusing glare.

"You don't know that," Ted insisted. She'd certainly stirred up enough trouble in high school. She'd also stirred his heart—*and* a lower part of his body—but he didn't like to acknowledge that these days.

"We're giving her the benefit of the doubt," Callie said. "You should try it sometime. Anyway, I'm guessing Gail will go, too." Gail DeMarco-O'Neal had grown up in Whiskey Creek, but she'd left for college and never moved back. After starting her own PR firm in Los Angeles, she'd married one of her clients—box-office hit Simon O'Neal—and was so busy she didn't visit often.

"Since when did Gail become friends with Sophia?" Ted didn't remember any type of rapport between them. Sophia had been part of a rival clique, was actually the leader of it—until the girls who were part of her posse moved away.

Eve cocked an eyebrow at him. "Gail invited Sophia to her wedding, remember?"

Seeing that the line to order food was gone, Ted stood up, intending to get his coffee. "I remember, but I thought it was strange then, and I think it's strange now."

Callie folded her arms. "Why?"

"Because Scott Harris was her big brother's best friend. She knew him well."

"I don't think you can hold Sophia responsible for what happened to Scott," Callie said. "She didn't *force* him to drive drunk."

He pulled out his wallet. "If it wasn't for her, he wouldn't have left the party."

Callie wasn't about to back down. "She was sixteen or seventeen, *Ted*. She made a mistake."

"Oh, well. Actions have consequences. Ask Scott's family about that the next time you see them, okay?" He'd given in to Callie's kind of thinking once before, and Sophia had made him sorry he had.

"She probably never dreamed her actions would lead where they did." Callie crumpled the napkin she'd used and dropped it on her plate. "Haven't you ever done anything you regret?"

He was already on his way to the counter, so he left her question unanswered. But he *had* done something he regretted.

He regretted ever getting involved with Sophia.

5

As Sophia had expected, hardly anyone attended the funeral. And those who came didn't have much to say. They filed past the casket, somber and subdued. Some managed a nod for her or Skip's parents. No one smiled but neither did anyone cry. Even Sophia didn't know how to act. Should she behave like the grieving widow? Or the hurt and angry spouse?

She told herself to behave as she honestly felt for a change. She was done with pretending. But Agent Freeman was there, watching her every move, every expression, and it made her nervous. How would he interpret what he saw? Would something she said or did make him decide that she was as guilty as her husband? He couldn't understand how Skip could do so much without her knowledge, but he had no idea what their marriage had been like.

Now she regretted telling the Brazilian police that they'd been happy together, that they'd been close.

When she twisted around to see who might've come in late, her eyes met Freeman's almost immediately, and she turned back. She hated having him there. But she couldn't have been honest with her emotions, anyway, or she would've seemed crazy—because she felt a little of everything. There were moments when she mourned the fact that she and Skip hadn't been happy together, that it had come down to *this*. Moments when she was grateful he was gone, that she no longer had to fear him. Moments when she felt so incredibly angry that she hoped he'd spend an eternity in hell for betraying them, especially after getting her hopes up with such beautiful promises of change and fresh commitment.

She'd muddled through the past ten days by focusing on doing what she could to shield Alexa, and by staying busy making arrangements for the return of Skip's body. She'd tried to arrange the funeral, too, but his parents hadn't liked some of her decisions, so they took over. That bothered her—they were always bossy and superior. The way they treated her made her want to drink. But her concern for her daughter had kept her off the booze. Her concern for Alexa had also enabled her to tell Agent Freeman that his interrogation would have to wait until she'd given Lex the chance to say goodbye to her father. She wanted to commemorate the things Skip had done *right* in his life, so the young girl he'd left behind wouldn't have to be completely devastated by his shortcomings and mistakes.

Unfortunately, however, the eulogy offered scant comfort. The clergyman, Rudy Flores, had known Skip all his life. This was where they'd gone to church every week, mostly at Skip's insistence. He'd demanded she attend whether he was home or not. But the reverend was obviously as disappointed in him as everyone else. Flores kept his comments almost entirely generic. Although he didn't refer to Skip's illegal and unethical activities, neither did he spare him any praise.

Sophia sat in her black Chanel dress, Manolo Blahnik heels and the Dolce & Gabbana sunglasses she'd put on to hide the redness of her eyes, and clasped her hands tightly in her lap. With her hair slicked back in a bun at her nape, she knew she looked like an ice princess. But she was doing her best to cope, didn't want anyone to know that she was shaking inside. If they understood how vulnerable she was, they might set on her en masse, like vultures. After what Skip had done, there were plenty of people in Whiskey Creek who were looking for a target. She had the feeling they'd be more than happy to pick her bones. Her own reputation wasn't helping. Thanks to her past mistakes, there was no one to champion her, no one to insist that she was too good a person to have cooperated with Skip.

"...just as Christ was raised from the dead by the glory of the Father, we too might walk in the newness of life...."

Reverend Flores's voice droned on, but Sophia tuned him out. She didn't want to hear what he was saying, didn't want to think about Skip being resurrected. She doubted anyone here—even his brokenhearted daughter and parents—would be too pleased to see him in the afterlife. *She* wouldn't. This was one time she wanted to believe that dead was *dead.* The sight of Alexa sitting beside her with tears dripping into her lap convinced her that Skip had had enough second chances. How often had she forgiven his violent outbursts and agreed to try again?

"Are you okay?" she whispered.

When Alexa nodded, Sophia slid an arm around her.

She wished she could've kept her from learning the ugly truth, but there'd been no way to preserve her innocence, not with the whole town talking about how Skip had used and tricked and cheated everyone. It was in the papers. It was on the news. It was on the internet, where strangers with various screen names like "chubbydate" and "village-itch" had posted nasty comments about how "vain" and "arrogant" she and Skip were to think they could "get away with it." "The wife has to be involved," some claimed. "It takes money to keep a woman as beautiful as that. He probably figured he'd lose her if he didn't give her the world."

Their lives had been torn apart in the most public manner possible, the wreckage strewn for all to see. Some kids, or maybe adults, had even thrown eggs at their house two nights ago.

"We could move," she whispered in Alexa's ear. The idea of a fresh start gave Sophia hope, but this suggestion just elicited *more* tears from her daughter.

"No, Mom. Please!" she begged. "I—I don't want to go. I can't leave my friends, and Grandma and Grandpa, and Uncle Colby and my cousins."

Sophia could understand why. Whiskey Creek was all Alexa had ever known. It was all Sophia had known, too. But that made it harder to face the many people Skip had wronged, especially when the presence of Agent Freeman seemed to signify that she might be as guilty as Skip. The longer he remained in town, asking his insidious questions, the more convinced everyone became that she'd been living the high life at their expense. Someone online had even accused her of having a "bundle" tucked away.

She wished she did have some money in a safe place.

Then she really *could* move, providing she could persuade Alexa. As it was, Sophia wasn't sure how she'd be able to scrape together the funds that relocating would require. She could sell her household furnishings and her wardrobe. They'd been expensive to begin with, but used items of that kind didn't retain their value. In any case, as soon as she sold her belongings, there'd be people lining up to get the money.

"Okay," she murmured, reassuring Alexa with a quick squeeze. "I just… I thought I'd make the offer."

"So we'll stay?" Alexa confirmed. "You promise?"

"We'll stay." At least as long as she could hang on to the house. The cars would go first. She had no way of making the payments. She'd learned this past week that every single one had a loan against it. So did the yacht. Sophia had tried to track down her wedding ring, but there was no record of where Skip might've taken it, and it was nowhere to be found in the house or the cars.

Alexa smiled her gratitude and Sophia managed to smile in return, but when she glanced around, she realized that more people were watching *her* than the preacher. Would the funeral never end?

Fortunately, Reverend Flores seemed to sense the unrest. He finally finished the service. Then the organ music swelled, and Sophia stood, eager to get out of the church and away from the expensive floral sprays his parents had insisted on ordering—since no one else was likely to send flowers. There was the graveside service still to go, but even fewer people would join her at the cemetery, and her time there would be limited to a short prayer. Soon she'd be able to go home, where she could find refuge from the prying eyes….

"I'm so sorry, Sophia. I'm sure that what you're

going through is just…awful." Gail DeMarco-O'Neal approached her first, with her movie-star husband, and gave Sophia a tight hug. It was a testament to how glum everyone was feeling that they weren't making a big deal of Simon's being in attendance. But, of course, they'd seen him around town on a number of occasions.

"Thank you." She swallowed hard, hoping to stave off the tears that burned behind her eyes now that someone had shown her some kindness. "It's nice of you to come. Truly." In recent years, she'd tried to join Gail's circle of friends, had loved having coffee with them. She would've kept going if not for Ted. Although she longed for his forgiveness, he'd made it clear that he couldn't or wouldn't forget the past.

"Is there anything we can do to make things easier?" Gail murmured.

Sophia had a feeling she'd need a good attorney and she had no idea how she'd pay for one. Even filing bankruptcy, which was inevitable, cost a couple thousand dollars. But that was none of Gail's concern. Although Gail and Simon were rich, Sophia had no right to ask for a loan or anything else. She and Gail had connected briefly one night before Gail got married. It wasn't as if they'd been friends for life. They hadn't been friends at all—until then. "No, but thank you."

"You'll call if something comes up?" Gail prompted.

What else could go wrong? She'd already lost everything. "Of course," she lied.

"Good. I'm afraid we can't stay for the graveside service. Simon has commitments in L.A. And we left the children at home. But I wanted to see you in person, if only for a few minutes."

"I appreciate it. I really do. I know you don't like to leave your babies."

"Ty is hardly a baby. He's almost eight! But he had school and the other two are more of a handful — definitely hard to manage on quick trips. Anyway, you're worth it." Gail handed her a sympathy card before moving on so that Simon and Levi, Callie's husband, could offer their condolences. Eve Harmon was with them, too, which was nice of her, given that Sophia was fairly certain her sympathies leaned more toward Ted than her.

They each spoke to her, but it was Callie who turned back. "I'm here for you, you know. I don't have the millions you need but…if you'd ever like to talk, you've got my number, right?"

"I do. Thanks so much." After accepting another hug, Sophia held her head high and let them go. Since they'd been the friendliest people at the funeral, she wanted to cling to them, to beg them to save her from the despair that threatened to consume her. Maybe she would have, if she felt she deserved their help, but she knew they had almost as many complaints against her as Ted did.

Although Agent Freeman didn't speak to her, he stood close enough to make her aware of him. When she'd been in Brazil and heard his deep, resonant voice over the phone, she'd assumed he would be young and maybe even attractive—not that it mattered—but that didn't turn out to be the case. Close to fifty, he had gray hair and sharp features, which contributed to a rather severe look. And his attitude reminded her of Javier, the police inspector from *Les Misérables*.

But that might just be her fear talking. Arms folded and lips pursed, he eyed the procession with obvious skepticism. The way he glared at the casket left little doubt as to how he felt about Skip. He'd spent two years pursuing the evidence he needed to punish a criminal, only to be denied the pleasure of seeing justice done. She figured that was why he wanted to believe *she* had some culpability in the fraud. Then he'd be able to prosecute at least one of the "bad guys."

In addition to Gail, Simon, Callie, Levi, Eve, Gail's brother, Joe, and the FBI, some of Skip's former schoolteachers had come to pay their respects. Apparently, he hadn't hit them up to invest. Or they hadn't had the money. Or maybe they just remembered him from a far more innocent time. His assistant, Kelly Petruzzi, had driven over from San Francisco, along with a handful of coworkers. Besides those with a connection to the business, there was the gardener who'd cared for their yard the past five years, Marta, who came in once a month to do the deep housecleaning (Skip prized his privacy too much to have anyone come more often), and the man who washed their cars. Sophia thought it was a sad state of affairs that a large proportion of the people in attendance were employees probably hoping to save their jobs by showing some support.

The rest of the funeral party comprised Skip's immediate and extended family, and they seemed eager to pretend she wasn't there. They looked past her, focused strictly on Alexa as if Sophia wasn't standing by her daughter's side. Or they spoke quietly among themselves, trying to console Dale and Sharon, acting as though Sophia wasn't entitled to their sympathy.

"I'm not willing to believe Skip did what they say. He wasn't the type."

This came from the cousin who'd pulled out a chair

for her once, spurring Skip to hit her so hard she'd had to have emergency dental surgery.

"The FBI's got to be wrong," an uncle agreed. "They're after his money or...something. We got a damn liberal for president. Maybe it's a new way of stealing from the rich to give to the poor."

"Then why did he go on the run?" his aunt asked.

"Because he knew they were setting him up," his brother said. "He knew they were after him."

"But if he was innocent, why wouldn't he have come to us for help?" This was the aunt again. "Or hired a good attorney? Instead, he put $100,000 in a waterproof pack and tried to swim to Brazil."

Finally, someone less blinded by love and loyalty.

"Or so they say," the cousin responded, once again infusing some doubt.

They had no idea that the real Skip bore no resemblance to the image he portrayed. And Sophia knew they wouldn't believe her, even if she tried to tell them.

"We'd better head over for the graveside service." Dale said this but as he looked up, he caught Sophia's eye and glanced away as if the mourners who'd be driving over together didn't include her. "Let's go."

Since the family had only been able to come up with four pallbearers, including Skip's father, they'd decided to have the mortuary provide this service so that wouldn't be obvious. But as anxious as Sophia was to be done with this day, she waved them off and lingered with Alexa after everyone had left. She thought that her daughter might need some private time to pay her last respects.

"Would it help to have a few minutes to...to say goodbye to your father?" she asked.

More tears spilled over Alexa's eyelashes, but she shook her head. "No. Daddy's not here. I don't even know who that man in the casket is."

"I'm sorry." Sophia hugged her again. No one knew him. Except maybe her. But she didn't add that.

Sharon poked her head into the church. "Alexa, would you like to ride over with Grandma and Grandpa?"

Lexi seemed hesitant, but Sophia gave her a nudge. "It's okay. You go. I'll join you in a minute."

With a sniff and a nod, her daughter hurried out, leaving Sophia alone with her husband's body.

"How could you?" she whispered when Alexa was gone. He'd always told her how vain and selfish *she* was. She'd allowed him to defeat her with that because she'd known in her heart it was true. She'd caused a lot of heartache in her teens. A young man had lost his life because of her immaturity and thoughtlessness. But no one could be more vain or selfish than Skip.

She was still clutching the card Gail had given her when the pallbearers came back. Needing a little more time before she could bring herself to join the others in the cemetery, she waited for them to carry the casket out to the hearse but stayed behind to open the card. She'd expected to find nothing more than a few words of consolation, but a check fell out and fluttered to the floor. No one else had given her money. She assumed everyone thought she'd already "taken" enough.

When she bent to retrieve it, she saw the amount. Five thousand dollars! She returned her attention to the card. "We all need a little help now and then," Gail had written. "I hope this will come in handy."

The words blurred before Sophia's eyes as, for the

first time that day, she broke down and started to cry. "Thank you," she said.

Gail couldn't hear her but maybe God could.

6

Agent Freeman knocked at Sophia's door two days after the funeral. She was impressed he'd waited that long. She figured she was lucky he hadn't followed her home the day they'd laid Skip to rest, hoping he'd get her to reveal something she might not have had she been emotionally stable.

"Do you have a few minutes?" he asked.

A knot of anxiety formed instantly in her stomach, or maybe it had been there since Skip first disappeared. Lately, she seemed to flinch at the slightest provocation. She didn't know when the next blow would hit or where it would come from, but almost every day held *another* nasty surprise, from news of the FBI probe, to the discovery of Skip's body, to the large number of people who'd been cheated, especially here in Whiskey Creek, to the unexpected coldness of his family.

Knowing it wouldn't do her any good to put off this interview, Sophia stepped back. "Come in."

He didn't react to her invitation right away. He angled his head up, as if he was taking in the size and grandeur of her home. Skip had spared no expense when he'd had the mansion built. He'd wanted to inspire jealousy and admiration, and he'd succeeded—which was coming back to bite her now that there was nothing to be admired.

"Is your daughter here?" Agent Freeman asked when he finally moved past her.

"No." That provided Sophia with a small measure of relief. She'd been careful to say nothing disparaging about Skip; she couldn't see how depriving Alexa of her father on a completely different level—destroying all the good memories she still had—would make anyone's life easier. But in the past week her daughter had heard plenty. Still, there was no need for Lexi to get another earful, especially in her own home. "She's back in school."

"So soon?"

"Because of the trip, she was off for over a week *before* Skip went missing. She brought her homework and was keeping up, but she and I both thought it might be better for her to jump into her usual routine as soon as possible. Circulating in town is…hard, with the way people are feeling toward us, but there's nothing for her to do here all day except remember her father and be sad." She motioned to the soft leather couch Skip had purchased in Belgium and had shipped over. "Would you like to sit down?"

She perched on the edge of a nearby chair while he took the couch, which afforded her less space than she'd anticipated when he rested his elbows on his knees and leaned forward. "Are *you* sad, Mrs. DeBussi?"

She didn't want to be called by Skip's last name anymore. She wasn't about to say so quite yet, but she wasn't a DeBussi and, in her heart, she hadn't been one for a long time. The way his family had behaved during the past couple of weeks convinced her that she'd never had anything in common with them, never shared anything, least of all love. "I look so unaffected that you can't tell?" she responded glibly.

He didn't smile at the joke. "You seem…disengaged, if you want the truth."

Because she *had* to be disengaged and stay disengaged or she'd never be able to tolerate the fear and uncertainty of the future. "Appearances can be deceiving."

"I would have to agree with that."

"Considering what my husband did, how would you expect me to feel?"

He rubbed his chin. "Betrayed, for one."

"There is that."

"What about brokenhearted?"

She was tempted to be honest and say she wasn't brokenhearted in the way he meant, but decided to keep that information to herself. She preferred to be sensitive to the fact that her daughter and Skip's family still loved him. Publicly breaking ranks with them would only leave her more isolated. She already felt like she was living on her own island. Besides, she'd rather be hated by the citizens of Whiskey Creek than pitied by them. If they knew how Skip had treated her, how unhappy she'd been since marrying him, her humiliation would be complete.

"Does this have any bearing on my guilt or innocence, Mr. Freeman?" she asked. "How sincerely I mourn the death of my husband? Don't tell me you think I strapped that money to his back and pushed him off the side of the boat."

A muscle flexed in his jaw. She was putting up a

fight and he hadn't expected it. "I'm merely trying to get to know you better. Opinions of you here in your hometown vary…greatly."

"You're saying I'm not well-liked. Your sympathy for my situation overwhelms me."

He shrugged off her sarcasm. "I'm not your friend, either. I have a job to do."

"And that includes making this week even worse by speaking to everyone I know about me on the heels of my husband's death?"

"You mean on the heels of your husband's *fraudulent* activities. He stole over $60 million from innocent investors, Mrs. DeBussi. These interviews help me build an accurate picture."

"How do you know it's accurate?"

He studied her. "The secret is not to rely too much on any one opinion."

But no one knew the whole truth. She couldn't see how the people of Whiskey Creek would have anything of value to contribute. She was no longer the girl she used to be, and they didn't know the woman she'd become. She'd been active in various charities and other community events, yes. But she'd been playing a role, fulfilling her duties as the wife of the richest man in town. She couldn't let anyone get close to her, despite Skip's absences, for fear of his jealous reaction once he got home. There'd even been a brief period when he'd hired a private investigator to keep an eye on her.

"What is it you're *really* after?" She wished she didn't have to suffer this intrusion. She felt as if she'd been violated—not physically but emotionally.

"How much did you know about Skip's business dealings?"

"Absolutely nothing," she replied without hesitation.

"Yet you told the Brazilian police you two were close."

She stared at him without blinking. "There are different kinds of close."

He cocked his head to one side. "The two of you never fought?"

She never fought back. She couldn't, or it would make things that much worse. "Our arguments weren't serious."

"Even the ones where he was upset about your drinking?"

When she stiffened but didn't attempt to explain, he continued, "Your mother-in-law told me you recently spent a month in rehab."

Her *mother-in-law?* Skip's family had acted so strange since his death. As if she was somehow to blame for what he'd done. As if she'd driven him to it. And now they were creating suspicion and undermining her credibility with the FBI? "I guess they need someone to blame besides their beloved son."

"What Sharon said isn't true?"

She sighed. "It *is* true. In case you haven't verified it, I completed a program at a clinic in Los Angeles right before our trip."

"Why so far from home?"

To minimize the embarrassment to the family, of course. But Agent Freeman didn't understand the dynamics of the DeBussis like she did. "Skip chose the facility. He always chose everything."

He paused when she said that but didn't follow up on it. "And have you remained sober since then?"

She remembered the long days of rehab, the hours

spent in group therapy, the journaling, the reading. She'd missed Lexi terribly during those weeks, and yet she'd felt protected at New Beginnings. Skip was unlikely to bother her there for fear she wouldn't complete her stay. "I haven't had a drink since."

He seemed disappointed by her answer. "Are you sure?"

"You don't believe me?"

"I spoke to a checker at Nature's Way."

Agent Freeman was nothing if not thorough. "And she told you that I came in the other night and bought several bottles of wine."

"Yes."

She'd almost broken down *so* many times. It was hard to walk the floors at night, worrying about what she was going to do without a drink to ease the anxiety. But every time she'd been about to uncork that first bottle, she'd thought of Lexi. "I dumped them out this morning. You can check the cupboards in the kitchen if you don't believe me."

He slid toward her until their knees almost touched, as if he wanted to make sure he had her full attention. "I hope that's true. I have no respect for a liar."

"I'm not lying," she said. "I *wanted* to drink them, but…"

"But?" he echoed.

"My daughter needs me."

"Yes, she does."

She wiped the sweat beading on her upper lip. Skip would've found that so unattractive. She was supposed to be perfect at all times. "If you think I had anything to do with Skip's business, you should talk to his employees instead of the townspeople," she said.

"I've done that, too."

"And?"

"I've taken notes."

"They told you I was rarely at the offices, didn't they? That I never gave an opinion or helped make a decision? I am exactly what I appear to be, Agent Freeman."

"And that is…"

She spread her arms with a dramatic flourish. "A trophy wife."

"Yet you claim you were happy."

"It doesn't matter now that he's gone."

He glanced around once again. "Mrs. DeBussi, would you be willing to allow me to search the house?"

Her mind flitted through what he might come across. She couldn't think of a single thing that would be incriminating. But she didn't know how he might interpret what he found. What if Skip had planted some papers in his home office designed to implicate her? He wouldn't like the idea of her moving on without him regardless of whether he was sunning himself on a beach halfway around the world with someone else.

"Do you have a warrant?" she asked.

"Do you have something to hide?" he replied.

"No, but since you could misconstrue what you find, I'm not taking that risk unless I have to. As I said, my daughter needs me. I can't go to prison."

"I see." He stood. "That will be all, then."

She hadn't expected him to accept her answer quite so easily. "Will you be coming back with a warrant?"

"Not unless there's some indication I need to go that far. For now, my business here is finished."

"You're leaving?" she asked in surprise.

"I am."

"Just my house or…Whiskey Creek?"

"I believe I've learned all I can in this town."

Could she finally be catching a break? She wasn't sure whether she could rely on that as she followed him to the door. "May I ask you one more question?"

He nodded.

"Is it reasonable to suppose I'm in the clear?"

"That'll depend on what turns up," he said. "But if you're as innocent as you say, you can relax. So far, I've seen nothing that leads me to think you played a significant role in your husband's illegal activities."

She sagged in relief. "I've made my share of mistakes in life, Agent Freeman. But I had *nothing* to do with what Skip did. I swear it. I was as blindsided as anyone."

"I hope that's true." He gave her another long, assessing look. "Thank you for giving me a few minutes of your time."

She held the door while he stepped outside, but then he turned back.

"Mrs. DeBussi?"

Her heart beat a little faster. Was *this* when the blow would come? "Yes?"

"Although it's none of my business, you need to be aware of a certain reality."

She tensed. "What is it?"

He softened his voice when he saw that she'd clenched her hands, bracing for the worst. "You *have* to stay off the booze."

Drawing a deep breath, she nodded rigorously to show she understood that. "Yes, yes, of course. I will. I came close a couple of times, like I said, but…I made it. I poured it all out."

"You can't buy more. You can't slip up even *once*."

Why was he making such a point of this? What concern was it of his? Whether or not she had a drink *now*, after the fact, couldn't relate to the case. "I don't know what you're getting at."

"That daughter you love so much?"

"Alexa."

"If you end up back in rehab, your in-laws will sue for custody."

The air rushed out of her. "They—they *told* you that?"

"They tried to convince me you weren't a good wife, and you're no better as a mother."

She felt her jaw drop open.

"Be careful of them."

"But…I *do* have a drinking problem. I told you as much. So…why…" She choked up, finding it impossible to finish.

"Why did I warn you? From what I've seen, you're the one who loves Alexa best."

She blinked rapidly to stem the tears. "How can you tell?"

"I have a kid of my own," he said with a reassuring smile. "Just hang in there. If you really didn't know what your husband was doing, you're the biggest victim of all. What happened isn't fair, but you have to stay sober or you'll lose the only thing you've got left and the one thing that matters most to you."

"Thanks." She watched him stride to his car, feeling shocked that he'd try to help her—and hurt that a complete stranger would show more compassion than her in-laws.

7

Ted sat in front of his computer and read what he'd just written, then proceeded to edit it. Nothing he wrote seemed any good today; he couldn't concentrate.

Shifting restlessly in his chair, he tried to devise a more believable method of getting his protagonist out of the building that contained the bomb. But every idea he came up with seemed so...*contrived.* It'd all been done before and, in his current frame of mind, he was pretty sure it had been done better. *Hot Pursuit* was turning out to be his weakest book—and yet he'd loved the premise when he first started the story a month ago.

What was wrong with him?

His cell phone rang, but he didn't bother to get up and find it. He didn't answer calls during the day. Refusing to be distracted was the only way he could finish his page quota and have any hope of meeting his deadlines. But someone had been trying to get through to him for the past hour. And after what Kyle and Callie had said at Black Gold Coffee last week about the possibility of Sophia DeBussi applying to be his housekeeper, he was afraid of who it might be. She had to do *something* to support herself and her daughter, didn't she? What else could she do except go after any menial job that might be available? In high school, she'd partied so much she'd barely graduated. She had no college credits, no work experience.

He supposed she could model. She was pretty enough. But she couldn't do that here in Whiskey Creek. And if her situation was as dire as he suspected from all the news reports, she wouldn't have a car—at least not for long. She wouldn't even have a house once the bank foreclosed.

Pushing away from his desk, he got up to stretch his legs, spotted his cell on a side table and scooped it up. The call he'd missed had come from his agent. Damn. He should've taken that one. But he'd deal with Jan Andersen in a minute; he had another call to make first. He'd limped along without any domestic help for the past ten years, since he started writing. He figured he could manage for a few more months, until whatever was going to happen to Sophia DeBussi happened, and he could interview applicants without fear that she might knock on his door.

Ed down at the *Gold Country Gazette* answered on the first ring. "What can I do for you, Ted?" he asked.

Caller ID, no doubt. "I'd like to cancel my ad."

"But it hasn't even run yet."

So far, he'd posted on Craigslist, but hadn't received much interest. A woman named Marta, who'd actually used Sophia as a reference, had applied; however she had a slew of other clients and couldn't focus strictly on him. Besides, she didn't cook, and she didn't know how to use a computer. He wanted someone who would act as maid, cook *and* secretary. An all-in-one assistant wouldn't be easy to find, especially since he didn't have time to sift through applications. So it wasn't *just* that he was afraid Sophia might apply for the job, he told himself. Delaying the process meshed better with his schedule.

"I'm aware of that," he said. "I'm planning to hold off until after the holidays."

"But the holidays are the busiest."

"I don't have time to interview, Ed. And I don't have time to train anyone. Just yank the ad, okay?"

"Does that mean you're pulling it from Craigslist, too?"

"Of course." He was walking to his computer to do that this very second.

"I'll take care of it. Let me know if you change your mind."

Another call was coming in. Ted said goodbye and switched over. He wasn't getting any writing done, anyway. "Hello?"

"Ted?"

It was his mother, Rayma, who'd raised him as a single parent after his father left them for his female law partner. He and his mother had moved to Whiskey Creek from affluent Atherton, south of San Francisco, when he was three years old and she was offered the position of vice-principal at the elementary school. She was principal now, and had been for twenty years, but recently she'd been talking about retiring and moving back to the Bay Area to be closer to her mother and sisters.

"What's up, Mom?"

"Rough day," she said. "Since when do sixth-grade students bring guns to school?"

"A twelve-year-old showed up *with a gun?*"

"The nephew of those trashy people in the river bottoms. Carl Inera and his clan."

"Drugs have a lot to do with Carl's situation."

"Chief Stacy said the same thing."

"So…what? Are you planning to retire even earlier than we talked about?"

"No. Nothing's changed there."

"Something's different. You don't normally call me while you're at work."

"Mrs. Vaughn over at the middle school wanted me to hit you up for a donation."

"For what? You usually reserve my resources for your own school."

"She's aware of how much you've done here and hoped you might see your way clear to helping over there, too."

"What do they need?"

"They're raising funds for a new gymnasium."

How could he say no? The school system had provided the job that'd enabled his mother to make a living and provide for him. And with the way schools were hurting these days, he helped out whenever he could.

"How much?" he asked.

"Could you do $10,000?"

"That's not exactly pocket change, Mom."

"Is it too much?"

He considered his bank account; he could afford it. "No, I'll do it."

"I'm proud of the man you've become, of your accomplishments. I hope you know that."

He smiled. "What are you talking about? You don't even like my books."

"All that murder…it's too graphic for me, but I can appreciate your talent."

"I'm glad. Because I'm proud of you, too," he said, and it was true.

"Have you seen Sophia since the funeral?"

He'd been heading to the window overlooking the same river that ran past Carl Inera's shack some miles away. But at this, he froze. "No. Why would I?"

"Just checking."

His mother was an attractive, strong, capable woman. Unfortunately, she was also highly opinionated and often stuck her nose in his business, which he didn't appreciate. "You mean you're worried that I might take up with her again now that she's available."

"I remember how much you loved her."

"*Loved, past tense,* being the key word. There isn't much I even respect about her these days."

"But let's face it. You're a sucker for a damsel in distress. And she's attractive. I can't deny that. Please don't feel you have to swoop in and save her from her misdeeds, though."

There was so much he wanted to respond to in what she'd said he hardly knew where to start. "You believe *she's* to blame for what Skip did?"

"She's the one who married him to begin with. I thought she was certifiable at the time. Just like her mother."

Ted winced. "That's kind of a low blow, don't you think? She can't help that her mother has mental problems. Even her mom can't help that."

"I'm sorry, but I've never liked Sophia, and I've never made any secret of it."

He scratched his neck. "Because you were afraid I'd marry her before completing my degree."

"And because her values are all screwed up."

"How do you know she hasn't changed? Grown up?" God, he was sounding like some of his friends. Only his mother could push him to the other side of an argument *that* easily. He loved her, but they were too much alike—both of them opinionated, take-charge people.

"It's obvious."

"A lot of people choose the wrong marriage partner."

Although he hadn't meant to imply anything about her own decision to marry his father, the silence that followed indicated she'd taken it that way.

He opened his mouth to clarify, but she spoke before he could. "At least I didn't marry for money," she said. "And it's how she went about getting engaged. Leading you on while she was seeing Skip on the side. She agreed to marry him before she broke things off with you. We were almost the last to know!"

"Sophia and I were young. I was away at school so we could only see each other on weekends, and with all my extracurricular activities, even those visits were few and far between. Anyway, she was pregnant and probably felt trapped. And it's time to let go of the past." He was glad Callie couldn't hear him now....

"You're *defending* her?"

He shoved a hand through his hair. "No, of course not. Just trying to keep it all in perspective. We were together for a couple of years almost a decade and a half ago. That's long enough to carry a grudge."

"I don't care how long it's been. Her character is flawed, and you need to remember that when she sets her sights on you again."

"How do you know she'll try to get me back?"

"She needs money, and I'm sure it hasn't escaped her notice that you're now a wealthy novelist. I'd like to see you get married, but I *don't* want you to end up with her. She caused you enough heartache the first time."

"You're being overprotective again. I'm an adult and perfectly capable of making my own decisions, thank you. Anyway, you have nothing to worry about. I haven't seen her and I don't plan on seeing her."

"Good."

Before he could respond, someone entered her office—he could hear it in the background—and she had to go. Which was fine by him. That interruption might've prevented an argument. Although Rayma wasn't telling him anything he didn't already believe, he didn't like her talking about Sophia.

His mother should've remarried and had other kids, he thought. Then she would've had to spread her attention around.

Determined to finish his pages for the day, he decided he'd get hold of his agent later and returned to the computer. But when he clicked over to check his email, as he often did before starting, he found a message that was being forwarded all over Whiskey Creek. Several of Skip's investors were trying to connect with others so they could band together and meet Sophia tomorrow night to talk about how they might recoup some of their losses. They mentioned the two Ferraris and how much they were worth. The Mercedes that Sophia drove. The art and sculptures in the house. When someone piped up to say that Skip had probably taken out loans against it all, another member of the group mentioned Sophia's clothes and jewelry.

Ted told himself to stay out of it. He hadn't invested, so this didn't pertain to him. But the idea of everyone ganging up on her bothered him enough that he called Kyle.

"Are you planning to attend the meeting with Sophia about her remaining 'assets'?" he asked.

"No," Kyle replied. "I don't want to take what little she still has. Her husband screwed her over. How's piling on going to make things better for any of us?"

"What about Noah? Will he be going?"

"I doubt it. He doesn't hold her responsible for what Skip did any more than I do."

Ted's mood improved after he hung up. His friends weren't party to the next evening's plans. But the image of Sophia being confronted by twenty or thirty angry men demanding her clothes and jewelry troubled him for the rest of the day.

Sophia had been grateful for Agent Freeman's understanding and advice. She'd resolved to take advantage of it. But the depression that set in the following week proved so debilitating she could hardly get out of bed. She would force herself to get up and fix Alexa breakfast, then crawl back under the covers and sleep until Alexa came home.

At least her daughter talked about school as if it was going well. Considering how cruel kids could be, that came as an unexpected relief. Alexa insisted she was being treated kindly and that her friends rallied around her whenever she wasn't. She seemed to be making the difficult adjustment. But the worry in her eyes whenever she took in Sophia's bedraggled appearance spoke volumes. It said: *You're all I have left and I'm terrified*

I can't rely on you. Look at you! I've never seen you like this. Maybe it even said: *I guess Dad was right.*

Sophia could remember all the times Skip had told her she was a bitter disappointment. Part of her believed she deserved to hear it. Perhaps that was what had stolen the fight out of her; she'd essentially defeated herself by giving him so much ammunition. But, regardless of the reason for her depression, she wasn't going to the gym anymore. She couldn't bring herself to clean the house. She couldn't even face showering on a regular basis or brushing her teeth.

Although she scolded herself whenever she was awake, pleaded with herself to do better—for Alexa's sake—she fell further and further into despair and self-loathing, and that made the craving for alcohol worse. She hadn't succumbed, but only because there was no alcohol in the house, and she wouldn't go out for fear of running into yet another Whiskey Creek citizen her husband had defrauded.

Soon they had very little food in their cupboards and were surviving on canned soup. But no one knew that the "Queen of Whiskey Creek" had fallen quite so far, because no one came to check on her. Although she didn't normally get a lot of visitors, there'd always been the domestic help. Now even they weren't coming since she'd had to let them all go.

Sharon had been her only visitor, and she didn't come because she was concerned. She came to collect Alexa that first weekend after the funeral. Fortunately, Sophia hadn't looked quite as bad then. Still, while waiting for Alexa to finish gathering her things, Sharon had stood in Sophia's doorway, shaking her head in disgust.

"This *can't* continue, Sophia," she'd said, her voice harsh and low.

Sophia had ignored her. She'd just been grateful Alexa had a safe place to go for a couple of days, so she wouldn't have to get out of bed at all. Part of her hoped Sharon would come back and take Alexa *this* weekend, too. If so, it might be possible to get a bottle of gin or tequila—anything. She could walk over to the liquor store late at night....

But when Friday rolled around again, Sharon didn't come. She didn't come the next day or the day after that, either. Alexa told her Grandma and Grandpa were putting their house up for sale and moving into a condo in a retirement village at Rancho Murieta fifty minutes away, so Sophia figured they were busy dealing with their own disappointments and concerns. Maybe they were being hounded by bill collectors, too. Although Sophia rarely answered the home phone—her cell had probably died; she didn't even know where it was—she could hear voices on the answering machine in Skip's office when someone left a message. Apparently, her late husband had been several payments behind on everything, including the mortgage.

That wasn't good news. It shortened the time she and Alexa would be able to live in the house and Sophia had no idea where they'd go.

"Mom?"

She had to fight to drag herself out of the black abyss. She was pretty sure this was a Wednesday but maybe not. "Yes?"

"We're out of food."

"I'll get some," she mumbled.

"When?"

"Soon."

"You always say that."

"Tomorrow."

"Why not *now?*" Alexa asked.

"I don't feel well."

"You've been sick for *two weeks.*"

"I'll be okay soon. Have some more soup."

Her daughter let out an exasperated sigh. "I'm tired of bean with bacon."

"It's better than going hungry, isn't it?"

Alexa didn't answer. She'd obviously heard the irritation in Sophia's voice. "Will you let *me* go?"

"By yourself? It's too far to walk."

"Nature's Way might be too far, but Mel's Quickie Grocery isn't."

Sophia didn't have the energy for this conversation. "They don't have much."

"They have more than we do! I could get bread, milk, cereal, cheese…"

She was *so* adamant. Why not let her go? Whiskey Creek was as safe a place as any. And Sophia wanted to be left alone. "Fine. But hurry back."

"What money should I use?"

Money. God, just that word made Sophia freeze in terror. Soon they wouldn't have a dime….

Alexa clasped her by the shoulder. "Mom? Did you hear me? Should I get your purse?"

Dragging her brain back to the problem at hand, Sophia thought of what she had in her wallet. Since she couldn't use her bank accounts, she'd cashed the check Gail had given her. But the gardener, the young man who washed Skip's cars and Marta, the once-a-month housecleaner—they'd all needed to be paid. Once Sophia had seen to that, there hadn't been much left—maybe fifteen hundred dollars.

Knowing it wouldn't last forever made the anvil of worry sitting on her chest feel even heavier, as if it would crush her.

"Take a hundred from my purse." She rolled over because she couldn't bear to face what her daughter had to be thinking.

Once Alexa was gone, silence fell, allowing Sophia to drift in and out of sleep. Then the phone rang, but instead of leaving a message, whoever it was hung up and called back, over and over again.

"Alexa?" Sophia wanted her daughter to put a stop to the noise. But then she remembered that Alexa wasn't home.

Rousing herself enough to move, she crawled across the bed to Skip's side and grabbed the handset from its base. She intended to set it down and ignore it, but the thought that her daughter might need help made her bring it to her ear.

"Hello?" God, she sounded drunk even though she hadn't had so much as a drop.

"Mrs. DeBussi?"

"Yes?" It was the piercing voice of Clarence Halloway, the undertaker who'd handled Skip's funeral.

"I haven't received a check from you for your husband's service," he said. "Can you tell me when I might expect to be paid? Or do you plan on ripping me off like you did everyone else in town?"

She managed to shove herself into a sitting position. "Ripping you off! It's Dale and Sharon who owe you. *They* made the arrangements." *She* hadn't wanted that expensive casket and headstone, or all those flowers.

She'd wanted to have Skip cremated and be done with it, but her in-laws had taken over, and she'd let them because she didn't have any money to insist one way or the other.

"I called them. They told me it's *your* responsibility. I guess Gail DeMarco-O'Neal gave you some money while she was here? Sharon said that was supposed to cover Mr. DeBussi's burial costs."

What? Anger flooded Sophia's system. She should never have told her in-laws about that kind gesture. Gail hadn't given her that money for any such purpose. It wasn't enough, anyway. Skip's parents were the ones who'd ordered everything. Sophia had been shocked by how much they were willing to spend, considering he'd cost them their life's savings, but she'd chalked it up to habit and that fierce DeBussi pride. They could never be honest about anything. Appearances were all that mattered. Perhaps she'd been guilty of the same thing earlier in her life. But she hadn't been guilty of racking up nearly $15,000 in funeral expenses!

"I'm afraid most of Gail's money is gone, Mr. Halloway," she said. "I—I had to pay the people who were working for me. And what's left is all I've got to take care of Alexa until…until I find a job."

"I have a family to support, too," he pressed. "I told you in the beginning I wouldn't perform the service unless you paid me in advance."

"Exactly. And you didn't change your mind until Skip's parents got involved. You were dealing with *them.*"

"They've been part of the community for so long I never dreamed they'd do this to me, but it seems Skip inherited his dishonesty from them."

Sophia didn't want to be seen as a crook. She supposed it was a good sign that she still cared enough for that to bother her. But he was just one of many who were clamoring for money. She couldn't possibly satisfy them *all*. "I'm sorry, I really am, but…I can't help you."

"I don't feel it's fair for me to take the loss," he said. "I buried your husband, didn't I? Now I'd like to stop by and pick up at least a partial payment."

She had so little left. But how could she say no? It *wasn't* fair that he shouldn't get paid for the funeral. She didn't want to be responsible for anyone else getting hurt.

"I can give you a hundred bucks," she told him.

"That's better than nothing. I'll be right over," he said and hung up.

With a sigh, she slumped onto the pillows. She had such a blinding headache, couldn't remember when she'd last eaten and was beginning to feel dehydrated.

She hoped Alexa would get home in time to handle Clarence, but the doorbell rang while her daughter was still gone. Summoning what remained of her strength, Sophia managed to get up and force her leaden feet to move. She pulled on a robe, collected the money from her purse on the kitchen counter where Alexa had put it, and went to the door.

The undertaker raised his eyebrows when he saw her, but he glanced away and took the money. "I'll come by next month," he said tersely and turned to leave without another word.

Sophia stood in the doorway, watching until she couldn't see his black Cadillac anymore. Next *month?*

Fine. That sounded like an eternity from now. She had no idea how she'd survive until then—and part of her hoped she wouldn't.

8

"What are you looking at?"

Eve Harmon glanced over as Cheyenne Amos came to stand next to her at the window. Since Chey had married Dylan, she didn't usually work late at the B and B, not like she used to. When she'd been living with her sick mother and troubled sister, she'd taken advantage of any reason to stay out of the house.

"I thought you'd gone home," Eve told her.

"I wanted to finish the new brunch menus."

"Dylan must be working overtime at the body shop."

"Aaron's closing tonight. Dylan's at the house, making dinner."

"God, he cooks, too?" Eve grinned. She often teased Cheyenne about her sexy husband. She was happy for her best friend—she'd never seen Cheyenne happier—but she couldn't help feeling left out, maybe even a trifle jealous. She'd never believed she needed a man in order to be fulfilled, but with so many of her friends marrying, she wished she could find someone to share her life with.

"It'll be steak," Cheyenne said. "That's what he makes whenever he cooks."

"There could be worse foods." Eve almost said something about inviting her over next time Dylan's brother, Aaron, would be there. She'd thought of mentioning it before. But Aaron had anger management issues. As gorgeous as he was, she'd be stupid to get involved with him, especially when Cheyenne's sister had already traveled down that road and it had ended in a broken heart.

"True," Cheyenne agreed.

Eve felt her smile wilt as she returned her attention to the scene outside the window.

Cheyenne looked out, trying to follow Eve's gaze, but the lonely figure Eve had noticed a few minutes earlier was sitting too far to the right, in the shadow of a large headstone.

"You didn't answer my question," Cheyenne said. "Don't tell me you're thinking of Little Mary again."

Six-year-old Mary Margaret had been strangled in the basement over a century ago. She was their resident ghost—*maybe*. Eve wasn't convinced that Mary hadn't moved on. "Not this time." She pointed to the newest plot in the Whiskey Creek cemetery. "Alexa DeBussi is out there."

Cheyenne frowned as she finally located the young teen, who had a grocery bag at her side. "Poor girl."

It was obvious that Sophia's daughter was crying as she sat there, huddled against her father's headstone.

"I wonder if Sophia knows she's here," Cheyenne said.

"I haven't seen Sophia for the past couple of weeks. Have you?" Eve had placed a few calls to Sophia's cell phone, including the one in which she mentioned the job Ted had available, but they hadn't been returned.

Cheyenne shook her head. "No. I sent flowers since I couldn't attend the funeral. And I've stopped by twice, but no one answered the door."

The fact that Cheyenne hadn't been able to come to the funeral reminded Eve of Wyatt. "How's your nephew doing?" she asked. Cheyenne's sister had the cutest little boy. He meant everything to his mother. He meant a great deal to Cheyenne, too, which was why she and Dylan had been at the hospital in Fresno, where Presley lived, instead of at the funeral.

"He's fine now. The pneumonia's gone. Thank goodness. I can't imagine what Presley would do if anything happened to him."

"Do you think his father will ever be part of his life?"

"I doubt it. How could she ever find him? You know he was just some loser she met in Arizona," Cheyenne said.

"It's just sad to think the guy's walking around out there and he doesn't even know he's a father."

"I don't think he'd be the type of guy we'd want in Wyatt's life, anyway."

Pulling her sweater closer around her—it felt as if the weather was about to turn—Eve shifted her attention back to Alexa, whose mother was only *sort of* their friend. Half the members of their group seemed to have forgiven Sophia for her past. But others, like Ted, definitely had not. Eve wasn't sure how she felt. She had bad memories of various catfights and backbiting incidents instigated by Sophia, but she hated to be the kind of person who harbored resentments. "What should we do about her?" She indicated Alexa. "We can't leave her out there alone."

"Maybe she needs time to grieve," Cheyenne said. "I know she was close to Skip."

"Death is so hard."

"Sometimes." Cheyenne's voice was thoughtful when she made that comment. The woman who'd raised her had also been laid to rest in that cemetery, but her death had been more of a release than anything else.

"Maybe I'll walk down and say hello, see how she's doing," Eve said. "You head on home to Dylan. You wouldn't want him to burn your steak."

"He doesn't burn meat. He barely cooks it," she said with a chuckle. "But it's so tender it melts in your mouth."

Once again Eve suffered a twinge of jealousy. "You're lucky to have someone who loves you so much."

Cheyenne touched her arm. "You're thinking about getting older, aren't you?"

"I'm thirty-four, Chey. And I want kids."

"It'll happen."

"Here in Whiskey Creek?" Eve gave her a doubtful look. "I know all the eligible men. Just about the only guy I haven't seriously considered is Aaron. Dylan's other brothers are too young for me." She laughed as if it was a joke, but she was secretly wondering how Cheyenne would react.

"I love Aaron, but...you don't want to get involved with him," she said.

Eve forced a smile. "Of course not." She jerked her head toward the window. "I'd better go."

"Would you like me to go down with you?"

"No need to overwhelm her. One adult she hardly knows is enough."

Cheyenne hugged her. "You're so good."

Eve missed the old days, when she'd had more time with Chey. Now Chey, Gail and Callie were all married. Even Noah had a wife and a baby on the way. Eve had never dreamed the biggest playboy in the group would settle down before she did. She felt like the last person to leave a party....

But she wasn't the *last*. Ted hadn't married. He hadn't even been serious with anyone since Sophia. Riley, Baxter and Kyle were single, too, but they didn't really count. Riley had a kid—he'd actually been the first to have one. Baxter was gay and in love with Noah, who wasn't. And Kyle had been married. His wife had revealed herself to be the spawn of Satan so they'd divorced within months, but at least he'd known *some* kind of romance. Actually, he was still in love with Olivia, who'd married his stepbrother. So why was *her* love life so uneventful?

She'd survive, she told herself. She shouldn't wallow in self-pity when there were people suffering from much bigger problems than a bout of loneliness. People like Sophia. She'd once been the most popular girl in school, the daughter of the mayor. And she'd married the richest guy in town. How would it feel to suddenly become a pariah after having all that? The reversal alone had probably given her whiplash. And what about poor Alexa?

Eve had such great parents. She couldn't even imagine what it would be like to find out her dad was a total douchebag.

Alexa was sobbing by the time Eve made it down

to her. She was crying so hard, in fact, that she didn't hear Eve's approach.

"Hey, kiddo. You okay?" Eve asked, putting a hand on her shoulder.

Alexa was too distraught to even be startled. She hiccuped and wiped her cheeks as she looked up. "Am I—" she glanced around the cemetery "—am I not supposed to be in here?"

Eve knelt beside her. "It's perfectly fine for you to visit your father's grave. I just didn't want you to be alone if you needed someone to talk to. You don't know me very well, but I'm a friend of your mom's."

"You are?" She sounded skeptical, and for good reason. Eve had never even been to Sophia's house. They'd had coffee together a few times at Black Gold with the others. That was it.

"We went to high school together," she said to bolster her claim.

With a sniff, Alexa again dashed a hand over her wet cheeks. "Oh."

"Are you going to be okay?" Eve gestured at the flowers adorning the grave. "I know it's hard to lose someone you love."

"Do you think it's true?" she asked.

Eve lowered her head to meet Alexa's eye. "Do I think what's true?"

"That he did all those terrible things? That he didn't love us like he said he did?"

Oh, boy… Eve took a deep breath as she tried to come up with an answer that would help instead of hurt. "Sometimes, when things go wrong, people panic and make foolish mistakes. I bet your father wasn't in the best frame of mind at the end. I'm sure he would've regretted his actions, had he lived. He loved you. There's no question about that."

"But he *did* steal everyone's money? And he was leaving us?"

Alexa's expression grew more beseeching. She seemed to be pleading for the truth, so Eve felt she had to be honest even if what she said would be painful to hear.

"That's what the evidence seems to suggest, sweetheart."

Two more tears slipped from her pretty blue eyes, eyes that were so much like her mother's. "And now I have no one," she said as if the world had just stopped turning.

Eve feared she'd gone too far. "You have your mom. She's not going anywhere."

Alexa's tears started to fall faster and she had to gulp for breath as she blurted, "My mom's not the same. She needs help."

"In what way?"

"Maybe she's drinking again. I don't think so because there's nothing in the house, but…she could be hiding it from me."

Eve felt a new measure of alarm. "You're saying she's drunk?"

Alexa shrugged. "She can't get out of bed."

Did Sophia have a drinking problem? If so, she wouldn't want anyone to know about it, which made Eve feel like some nosy, intrusive bystander, gawking at the scene of a car crash. "She's grieving, like you. The process affects us all differently."

"It's more than that," Alexa insisted. "She won't eat, won't let me open the drapes, hardly ever talks to me."

She plucked a blade of grass. "I'm going to have to call my grandma, but—" she turned her watery gaze to her father's elaborate marble headstone "—then she'll make me come and live with her." Getting to her feet, she picked up her bag of groceries. She seemed so weary she could hardly move.

Eve couldn't let her go home by herself. "Why don't I come with you?" she said. "I'll check on your mom, see if there's anything I can do."

She'd expected Alexa to be relieved to have reinforcements, but her lips slanted into a frown. "Thanks, but...you'd better not. No one's supposed to know," she said and started off, all but dragging those groceries along.

Eve wasn't sure what to do. She stood where she was and watched her for a few seconds, then jogged to catch up. "Lexi, I'm your mom's friend, as I told you. And it sounds like she could use a friend right now."

"But then she'll find out I told you," Alexa said.

"You only told me because you love her and you want to get her the help she needs." Eve took the bag of groceries. "So let's put these in my car and drive over together, okay? We'll do what we can to get her back on her feet."

Alexa looked as if she was afraid to even hope, the poor girl. "You think it might work?"

"Sometimes we have to fight for those we love. What I think is that we need to stage an intervention."

Alexa remained skeptical. "Is an intervention like rehab? Because she's already done rehab. That lasted the whole month of September."

Eve secretly winced at the information the innocent Lexi had revealed. But at least it enabled her to view

Sophia in a far more sympathetic light. Sophia had always been the girl who had it all. But maybe she was just more skillful at hiding her troubles. "It's not rehab. It's where your loved ones get hold of you and shake some sense into you, get you turned around and heading in the right direction."

For the first time since Eve had confronted her, Alexa lifted her chin and seemed to overcome her tears. "Will it work?"

"We won't know until we try."

Her sniff sounded more decisive than before. "Yes," she said with a nod, "I want to stage an intervention."

Eve reached out with her free hand. "Let's do it," she said, but before they left the inn, she checked the sack, found it full of cold cereal and snack items and decided to grab a few ingredients from her own pantry.

9

Voices carried up to Sophia. At first she imagined she was still in rehab, that some of her fellow "inmates"—as they'd jokingly referred to themselves—were talking in the hall outside her room. But when she opened her eyes and blinked at the ceiling, she realized she was at home. Then the rest of what had happened during the past month came rushing in on her. Skip was dead but he hadn't just stepped out of her life like she'd long hoped he would; he'd done everything he could to ruin her first. She had a thousand dollars or so to her name and no way to earn more. Alexa needed her but she was turning out to be as terrible a mother as Skip had always accused her of being. And all of that reminded her of why she didn't want to wake up. She was going to lose her daughter. Agent Freeman had warned her. There didn't seem to be a damn thing she could do about it, though. Except sleep. Sleep was her only escape.

She almost drifted off again, but Alexa was talking to someone in the cathedral-like entrance of their house, and curiosity got the better of her.

Had her daughter brought home a friend from school?

No, she'd come back a while ago. Alone. She claimed she was being treated as well as ever, but Sophia hadn't seen any proof of her life returning to normal. Where were the girls who used to hang out with her? The girls who liked to come over and play in the game room? Or visit the garage to see the two Ferraris Skip owned? Or make an ice-cream creation at the soda fountain in the basement?

Sophia couldn't think about that, *wouldn't* think of it. It hurt too badly to suspect that her daughter might be suffering more than she said. That she might be hiding her pain because she was worried about Sophia.

She'd left after school to go to the store. She must've run into someone there.

"Alexa?" Sophia called.

The talking quieted for a moment, then her daughter responded. "What?"

"You got home okay?"

"Yes."

"Who's with you?"

"I brought a…a friend."

Good. She needed one.

When they moved into the kitchen, Sophia couldn't hear them anymore, so she pulled the blankets over her head. At least her daughter was safe. At least Lexi had something besides soup to eat. Now Sophia didn't have to regret letting her go out alone.

The pungent smell of garlic and tomatoes woke Sophia some time later. She didn't think she'd been sleeping long, but she knew her daughter didn't have the cooking skills to create such a delectable smell—like an Italian restaurant. Maybe her friend was helping her…. She was about to call Lexi's name, to find out what was going on, when she heard a light tread on the stairs and saw a woman, not a girl, poke her head into the room. "Hey."

Sophia squinted, trying to identify this person, but it was too dark to see. She'd been keeping the blinds shut. The sun had set since the last time she'd fallen asleep, anyway. The digital clock on the nightstand told her that. "Who is it?"

"Eve."

"Ted's friend?" Sophia definitely didn't want anyone connected with him to see how badly she was faring.

"*Your* friend."

That couldn't be true. She didn't have any friends. She'd alienated them when she was a teenager, right before making the biggest mistake of her life by marrying Skip. But she didn't want word of her diminished state to get back to Ted, so she struggled to put some energy into her voice. "Oh, hey. Sorry I'm not feeling well. Maybe you could come back another time."

"But then you'd miss the amazing dinner Alexa and I cooked for you. Where's your robe?"

"What?" She'd expected Eve to apologize and excuse herself. That was what most people would do. It wasn't as if they knew each other all that well.

"You have a young lady downstairs who's setting a beautiful table, just waiting to show her mother all the wonderful things she helped make. So I'm going to wrap you up in your robe and walk you down the stairs. And you're going to have dinner. Maybe once you've got some food in your stomach, you'll have the strength to shower."

"I can't," she said. "I—I'm sick."

"Then we'll take you to a doctor."

She didn't want a doctor. She was terrified of what a doctor might tell her, terrified she'd wind up like her mother. She just wanted to continue hiding from the world until she could get back on her feet. "I'll get up later. Maybe another day."

"You can't put it off, Sophia."

She raised her head. "Why not?"

"Because it'll only get harder."

There was truth in that. Sophia knew it. How had she even arrived at this dark place? It was humiliating to feel so lost, so helpless. Skip would never have stood for it. She was embarrassed herself. She had so many enemies who would take pleasure in seeing her crushed and broken and, for all she knew, Eve was one of them. "You don't have to trouble yourself," she muttered. "I'll be fine in a few days."

"That's what I hope. Are you hungry?"

She should be, but... "I can't tell."

"That means you've been hungry for too long. Let's get some food into you."

The light went on. Sophia covered her face against its painful brightness as Eve collected her robe and slippers, then helped her put them on. "You ready?"

"For what?" Sophia couldn't believe this was happening. Eve had never shown any interest in her before, not since high school, and they certainly hadn't been friends back then.

Eve slipped her head under Sophia's arm so she could support the majority of her weight as they stood. "For a trip to the dinner table."

Sophia's chest grew tight as she leaned on a woman who had no particular reason to care about her. She hadn't cried since she'd taken to her bed. It felt like

she'd been numb since the funeral. But she was starting to feel more acutely again—and the burning and
prickling sensation of coming alive stung so badly she
could hardly bear it.

"Eve?"

They took a few careful steps toward the door.
"Yes?"

"Why are you helping me?"

"Because life is hard enough without trying to manage the worst of times alone."

She swallowed the tears that were welling up. "Do
you believe I knew what Skip was doing?"

"Did you?" she asked as they entered the hall and
approached the long, sweeping staircase.

"No."

Eve paused, staring into Sophia's face. "Then *stop*
letting him get the better of you," she whispered. "What
he did was terrible. But you can still make a good life
for yourself and Alexa *if you fight.* Do you understand?"

She nodded. Eve was right, of course. Sophia had to
change her thinking, had to get past the despair. "How
do I start?" she whispered.

"By taking it one day at a time. Or, if that's too
much, one hour at a time." Eve squeezed her tighter.
"Will you try?"

"I will," she said and meant it.

"Then you'll be fine." Eve helped her down to the
dining room, where Alexa was waiting with a hopeful
smile on her face.

"Doesn't the food smell good, Mommy? And doesn't
the table look pretty?"

Sophia shifted her gaze from the antipasto, to the
spaghetti and meatballs, to the salad and garlic bread.

Alexa had set out their best crystal, china and silverware for this Italian feast. There was even a slice of lemon in her water glass.

This meal signified something, she realized: It signified a new beginning.

"It does look pretty," she breathed and made herself a promise as she sat down. No matter how bad it got, she wouldn't give up. Wouldn't allow her mother-in-law to take custody of Alexa. Wouldn't allow alcohol to ruin her. She'd prove Skip wrong, damn it. The whole town, too. She'd prove she had more backbone, more strength, than anyone imagined. And she'd do it by getting a job and working herself out of the mess he'd left her in.

But just after she'd eaten and had begun to talk and laugh and feel a sense of well-being for the first time since Skip went missing, there was a knock at the door.

Sophia was in no position to see anyone, so Alexa answered it.

"Who was it?" Sophia asked the moment Alexa returned.

She handed Sophia an envelope. "He said his name was Mr. Groscost."

"The guy who bought the tractor place from Noah's dad?" Eve said.

When Alexa shrugged, Sophia exchanged a glance with Eve and opened the letter.

"What does he want?" Eve murmured as Sophia skimmed the contents.

Feeling some of the old panic, Sophia swallowed hard and read the letter more carefully. "A 'certain number' of Skip's investors want to meet with me."

Eve blanched. "What for?"

"To discuss their 'options.'"

"What options?"

"Repayment of some kind, I guess."

"When?"

"Tomorrow night."

"Don't tell me they're coming here," Eve said.

"No. They want to meet at the church."

Eve took the letter and read it for herself. Reverend Flores was among those who'd signed it. He must've lost money investing with Skip, too, which was why he'd offered the church as their meeting place. "You don't have to go. As a matter of fact, I suggest you don't."

"Listen to Eve, Mommy," Alexa begged.

Sophia hated seeing the haunted look back in her daughter's eyes. "Maybe it'll help," she said.

"How?" Eve asked.

"I can't hide in this house forever. We just established that, didn't we?"

"But I have no idea how these people will treat you. Actually, I *do* have an idea. That's why I'm worried."

"Maybe if I give them a chance to vent their anger, to throw whatever punches they're dying to throw, they'll begin to heal so I can, too."

Eve sighed as she slouched in a chair. "I don't like the sound of that."

"In order to get past what happened, I have to confront these people sometime," Sophia said. "It might as well be now."

Eve nibbled nervously on her bottom lip. "Then I'm going with you."

Ted knew he had no business attending this meeting. He needed to stay as far away from Sophia DeBussi as possible. Maybe he didn't like her, but he was still attracted to her, which was a dangerous combination. So when he first pulled into the church, he almost turned around and drove off—until he saw the number of cars in the lot. Once he realized how outnumbered she'd be, he parked. He didn't believe in kicking people when they were down, even if they deserved it. Especially a woman. And, beyond that, a woman with a kid. He wanted to make sure this didn't get out of hand.

It took a moment for his eyes to adjust. He'd been driving right into the sunset. But from what he could see when he walked in, she hadn't arrived yet. He stood at the back of the church, listening as the boisterous, angry group congregating near the pulpit talked about her as if she were pure evil. They wanted to believe that she, and not Skip, had stolen their money. Ted heard Eric Groscost say that Skip never would've done what he did if she hadn't demanded he keep her in luxury, and several others readily agreed.

Ted rolled his eyes. Although Sophia had no doubt enjoyed Skip's money and the prestige it afforded her, he was pretty sure these people were conveniently forgetting how arrogant and egotistical Skip had been.

Reverend Flores spotted him before any of the others did. "Ted," he said, hurrying down the aisle to greet him. "I'm so glad you could come. I had *no* idea you were caught up in this, too."

He grunted so he wouldn't have to explain why he'd decided to attend if he *wasn't* an investor, and took a seat in the back row.

"Don't you want to join us up front?" Flores asked. "Sophia should be here any minute."

If she knew what was good for her, she wouldn't show. But he'd had coffee with his friends this morning and Eve had mentioned that they were both planning to attend. "I'm fine back here," he said. "Maybe you could just tell me… What do you guys hope to accomplish tonight?"

"What do you mean?" Flores replied. "We're hoping to get back as much of our money as we can."

Eve had made Sophia's situation seem dire. Didn't they realize that Skip had cheated her far more than he'd cheated them? "From where? You know the old saying about getting blood from a turnip."

"She's hardly a turnip, Ted. Her wedding ring alone has to be worth enough to pay off half the people in this room."

"You expect her to sell her *wedding ring?*"

"Yeah, I expect her to sell it. Why should she be walking around with a rock like that when I lost my life savings? She has other things she could sell, too."

Ted gestured at the crowd. "Enough to satisfy everyone here?"

"*Something* is better than nothing. It might sound cruel, but it's only right that she try to make amends. That's the Lord's way."

"I thought forgiveness was the Lord's way," Ted murmured.

"She has to bring forth fruit meet for repentance first." He raised his chin as if he'd just put Ted in his place, but Ted wasn't willing to let it go that easily.

"Which entails…"

"Doing what she can, like I said. What about the Ferraris Skip drove?"

"They're probably encumbered. A man would have to be desperate to do what Skip did. I'm sure he exhausted all of his resources before giving up his house, his wife and his daughter to start a new life."

"Maybe that's true, but now we'll at least have a chance to hear it from her own lips. You've got to be curious as to whether she knew what Skip was doing."

"I *am* curious about how he got away with so much. But I don't necessarily believe she's responsible for his actions. And dragging her in front of half the town won't do any good. Even if she knew, even if she masterminded the whole thing, she has to proclaim her innocence. Doing anything else might turn this crowd into a lynch mob."

Reverend Flores made a calming gesture. "No, this is a peaceable gathering. Chief Stacy is planning to be here to make sure of it."

"Just to keep the situation under control? Or to help pressure her into selling her jewelry?"

"He invested with Skip, too. He'd like to get his money back same as we would. He has a boy and a girl to put through college, you know."

Ted started to say something about the foolishness of investing money that was needed for living expenses, but he didn't get the chance. When he heard the door open behind him and saw the reverend's face, he knew Sophia had arrived.

Turning, he saw that she looked beautiful, as always. She was dressed to impress, too. But there were a few telltale signs that indicated she wasn't doing as well as she wanted it to appear. For one, she was white as a ghost. He could see the blue veins under the alabaster skin of her cheeks. For another, she'd lost weight.

As she walked in, she held her head high, but she didn't remove her sunglasses. Eve held on to her arm.

She'd been pretty defensive of Sophia this morning, had even tried talking some of them into attending—to give Sophia moral support. But, considering how much Noah and Kyle had lost, that didn't go over too well. None of them were hoping to make Sophia's life miserable, but they weren't ready to champion her, either. Cheyenne and Callie were two exceptions, but they both had other plans tonight.

"Mrs. DeBussi, thank you for joining us," Reverend Flores said, not bothering to address Eve. Ted wanted to believe it was because Eve was agnostic and didn't worship here on Sundays, so Flores wasn't familiar with her. But he guessed it had more to do with the fact that Flores wasn't interested in anyone other than Sophia. "I'm Mrs. DeBussi to you now, Reverend?" Sophia smiled coldly. "Does that give you the distance you need in order to feel better about what you're here to do?"

"I'm not doing anything wrong. I'm trying to *right* a wrong."

"I wish you could right it for me, too," she murmured.

When Eve recognized Ted, her eyes widened, but she was so distracted by the men who were streaming down the aisle toward them that she didn't say anything. Sophia didn't even glance at him. She stiffened as if she wanted to run but wouldn't let herself. Instead, she moved purposefully toward them.

"I've left my daughter at a friend's, doing her homework. I'd like to get through this as soon as possible so she doesn't get to bed too late."

"It won't take long," Mr. Groscost assured her. He was far more solicitous now that he was confronting the beautiful Sophia face to face, but Ted knew nothing would deter him from his purpose. "Have a seat."

"I prefer to stand if you don't mind." No one else seemed interested in sitting, either. They were too keyed up.

"Fine." Groscost cleared his throat. "We wanted to meet with you to see what you plan to do to make things right for the people you and your husband cheated."

She didn't claim that she hadn't been involved, didn't try to defend herself. She merely lifted her keys and, when he held out his hand, dropped them into his open palm. "These are for the house. The furnishings, my clothes—that's all I have left. Take what you want. I ask only that you stay out of my daughter's room."

She'd given in so quickly that Groscost didn't seem to know how to react. His eyebrows shot up as he turned to Flores, who blinked and stammered, "Why—why, thank you for making this easy, Mrs. DeBussi. But I think I speak for everyone when I say we're most interested in your wedding ring."

"If you can find it, you can have it," she said. "Skip took it several weeks ago. He told me he was having it appraised for insurance purposes. He didn't give it back, and it isn't in the house."

God, he took her wedding ring, too....

"I see." Obviously deflated, Reverend Flores exchanged another look with Eric Groscost. He obviously didn't know whether or not to proceed, but Groscost shored him up.

"You have many other lovely things that must be worth quite a bit."

"As I said, Mr. Groscost, I have household furnishings and clothes."

"That's a start. I'm sure it'll go a long way toward mollifying your friends here in Whiskey Creek."

She gazed around at them. "I don't have any friends in Whiskey Creek."

"Maybe it's because you don't deserve them," someone else snapped.

"Maybe I don't," she agreed. At least, that was what Ted thought she said. She'd spoken in such a low voice he could barely hear her.

Eve squeezed her arm as if to say that wasn't true. Then the place erupted in chaos. Chief Stacy, the enforcer, hadn't even arrived yet and already Sophia was opening her gorgeous home and allowing them to take whatever they wanted.

Excitement replaced anger. She wasn't asking for proof that they'd ever been Skip's investors. Neither was she requiring proof of the amount owed. She was simply opening her doors and letting them take their revenge.

This was crazy. Ted almost stood up and told everyone to go home and leave her be. She'd lost her husband. Worse, he'd died in the process of abandoning her. He couldn't think of two more hurtful blows. To top it all off, Skip had left her broke when she'd had money her whole life and wasn't exactly primed to make a living.

But just as he was about to speak up, she turned and saw him. She flinched when she realized who he was, as if his presence was like another stripe across her back. Then she nodded politely, resolutely, and walked past him.

Eve hesitated as though tempted to stop and say a few words to him, but he could tell she didn't dare leave Sophia's side. Although she tossed him a smile, he could see the tears in her eyes. She felt the same way he did about this, found it a cruelty she could hardly stand to witness. While she reacted with tears, he got angry.

That anger motivated him to drive over to Sophia's house, where he was again tempted to intervene. But what was happening was none of his business. He had no responsibility for Sophia. He hadn't even invested with Skip—so how could he tell these people how they should react? They felt hurt, betrayed, and maybe the loss had damaged some more than others.

Forcing himself to remain in his car, he watched his fellow townspeople carry away her belongings. Several left and returned with trucks so they could take the furniture. From what he could see, they were stripping the place, and she was doing nothing to stop them. She probably *couldn't* stop them at this point; it had turned into a frenzy.

Where was she? Was she standing in her living room as all the people who'd admired her for so long grabbed as much as they could carry? He'd seen her go in with Eve, but neither of them had come back out.

Chief Stacy showed up after an hour. Ted saw him walk by and rolled down his window. "Hey, Chief," he called. "You're a little late to the party."

Stacy frowned as though he regretted that and shook his head. "Got held up at a traffic stop. The driver had a bag of pot on him. You wouldn't believe what some tourists bring through here."

"Good thing you're around to keep our streets safe."

This was exactly what he wanted to hear. His chest swelled out and he clicked his tongue. "That's my job."

Ted wasn't buying the false humility. He'd never particularly liked Stacy. He liked him even less after hearing about some of the things he'd done over the past few years—to Cheyenne's husband, Dylan, Dylan's brother, Aaron, and Callie's husband, Levi.

But surely he wouldn't want everyone ganging up on a woman, especially one who was already going through hell.

"So now that you're here, you'll put an end to this circus, right?"

Stacy seemed taken aback. "What circus?"

"All these people carrying off everything Sophia DeBussi owns."

"From what I've heard, she owes them that and more."

"Maybe she didn't know what Skip was doing. Maybe she had no part in it."

Stacy ran a finger over his chin. He looked less bloated since his divorce; he'd finally lost some weight. "She certainly took part in spending our money."

"Not knowingly."

"You sure about that?"

"In any case, I think she's suffering enough. And her daughter's what…thirteen? At that age, it's highly unlikely *she* had any part in it. How will they get by when this is over? Does anyone care about that?"

Stacy made a face that said Ted was worried about nothing. "She's probably got a fortune we don't know about. Anyway, she doesn't need a twenty-thousand-dollar couch to *get by.* We've all been getting by with a lot less than that, haven't we?"

He walked off, and fifteen minutes later, reappeared, pockets bulging, as he carried a painting to his cruiser. After that, Ted couldn't bear to watch. With all the things coming out of that house, he couldn't imagine there was much left. Some people were even taking

Sophia's silverware, dishes and small appliances. Why wasn't Eve putting a stop to it?

He texted her, telling her to do just that, and drove away, but he was too upset to go home. He went by the high school, and parked in front of the gymnasium, where he'd given so many speeches as student body president—and taken Sophia to the prom. Then he headed to the river and hiked down to the rope swing where he and Sophia had gone skinny-dipping the summer they were seventeen. He even visited the abandoned gold-mining shack where they'd made love for the first time. He wanted to remember all the reasons he should hate her. And visiting these places should have helped because they reminded him of how much she'd meant to him. Reminded him that she'd ruined all their plans by getting serious with Skip while he was away at college. She'd never mentioned that she was seeing someone else. She'd pretended she wasn't. Then his mother had heard, via town gossip, that she was pregnant.

He'd been furious with her for so long. Over the past decade and a half or so, there'd been plenty of times he'd found himself wishing she'd realize what she'd lost, what she'd cost them both. That was pride talking, of course. Like any spurned lover, he wanted her to regret choosing someone else. But despite everything he held against her, he'd never wanted to see her devastated.

He hated seeing it now.

Maybe that was the truest testament to how much he'd loved her.

10

"I'm stunned that you've agreed!"

With a grimace at Eve's reaction, which he considered a bit over the top, Ted pivoted at the window and headed back across his living room. He'd been pacing ever since he'd returned home. And although it was approaching midnight, too late to be calling someone even on a weekend, he'd broken down and called Eve.

"Don't sound so surprised," he said. "I'm not *completely* heartless."

Just crazy. What had happened to his conviction? He'd told himself he would never have another thing to do with Sophia. He'd already forgiven her once, when he'd taken her back after Scott's death. She'd come to him in tears, insisting that she still wanted to be with him, that he was the only boy she'd ever love. And he'd stood by her despite the negative reaction of almost everyone else in town. So what did she do after that? She proved her love by getting pregnant while he was away at school and marrying the other guy.

Yet here he was, suggesting she call him about his housekeeper position, even though he'd removed the ad from Craigslist for fear she'd apply!

His mother was going to have a fit. He felt a little guilty about that, since she'd always been such a stand-out mom. His father had never taken much interest; he'd been too involved with his second family. That made Ted feel he owed the parent who'd stuck by him more than a normal kid would owe his mother. But he insisted on making his own decisions, especially about *this,* even if it proved to be a mistake.

"What changed your mind?" Eve asked. "You haven't had anything nice to say about Sophia in years."

"I'm not saying anything nice about her now," he clarified. "I barely know her anymore. I just… I can't imagine how she'll ever get back on her feet without *some* help. And I don't see Skip's parents or anyone else taking pity on her."

"Ugh, if only you knew how badly they were treating her," Eve said. "I'd give you details, but I feel like that would somehow be…breaking a confidence."

Her comment irritated him because it suggested she had strong loyalties to Sophia, when *he* was the one who'd hung out with Eve since grade school. "Suddenly you're better friends with her than you are me?"

"No! Of course not. But she's vulnerable right now, fragile. And you…you have everything under control. Let's face it. No one manages life—or anything else— quite as well as you do."

"It's because of that inflexibility you tease me about," he said dryly.

She laughed. "It is! But that inflexibility could also be called self-discipline. You've always been the over-achiever in the group."

"Stop trying to appeal to my vanity. You're throwing me over for Sophia."

"I am not!" she said. "But I don't mind telling you that what you're offering her is really wonderful. You should've seen her tonight while everyone was rummaging through her house."

He wasn't sure he wanted to hear the details. It'd been difficult enough to watch it from outside. But he couldn't help asking, "Was she crying?"

"No. I wish she *had* been. Crying would've been a normal reaction to sadness and pain. Crying is how most people cope with disappointment. But what she's suffering goes deeper than that. She's depressed. Numb. Completely lost. She sat on the back steps, smoking a cigarette, believe it or not, and staring off into space. She didn't try to protect any of her possessions, even the ones with sentimental value."

He felt a tightness in his chest, which he didn't want to acknowledge, and opened his mouth to bring the conversation back to the practical—the details of the job—but she kept talking.

"You know what they say about people who lose all their belongings in a fire."

That distracted him. "No. What do they say?"

"It's one of the most catastrophic things that can happen to a person. One minute her house looked like she was used to seeing it, the next almost everything was gone."

Including her husband, he thought. He wondered if she missed Skip, if she'd loved him—although he couldn't understand how anyone could care too deeply about such a pompous ass.

"The people who came were like locusts," Eve was saying. "They took practically everything."

"You didn't put a stop to it?"

"Eventually. I wish I'd acted sooner. I just… I don't know her all that well, so I didn't think it was my place until you sent me that text. Then I got mad at myself for not standing at the door and refusing to let them enter in the first place."

He remembered his brief exchange with Chief Stacy. "It's a difficult situation. They felt justified in what they were doing."

"I heard one person say, 'I paid for it, why shouldn't I have it?'"

"They're happy to see her deprived of all the things they've envied."

"I guess. It sucked—that's all I know."

"So when did she start smoking?" He couldn't recall Sophia ever having a cigarette. They'd certainly never smoked when they were younger.

"I guess she started tonight," Eve said. "She made me stop at the Gas-N-Go on our way to the house. When she came out toting a carton of cigarettes, I asked her why, and she said, 'Because I can't drink.' She began to add that she hoped they'd kill her and put her out of her misery but when she saw my reaction, she clammed up."

"Why can't she drink?"

There was a slight hesitation. "Um…I didn't ask."

"Well, she can't smoke in *my* house." He hated the smell. He was willing to provide employment so she could get over this rough patch, but he planned to keep everything very professional. There'd be no allowances.

"She won't. She'll do everything she can to make you happy." She groaned. "God, I'm so relieved. Before you called, I was sitting here going over my books, trying to figure out a way to hire her at the B and B. But…it's just not in my budget to add another employee, especially going into the off season."

"She can start on Monday if she wants. If she's not ready, it can wait until later in the week or the following Monday."

"Judging by the state of her cupboards, I think she needs to start as soon as possible."

"Don't tell me they carted off her food, too!"

"She didn't have much to begin with."

"Shit." He could already feel the situation getting stickier than he'd bargained for.

"But now everything's going to be okay." She laughed. "You're such a softie, you know that?"

"Don't let it get out. I can only take on one charity case at a time."

"She'd hate to hear you say that."

He heard the displeasure in her voice. "She won't hear it, because you won't tell her."

"Is that the *only* reason you're giving her a hand? For the sake of helping someone who's going through a rough time?"

"Of course," he snapped, irritated again. "Why else would I be doing it?"

"Sometimes I wonder if you still have feelings for her."

His other friends wondered, too, which made what he was doing even more problematic, since he'd have to deal with their reactions. "The answer is no."

So what if the idea of peeling off her clothes caused a visceral excitement, even after this many years? That didn't mean anything. Lots of people harbored desire for an ex.

It was just that he hadn't been in a relationship in

forever. He needed to quit worrying about work and get back to dating. "And don't bring that up again."

"Got it. There will be no questioning your motives."

"Smart ass," he grumbled. "So do you think she can get by on $2,500 a month? It's not a lot—pennies compared to what she's used to."

"But it's the most she'll be able to make, especially in Whiskey Creek. There aren't many jobs."

"Why doesn't she move somewhere else?"

"She won't uproot her daughter. Alexa wants to stay where it's familiar. Where her friends are."

"Sophia cares about that?"

"Of course! Alexa is everything to her."

"Maybe she's not as terrible a person as I thought."

"Ted, stop."

He rolled his eyes. "Fine. I hope her salary will cover the basics. And I'll be flexible about hours. As long as she's not too loud while I'm trying to write, Alexa can come here after school. Sophia might as well make one dinner for all of us. They can eat before they leave. I'll eat after they go home."

"Heaven forbid you should ever eat together."

He rubbed his neck. "You're already making me regret this."

"Don't, because what you're offering is more than fair. I just...I wish you could forgive her and start over—as friends. She's different than she was."

"Sure she is."

"It's true!"

"Don't worry. I'll be perfectly polite."

There was a slight pause, but she must've decided not to challenge him further. "I can't wait to call and tell her the job I mentioned before is still available if she wants it!" Eve said. "It was so hard to leave her sitting in that empty house once I got everyone out of there. You should've seen Alexa's face when she came home. She's every bit as lost as her mother, you know. I found her crying in the cemetery yesterday."

She'd told them at coffee, but he let her tell him again. "She just lost her father in one of the worst ways possible. Of course she's going to cry."

"But she wasn't crying over her father. She was crying about her mother!"

She hadn't made such a point of *that*.

He sighed. He'd justified making this call by telling himself he wouldn't get *too* involved. He'd give her work. That was it. Anything beyond money for services rendered would be…foolhardy. "I'd rather not hear about it, if you don't mind. I'm in the market for a housekeeper. I figure she can have the job until she finds something better."

"Understood," Eve said. "No emotional involvement."

"Now you've got it."

"So what should I say her duties will include?"

"Meals. Cleaning. Errands. Some computer work. She knows how to use a computer, doesn't she?"

"If she doesn't, Alexa will," she joked. "Kids are all computer-literate these days."

"Not funny. Alexa can't manage what I need done."

"Fine. I'll tutor Sophia if I have to. Or do your secretarial stuff myself while I'm working at the B and B. I have an office with a computer off the kitchen, and I'm a hell of a typist."

He parted the blinds to see the moonlight glinting

off the river behind his house. "Why would you take that on?"

"Because I'm willing to do my part."

"For the sake of charity?"

"It's not quite that impersonal for me. I want to help *her!*"

So it was going to be okay, wasn't it? They were both just doing a good deed.

Somehow he managed to convince himself so he could breathe a little easier. But when Sophia called him the next morning, the sound of her voice carried him right back to high school.

This wasn't going to be a comfortable conversation. Sophia was so nervous she had butterflies in her stomach, which was silly. She was thirty-four years old! But she hadn't had a real conversation with Ted since he'd confronted her after hearing about her engagement to Skip. He'd been so hurt and angry to learn she was pregnant that he hadn't allowed her to say much.

She'd tried several times since then to apologize. She felt guilty for hurting him, but back then she could see no other way out of her predicament. She couldn't get an abortion, not with her religious upbringing. She couldn't raise a child on her own, not without a job or some way to earn a living. And she could no longer rely on her parents, who'd always been her rock, because their lives were crumbling in front of her. As much as her heart rebelled, Skip had seemed like her best option. And he was so determined to have her, so confident that she'd be making the right choice in becoming his wife.

The promises he'd made were very different from the reality, but she hadn't known he was abusive *before* the wedding. She'd only known that Ted wasn't ready for marriage and that trying to stay with him would mean asking him to accept a child who wasn't his. Skip wouldn't have let that happen anyway.

"Eve just called. She said—" she had to clear her throat to continue talking "—she said you have a…a possible job opportunity?" Eve claimed she'd called about the housekeeper position before, but Sophia hadn't gotten that message. She'd never listened to the messages that had come in the first couple of weeks after Skip died; she hadn't seen any point, since she'd expected them all to be bill collectors.

The silence stretched so long, she began to fear that Eve *hadn't* left that message. Had Eve set her up? Maybe Ted hadn't said anything about a job, and she'd called him up out of the blue. That was how little she trusted human kindness these days. But then he spoke, addressing her for the first time in years—other than a few brief comments when she'd gone to coffee with him and his friends. He preferred to ignore her if he could.

"That's true. I'm looking for a housekeeper slash assistant. I thought you might be capable of filling the position. If you're interested."

Her mouth went dry. "I'm *definitely* interested."

"Can you cook?"

"What kind of meals would you want me to make?"

"Nothing too complicated—healthy food that tastes good."

"Those things don't always go together," she joked but he didn't laugh. His determined reticence told her his resentment was alive and well. That hadn't changed. So why was he bothering to help her?

"Just basic meals," he said. "Lean meat. Vegetables. An occasional dessert."

She used the same clipped tone he had—all business. He obviously preferred the distance that allowed them. "I can handle meals."

"Can you clean?"

"Of course. I—I had a woman who came in once a month to do the deep cleaning—windows and cupboards and closets and such. But I did all the other stuff myself." She bit her lip as she finished because she was afraid that had sounded as if she had something to be proud of when *anyone* could clean.

"You may have to do a few windows here. And closets, too—for both the main house and the guesthouse in back. There won't be someone like Marta coming in."

"You know Marta?"

"She applied for the position."

"She's good."

"But not what I'm looking for."

So what *was* he looking for?

Suddenly the thought that had come to her before, the thought she'd discarded in her hope, popped back into her mind. Was he hiring her out of spite? To lord his success over her? To take some sort of revenge?

She hated to think that might be true....

But what did it ultimately matter? She had no choice other than to accept his offer. Who else in Whiskey Creek would hire her? Before long she wouldn't even have a car, so it wasn't as if she could commute elsewhere. "Of course. I'll do whatever you ask. I—I appreciate the opportunity."

"Then we should get along fine. Do you have a laptop you can bring?"

She pressed her fingers to one temple as she remembered last night. Although he'd been at the church, which made her wonder if he'd also invested with Skip—heaven forbid—she hadn't seen him at the house, so it was highly probable he wouldn't know what she'd had to let go.

"I did, but…it's gone," she said simply. No way did she want to address how or why or even acknowledge that she'd seen him. Having him as a witness to her shame had been so humiliating that she didn't want to think about it, let alone *talk* about it.

"That's okay. I have one here you can use." He sounded gruffer than a moment before, although she couldn't identify the reason for it.

She hoped she hadn't said anything wrong or come across as too needy. This job was the only bright spot in the past several weeks—and not just because of the money. Maybe she'd eventually have the chance to apologize to Ted. And maybe, after a while, he'd be able to forgive her, and the regret she felt would fade.

"So you know how to use one, right?" he clarified.

"I'm probably not your best bet on the clerical side," she admitted. "I have no experience there. But I can learn. I'm a fast learner." She wasn't sure why she added that. Desperation, she supposed.

"Can you write a decent email? That's not quite as easy to teach."

"I should be able to. I'm not *stupid*." Maybe *he* thought she was. She didn't have a college education, like him.

"Then we'll give it a shot," he said. "When would you like to start?"

A shot? That didn't sound too definite. "Eve said something about Monday."

"Monday is Halloween. But you can take off early if you need to."

Alexa hadn't mentioned having Halloween plans, but Sophia figured she should be prepared, just in case. "Thanks. I'll work until three."

"Okay. Come here as soon as you get your daughter off to school. What time will that be?"

"We leave the house at seven-thirty."

"Eight, then?"

"That should be fine."

"See you Monday."

She hurried to catch him before he could hang up. "There's one more thing...."

"What is it?"

"A clarification, actually. Eve said Lex can come to your place after school until I get off work. Is that true?"

"It is. You can have dinner here so you only have to make it once."

"I appreciate that."

"Not a problem."

Her brain conjured up the memory that came to her whenever she saw him—at coffee or even in town. It was of Ted during his first trip home from college. They hadn't seen each other for almost a month and could hardly breathe, they were so eager to touch, to kiss, to get naked. She'd never had a more exciting sexual encounter than when he'd taken her directly to the shack. She could still feel the pressure of him, pinning her to the old mattress they'd brought there months before.

"Sophia?"

She gripped the phone more tightly. "What?"

"Is that all?"

"Yes, thank you." She had to forget about that night

and all the other times they'd been together, she told herself. She couldn't blow this opportunity, or Skip and what he'd done would destroy her yet.

11

The weekend went fast because Sophia had something to look forward to. She knew working wouldn't be easy, especially working for Ted. He could be critical and demanding, and he didn't like her to begin with. But just knowing she had a job— that she'd be making $2,500 a month and should be able to get through the winter— lifted the heavy cloud of doom that had hung over her. She could get out of bed in the morning. She could shower and dress and put on her makeup. She could even clean the house—which was easier to do now that it was almost bare.

Fortunately, she still had a few of her belongings. Eve had lost her temper and ordered everyone out once they started getting into her cupboards and trying to take things she'd be hard-pressed to live without. Thanks to that timely intervention, Sophia had the basics— a kettle, toaster and so on. And she finally felt energetic enough to spend time with Lex. She wished she'd been more supportive of her daughter over the past two weeks, but she had to ward off that regret, along with any other negative emotion, or she risked a setback.

She had to move forward, do the best she could.

They used some of the money she had left to go grocery shopping and restock the cupboards. Sophia even splurged and took Lex to Just Like Mom's for a milkshake on Sunday night. To her, it was a celebration of the hope and kindness that had come to her rescue.

"You seem to be feeling better." Alexa eyed her while spooning ice cream into her mouth.

Relieved to have her energy back, Sophia smiled. "I am."

"You'll be able to go to your new job, then? The way you are right now...happy...it will last?"

The poor kid didn't know *what* she could count on.

Sophia was just as frightened that the despair would return, but she tried to reassure Alexa. "Don't worry, honey. I'm back on my feet. Everything will be okay." Having the chance to rebuild, to break her fall before it was too late, brought a lump to her throat. She'd almost given up!

How ironic that Eve had become involved, since they'd never really been friends, and that Ted had offered her the job she needed despite their history. He hadn't even made her apply for it. Not really.

She could dwell on Eve's kindness, which she was so grateful for—hers and Gail's—but not Ted's. Gail had called to check in with her just yesterday. She didn't want to get her hopes and expectations up where Ted was concerned, didn't want to imbue this job offer with more meaning than it had. But...it was tempting. She'd often felt such revulsion when Skip was making love to her that she'd imagine he was Ted just to get through it, especially when he demanded that she moan and writhe and pretend to enjoy herself. She knew those fantasies would complicate her situation if she let them.

A group of preteens entered the restaurant. They noticed Alexa but didn't come over to say hello. They whispered behind their hands and giggled, as if it was funny to see her sitting there.

The moment Alexa noticed them she dropped her spoon, even though she'd barely started on her shake. "Can we go?"

Sophia tucked her own hair behind her ears. It wasn't comfortable for her to be out in public, either. She felt so disliked and unwanted. But letting Skip's investors strip the house seemed to have neutralized her worst enemies. When they'd gone shopping at the grocery store, and even now, she felt a tentative truce between her and the citizens of Whiskey Creek. No one acted pleased to see her, but they didn't glare at her like before. They usually glanced away.

"You're ready to go?" Sophia asked. "But you were so excited about coming here. And that's your favorite shake."

"I've had enough."

The girls were crowding into a booth along the wall. Sophia recognized them; they'd been over to the house several times in the past, although not since Skip's death. "Aren't you part of that group anymore?" Sophia asked.

Alexa shook her head.

"But you said everything was going well at school."

Alexa shrugged, keeping her eyes on her food. "It's fine. I can deal with it."

"So…is this about what Daddy did? Or is it something else?" She knew what life was like at that age, how girls who were best friends one day weren't even friends the next. They were trying to figure out the ins and outs of relationships and seemed to try just about everything on for size. But the timing of this was certainly suspect.

Alexa slumped in her seat. "Do we *have* to talk about it?"

"Isn't it better if we face our problems together?" Sophia lowered her voice. "You helped me when *I* needed *you*."

That elicited a faint smile, and a grudging response. "Amberly's dad invested in the fund."

The *fund.* The infamous SLD Growth Fund. What other seventh-grader would be so familiar with that investment term? "I didn't see him at the meeting the other night." He hadn't called her, either—not that she knew of, anyway.

"I don't know why," Alexa said, "but he told Amberly she can't talk to me anymore. Clara's parents lost money, too."

Sophia hated knowing that her daughter was being treated as an outcast. She'd wondered, of course, but as long as Alexa was denying it she'd been able to avoid the reality. "Have *all* your friends turned on you?" she asked softly.

Her daughter's cheeks reddened. "Not *all* of them."

When Sophia kept staring at her, insisting on the truth, she laughed without humor. "Just the popular crowd."

"But those were your closest friends."

Lex took another spoonful of ice cream but her downcast expression didn't change. "Doesn't matter. There's still Emily from my softball team."

"That's who you eat lunch with every day?"

She nodded.

Emily hadn't even been her daughter's favorite. "Go ahead and wait in the car while I take care of the check, okay?"

Alexa hurried out of the restaurant without even glancing over at her former friends, but that didn't stop them from gossiping.

"My aunt Linda said she deserves what she's getting for thinking she's too good for the rest of us," she heard one of them say. Sophia guessed they were talking about *her* now, but she didn't care. Not about herself. She was dying to tell them to leave her little girl alone, though. Now that she was beginning to rally, the hurt she'd been feeling was turning to anger. She wasn't sure that was a *good* thing; it would probably cause an even deeper rift between her and everyone else. But she and Alexa weren't to blame for the losses Skip's investors had sustained. They hadn't asked him to do what he did. And anger was better than despair. It gave her the strength she needed to fight back, to find herself, to provide a foundation for her daughter instead of giving way.

Suddenly, she wanted to flip off the whole world. She couldn't believe she'd let the citizens of Whiskey Creek, not to mention Skip's parents, treat her so badly these past few weeks. She almost marched over and told those kids exactly how she felt. She would have, except verbally attacking thirteen-year-olds wasn't going to rectify the situation. Her interference would only make matters worse for Lex, so she held back.

She was just putting some money on the table so she could leave when Chief Stacy walked into the restaurant. His eyes narrowed the second he spotted her, and he made a point of walking past her, even though the hostess guiding him to a table had circled around a different way.

"Out and about already, Mrs. *DeBussi?*" He said her last name as if it had become some kind of curse.

According to Eve, he'd carried off quite a bit of her jewelry, had been one of the greediest of those who'd come to the house on Friday, although he'd admitted to investing far less than the others. She'd even heard Reverend Flores say something to him about that.

"Is there any reason I can't be here?" she asked.

"If I were you, I wouldn't show my face in public. People might think you're not remorseful."

"I had nothing to do with what Skip did."

"I'm not sure I believe that," he said. "And even if I did, you certainly didn't seem to have any trouble having fun on other people's money."

He was heaping on the persecution because he thought she wouldn't do anything about it. But she'd had enough. "I do know how to have fun," she snapped. "Particularly with *your* money. Thanks for investing."

His eyes bugged out and he came to a sudden stop. He was probably surprised that she wasn't the cowed, tolerant woman he'd seen at the house after that church meeting. "You really think you should provoke me?"

Sophia poured all the contempt she was feeling into the look she gave him. "I'll do as I please. And as long as it's not against the law, there isn't a damn thing you can do about it."

"Watch yourself," he murmured, his voice gruff. "You don't want to give me a reason to make your life any more difficult than it has to be."

"By doing *what?*" she asked. "Carting off more of

my jewelry? I don't have anything left to lose, Chief, except Alexa. And if anyone hurts her, they're going to be sorry they ever met me, and that includes you."

He grabbed her arm so she couldn't walk away from him. "I'm *already* sorry I met you. The whole town is."

"Go to hell!" Jerking away, she marched out to her car.

"What happened?" Alexa asked as she climbed in.

"Nothing." She started the engine of her beautiful Mercedes. She missed who she used to be. Missed the admiration and respect. She was going to miss her belongings, too. But her encounter with the arrogant chief of police reminded her that she wasn't going to miss Skip. She'd *never* let another man control her.

"Are you sure?" Alexa said. "Because you're breathing hard. And—and your face is all…splotchy."

She put the car in Reverse. "Chief Stacy and I had a little…disagreement."

"Did he hurt your feelings?"

She patted Alexa's leg before shifting into Drive. "Don't worry. I'll survive. We'll survive this together." He hadn't hurt her feelings. He'd made her so angry that telling him off had felt damn good.

Fighting back beat the hell out of crying and feeling sorry for herself, she decided.

She was done being a victim.

When Sophia showed up for work on Monday morning, she was still angry—at Skip, her in-laws, Chief Stacy, almost everyone. She wasn't going to let them push her around anymore. But just before she knocked on the door, some of that anger faded, and the fear and uncertainty returned. The job Ted had offered her was the only thing standing between her and complete disaster, the only thing that made it possible for her to fight back—because now she had a way to provide for herself.

But what if he didn't like her cooking? Or she couldn't manage the clerical tasks he expected her to do? Or being around each other was simply too awkward?

She wasn't sure she could take any more disappointment or rejection.

Especially from him.

Maybe he was giving her the job so he could take it away, dash her hopes and send her packing. Hurt her the way she'd once hurt him.

She twisted around to look at her Mercedes, parked in a gravel lot to one side so she wouldn't block his driveway, and nearly walked back to it. She was crazy to think any type of arrangement with Ted Dixon would be successful. She'd be working for her old boyfriend, of all people. They had too much history, would never be able to put the past behind them. He'd barely been civil to her the mornings she'd joined his friends at Black Gold Coffee....

But before she could take a single step, the door opened and he stood in the entryway, looking more handsome than ever. He'd always been tall and thin, with a rangy, rock-star build. Truth be told, he was a little *too* thin, even at thirty-four, but he'd put on a good twenty pounds over the past decade. The added muscle was apparent beneath the tight-fitting thermal shirt he wore with a pair of faded jeans and expensive-looking house shoes.

He'd also grown into his hawkish features. She'd noticed that before, of course. Although his face retained a sort of raw-boned quality, his eyes were so intelligent and his mouth so expressive and dynamic that he drew immediate interest, if not admiration.

His looks appealed to Sophia, but not as much as his blatant sexuality. He had a way of taking command of...*everything,* including a woman's body, without becoming an insufferable, selfish pig—a distinction Skip had entirely missed.

Anyway, the zing that went through her the moment she laid eyes on him worried her. It was too risky to feel so...*aware* of her new employer.

"You're early," he said.

She'd been afraid she might be late when she dragged Alexa out of the house at seven-fifteen instead of seven-thirty. She was already getting off at three today, for Halloween. "I'm sorry. I came as soon as I dropped Alexa off."

"It's fine. Come on in."

His house was a converted sawmill that appeared to have four levels, all of them open except for the top one—most likely his bedroom. It was loft-like, artsy and unique with brick walls and a wood-beamed ceiling.

She loved the pop art he had hanging all over, too. "Nice place."

"Thanks."

There had to be a story behind his home. She'd known when he converted the old sawmill. She'd heard his friends talk about it at coffee and had secretly driven past several times when Skip was out of town. But she didn't know what had inspired him to buy the property and make such radical changes to it, and he didn't volunteer any details.

"You can leave your purse and coat over there." He indicated some rolling shelves of corrugated metal that had hooks on one side. "I'll show you where the kitchen is."

They descended half a flight of stairs and then another half a flight before entering a gourmet kitchen with a floor of polished rock, windows that overlooked the river and copper pots hanging above an extensive woodblock island. Somehow this part of the house managed to be cozy, even though it was large and reminded her of a medieval manor. There was a fire burning in the hearth at one end, a pantry off to the other side and stairs leading down to what she guessed would be a wine cellar. She inhaled the aroma of fresh mint hanging on a drying rack not far from the oak table and the rich smell of coffee.

These would be very pleasant surroundings....

"I put on a pot of Black Gold's finest," he said. "Feel free to pour yourself a cup."

She was far too nervous to eat or drink. "Maybe when I take a break midmorning."

He paused for a second, and his eyes ranged over her. She wondered if she was inappropriately dressed. She'd put on a pair of jeans, a lightweight sweater and tennis shoes, and she'd brought an apron in case he didn't have one. "Is this okay?" she asked.

"Is what okay?"

"What I'm wearing."

He averted his gaze as if he hadn't really been looking at her in the first place. "Of course. Dress however you like. I rarely get company during the day when I'm working."

So it would be just the two of them in his secluded house for hours on end....

She rubbed sweaty palms on her thighs. "When's your next deadline?"

He was leading her back up the stairs. "End of December."

"Will you be able to meet it?"

"Maybe."

"I'll do everything I can to help."

Instead of thanking her, he turned and gave her another assessing look before continuing the tour. As they passed through the dining room, which was quite formal, she guessed he typically ate in the kitchen. His living room had more of a lived-in feel. So did the game room, which included a pool table, darts and video game systems, along with a big-screen TV. The only thing he didn't show her was his bedroom. It had to be on the top floor, as she'd initially guessed.

On the third level, double doors separated his workspace from the rest of the loft. Inside, Sophia saw an extra desk. He said that was where she'd be handling the clerical tasks he assigned her and gestured at the chair. "I'd like you to take a typing test, if you don't mind."

"Right now?" she asked.

One dark eyebrow quirked up. "Is there something wrong with right now?"

"No." Except that her anxiety had her feeling queasy. "What do you want me to type?"

He grabbed a research book from the shelves lining the two walls that weren't glass. "How about half a page from this? I just want to get a general idea of your speed."

She was a far better cook than she was a typist. She

preferred to start proving herself in the kitchen, but she couldn't say that, not without sounding as if she was making up excuses. At home, she'd used a laptop to surf and shop on the internet. She could limp along on a keyboard but wasn't what anyone would consider a crack typist.

He held the book while she tried to copy it. But having him so close, watching her, brought out the worst of her nerves. Her hands shook so badly she couldn't avoid making mistakes. Soon her eyes were burning, too, with the tears she was holding back, and that made it difficult to read. Terrified that he'd notice she was about to break down, she blinked and blinked and consequently finished the paragraph by slaughtering almost every word.

He shut the book. "Maybe we can get you an online typing tutor."

She curved her lips into a smile. "If you don't mind letting me borrow this laptop, I'll take the clerical work home and do it on my own time since I'm slow, if that's okay."

He pinched the bridge of his nose—as if hiring her was the worst mistake he'd ever made. "That's fine."

"I'm not as bad as I seem at the moment," she insisted.

"It's fine, like I said. This is just a stopgap until you find something more suited to your, uh, skills. We can work around…whatever."

In other words, he'd put up with her until he could conscionably get rid of her.

"And what do you think would be better suited to me?" she asked.

He shrugged as if he didn't care as long as she eventually secured alternate employment. "There's always retail. Or…maybe you should take some online classes while you work here to gain skills in other areas. Medical transcription or…or web design. Something like that."

She winced but hoped he couldn't tell. "Thanks for the vote of confidence."

If he heard her sarcasm, he didn't respond to it. With a nod, he went to his own desk. "I'm going to get a few pages done. The cleaning supplies are above the washing machine. Maybe you can start with the house."

She curled her nails into her palms. His tone said, *Anybody ought to be able to do that.* "What time would you like breakfast?"

He was opening his document. "I had a piece of toast with my coffee earlier."

"So skip breakfast?"

"Right."

"And lunch?"

"I'll eat at one and five, just to give you a rough schedule. Lunch you can bring up and set on that desk." He indicated the desk she'd been using. "I'll get to it when I can. Dinner should be ready at five so you can eat with Alexa before you go home. I'll have the leftovers when I finish up for the day."

He wasn't planning on seeing much of her, despite the fact that they'd both be in the house, she realized. Since she couldn't type, she'd been relegated to the nether regions. "Got it."

When she didn't immediately leave, he turned to look at her. "Is there anything else?"

"I might not be quite as worthless as you think," she said and walked out.

12

He was an idiot. He'd thought he could employ Sophia for a few months without finding it too much of a sacrifice, but that was a joke. She was *in his house* where he'd have to face her every time he left his office. And she was going to be there all day every day, except weekends.

Instead of writing, Ted spent the next hour cursing his own ridiculous response to recent events. So when his phone buzzed, it was a welcome distraction rather than an interruption. He couldn't create a good story, not in his current frame of mind. He might as well answer.

But when caller ID showed it was his mother, he almost put down the phone. She'd told him not to get involved with Sophia, and he'd done exactly the opposite. Now he'd hear about it. But if he didn't answer, she'd just keep trying until she got through. Why not break the news, if she hadn't learned it yet, and get that over with?

He pushed the talk button. "Hello?"

"Tell me it's not true," she stated flatly.

She'd learned, all right. "Who told you?" he asked.

"I ran into Sharon DeBussi at the gas station. She said her granddaughter told her they were going to be okay because of you."

"Everyone needs a hand now and then, Mom." He pretended his actions were perfectly logical and defensible. But he'd lost a lot of confidence since Sophia had arrived. Hiring her had been a mistake. She couldn't even type, which suddenly seemed more significant than it had when he was feeling sorry for her. He sincerely doubted a woman who'd been *that* rich could cook or clean, either. She'd stupidly settled for being nothing more than Skip's arm candy. So what had *he* been thinking? It wasn't *his* responsibility to save her from her own poor choices, but he'd jumped in despite that, and now he had to deal with the fallout.

"Why not let someone *else* give her a hand?" his mother asked.

"Because no one else stepped up!" At least that was true. He wouldn't have offered her a job if he felt she'd had a better option—or even *another* option. "From what I could tell, our fellow Whiskey Creek residents just wanted to…pile on."

"There's a reason for that."

"She inspires a great deal of resentment. I get it. But enough is enough." That was true, too, and stating it so emphatically seemed to bolster him, if only slightly.

"I knew she'd draw you back into her web."

His mother's tone got on his nerves. She could be so smug. "Stop it. I'm not *in her web.* I'm trying to do something kind for another human being."

"The same human being who broke your heart when she chose that bum over you?"

"Thanks for the reminder. But have you forgotten how hard it was when Dad left us?" he asked. "And you had child support, an education and a good job. What does *she* have?"

"The uncanny ability to prey on your sympathies, apparently."

His mother wasn't softening at all. She didn't forgive easily as a general rule. She was too demanding of herself and others. Expecting her to forgive someone who'd wronged *him?* Forget it. They could fight between themselves, butt heads all the time, but she'd die defending him. That was what made their relationship so damn complicated. It was difficult to tell someone *that* devoted to quit meddling when the line between "meddling" and "loving" so often blurred.

"She didn't come to me for the job, Mom. I offered it."

"You're kidding."

"No."

"Then you deserve exactly what you're going to get!" A dial tone buzzed in his ear.

Ted couldn't remember the last time his mother had hung up on him. She was *really* upset about this. But she had no right to be. He was an *adult,* for crying out loud. He could make his own decisions.

Slumping into his chair, he set the perpetual motion skier his editor had sent him for Christmas into action. He needed to get back to work. He couldn't lose another day, not if he wanted to meet his deadline. But he was so distracted....

He stopped the skier as a new thought occurred to him. Was there any chance he could foist Sophia off on someone else, someone in Sacramento or the Bay Area?

That might be possible...*if* she had any marketable job skills.

He was still searching for a way out when a pleasant aroma began to waft into the room. Closing his eyes, he breathed deeply, trying to decide what Sophia was baking. Cookies? A cake? Muffins?

He didn't have to wonder long. A few seconds later, he heard a bump against his office door and swiveled around to see her standing on the other side, holding a plate and a glass of milk. She must've used her knee to hit the door because she didn't have a free hand.

When he drew close enough to see what was on the plate, he realized she'd brought him some banana bread. It was an eternity since he'd had anything like that. He took his mother to Just Like Mom's almost every Sunday, and the meals he got there were always good. But he couldn't remember the last time he'd had banana bread, let alone smelled it baking.

He doubted Sophia could've brought him anything he'd find more appealing...at least not in the realm of food.

"I don't want to interrupt," she said. "I just thought you might enjoy a midmorning pick-me-up since you didn't have much for breakfast."

Her tentative smile and the way she hung back to ascertain his response reminded him of an animal that was eager for affection but feared it would be kicked instead. She'd never had that haunted look in her eyes when he'd been part of her life. He'd sensed the change in her at the church, too, during that meeting with Skip's investors. She no longer knew what she could count on, what kind of response she'd get—from *anyone*.

"Smells good," he said.

That was the positive sign she'd been waiting for. Her smile relaxed as he held the door so she could come in, and she put his lunch on the desk where he'd told her she should leave it.

"It'll be here whenever you're ready. I'll get the plate later."

She scooted out of the room so fast he didn't have a chance to say anything except thanks before she closed the door. But once she was gone he wasted no time in trying what she'd made.

The sweet bread, slathered in butter, nearly melted in his mouth. He groaned as he downed both slices and wished she'd brought him the whole loaf.

His cell phone buzzed as he swallowed the last bite. It was a text message—from Eve.

How's she doing?

Better, he wrote back and went down to the kitchen for more.

By the time Sophia finished cleaning two of Ted's four bathrooms, she was tired even though it wasn't quite noon. It'd been a while since she'd engaged in such strenuous activity. She'd *never* scoured a sunken bath—especially as large as the one he had off his bedroom. Her showers and baths were big and fancy, too, in a more elegant way, but Marta had handled keeping them clean.

At least she liked being busy. Maybe with some real effort and elbow grease, she'd be able to prove herself. This afternoon she'd take a few minutes and borrow that laptop he had on the desk in his office so she could search the internet for tips on how to keep a house clean and organized. She could even look up various recipes for healthy meals.

Determined to give her new position everything she had, to convince Ted he was wrong about her abilities, she returned to the kitchen. It was time to start lunch. After that, she'd clean the laundry room and do the laundry. From what she'd seen in Ted's bedroom, he didn't have a lot of dirty clothes, but some of his slacks and shirts would need ironing. And there was a far better way to organize his closet. She'd learned that from the specialist who'd come to organize hers.

She hoped he wouldn't mind if she changed things around.... He'd given her so little direction. She was supposed to cook and clean, but he hadn't told her specifically what he'd like cooked or what he'd like cleaned. She figured she'd just do the best she could, and if he disapproved of something, he'd have to let her know.

She rolled her eyes as she recalled his obvious disappointment at her typing skills. He certainly had no trouble being direct.

Grabbing a cookbook from a shelf near the pantry, she carried it to the kitchen table and sat down to pore through the recipes. She almost didn't notice that the loaf of banana bread was nearly gone, but when the small chunk that was left caught her eye, she couldn't help feeling vindicated. He'd liked it. He hadn't said anything to her, but the proof was right there. He'd eaten enough for *five* people.

Maybe she'd be that lucky with his lunch....

The picture of an almond-and-berry salad with poppy-seed dressing caught her eye as she turned the pages. That looked healthy *and* delicious, which were the two stipulations he'd given her so far. She'd make the salad for lunch. For dinner she'd do a savory soup. It was growing so chilly in the evenings that a warm bowl of broccoli-cheddar served with sourdough bread might be perfect. Again, it was healthy, so she should be on track there. She just hoped he liked broccoli....

She considered asking him. She had to interrupt him anyway, to see if she could go to the grocery store for ingredients. But before she could make it out of the kitchen, the doorbell rang.

Figuring it was her job to answer—the whole point of having a housekeeper was to allow Ted more time to write—she hurried up the stairs and nearly bumped into him on the landing.

"Oh, did you want to get it?" she asked.

He lifted his hands. "Sorry. Force of habit."

"So greeting any visitors while you're working would be my job?"

"That's right."

"Understood." She reached for the handle. "Are you expecting anyone?"

"No. Like I said, I don't get many visitors during the day." His tone confirmed that he had no idea who it might be.

She opened the door to find the answer to that question: Chief Stacy was standing on the front stoop.

Recalling their exchange last night, and how unpleasant that had been, Sophia stood rigidly as he looked her up and down.

"So it's true," he said.

She felt her pulse kick into a higher gear. "*What's* true?"

"Ted hired you." He shook his head. "Some people never learn."

Ted, hidden by the door, pulled it from her grasp and, nudging her off to one side, replaced her in the opening. "What the hell is that supposed to mean?" he asked.

"You, of all people, should know she can't be trusted."

A muscle flexed in Ted's cheek, but instead of responding, he glanced in her direction. "You can go back to work."

She knew she should do exactly that. He was her boss. But the anger she'd felt at Just Like Mom's welled up again. Was Stacy here to sabotage her first break since the night Skip had disappeared from their yacht?

"If he's here to complain about me, he can't claim I owe him anything," she said. "From what he told Eve when he was at the house on Friday, he invested $5,000 with Skip. But he took items worth at least that much from my house. Maybe I can't pay back *all* the investors, but he should be satisfied."

"You don't know anything," Stacy said.

Ted didn't even look at him. "I'll handle this," he told Sophia.

Would he give her the benefit of the doubt, no matter what Stacy had to say? Or was she crazy for even trying to keep this job?

Part of her said she was crazy—the same part that suggested she walk out before he could fire her. But if she did that…then what? She'd go home to a stripped-down house with little food and no money—and possibly fall back into the terrible depression that had so recently taken control.

That would be the worst thing that could happen, for her *and* Alexa. She was afraid she wouldn't be able to pull out of another nosedive like the last one. She hadn't been drinking for just that reason—because she couldn't afford to take the risk. She had to do everything in her power to avoid depression, even if that meant trusting Ted—a man she'd once scorned —to somehow see the best in her.

"I have to go to the grocery store," she mumbled. "Maybe now would be a good time."

Ted pulled a wad of bills from his pocket. After peeling off two hundreds, he handed her the money and said to get whatever she needed.

"You sure she'll come back with the groceries?" Stacy quipped.

Difficult though it was, Sophia managed to ignore him. He was *trying* to provoke her.

"Thanks," she told Ted. Then she retrieved her purse, shoved the money inside and slipped past both of them. She was eager for a few moments of freedom, a few moments when she wasn't worrying about whether she was cleaning the right thing or cooking the right thing or if she'd only end up disappointing Ted like she had with her typing.

She could feel Chief Stacy's gaze follow her all the way to her car. But then he disappeared inside the house and she drove off.

"What can I do for you?" Ted asked as Stacy took a seat opposite him in the living room.

The police chief pursed his lips and gazed around Ted's house. "This is kind of different, isn't it?"

He obviously didn't approve. "You came to see my house?"

"No, I came to talk about Sophia."

"With *me?*" Ted brought a hand to his chest. "Why?"

"I'm thinking you might be able to help. She owes me money—like she does a lot of other people."

How could *he* help that? "I can't garnishee her wages, not unless you get a judgment against her and go through the proper channels. And why would you waste your time? I'm guessing she'll be forced to file for bankruptcy. She can't make enough money to pay anyone. You're lucky you came out of this as well as you did."

"As well as I did?" Stacy repeated. "I've got more skin in the game than you realize."

"How's that? Was Eve wrong about the amount you invested? Or don't you think the jewelry and other stuff you took from Sophia's house has much value?"

"Neither. I've been seeing Pam Swank for the past four months. And I don't mind telling you that we're getting pretty serious."

How did *this* relate? "Who's Pam Swank?"

"Lives in Jackson. You don't know her?"

"Never met her."

"She invested, too—to the tune of a quarter million dollars. Everything she inherited when her parents died a year ago."

Ted flinched at the size of *her* loss. "That's *really* unfortunate. How'd she meet Skip?"

"Has family in town. Knows most everyone."

"So she believed all the stories she was hearing about making a huge return and stepped up."

"Skip told her he could double her money within a year. That gigantic house of his convinced her that he knew what he was talking about. So she signed it all over."

Ted was beginning to understand Stacy's enmity toward Sophia. He was talking about a quarter of a million dollars he would've had access to if and when he married Pam. The police chief felt that Skip, and by extension Sophia, had robbed him of a nice chunk of change his potential new wife would presumably share with him.

"Skip was a bastard," Ted said. "We can agree on that. I feel sorry for everyone who got hurt by him. But…the FBI looked into Sophia's culpability and found no indication that she was involved. After seeing how devastated she's been, you must know there's nothing she can do for you."

Stacy leaned forward. "I'm not so sure about that. A man doesn't walk off and leave a gorgeous woman like that behind." He lowered his voice even though there was no one in the house to overhear them. "Skip once told me she gave the best head a guy could imagine." His laugh took on a lascivious edge. "Doesn't it make you hard just to think of it?"

Ted was tempted to throw Stacy out of his house. But first he wanted to find out what had brought him over in the first place. He still didn't understand. "More proof that Skip was a prick. What kind of man speaks so crudely of his own wife?"

"I agree, but that boy liked to brag. Remember what he'd make her do every Fourth? How he'd insist she ride on top of that damn float dressed in some skimpy evening gown just to show the rest of us what we were missing? He would've put her in a bikini if he could've gotten away with it."

Ted remembered, all right. When he'd bothered to attend the parade, he'd tried to ignore the spectacle she made, but it hadn't been easy when she wore such revealing clothes. "That was *his* idea?"

"It wasn't hers. I heard them arguing about it once, right before the parade was supposed to start. She said it was too embarrassing, begged him not to make her do it, but he wasn't about to let her off the hook. Making us envious was *way* too much fun."

That Skip had treated Sophia like a prize cow infuriated Ted. But it was none of his business. He had to remind himself of that—again. "She was stupid to ever get with him."

"Rich as he was? I don't know if you could call it stupid or calculated, but it certainly came at a price." Acting as if he had all the answers, Stacy rocked back. "Skip dictated her every move. She came up to me once on the street, said she wanted to file a police report. She looked fine to me so I asked her what was going on, but before I could get an answer, Skip swerved to a stop in front of us and demanded she get in." He chuckled. "You should've seen her jump. She didn't even say goodbye, she was in such a hurry to climb into that car."

Ted had heard his friends talk about various bumps and bruises. They said she always had a good excuse for the injuries, but…there'd been speculation that maybe Skip was to blame. "Any idea what she wanted to report?"

"Who knows? He was probably trying to put a lid on her spending or something," he said with a chuckle. "The point is…she knew he was boss. *My* wife? She was the exact opposite—so damn difficult. She's even worse now that we're not married." He scratched his neck. "Man, am I glad to be rid of her."

Ted could only imagine how happy she was to be rid of him, too.

"Anyway," Stacy continued, "I can't believe Skip would give up a woman like Sophia. Beautiful. According to him, a dream in bed. Obedient." He ticked these things off on his stubby fingers. "So I suspect that when he decided to disappear, he had a plan that included her."

"An interesting hypothesis. Considering that it's obvious he tried to abandon her."

"He *couldn't* tell her what he was up to, not without worrying that she'd give him away if the police pushed hard enough. You understand that, don't you?"

Ted was losing patience. He doubted Skip had any kind of plan other than to escape with as much money as possible—at the expense of those he'd cheated *and* abandoned. He'd even robbed his parents. That didn't suggest he had any hope of reconnecting with his past. In Ted's opinion, he was kissing it *all* goodbye.

"What are you getting at, Chief? Why are you here?"

"I believe Mr. DeBussi was heading to some remote corner of the world where he could change his identity and set himself up before sending for her and the kid."

"And how was she supposed to get by in the meantime?"

"There must be some money for her somewhere. She just needs to find it. And when she does, those of us who've been hurt should be able to collect our share."

"With your girlfriend at the front of the line."

"Why not? No one else lost as much as she did."

"That we know of."

"That we know of," he agreed.

"So you're hoping I'll keep an eye on her in case

she stumbles across the key to a safe deposit box filled with currency?"

"Exactly. I don't mind telling you that Pam's beside herself over losing all that money. Absolutely inconsolable. I'd like to help her, and the others, if I can."

Ted suspected the person he most wanted to help was himself. "And what about Sophia's well-being?"

"Far as I'm concerned, she's had her taste of the good life. That party's over. Now she gets to work for a living like the rest of us. She's finally been put in her place, right? And I can promise you, you're not the only one who's been waiting for it."

"How do you know what I've been waiting for?" Ted asked. It wasn't as if he and Stacy had ever been friends. There was a decade between them; they didn't know each other all that well.

"It's never been a secret how you feel about Sophia, Ted. Six months ago, you quit the task force the mayor and I organized to clean up the mine tailings the moment she joined."

"I was on a tight deadline, and you had enough people."

"Come on—you didn't want to work with her. And I don't blame you. I told you Pam has family in town."

"Yes…"

"Well, she's Scott Harris's aunt." He grew somber, as if Scott had just died yesterday. "You remember what she did to him."

"I remember what *he* did."

"Oh, stop pretending." Stacy adjusted his gun so it wouldn't cut into his stomach. "He never would've gotten behind the wheel if not for her. She caused the death of the best athlete ever to come through Eureka High. His entire family hates her, and I can see why."

That argument could certainly be made; Ted had made it once or twice himself. But Chief Stacy's sudden reversal bothered him. When Sophia had joined the mine tailings task force, he'd been her most ardent supporter. He was switching sides now because it allowed him to press for his girlfriend's money. "Sophia's had her share of detractors over the years, but I didn't know you were one of them."

Because he hadn't been, not until now. The police chief had kissed Skip's ass at every opportunity. Sophia's, too. He'd been in awe of their money and the power that money gave them.

"If she eventually does the right thing, I'm sure we'll get along just fine." Stacy came to his feet. "I'll let you return to work. I wanted to see if you'd keep an eye on her for the rest of us, now that you're aware of what's at stake. Since you'll be seeing her every day, you'll probably be the first to know if she comes into some money."

Ted followed him to the door. "And you think I'd tell you, just because you came out here and asked me to?"

Stacy turned around. "A lot of innocent people have lost money. You'd be a hero if you could get even some of it back. Why wouldn't you want to do that? You have no loyalty to Sophia, no more reason to like her than the Harrises do."

"I hired her, didn't I?"

"I assumed the idea of her scrubbing your toilets appealed to you. That you enjoy having the upper hand, for a change."

Ted scowled. "It has nothing to do with being so petty."

"Then what's going on?" Stacy narrowed his eyes, obviously reassessing the situation. "You can't be making a play for her, not after what she did to you…."

"No." Ted denied it immediately and, possibly, too emphatically.

"Then you want to get in her pants? Make her pay on her back? That's between the two of you. I'm just looking to recover what I can of Pam's money."

"Wait." Ted got him to hold up. "For the record, I'm not trying to punish her. I'm not still in love with her. And I can find plenty of other women to sleep with. I need a housekeeper. It's that simple."

"Sure it is," Stacy said and laughed as he walked out the door.

13

Sophia stood near the glass doors of Ted's office, watching him at his computer. She had his lunch on a tray, the salad perfectly arranged. With the colorful berries and white poppyseed dressing it looked as appetizing as it had in the cookbook. But she was nervous again. She didn't know what to expect from one encounter to the next. And she was curious as to what Chief Stacy had wanted when he came by earlier. Had he managed to convince Ted that she was even more of a villain than he already thought?

She couldn't guess the answer to that question, because Ted had been in his office since she returned from the grocery store. She hadn't dared interrupt him. She'd also been in a hurry to get lunch on—she was running thirty minutes behind schedule as it was, didn't want *that* to count against her, too.

When she bumped the door with her knee, he got up to let her in.

"If you don't mind leaving that door open a crack, I could deliver your food without disturbing you," she said as she carried the tray past him.

"Good point."

"Do you shut it when you're home alone?"

He seemed too preoccupied—or too diplomatic—to answer as he cleared a spot on her desk. Maybe he felt that if he left the door open she'd take it as an invitation to drop in and chat. Or she'd be too noisy.

"Looks great," he said.

He sounded mildly surprised, so she took that to be a sincere compliment. "I hope you like berries."

"I do. I like most foods."

"Including broccoli?"

"Broccoli's a personal favorite."

"Good news for dinner. Remember I'm leaving as soon as Alexa gets out of school, so you'll have to get it out of the fridge and warm it up."

"Don't make anything for tonight. I've got a Halloween party."

She knew which party he was referring to. His friends always got together on Halloween. Sometimes, depending on who was hosting and whether Skip was out of town, she'd attended. She didn't go last year because it was here at Ted's.

"I'll make it tomorrow, then." She put the tray down but backed up instead of turning to go. "Before I leave you to your lunch, could I ask what Chief Stacy wanted? I mean, if his purpose in coming involved me?" She clasped her hands behind her back so that he couldn't see what she'd done to her cuticles. She couldn't have a drink. And, after Friday, she'd decided that smoking wasn't for her, either. Because of the smell, she couldn't hide it from Alexa and didn't want to set a bad example. Her latest bad habit was destructive, too, but at least it relieved some of her stress and anxiety without hurting anyone else. Now that Skip was gone and could no longer belittle her, she could do whatever she wanted.

Ted met her gaze. "He thinks you have money hidden away."

"And I'm working as a housekeeper because…"

"You haven't found it yet."

"I see. But…why would he want to meet with *you* about that?"

"That was my question. The answer? He's hoping I'll be the first to notice if you come into money. So if you happen to stumble across a pot of gold lying around the house, be sure and tell me so I can spread the word."

He'd always had a dry sense of humor. She could tell he was joking, but it bothered her that Chief Stacy was creating false hope. If the people of Whiskey Creek were expecting to recover their money, they were going to be disappointed. She didn't think that was fair—to her or to them. The money was *gone*. Skip had burned through it trying to maintain a lifestyle that cost far too much. She'd heard Captain Armstrong say that the yacht alone required over ten grand *a month* to own and maintain.

Chief Stacy and the others needed to accept the truth and heal, get beyond the losses they'd sustained. And she wasn't being glib; she had to do the same. Skip had put everything he could salvage on his back, and he hadn't cared about the damage it would cause her or Alexa when he'd jumped into the ocean.

He hadn't even left a note.

"Don't worry, you won't have to sound the alarm," she said. "If I so much as buy a gallon of milk, it's like bleeding in shark-infested waters."

"It's still very new," he said, watching her curiously.

She straightened her spine. "Is that why you hired me? So you could keep an eye on me and what I might or might not have? Did *you* invest with Skip?"

Although he'd taken a seat at her desk to start eating, he hesitated before picking up the fork she'd put on the tray. "No, to all three questions."

"You're *not* an investor."

"I'm not."

"Then…why were you at the church with the others?"

He suddenly became much more interested in his lunch. He took a bite and spoke around it, which made it difficult to hear every word. "Eve asked me to come, to…"

She didn't catch the rest. *"Why?"*

"To make sure there was no trouble."

"I see. So you did it as a favor to her."

"More or less." He swallowed and took a drink of his iced tea. "You honestly don't know who they are?"

"They?"

"The investors."

"How would I?" she asked. "Skip kept his business affairs to himself. I might be able to get a list from the FBI or Kelly, his assistant—"

"The offices are still open?"

"No. Kelly called me over the weekend. He said they've been shut down. The FBI will liquidate what's left of the assets, even the furniture, and that will be that. But he might have a list of investors on his personal computer. It depends on how much work he took home, and whether or not he had reason to save it. I didn't ask. I'm not sure I want to know all the names. I doubt anyone will ever believe this, but I feel bad enough as it is, and not just for myself."

"Maybe you should call Chief Stacy and tell him that. His girlfriend lost over a quarter of a million dollars, her entire inheritance."

"I ran into him at Just Like Mom's last night. It didn't go very well. I'm not going to call him. He wouldn't believe me, anyway."

"You're probably right. He's convinced that Skip would never leave you without a plan to reunite. And I don't see him giving up on that anytime soon."

She could understand why the police chief might think as he did. Skip had loved possessing her, loved *dominating* her, and he'd made a show of it. At first, even she could scarcely believe that he'd just get up and leave, that she could be free so suddenly and easily after thirteen years of wishing for a "do-over."

But she'd since realized that he'd had no choice. Not if he hoped to avoid prison. "Knowing my husband, he measured the odds and decided his best chance was to cut loose and start over. At that point, I was just…excess baggage to him. Alexa, too."

"Did he say that?" Ted asked. "Did he ever indicate he might do something like what he did?"

"Never. I had no idea we were in financial trouble. He kept that from me—had all his bank statements and even household bills go to his office. It was our anniversary. We were supposed to be—" she winced "—celebrating."

His fork hung suspended halfway to his mouth. "He stole your wedding ring and all the money you had between you and jumped ship—literally—on your *wedding anniversary?*"

She forced a smile. "It gave a nice cover for taking the yacht to Brazil."

He shook his head. "God, Sophia. He really did a number on you."

For a second, the walls they'd erected seemed to come down, but that changed quickly. She could sense the shift and couldn't help feeling stung by it. "Yeah, well, we all have to pay for our mistakes, right?"

"I'm not taking any pleasure in your situation. I hope you know that."

"I wouldn't blame you if you were." She managed another smile and hoped it didn't look as wobbly as it felt. "I'll pick up the tray later."

Sophia was several payments behind on her iPhone. But AT&T hadn't yet shut off their service. She'd gone online and made a small payment with a prepaid Visa card she'd bought at the grocery store over the weekend. She hoped that would suffice until she got her first paycheck, especially since their home phone was no longer working. How would Ted notify her if he wanted her to arrive early or pick up something on her way in if he couldn't reach her?

Occasionally, partly to make sure she could still make calls on her own phone, she tried Skip's number. His voice mail picked up right away and would as long as they had an account, even though the actual device was probably lying on the bottom of the ocean. It felt so odd to hear his voice…but she liked leaving him messages. It wasn't important that he'd never hear them. At least she got to say all the things she'd never said. She got to tell him what she thought of him and how sorry she was that she'd ever married him. That Alexa was the only good thing to come out of their years together, and he was missing out on raising her. That stealing had cost him more than he'd ever gained. She also got to tell him that she finally had a job, and there wasn't a damn thing he could do about it. She figured that had to be therapeutic. So when her cell rang as she was pulling to a stop at the corner a couple of blocks from the school, where she picked up Alexa to avoid the crush in the parking lot, it was already out of her purse and on her console. She'd just used her Bluetooth headset to leave him one of those messages—the one about having a job.

According to caller ID, Eve was trying to get hold of her. Sophia remained in her car, enjoying the oven-like warmth it provided against the cold, windy afternoon, while she waited for Alexa and answered.

"How was your first day at work?"

Eve sounded chipper, was obviously trying to keep Sophia's spirits up. Sophia appreciated the effort—and responded with enthusiasm. "Fine," she said but then she laughed as she remembered certain parts of it.

"Was that a loaded response?"

"We both survived it. Let me put it that way."

"Give me more details! What was the worst moment?"

She thought of Chief Stacy's visit but decided not to mention it. That was *too* negative for a festive night like Halloween. "When I failed my typing test shortly after I arrived."

"Oh, no!" She started laughing, too. "Ted gave you a typing test?"

"He did. And I can tell you he wasn't impressed with the results."

"I'll help with the clerical stuff, if you need me to. What does he want typed?"

"He didn't say."

"Then it must not be too important."

"Or else he did it himself."

"I'll talk to him about it. And…the best moment of your day?"

She considered the hours she'd spent in the kitchen. They'd been enjoyable. She loved his house. It was different enough to feel free-spirited, definitely didn't resemble the gilded cage in which she'd lived with Skip. "He seemed to like the food I made. He ate enough of it. So…I have *that* going for me—at the moment, anyway. Who knows what tomorrow will bring."

"Don't worry, you'll hit your groove once you get used to the demands of the job."

"I hope it gets easier."

"The first day is always the toughest."

Sophia wouldn't know. She'd never worked for anyone except her father, who'd had her create and deliver flyers for various charities or serve at community events when he was mayor. He'd paid her for her time, to augment what he gave her, which was too much to begin with.

However, she didn't want to point out her lack of experience. She'd felt like an exception to the rule in Whiskey Creek for too long. "Are you going to the Halloween party tonight?"

There was a slight pause. "I am. Would you like to come?"

"No. I wasn't fishing for an invitation. Alexa and I have plans." That wasn't necessarily true. Alexa was going to see about trick-or-treating with Emily, her softball buddy. But in case that didn't pan out, Sophia wanted to be there for her. "I was wondering if you needed a costume."

"I was planning to be an old-fashioned barmaid, like I was last year. Or maybe an elderly lady in a robe and curlers. I couldn't bring myself to spend any money this year. Thanks to the owners of A Room with a View constantly undercutting my prices, I'm having trouble turning a profit at the inn."

"Even after the remodel and the grand reopening?"

"It's gotten better the past couple of years, but…it's still a struggle."

"I'm sorry. I hope *you* didn't invest with Skip."

Eve laughed again. "No. You're safe there. I'm just being conservative."

"I'm glad you're not an investor. And it's a good thing you didn't buy a costume because I have some really great ones, and you can borrow any of them. Would you like to come over and take a peek? You're a few inches taller than I am, but we could find something that would fit. I could do your makeup, too." She held her breath as she awaited Eve's response. She'd made overtures toward Ted's friends before—overtures that'd been politely but not warmly accepted. Eve pitied her, so she was trying to help; that didn't mean she was willing to embrace a full-fledged friendship. Considering how most people felt right now, Eve would be justified in keeping her distance.

"You mean the scavengers didn't take those, too?" she asked.

"Far as I know, they're in the attic. They didn't get into my holiday decorations. And I didn't suggest it."

"Thank goodness! You were offering up everything else. I finally had to stop them when they got to your underwear drawer."

They hadn't really gone that far, other than to dump

them out and carry off the furniture, but Sophia was grateful she and Eve could joke about it. Laughter eased the heartache. "I owe you a big thanks for that."

"Yes, you do," Eve teased. "So this can be it. I'll come right over."

Sophia smiled as she hung up. That exchange had felt good—natural, real—at a time when not many things did.

Alexa was coming down the street. She was later than usual, but Sophia wasn't concerned. She was excited about spending the evening with her daughter. She'd just finished her first day of work *ever* and felt proud that she hadn't been fired. But when Alexa drew closer, Sophia realized why she was late: there were marks on her face, and her shirt was torn.

"Oh, no," she whispered. "Not *her*."

14

Ted was too distracted to have much fun. Maybe it was because he'd been coming to the same party—if he wasn't hosting it—for too many years. He liked getting together with his friends. Gail and Simon couldn't make it, and Baxter hadn't yet arrived, but all the others were there: Callie, Levi, Adelaide, Noah, Brandon, Olivia, Kyle, Riley, Cheyenne, Dylan and Eve. There was just something…anticlimactic about this event. As he sat on Cheyenne and Dylan's sofa, his mind kept wandering back to Sophia and what he'd learned today. How Skip had abandoned her on their wedding anniversary. How he'd made her ride on a float each Fourth of July, as if she was a Barbie doll he could dress up and pose at his whim. The fact that she'd wanted to file a complaint with the police and he'd intervened before she could.

Had he been abusive?

Most of the people at this party thought so. They'd debated it before, had seen the bruises. Ted had chosen to believe Sophia when she said her injuries were the result of bumping into a door or a cupboard, but—

"You're quiet tonight, Sir Dixon."

He glanced up to find Eve smiling down at him and moved the sword of his Knight Templar costume so she could sit beside him.

"What's going on in that head of yours?" she asked as she handed him a glass of wine.

"Nothing much."

"There's always *something* going on. You're our resident intellectual. Are you busy plotting your current manuscript?"

"Maybe." He grinned and clinked his glass against hers. "Nice costume, by the way." This year Cheyenne had asked everyone to contribute $5 so the person with the best costume could win a jackpot. Knowing there was a competition made it more interesting to dress up. He doubted he would have bothered otherwise. He wasn't much for that sort of thing, despite participating in the past. For tonight he'd spent nearly $200 to make sure his costume looked authentic instead of cheesy, and he'd accomplished that. But even an authentic-looking Knight Templar couldn't compete with Catwoman— not *this* version. He could hardly take his eyes off Eve in that tight-fitting black leather bodysuit.

Since when did Halloween costumes get so damn *sexy?*

"Why are you looking at me like that?" she asked.

"Like what?"

She pointed to her face. "My *eyes* are up here."

He'd never ogled Eve's breasts before. It felt odd to be doing it now. They'd been friends for too long. But having Sophia back in his life made him restless and suddenly dissatisfied, as if he should've been doing more all along. Dating. Socializing. Making the most of his youth. All he could think about was how long it had been since he'd had sex....

"You're the one who wore that costume," he grumbled. "I can't be the only man who's tempted to stare."

"I was a barmaid last year."

"So?"

"So that costume showed a lot *more* cleavage, and you didn't give me a second glance." She fluffed her hair. "Maybe it's the red wig."

He knew she was teasing, but he answered her seriously despite that. "It's definitely *not* the wig." He drained his glass. "It's that I haven't gotten out of the house enough this year."

She lowered her voice so the others couldn't hear. "You mean it's too long since you've gotten laid."

When she said that, he could tell she'd had too much to drink. Adelaide, being pregnant, was a designated driver. So was he, since he usually didn't drink much more than a glass of wine. That meant even those who didn't live within walking distance had a safe way to get home. "That, too," he admitted. "How'd you guess?"

Her expression suggested it had been all too easy. "We live in the same small town. We basically have the same problem."

He shifted in his seat. He guessed she normally reserved that kind of remark for Cheyenne or another female member of the group because she'd never been *that* candid with him before. But he had no chance to comment. The doorbell rang and Callie cried, "It's Bax!"

This was the moment they'd all been waiting for. After spending his whole life pretending to be straight, Baxter North had come out of the closet a year ago, and he'd done it by declaring his love for Noah, who wasn't the least bit gay. That had disrupted their friendship, which had lasted since early childhood, and it had sent shock waves through the whole group—until everyone who was part of it could adjust. For a while, no one was sure Baxter would be able to come to grips with his true identity. But he seemed to be doing better since moving to San Francisco, where he'd already been working as a stockbroker for a number of years. Fortunately, he and Noah were friends again. Ted didn't talk to Baxter as often as some of the others, like Callie, but he knew that much. Even Adelaide, whom Noah had married nine months ago, liked Bax.

Everyone liked Bax and had been looking forward to seeing him. But they hadn't expected him to bring a friend. He hadn't mentioned it. So when he walked in holding hands with a man who strongly resembled Noah—a man who was even dressed in biking shorts and a biking tunic with Noah's store logo—the room fell silent.

Noah seemed determined to ease the awkwardness when he stepped forward to hug his best friend and shake hands with his doppelganger, whom Baxter introduced as Skye. "I like your shirt," he said, grinning. "But *I* look better in Spandex."

They all laughed and followed his lead.

"Nice to meet you," Ted murmured when it was his turn to be introduced.

After that they all stood blinking at one another, trying to ignore the fact that Baxter's boyfriend was almost a carbon copy of Noah—the man he'd loved his whole life.

Probably feeling desperate to get the party back on

track, Cheyenne cleared her throat. "You two have a seat. What can I get you to drink?"

Baxter swung the hand that was clasping Skye's as they cut through the crowd toward the living room. But then Baxter let go. "Gotcha!" he cried and announced that Skye was only a friend he'd met at work. He wasn't even gay.

"He was nice enough to dress up like Noah and help me pull off this gag. I *knew* it would freak you out," he said, laughing. "It's uncanny how much they look alike, right?"

Callie was laughing, too. "But how'd you get one of Noah's tunics?"

Baxter gestured as if that was the easy part. "He gave that to me ages ago."

Once everyone realized he hadn't fallen for a Noah stunt double, as he'd pretended, they could all enjoy the joke. The tension dissipated and everything grew comfortable again. As usual, they talked, watched a horror flick and played games.

Thanks to Skye, Eve *didn't* win the costume contest. No one could outdo a Noah look-alike who resembled him more than the fraternal twin who'd died on grad night. They just wished Noah had dressed up in biking clothes, too, so they could get a picture of both of them together.

At the end of the evening, when the party was breaking up, Ted invited anyone who'd remembered to bring a swimsuit to get in his hot tub, and a handful of stragglers followed him home.

It was nearly two o'clock by the time everyone left Ted's place. Only Eve remained, and Ted wasn't disappointed about that. Since he got home, he'd had more to drink. And she was in a bikini.

He kept asking himself why he hadn't noticed what a beautiful body she had until tonight....

"That was a shocker," she said as she leaned against the back of the Jacuzzi. The water bubbled and foamed about her breasts as she finished another glass of wine.

"Skye?" He leaned over to pour her some more from the bottle sitting near his elbow.

"Yeah. I thought that was really cool of Bax—to poke fun at himself like that. To laugh and let *us* laugh, so we can finally feel as if he's come to terms with his crush."

"It's always better to tackle that sort of thing head-on and get it out of the way. Skye made for a great ice-breaker. But I bet Noah just about had a heart attack when they walked in."

Her laugh sounded relaxed and husky as she let her head rest on the edge of the hot tub. She was drunker than he was, but he was getting there fast. "Adelaide, too. Bax came out just after she returned to town and started seeing Noah. She must've felt some anxiety, if only for Noah's sake, when Baxter showed up with Skye."

Ted took another sip of his wine. "Do you think Bax is over Noah?"

"Probably not. But he's reconciled to the fact that he'll never be with him in that way. And he's willing to remain friends, which is more than most people in his situation would be capable of. It's hard to love someone who doesn't love you back. I hope he finds the happiness he deserves."

"Finding that happiness would be easier if his parents would accept him for who he is," Ted said. "But I don't get the impression his relationship with them has improved, do you?"

"Maybe it hasn't improved *a lot,* but he told me they're starting to come around. That's hopeful."

They gazed up at the stars in silence. It was cold out, but the wind had died down. "Speaking of old love interests," Eve eventually said. "Will you be okay with Sophia working here?"

He didn't want to talk about Sophia. He understood all about unrequited love and how long it could take to get over someone. He wasn't about to fall back into that pit now that he was free of it, but whatever had drawn him to her in the first place was still lurking beneath the surface. He'd have to fight that magnetic pull, make sure he didn't take so much as one step in her direction. Tonight, probably due to the wine, there'd been a brief few seconds when he'd wondered what it would be like to try again with her now that Skip was gone. She obviously needed help; he could provide it. And no matter how much he tried to deny the truth, he hadn't lost his craving for the taste and feel of her.

But he didn't want to become her new sugar daddy. That wouldn't make her love him any more deeply than she had before. Besides, dating Sophia would ruin his relationship with his mother, who would consider him the biggest fool on earth. And she'd be right. Because he'd *have* to be a fool to get involved with Sophia again.

His gaze shifted from the stars to Eve. Why couldn't he fall for a nice girl like her? He'd known her for so long, could absolutely count on the strength of her character. Maybe he'd missed what was right in front of him. Friends could become lovers; it happened all the time. For some, finding a mate had more to do with mutual respect than physical chemistry. Maybe those were actually the best relationships.

That was what a lot of people said....

He took a deep breath as he considered her question about Sophia, and decided to keep his answer short and sweet. The less he said on that subject, the better. "It'll be fine. Because of her situation, I don't have any choice except to keep her on until she can come up with something else. But...I'm hoping that won't take too long."

"You're over her? It doesn't have any impact on you *romantically* to have her coming to your house every day?"

He could guess why she was asking. They were both wondering why they couldn't be that special someone in each other's lives. Eve was sweet, attractive, loyal and capable of real commitment. She wanted to get married and have a family, and so did he. They were in their mid-thirties and hadn't met anyone. They lived in a small town, so they didn't come into contact with many strangers.

Could they somehow transform their relationship?

Should they even try?

"It's just a job." On some level he knew that wasn't *entirely* true. But he wanted reality to be as he'd represented it, so he promised himself that this time he'd choose the path less likely to end in heartbreak. He had the self-discipline. He just wished he wasn't still tempted by her....

Eve swished the bubbles over to one side. "She mentioned that she didn't do too well on her typing test."

"No," he said with a laugh.

"What can I do to fill the gap?"

"I think we can limp by. Don't worry about it."

"I don't mind helping out. Let me know if something comes up."

"I will."

"She seems to have changed a great deal," she said. "For the better."

Eve—honest, as always. She was making an effort to be fair to Sophia. "Everyone seems changed when they're down-and-out," he said. "Being broke is a humbling experience. Makes you more tractable."

"She used to be hell on wheels, didn't she? Charismatic and beautiful but…ruthless. I've always seen her as a Scarlett O'Hara."

He agreed with that comparison. But he wasn't sure her ruthlessness stemmed from anything more than being spoiled. She'd been gorgeous from the moment she was born, had received far more attention than was healthy for any child. On top of that, he doubted her doting parents ever used the word *no.* Since they'd never placed any boundaries on her behavior, she hadn't realized there *were* boundaries. She'd thought that only applied to others, that she was somehow exempt because her daddy was the mayor.

"I wonder if she regrets any of it," he said.

"I think she does," Eve responded. "That costume I wore tonight? She lent it to me. She had me come over and pick it out from a wide array of really nice costumes she had stored in her attic. Then she got me all fixed up with makeup and a wig."

"What was *she* doing tonight?" he asked, curious in spite of himself. If she'd still been meeting them for coffee every Friday, she would've been invited to Cheyenne's party, but he purposely hadn't extended the invitation himself. Bad enough that he had to see her during work hours. He wasn't going to include her in his social life, too.

"From what I could tell, she didn't have any plans, but we didn't talk about it. She was too upset when I was there."

"About losing her dearly beloved?" He'd been curious as to how much she missed Skip, if she was sad to have him gone from her life or more distressed about the loss of money and status.

Again, the question of whether Skip had abused Sophia popped into his mind, but he didn't ask Eve. It was better if he didn't find out. Sympathy was what had landed him in his current position.

"No, this was about Alexa. Some kid jumped her after school."

He sat up so fast, the water sloshed. "*Which* kid?"

"Sophia doesn't know. Lex wouldn't say."

"Did Lex say why?"

"Because of what Skip did, of course. Kids often imitate the attitudes and behavior of their parents."

He finished his wine. "So his daughter's being picked on now, too? As well as his wife?"

"I guess."

He flipped his wet hair off his face. "That's too bad. It's Halloween. She should've been looking forward to trick-or-treating—not getting beaten up." And maybe Sophia should've been invited to Cheyenne's....

"It made me feel terrible. Poor Sophia has enough problems."

"No kidding."

They remained silent for a few seconds. Then she stood. "Well, it's getting late. I'd better go."

He watched as a drop of water rolled between her breasts. "You can't go."

She seemed surprised. "Why not?"

She didn't have her car, for one. She'd ridden over with him. "You've had too much to drink, and I can't drive you because *I've* had too much to drink."

A sexy smile curved her lips. "And that means…"

He smiled, too. "You'll have to stay over."

Her eyes locked with his. "Where will I sleep?"

He gestured to the mother-in-law quarters off to the right, where he suspected his own mother would live when she got too old to take care of herself. "There's always the guesthouse." His mouth went a little dry at what he was about to suggest. "Or…"

"Or?" she prompted.

"You could sleep with me."

She caught her bottom lip between her teeth as she stared at him.

"You're thinking about it," he said.

"It's been a long time since…since I was with a man. I miss it."

"I can solve that problem."

"But this is pretty scandalous—"

"Why?" He broke in before she could come up with too many reasons they shouldn't. "We've known each other our whole lives. And we love each other."

"It's not that kind of love."

"Maybe it could be."

She didn't seem convinced. "You remember what happened with Callie and Kyle. I've talked to her. She's sorry she slept with him, says it was a mistake."

"Kyle was on the rebound. He was in no shape to take on another relationship. Then Callie was diagnosed with liver disease and trying to cope with knowing she might not make it through the summer. They weren't doing it for the right reasons."

"Would it be any different for us?"

"We're both ready for a relationship."

"We're also a little drunk and sex-starved," she said with another laugh.

"We have to take charge of our lives sometime, go for what we want. I can't imagine finding anyone better than you."

What was he doing? Part of him felt as if he was racing full-throttle toward a cliff just to escape Sophia. But the other part, the more insistent part, said there was no reason he couldn't love the right woman for a change.

She peered more closely at him. "You're not talking about just one night?"

"Of course not. I would never use you that way. We could be a couple, couldn't we?"

Her tongue darted out to wet her lips—evidence that he was making her nervous. "That's a sweet offer. I adore you, you know that. And you're gorgeous. I won't pretend I've never noticed. But…why now? We've known each other for ages, and you've never hit on me before."

"Maybe we've both been waiting for love to just come upon us. And maybe it doesn't work like that, at least not for everyone."

"You're looking at the situation pragmatically. We're getting older. We both want a family. We already have a great relationship, so…why not."

Using the "we haven't found anyone else" logic wasn't the most romantic approach, so he tried to soften it. "I'm just saying…who knows what might develop? Why not give it a chance?"

Her laugh sounded more like a giggle, something he wasn't sure he'd ever heard from her. "I don't mind telling you that my heart is pounding like crazy."

"So is mine." He reached out to her. "Come here. Let's see what it feels like to touch you."

She moved closer, and straddled him when he pulled her into his lap.

"What do you think?" he asked. "Do we fit together well enough? Could we get in to this?"

She closed her eyes and pressed up against his erection. "You feel good," she admitted. "So good I'm not thinking clearly. What about our friends…"

He dropped his head back as she increased the pressure. "What about them?"

She kissed his neck, tentatively at first but then with more abandon. "They'll kill us if we wind up hating each other and refuse to be in the same room together."

"Most of them are married. They have better things to worry about than what we're doing. Besides, I could never hate you."

He was afraid that he was going too far in his efforts to convince her. But she was so warm, so soft and pliable. He was dying to lose himself in her body, to do something, *anything,* to stop thinking of Sophia.

"I couldn't hate you, either." She rocked against him, creating sparks of pleasure. He could make love to her without a problem, just as he'd thought. But could he commit to her, as well? Because taking Eve to bed would be different from being with anyone else. He wouldn't be able to move on afterward, not if there was any danger it would hurt her.

For a second he panicked, realized he'd be trading away too much. He loved Eve, but he didn't feel the intense romantic attraction he'd experienced with Sophia. *That* was what passion felt like. *That* was what falling in love felt like, falling in love so deeply he didn't care if he drowned. But Eve was a good woman, a woman who deserved to have the husband and babies she wanted. He could give her that, couldn't he? Maybe, with time, he could feel about her the way he'd felt about Sophia.

Either way, once she untied her bikini top and let it fall, it was too late to back out.

15

Sophia was still worried about Alexa when she arrived at work the following morning. Her daughter had insisted on going to school despite yesterday's attack. She was afraid she'd fail math if she didn't. Her grades were slipping, which was no surprise given everything they were going through. But Sophia didn't feel good about letting her go to class. Late last night, after spending the entire evening with her and not going out for Halloween at all, Lex had finally broken down and explained what had happened. Babette, the girl she'd hung out with most before Skip died, had turned on her. She'd told Connie, a girl who was often kicked out of school for fighting or ditching, that Alexa had said all kinds of terrible things about her. It was a lie, of course, but Connie had exacted her revenge while everyone else stood around, sealing off Alexa's retreat and cheering the other girl on.

The whole encounter was senseless and stupid— mean, catty games. Babette enjoyed being the leader of the popular group now that Alexa had been deposed, and Connie was probably enjoying the notoriety her actions brought.

Sophia feared yesterday's incident might not be the end of it. So she again brought up the possibility of moving. This time, Alexa was amenable to it, but Sophia knew they couldn't go just yet. Relocating required money they didn't have. There'd be rent and a car payment, neither of which Sophia was paying now. She would also need some assurance that she'd be able to get a job in their new town or city. She couldn't risk giving Ted notice until then.

Bottom line, leaving Whiskey Creek wasn't a viable option at the moment. But she'd promised Alexa they'd shoot for that. Eventually they'd leave and start over somewhere else.

She was so preoccupied when she arrived at Ted's that she didn't think too much of it when he didn't answer the door. Her impression from yesterday was that he preferred to go about his business and leave her to cook and clean as she saw fit. So when she tried the handle and found it unlocked, she let herself in. She was looking up at the third level to determine whether he was on his computer, or maybe showering, when she saw several puddles of water on the floor.

She got a towel out of the cleaning closet and wiped up each one. They led up the stairs, past his office. She assumed he'd been in the hot tub last night and hadn't bothered to dry off before coming inside, because they led all the way to his bedroom.

Then she spotted something else—a bikini top slung over the bannister. The bottom of the same suit was right outside his bedroom door, in the biggest puddle of all, as if it'd been cast off en route to his bed.

Holy shit! She turned to hurry back down the stairs. She didn't want to see him with someone else—didn't want to face the way it would make her feel. But his bedroom door opened at that moment and *Eve,* of all people, emerged. Wearing *his* sweats.

"Sophia, I'm sorry," she said when they both froze and gaped at each other. "We couldn't tell if that was the doorbell. We...we were groggy...not quite awake."

We. Sophia felt as if Eve had slugged her in the stomach. She wasn't sure why. Ted had the right to take whoever he wanted to bed, even a close friend. She'd always assumed he was sleeping with other women. He was a single, virile man in his thirties. *Of course* he was sleeping with other women. He wouldn't remain celibate all his life just because *she'd* married someone else.

But she'd never had to encounter him with a love interest. He hadn't had a single steady girlfriend since they broke up, not one she'd known about. And she'd certainly never dreamed he was sleeping with *Eve!*

When her cheeks flushed hot, she hoped Eve wouldn't notice—but Eve seemed equally embarrassed. "It's no problem. I...I didn't see your car outside or I wouldn't have let myself in. I figured Ted was in the shower."

Eve's hands kept messing with her hair, tucking it behind her ears or smoothing it down—more evidence of her self-consciousness. "My car's not here. I—I rode over with Ted last night."

Sophia nodded. The towel in her hands made what she was doing obvious, but she still felt compelled to explain her presence outside his bedroom door. "I only came up here because I saw the water on the floor and was trying to—to dry it before someone could slip." She picked up the bikini and handed both pieces to Eve. "I'll get breakfast and make enough for two." She headed down the stairs but paused on the landing. "Should I set places in the dining room or would you like me to bring the food up on a tray?"

"I wasn't planning to stay," Eve said. "I need to get home so I can dress and go over to the B and B."

Sophia willed her pulse to slow, but that seemed futile. "Are you sure? Because I could whip up some eggs really fast."

"Ted's getting in the shower. That'll take a few minutes, so…I'll go to work and eat there. Maybe the three of us can have a meal together another time." She smiled as if that was a possibility but Sophia knew it wasn't.

"Absolutely. Do you need a ride?"

Eve dangled a set of keys. "Ted's letting me take his car."

"I see."

"Your costume's folded on a chair in the game room, by the way. Thanks for lending it to me. Last night was a lot of fun."

Sophia didn't doubt it. How many times had she imagined herself back in Ted's bed? Those fantasies, and a great deal of alcohol, had pulled her through thirteen years of being married to the wrong person.

A flash of pain warned Sophia that she was digging too deeply at her cuticles, but the pain didn't outweigh the relief it somehow gave her. Even the knowledge that she was making her hands ugly didn't stop her. "I'm glad I could help. You—you've been so good to me."

Sophia heard movement in the room behind Eve. Afraid that Ted would appear wearing nothing but a satisfied grin and a pair of boxers, she made a concerted effort to get away. She didn't want to see him kiss Eve goodbye. Nor did she want *him* to see her standing at the bottom of the stairs, gaping up at them in envy. "I'll go and start the coffee."

Once she reached the privacy of the kitchen, she sank into a chair and rested her head in her hands. *What did you expect? That he'd choose you?*

Of course he wouldn't. Why would he? Besides, she liked Eve and wanted her to be happy.

"I'll see you later."

She jumped as Eve, still dressed in Ted's clothes since she was returning the Halloween costume, ducked her head into the room. "Have a—a good day," Sophia managed to stutter.

Eve paused. "Everything's going okay for you here?"

"Oh, yes. Great." Pasting yet another smile on her face, she prayed Eve wouldn't realize that she hadn't started the coffee. She hadn't done a damn thing except try to regain her equilibrium.

"I'm glad to hear it." With a wave, she was gone. But it wasn't long before Ted came down, showered and wearing a T-shirt with a darker pair of jeans than he'd had on yesterday. He hadn't shaved, but that made him look better instead of worse. Fortunately, by the time he appeared she had coffee brewing and was scrambling some eggs.

"Morning," he said.

She didn't look up. "Morning."

"You okay?"

At first, she assumed he'd read what she was feeling. But then she saw that her thumb was bleeding and grabbed a paper towel to wipe the blood. "Fine."

He came closer. "Did you cut yourself or…"

She hid her hands behind her back. "No."

Two lines formed between his eyes. "I thought I saw blood."

"It's nothing. I'll get a Band-Aid."

When he sat down at the kitchen table, she cursed silently. He was going to stay until she'd cooked breakfast. She hadn't done so well when he'd been watching her type, so she tried to pay particular attention to what she was doing now.

"Eve told me what happened to Lexi yesterday," he said. "I'm sorry about that."

She kept her eyes on her skillet because she couldn't bear to look at him quite yet. "Thanks. Um…you can get to work if you want. I'll bring this up when it's ready."

"I'll go in a second." His chair squeaked against the floor, but he didn't get up, even though she'd just given him the perfect opportunity to flee the kitchen. "Will you be able to get the details?"

"Excuse me?" She forced herself to glance at him.

"I'm talking about the fight—what happened to Alexa."

She returned her attention to the food. "There's nothing I can do about that, even if I learn the details."

"You can go to the school, talk to the principal."

"Lex begged me not to. She said that would only make the kids treat her worse."

"So is she at home today or…"

"She couldn't miss math. Her—her grades are…not what they should be. We're both afraid she'll end up having to repeat seventh grade if we're not careful, and we don't want that."

"Of course not."

Thankfully, the eggs were done and she could scoop them onto a plate. "Would you like some toast?"

"Please."

She put two slices in the toaster and poured him a cup of coffee, which she carried to the table before bringing over his eggs. She didn't bother with cream or sugar. She knew he liked his coffee black. "I could cut up some fruit, too, if you like."

He caught her hand as she let go of his plate and frowned when he saw the damage to her fingers. "What are you doing to yourself? Doesn't that *hurt?*"

"Not really," she lied, pulling away so she could hide her hands again.

"They look sore."

"They're fine. I'll take care of it tonight."

"Why don't you take care of it now? There're some Band-Aids in my bathroom."

She gestured as if she'd do anything to get him to stop pressing her. "Okay. I—I'll bring you a new box tomorrow."

"I'm not worried about the price of a box of Band-Aids."

His toast popped up and she hurried over to butter it. She planned to put the rest of his breakfast on his plate and get out of there until he finished eating, but he spoke before she could clear the door.

"Did he abuse you, Sophia?"

She knew about the rumors that'd gone through town, knew he was talking about Skip. The tone of his voice, itself a request for her to level with him, tempted her to admit the truth at last. She'd had to lie for so long. But she didn't want word of what she'd suffered to get back to Lex.

Besides, she was pitiable enough in her current situation. "No."

"How do you explain the bruises?"

She couldn't meet his eyes. Every time she did, she pictured him with Eve. "I guess I'm just clumsy."

Ted was back at his desk, but he wasn't doing any more writing than yesterday. He kept thinking about last night and the fact that he'd slept with Eve. He'd known what he was doing. He'd made a conscious decision to take Eve to bed. So why did he feel so crappy today?

He listened to the sound of the vacuum as Sophia cleaned the house. She was working hard and fast, reminding him of the white tornado he'd once seen on a commercial. He couldn't even convince her to stop and have lunch.

And her hands. Shit, she was *destroying* them.

He thought about how she'd responded when he'd asked if Skip had abused her. Her mouth said no, but her eyes—

His phone rang. For a change, he was hoping it'd be his mother. He wanted to tell her that he was dating Eve, wanted to hear her excitement now that he finally had a serious love interest—one she and everyone else could be happy about. He thought that might erase the doubts nagging at him, help him believe he'd made the right choice.

But it wasn't Rayma. It was his new girlfriend.

"Hey." When he answered, he infused his voice with more excitement than he felt. "How are you today?"

"Fine. You?"

"Great. Why wouldn't I be great?" He rolled his eyes. He was acting odd, and even he could tell.

"You're not freaked out?" She sounded hesitant, eager to be reassured.

He kneaded his forehead. "Of course not."

"That's a relief. Because last night was—" she laughed "—last night blew my mind. And it's going to blow everyone else's when they find out we're together now. But I'll just say this—if I'd known you were *that* good in bed, I would've jumped your bones a long time ago."

She wasn't bad herself. And it was nice of her to stroke his ego. So why did he feel like crawling under his desk? "It was…amazing," he said weakly.

"We could have another amazing night."

He felt himself cringe. "When?"

"You could come over for dinner."

Tonight? No. He didn't want to see her again so soon. He needed time to regroup. But he wasn't about to admit it. He'd made himself a promise that he'd see this through no matter what. "I have to work late but… after?"

"Fine. We'll have dessert."

"Okay."

"Eight-thirty work for you?"

"Yeah. But you have my car."

"I'll pick you up."

"Perfect."

"Um…"

He clenched his jaw when she didn't say goodbye. *Please, God, don't let her say she loves me. Anything but that.* "What is it?"

"When are we going to tell the others?"

His chest tightened until he could scarcely breathe. It felt as if someone was smothering him. He got to his feet. *Relax...you're not engaged yet.* "Let's give it a couple of weeks. *We* should adjust to the change in our relationship before we ask them to, don't you think?"

"Good point."

"See you tonight?"

"One more thing."

He shifted the phone to his other ear.

"Are you sure you don't regret it?"

"Do *you?*" he asked.

"Not at all!"

"Me, neither."

"In fact, I hope I'm pregnant."

He was glad he wasn't eating anything, because he would've choked. "Why would you say *that?* We used a condom. Is there some reason you—"

"No. I just...I want a baby."

"I'm definitely not ready, Eve," he said.

She chuckled. "I know. I'm probably scaring you to death."

She was certainly doing that. "Promise me you won't talk about babies for a while."

"All right," she said. "But it's not as if you didn't know."

True. She'd brought it up more than once in the past couple of years; she'd been afraid she wouldn't get the opportunity to have a family.

"Is Sophia okay?" she asked.

He hated that just the mention of Sophia's name made him tense up. "She's fine. Why wouldn't she be?"

"I was so embarrassed when she showed up this morning and I was still there. *She* was embarrassed, too. I could tell. She could hardly look at me. Did she say anything to you about it?"

He walked over to the glass walls of his office and gazed down into his house, to where Sophia was vacuuming the living room a level below. Completely unaware that she was being watched, she stopped long enough to wipe sweat from her face, then went back to work as energetically as before. It was as though she'd gone into fast-forward this morning and gotten stuck there. "No. Nothing. She knows it's none of her business." She didn't care, anyway. Why would she? She'd been sleeping with someone else for fourteen years.

"Sometimes, at Black Gold, I'd see a nostalgic expression on her face when she looked at you and—"

"Stop. You were imagining things."

"You didn't see her when I came out of your bedroom this morning. She seemed so...stricken."

"A lot of people will be shocked when they find out about us." Shocked and stricken weren't exactly the same thing, but he purposely glossed over that.

"True."

Suddenly, Sophia turned and glanced up—and when she realized he was there, watching her, she grabbed the vacuum and hurried out of sight.

"Everything will be fine," he said. "We'll just...take it slow." Was he saying that to allay her fears—or his own?

"Okay," she said.

He quickly changed the subject. "Want me to bring something tonight?"

"Condoms would be nice," she said and hung up.

He stared at his phone. "God, what have I done?" he mumbled and knocked his head against the glass.

16

Sophia kept her earphones jammed in her ears, her iPod on high and her hands busy. She didn't want to worry about anything—not what her little girl might be facing at school, whether her car would be repossessed today or why she felt so sick every time she thought of Ted with Eve. She just wanted to zone out to the music while she worked, fill the hours with so much industry that they passed with lightning speed. Then she could go home and be with Alexa and reassure herself that her daughter was safe. Her car would be in more jeopardy at home—it could disappear anytime it was located where a repo company could easily find it—but maybe getting away from Ted would enable her to gain some perspective on his unexpected relationship with Eve. She knew better than to hope *she* could ever get him back. But she'd been so happy to think she'd *finally* found a friend in Eve. Although Eve had been wonderful to her the past week, Sophia could never be close to someone who was sleeping with Ted. She'd feel too guilty about her own thoughts and feelings.

She spent the morning vacuuming, dusting and

cleaning closets. Ted kept his house picked up and somewhat organized but, like most men, he didn't do much deep cleaning. She felt she was making some real headway with that, but she had to break away to fix lunch.

Once she was back in the kitchen, she decided to serve him a grilled panini sandwich with sliced fruit on the side.

It didn't take her long to prepare it. She tried to deliver his lunch and leave without his noticing so she could return to her music and her war on dirt. But he stopped her just as she was about to shut the door and said he wanted to go over some clerical work he needed her to do.

"Sure. I'll give it my best," she said and transferred his meal tray to the coffee table so she could sit down.

He took half his sandwich and came over. "You know how to boot up a computer, right?"

She gave him a look that said she wasn't an idiot and turned on the laptop. He ate as it went through its paces but he didn't say anything. He grabbed the rest of his sandwich while she searched for the Excel document he asked her to locate.

"This is delicious," he said.

She didn't look up. "Glad you're enjoying it. You should tell me when you like one meal more than another so I can make a list of your favorites."

"So far, the salad and sandwich have been perfect. Maybe you could try some sort of pasta tomorrow."

"I can do that."

She managed to open the document he wanted, but she'd never worked in Excel, didn't know the first thing about it, so the nerves she'd experienced during her typing test began to reassert themselves.

"This won't be as hard as it looks." His voice was encouraging; he could tell she was a bit overwhelmed.

He brought over a thick stack of paper slips and explained that these were from people who'd signed up to be on his mailing list at the state fair and various other events. He wanted her to add them to an Excel spreadsheet so he could send out a newsletter.

"I'm just inputting names and email addresses?" she asked.

"That's it. Data entry. Be careful not to type the name or email address incorrectly, though."

She didn't think that would be a problem, as long as she could read the handwriting. She'd double-check each one. "What column should I put the names in?"

"I'm about to show you." He helped her format the page. She could smell his cologne, even feel the warmth of his body as he bent over her and used the mouse to demonstrate how to title the columns and widen them when necessary.

Fortunately, he was right. It took only a few clicks to get her going. Then the work was tedious and repetitive but easy.

As soon as she was sure she had the hang of it, she put a rubber band around the slips and started to close down the computer.

He'd gone back to his own desk by then, but turned when he heard the squeak of her chair. "What are you doing?" he asked.

"I haven't finished cleaning up from lunch. I thought I'd go do that and wrap up a few other things. But don't worry. I'll take this home with me so you'll be able to send out your newsletter tomorrow."

"There's no need to work at home if you have time here. The cleaning's not going anywhere."

She felt she should at least put her sandwich in the fridge until she could eat it, but figured it would be okay for a while. With a nod, she opened the computer again and went back to work.

More than an hour passed with Ted sitting about eight feet away from her. She'd glance up every once in a while, thinking about how handsome he was and how different her life would've been if *he'd* been Alexa's father—and then she'd catch herself. There was no guarantee they would've had a child or even gotten married. And she couldn't change the decisions she'd made. She had to live with the results, especially now that he was seeing Eve. Eve seemed to be everything a man could want. Why would he walk away from her?

At two, Sophia began to watch the clock. Alexa would get out of school in an hour. Then, hopefully, she could breathe easier where her daughter was concerned. But it was only five minutes later that her phone rang.

Caller ID indicated it was the school.

She didn't want to disturb Ted while he was writing. He'd already looked back at the noise. So she answered softly as she let herself out of the room.

"Hello?" Anxiety roiled in her stomach but she tried to sound like her usual self.

"Mrs. DeBussi?"

"Yes?"

"This is Mrs. Vaughn, the principal at Whiskey Creek Middle School. I'm afraid we need you to pick up your daughter as soon as possible."

The nails of her free hand curved into her palm. "Why? She's okay, isn't she?"

"Physically she's fine. But she's been suspended from school."

"What?" When Alexa was part of her former group of friends, she'd had the tendency to socialize too much and not pay enough attention in class. On Back to School night in September, several teachers had commented on how much she talked. But Alexa had never done anything that had gotten her sent to the principal's office.

"She attacked another girl in her fifth-period class," Mrs. Vaughn explained. "You should see how badly she scratched her face."

Sophia wanted to ask if Mrs. Vaughn had seen the damage to her own daughter's face from yesterday but was still trying to get over the word *attacked*. She couldn't imagine Alexa being the aggressor. "Who was it?"

"A student who's only been in the area a couple of years. Her name is Connie Ruesch."

Maybe Connie hadn't been in the area long, but from what Sophia had heard, she'd been causing trouble since the day she moved in. "That's the girl who jumped Alexa yesterday after school," she said. "Lex was walking to the corner where I pick her up when it happened. So…are you *sure* she's the one who started the fight?"

"According to witnesses, this was an unprovoked attack."

"Connie hit her several times yesterday. That hardly makes it unprovoked!"

"Whatever happened yesterday happened off school

grounds. There's nothing I can do about it, *even* if events unfolded exactly as your daughter claims."

The skepticism in Mrs. Vaughn's voice really bothered Sophia. "*Claims?* You doubt her word? You think she's lying?"

"I think she'd rather Connie be the one to get into trouble."

"She's not like that, not…conniving."

"Trust me, I've seen it all."

"But you know me, know *her.*"

"She's well-loved. I applaud you for that, but no child is perfect. And I do not allow parents to rescue children from the consequences of their actions. That's not how discipline works here at Whiskey Creek Middle School."

Sophia pressed her fingertips to her forehead. "You mentioned witnesses."

"Most of the class saw what happened."

"Including the teacher?"

"The teacher had stepped out for a moment. But she saw what was going on when she returned and pulled Alexa off Connie. We have the accounts of several students to verify what occurred before that. Ella, a child I trust, was one of them."

But Ella was part of the popular crowd, and she'd been among the girls snickering at Alexa that Sunday at Just Like Mom's. "Was Babette in that room, too?"

"I'm sorry. I shouldn't even have mentioned Ella's name. We can't give out that kind of information on someone else's child."

"*What* kind of information?"

"Private information."

Sophia couldn't help laughing. Mrs. Vaughn

would've given her the entire class roster if she'd asked for it a month ago. The school had had no trouble coming to her when they were short of computers in the learning center. Or for the annual crab feed, when they'd needed an organizer and some large-ticket items for the live auction. Last year, she and Skip had donated a trip on their yacht.

The principal's voice grew even starchier when Sophia didn't seem to be taking her seriously. "Those are the rules, Mrs. DeBussi."

"When they're convenient," Sophia muttered.

"I didn't call you to argue. I'm merely trying to inform you that your daughter started a fight, and now she has to be punished just like anybody else."

Sophia was *so* close to letting the anger inside her erupt, but she ordered herself to override that impulse. She had to consider how her actions would affect Alexa.

Keeping a tight rein on her temper, she tried a different approach. "Mrs. Vaughn, I don't have to tell you that Alexa recently lost her father. Whatever you hold against him, or me, *please* don't let that influence how you treat *her*."

"I'm offended that you'd even suggest I could be capable of taking out what I feel for a child's parents on the child," she responded.

But that was precisely what she was doing. Couldn't she see it? Before Skip cheated everyone, this wouldn't have been a problem. Mrs. Vaughn would've believed Alexa immediately. "I'm not suggesting anything," she said. "I'm just asking you to be aware of the potential for prejudice and to guard against it. I mean…isn't there something else you could do to punish Alexa? Give her a detention after school or—or have her come in during lunch? I know she's not responsible for that fight. I *know* it. It doesn't seem fair that she'll be punished so harshly. For one thing, she'll fall behind in her classes if she misses the rest of the week. She's already struggling…in more ways than one."

"Maybe that's why she acted out. Makes sense, doesn't it? I'll see you in a few minutes."

When Mrs. Vaughn hung up, Sophia wanted to throw her phone. Instead, she pounded it against her forehead. "Damn it," she whispered as she lost her battle with the tears that had welled up. "Can't *anything* go right? Can I really be so terrible as to deserve all this?"

"What's going on?"

Dropping her hand, she whirled to see Ted standing behind her. She hadn't heard him come out. How long had he been listening?

She dashed a hand across her cheeks. "Nothing. Alexa needs to be picked up from a school a little early, that's all." Hoping to escape the scrutiny of those dark eyes, she moved away from him. "I hope you don't mind if I go now instead of in forty minutes."

She couldn't even make herself wait for an answer. She hurried down the stairs and out the front door as fast as she could without breaking into a full run. But before she could get in her car, Ted came jogging out after her.

At the sound of his footsteps, she glanced back and he gestured toward the passenger side door. "Unlock it. I'm going with you."

Ted took a seat in the principal's office next to Sophia while Mrs. Vaughn closed the door. Alexa was already there, in a chair set off to one side, looking like a condemned prisoner. She didn't get up and rush into her mother's arms, as Ted thought she might. She didn't plead her case. She just peered up at them through her brown bangs with swollen eyes and a tear-streaked face.

Certain injuries were evident. Ted suspected the scrape on her cheek was new—it was bleeding—but the swollen lip and the bruise didn't seem as recent.

"I'm sorry to have to call you in under these circumstances." Mrs. Vaughn looked at him as if she couldn't fathom how he was involved, but he didn't trouble himself to explain. He wasn't sure he could. He just acted as if he had every right to be there, and she didn't try to shut him out.

When Sophia turned to her daughter and started to blink rapidly, he knew she was fighting tears, just as she'd been fighting them on the way over. She opened her mouth to respond to the principal, but Ted squeezed her arm to tell her he'd handle this. "It's unfortunate. Has Alexa been in trouble often?"

Alexa's gaze shifted to him. She seemed confused by his presence, too, but didn't say anything. She just bowed her head and stared at the floor.

Mrs. Vaughn took her seat behind the desk. "Never."

"So this is her first infraction?" He knew it was. Sophia had explained the whole situation in the car. He merely wanted to remind Mrs. Vaughn that this was a kid who'd never caused trouble before. Maybe she'd see that suspension was a bit extreme, that maybe there'd been more provocation than she'd been told, since this wasn't typical behavior for Alexa.

"Yes. But as you know—" Mrs. Vaughn's eyes cut to Sophia "—there's been a lot of disruption at home."

"None of which is Alexa's fault," he pointed out.

"Oh, no," she agreed. "I wasn't implying that."

He addressed Alexa. "Lex, can you tell me what happened?"

She didn't say anything until Sophia encouraged her. "This is a friend of mine, honey. Can you answer him?"

"She kept shoving her pencil into my back," she mumbled.

"She being…Connie?" Ted said.

A nod confirmed this.

Sophia made a sound that led him to believe she'd jump in, but he squeezed her arm again. "And she poked you *before* the fight broke out?" he asked.

Another nod.

"Did it hurt?"

"Yes!" Alexa spoke louder. "It was the pointy end!"

"Then it probably left some marks. Do you know if it did?"

"No," she said. "I can't see my own back."

"Can *we* take a look?"

After a silent confirmation from her mother, she got up, turned around and let Sophia lift the back of her shirt. Sure enough, there were several red marks, one where the point had broken the skin.

"Did you tell the teacher?" Ted asked.

She tugged her shirt down. "I couldn't. She wasn't there. It wouldn't help, anyway."

"Because…"

Her voice filled with indignation. "Then Connie and the others would be even meaner. A bunch of them followed me off campus yesterday, and Connie hit me lots of times."

"So you'd already had a bad experience with this girl."

Her chin bumped her chest as she nodded.

"What did you do when she kept poking you today?"

"I asked her to stop. But Babette and Ella kept laughing and egging her on. They said they'd give her a dollar to do it again. Then they offered her a cookie and a bag of chips. She was pulling my hair when she wasn't poking me." Alexa held out her white blouse. "She even marked my shirt with her pen and said I'd have to get another one from a thrift store since we don't have money anymore."

Ted knew this wasn't *his* battle, but he was glad he'd come. Sophia was so emotional. She'd break into tears if she tried to speak.

When he looked up, Mrs. Vaughn cleared her throat. "A sympathetic story. But the other kids say most of it isn't true. They maintain that Connie made some comment about Alexa having to get her clothes from a thrift store and that was all it took."

Ted stood and gestured toward Alexa. "And those marks on her back? How did they get there?"

The principal couldn't argue with that. Alexa couldn't have hurt herself in that way. "She should've gone to the teacher, like you suggested."

"Tell me something, Mrs. Vaughn." Ted rested his hands on his hips, knowing it made him seem more imposing. "What would you have done in her shoes?"

"Stop baiting me, Mr. Dixon. I can't condone her actions. Fighting doesn't solve anything."

"That's true. So what's Connie's punishment for instigating this?"

She straightened her blotter. "I've assigned her after-school detention."

"And Babette and Ella?"

"Babette and Ella?" she echoed. "This is the first I've heard of their involvement."

"Now that you know they have some culpability, I mean."

"Unfortunately, it's impossible to be perfectly fair to every child who *might* have been involved. I wasn't there. I can only go by eyewitness accounts, and I have to draw a hard line when students get physical. Alexa's the one who crossed *that* line."

"She just showed you the marks on her back. That looks pretty physical to me."

"But I have no idea how they got there. Maybe she poked first, because what she's saying goes against everything I've heard so far."

Ted caught Alexa's eye. "Lex, could you wait outside and let your mother and me have a few words with Mrs. Vaughn alone?"

After the door closed, he lowered his voice so she couldn't hear him in the anteroom. "I'm sorry to learn that you condone bullying here, Mrs. Vaughn. With my mother being a principal herself, I expected more from you and our school system."

She drew herself up taller. "I don't...*condone* bullying, Mr. Dixon!"

"Then why are you punishing the victim instead of the perpetrator?"

"Consequences follow behavior. One child struck another, and now she must face the consequences."

"It doesn't matter to you that the child you're suspending is the one who was first teased, poked and tormented?"

Her nostrils flared, but she didn't answer.

"I believe I've committed a sizeable amount to funding the new gymnasium. As disappointed as I am in the way this school is being run, however, I'm afraid I'll have to withdraw my support from that project." He motioned to Sophia. "Let's go."

Mrs. Vaughn hurried around her desk. "You'd penalize the *kids* for something you feel *I've* done?"

"Why not? You're penalizing Alexa for something Connie did."

"But we've already lost the money Mr. DeBussi pledged to the project!"

"That explains a lot, doesn't it?"

They glared at each other for several seconds, until she lowered her gaze. "I apologize if you feel I've been unfair."

"I don't *feel* anything. I'm convinced of it." Whether she'd acted consciously or not, she'd known that Sophia was in no position to defend her daughter. In his opinion, Mrs. Vaughn thought she'd be able to get away with punishing Sophia and Alexa for Skip's sins, just like Chief Stacy seemed eager to do.

"What do you suggest as a more fitting punishment?" she asked grudgingly.

"You assigned Connie detention. Maybe Alexa should have the same." Ted turned to Sophia. "Don't you agree?"

She nodded.

"I don't mind telling you that it's a mistake to keep rescuing a child," Mrs. Vaughn said, her voice and demeanor full of reproach. "It teaches the wrong principles."

Ted straightened the nameplate at the edge of her desk. "Didn't you admit to me that this is the first time Alexa has ever been in trouble?"

She didn't reply to that question. With a sigh, she wadded up the sheet she had ready for Sophia to sign and threw it in the wastebasket. "Fine. She'll serve detention for five days after school, starting tomorrow. But it's not *my* fault that she'll be doing it with Connie. And I will not tolerate either one of them acting out again."

"Will a teacher be present at all times?" Sophia asked. "I don't want her left alone with that girl ever again."

It was easy to see that Mrs. Vaughn was loath to reassure her. She preferred to insist that the way *she'd* chosen to handle the situation would've been better. But Ted wasn't about to back off. He was tired of the prejudice and injustice that'd been heaped upon Sophia, and he was angry that everyone else's reaction to what Skip had done kept drawing him into her life. He wouldn't have gotten involved with one of his best friends if not for Sophia. But he didn't want to think about that, didn't want to feel any regret because it was too late to change anything.

"There will be a teacher," the principal said.

Sophia lifted her chin. "Thank you."

Mrs. Vaughn followed them into the reception area, where they waited for Alexa to retrieve her backpack. "Does this mean we can count on you to help with the gymnasium?" she asked.

Ted could see Alexa in the principal's office, wiping her eyes before pulling her backpack over one shoulder. "We'll see how school goes this coming week," he replied. "As long as Alexa remains safe, I'm happy to donate."

Her lips pursed. "So…are you and Mrs. DeBussi… *seeing* each other?"

She was still perplexed as to why he was there, was trying to put it into some sort of context. "No, Mrs. De-Bussi is working for me."

"Since when?"

He pretended not to hear her. Alexa joined them at that moment, and they walked out.

"Thanks for your help," Sophia murmured as they navigated the front steps.

He didn't respond to that, either. He was drifting closer and closer to her; he could feel it. But he didn't know how to stop what was happening between them. Being with her, standing up for her, felt too damn... natural.

17

"Once you drop me off, you can head home," Ted told Sophia as he drove them back to his place. He probably should've let Sophia take the wheel. The Mercedes was, after all, her car—until the repo company took possession of it, anyway—but driving gave him something to concentrate on besides his new housekeeper and her daughter.

"I'll finish that project you gave me first," Sophia said. "And make dinner. Alexa can do her homework. We were planning to have her come over after school, anyway, so nothing's changed."

"Except that it's been a rough day for both of you. Why don't you go home and recoup?" He hoped to convince her, especially because he needed to do the same, needed to get her out of his system before Eve picked him up. The last thing he wanted was to be thinking of Sophia the whole time he was trying to talk himself into loving the person he'd chosen to pursue.

"No, I'll finish out the day. I don't want you to feel my problems are taking a toll on my work."

"I don't mind."

She raised a hand. "Please, I need to finish...for me, if not for you."

"Right. Okay."

"I have to do my part," she explained. "I hope you understand."

"I do. And I appreciate that," he said, but when they went into the house so she could get Alexa set up at the kitchen table, he saw her lunch and knew she was try- ing *too* hard. When she'd brought up his tray and he'd waylaid her without realizing she hadn't eaten, she'd never said a word.

She should've spoken up.

"Get started with your math," she told Lex. "I'll be up in the office for a while, but I'll come down and see how you're getting along when I make dinner."

"This is a cool place," Alexa breathed as she put her backpack on the floor. "I *really* like it."

Ted smiled. Lex seemed pretty damn sweet and down-to-earth for being Skip's only child.

She sent him a shy glance. "You're the author, right? I've seen your name. My mom reads your books *all* the time. She *loves* them."

Sophia tried to duck out of the room and head up- stairs, but Ted cut her off before she could reach the door. "Oh, no, you don't." He pointed at her waiting sandwich. "You might want to throw that away since it's been sitting out for so long, but you need to eat *some- thing* before you return to work."

"I'm sure my sandwich is fine," she said and nuked it before taking it up with her.

Ted sat at the table across from Alexa, who was busy getting out her books. "What kind of homework do you have? Just math?"

"I wish," she said. "I've got social studies and English, too. Tons of English." She made a face. "I have to write a persuasive essay."

"Believe it or not, I hated English homework when I was a kid, too."

"And you turned out to be a writer?"

"It's a lot more fun when *you* get to decide what to write." Sophia hadn't offered her daughter an after-school snack; she was probably worried that would make her appear too free with his food. "Would you like some cookies and milk before you get to work?"

"Sure, if…if that's okay." She checked the doorway as if she expected her mother to pop in and tell her whether she was allowed to accept his offer.

"It's okay," he assured her and got some Oreo cookies out of the cupboard.

"Oh, my *favorite,*" she said when she saw them.

"We have that in common."

"Do you ever put them in ice cream?"

"All the time." He peered more closely at her. "I have some ice cream. Would you rather I made you a shake?"

"Oh, no. I was just saying they're good that way, too."

"I've got plenty of ice cream," he said, tempting her.

"Really?"

"Yeah, really. As far as I'm concerned, you deserve ice cream after a day like today."

"It *was* one of the worst," she agreed. "But lots of days have been bad lately."

"I can imagine." He could feel her watching him as he worked. "I'm sorry about that."

"*You* didn't invest with my dad," she said as if that was a given.

"No."

"That explains it."

He crushed several cookies. "Explains what?"

"Why you're so nice."

"What happened wasn't your fault. I certainly wouldn't take it out on you."

She prodded her sore lip with her tongue. "I wish everyone felt that way."

"They're hurt and angry, and that makes them want to place blame. Things will get better."

"We're going to move, anyway," she said.

Sophia hadn't mentioned anything about leaving town. "When?" he asked.

"As soon as we get the money." She took her shake with a smile. "My mom says we need to start over."

"Where will you go?"

"Anywhere but here," she said with a roll of her eyes.

He could tell she was repeating the words and sentiments of her mother. "I see." But, somehow, he didn't like the idea of their leaving, despite all the reasons he'd been hoping for just that.

"How many books have you written?" she asked while she shoveled ice cream into her mouth.

"Fifteen so far."

"Maybe *I* could read one."

He finished mixing his own shake. "You're a little young."

"So they have sex in them?"

He hadn't expected her to be quite so blunt—not at thirteen. But now that he was faced with that question, he had to be equally honest. "Sometimes."

"*That's* why my mom had to hide them!" Her laugh suggested she finally understood a great mystery.

"From *you?*" Ted asked.

"No, from my dad."

Ted was pretty sure there were other reasons. His name on the cover, for one. But it was good to know she'd been interested in his work. He'd often wondered. "Was it just my books or other people's, too?"

"I don't know. But once he found your book on the nightstand and got *so* mad. After that, Mom could only read books he approved of. He'd give her a list."

Ted felt his jaw tighten. "Really!"

"Yep."

"What types of books would be on that list?"

"Books about God and cookbooks mostly."

He jammed the spoon through another cookie to break it up. "Hard for those kinds of books to lead you astray."

Again, she missed his sarcasm. "Except the cookbooks."

"How can cookbooks be harmful?"

"They can make you fat if you cook and eat all the food!"

"Did she get in trouble for eating too much?" He was being facetious but Alexa took the question at face value.

"If it was dessert."

"Your mother's never been fat."

She was scraping the sides of the glass when she answered. "Because she didn't want to get in trouble."

"Would *you* get in trouble if you gained weight?"

"Probably," she said. "My dad hated fat women."

Ted remembered Skip as having a paunch. He longed to point out the double standard but bit his tongue. "You and your mom are going to get by just fine. You know that, right?" He wanted to add that at least they didn't have anyone policing what they ate or what they read these days, but that would be out of line.

"My mom's doing better than she was at first," she conceded. "I think it's because you gave her a job. So… thank you."

"You're welcome."

Sophia appeared as he was carrying their empty glasses to the sink. She seemed surprised to find him still in the kitchen, but she spoke to her daughter. "You haven't started your homework?"

"Not yet. Mr. Dixon made me an Oreo shake. It was *delicious*."

Alexa's smile made him glad he'd taken the time.

"That's very nice of him," Sophia said, "but Mr. Dixon has a book to write. I hope…I hope you didn't detain him by asking for anything."

"I didn't!" she said. "I promise!"

He put their glasses in the dishwasher. "I offered."

Sophia rubbed her hands on her thighs. "I'm sorry if you felt you had to look after her."

"Calm down," he responded. "I'm not criticizing you."

He thought she might ask what he meant by that, but she didn't. She waited for him to head to his office. Then, a few minutes later, she joined him and worked silently at her own desk.

Somehow, he managed to write a few pages—a marvel considering how distracted he was. "It's five," he told her when he noticed the time. "You can quit."

She kept working. "I have a few more names."

"You can enter them tomorrow." He scowled, hoping she'd hear the firmness in his voice. He was ready for her to leave. He'd been so conscious of her sitting behind him for the past couple of hours. It was almost as if he could hear her *breathe.* And if he wasn't focusing on that, he was thinking about the fact that she was planning to move.

But Sophia was so determined to finish, she didn't even glance up. "It'll just take a minute."

Once she returned the mailing-list additions to his desk, he thought that was that. But no. She went to the kitchen and prepared dinner. If he listened carefully, he could hear her downstairs. He knew she had to be tired, with everything she'd done today. He considered going down and ordering her to go home. But he refrained because he knew she was struggling to feel good about herself, and she'd indicated that her work here was part of that.

An hour later, she brought up a steaming bowl of the most delicious broccoli-cheddar soup he'd ever tasted.

Sophia had stayed longer than she was supposed to. But she was finally satisfied with what she'd accomplished today. She'd even finished the data entry project he'd given her.

"Your boss is really nice, isn't he?" Alexa said as they climbed into the car.

She tried not to envision Ted from behind as she'd seen him all afternoon. She'd memorized the size and shape of his shoulders, taking note of every change in his body—a body she'd once been so familiar with. "He's a good man."

"He doesn't have a wife?"

When Sophia looked over at her daughter, she saw that Alexa was playing with the zipper on her backpack. "No, but he has a girlfriend. You know Eve."

"He's with Eve?"

"He is."

"Wow. She's nice. But…it's a bummer that he's taken. He's *so* cute, don't you think?"

Sophia rested her hands on the steering wheel instead of starting the car. "Lex, I think maybe it's time I explained something. I heard you tell Ted that Daddy got mad when he found his book on the nightstand."

"He did!" she said, suddenly defensive.

Sophia knew she expected another lecture on keeping quiet about what happened inside their house. Skip had been so obsessed with maintaining a certain image that they weren't allowed to reveal anything that might not show him in a positive light. He'd been so adamant about that, and got so angry if they ever made a mistake, they'd both been afraid to say anything.

She softened her voice to let her daughter know this wasn't one of *those* conversations. "That's true. But it wasn't the genre of the book he objected to."

"It wasn't?"

"Not entirely, although he tried to make a big deal out of that, too."

"So what was it?"

She'd caught her daughter's interest. "Ted and I used to be friends before your daddy and I got married. Actually, for about two years, we were…more than friends."

Her eyes grew wide. "*Ted* was your boyfriend? Why didn't you ever tell me?"

Because just mentioning his name would've been enough to start a fight with Skip. "There was no point. Ted wasn't part of our lives. But now…"

"Now he is." She seemed happy about that.

"Yes, but I need you to be aware of the past and how

that might make Ted and me feel awkward if you…if you say the wrong thing."

She was silent as she considered that. Then she said, "I'll be careful."

"Thanks."

"But do you think you two might ever get back together?"

"I told you, he's seeing Eve."

"That doesn't mean he'll marry her."

"You want me to start *dating?*"

"Why not? You don't owe Dad anything. Not after what *he* did."

This was an interesting twist. Alexa had always been a daddy's girl. "We have to try to remember the good things about your father, Lex. He loved you. He—"

"Was desperate when he jumped ship. I know. You told me before. But…"

She didn't sound impressed. "What?" Sophia prompted.

"How could he love us and do what he did?"

"He was confused on top of everything else."

"*Confused?* About what? About whether he wanted to be part of our family? Look at what happened at school! I'd still have my friends if he hadn't hurt so many people."

Sophia couldn't argue with that. "True, but—"

"Why do you always defend him? He wouldn't have said any nice things about *you* if you'd jumped off the yacht."

No doubt that was true. But she wasn't Skip—and she didn't want to be anything like him. "That's beside the point."

Alexa slumped in her seat. "So why?" she asked again. "Why do you defend him?"

"I don't do it for him. I do it for you. I'd do *anything* for you."

"Even give up drinking?"

"That's right."

She reached over to take Sophia's hand, and Sophia couldn't help smiling. Maybe the past weeks had been pure hell, but there was something new and fresh and exciting being forged in that fire. For one thing, she and Alexa were pulling together, growing closer than they'd ever been. It made Sophia feel good to be the parent to come through for a change—made her feel better than she had in years.

"You're a good mom."

Hearing the conviction in Alexa's voice filled Sophia with warmth. For a second, she was glad that Skip had shown who he really was. Without that, maybe she wouldn't have found out who *she* really was.

"And you're a wonderful daughter." She gave Alexa's hand a squeeze. But that special moment didn't last much longer than it took to start the car and drive home. As Sophia crested the top of the hill where they lived, she saw that the battle they were waging was far from over.

18

Ted left Eve's determined to overcome the rebellion of his own heart. She'd make a great wife, a great mother. With her, he'd never have to deal with trust issues. So why *not* pursue a more serious relationship?

Maybe he'd been hanging back all these years, feeling he couldn't get over Sophia, when that wasn't the case at all. Maybe he simply hadn't tried hard enough. These days, half the people in his group of friends were married. He was ready to make the same transition, to embrace the next phase of life. And he could be happy with Eve. They'd had a really nice time tonight.

Well, *overall* they'd had a nice time. There were a few moments when he'd felt a little spooked by the possessiveness in her touch. And it was a bit odd that, even though they'd kissed, he hadn't been in the mood to make love.

But she hadn't pushed him.

See? Even in that she was perfect. He'd said that it had been a hell of a day and he was exhausted, and they'd had a piece of pie and watched TV. With her, life would be simple. So what if he didn't want to jump into bed all the time? He just needed a chance to acclimate to being physical with someone he'd never previously viewed in a sexual way. Ignoring that slight resistance wasn't quite so easy when you were sober.

He was almost home when he checked his phone and saw that he'd missed a call from Sophia. It'd come in not long after she'd left his place.

Curious, he pulled over to listen to her message.

"Ted? Um…sorry to bother you. I was wondering if you have a gun you could lend me. But…I'll figure out something else. Don't worry. No need to return this call."

A *gun?* Why would she need a gun?

He considered calling her back, but it was close to midnight. He doubted she'd be up this late. He hoped not. With the way things had been going for her, she needed the rest.

Right now he felt like he could use some rest, too. Since she'd come to work for him, his life hadn't been the same, and he had a feeling it might never go back. If he continued seeing Eve, he could be married this time next year.

Putting the transmission back in Drive, he turned around. He figured he could go by Sophia's. If there were any lights on, he'd return her call, make sure everything was okay. The fact that Chief Stacy had been so antagonistic toward her, when he held so much power in Whiskey Creek, was disconcerting. Then there was that incident with Alexa at school. Maybe Connie had gone home and told her parents the same story she'd told Mrs. Vaughn and they'd decided to get nasty. After all, Sophia and Lex were in that huge house all by themselves, and everyone knew where they lived. Ted didn't think his fellow residents would do anything to cause *serious* harm—but Sophia *had* asked for a gun. There must've been a reason.

He snapped off his headlights as he arrived at the top of the hill and turned toward the house. The DeBussi mansion was the only residence up here. It wasn't as if he'd be disturbing any of Sophia's neighbors. He just didn't want to shine bright lights into her windows, didn't want to scare her if she happened to be up.

Not only that but, truth be told, he preferred she not know he'd come to check on her. This was strictly for his own peace of mind.

He barely pressed on the gas; mostly he let the engine idle as he rolled toward her house. Several strips of toilet paper fluttered from the tallest trees, as if they'd recently been T.P.'d and whoever'd cleaned up couldn't reach that high, but other than the dim pagoda lamps strategically placed in the landscaping, no lights were on.

This had been a waste of time. Sophia and Alexa were in bed, as he'd imagined.

Reassured, he nearly made a U-turn at the end of the court so he could go home. He would've hurried out of there; he was seconds away from doing just that when he spotted a dark shape on the porch.

Because that shape looked human, he hit the brakes instead of the gas.

Were Sophia and Alexa getting T.P.'d again? Or was that someone trying to get in?

Whoever it was didn't turn at the sound of his engine. After pulling into Sophia's circular drive, he parked and walked quickly toward the house. He'd almost decided he'd been wrong. What he saw couldn't be a human. There was *still* no reaction to his approach.

But then he realized why. It wasn't *someone;* it was Sophia. She was sitting on a metal fold-out chair, since her lawn furniture had been taken from the house. Fast asleep, her breath misting in the cold air, she had a blanket wrapped around her shoulders—and a rifle in her lap.

Obviously she'd found a gun. But…what was she doing?

He reached out to give her shoulder a shake, pausing when he noticed the broken window. An object had been thrown through it. Then he saw what looked like the word *Bitch* spray-painted across her front door. A symbol had been drawn on the porch, too. It seemed to be some kind of rocket….

Someone had done more than T.P. the property. Had this happened tonight? Judging by Sophia's attempt to defend her house, he guessed it had.

"Shit," he muttered and shoved his hands in his pockets as he surveyed the rest of the damage.

His voice finally woke Sophia. She leaped out of her seat and grabbed for her gun, but he whipped it away.

"Calm down," he said. "It's me."

"Ted?" The blanket had slipped off. Although she was fully clothed in sweats and tennis shoes, he could see the rapid rise and fall of her chest as she struggled to cope with the shock.

"What are you doing out here in the cold?" he asked.

It seemed to take her a moment to realize she wasn't under attack. She blinked, then peered out at the lawn and beyond, as if she still wasn't convinced. "I could ask you the same thing," she said when she returned her attention to his face.

"On my way home, I saw that I missed your call. I was concerned because you asked for a gun, so I decided to drive by and check that you were okay."

She drew a hand through her hair. "I'm sorry to put you to the trouble. I shouldn't have bothered you. I wouldn't have if...if I thought I could borrow a gun from someone else."

He motioned at the guard post she'd set up. "What's this all about?"

"I was...I was making sure they don't come back."

"Who are *they?*"

She picked up the blanket. "How would I know? They weren't here when we got home. But they left me some nasty surprises." She pointed at the broken window. "That's part of it. So is the penis you're standing on."

"Penis?" He looked down at the porch floor. The rocket. Of course.

"They spray-painted swearwords in various places and broke some stuff, too. But it was the message they left that...that really upset me."

"What'd it say?"

Grasping the blanket with one arm, she dug the house key out of her pocket and gestured with it toward the door. "You can see for yourself. It's inside."

He stepped aside while she let him in. "Who gave you this?" he asked, hefting her gun.

She shoved open the door. "No one. I got it from the attic."

"You have *guns* in your attic?"

"It's not real."

When she flipped on the light, he examined it. It looked pretty damn real to him.

"That's one of Skip's paintball guns." She closed and locked the door. "It's expensive as far as toys go, and high-powered, so it hurts. But it's not going to kill anyone."

"This thing could put your eye out." He grinned at her when he said that. He could hear his mother warning him in exactly the same way when he was a kid.

"If they're going to attack me in my own house, I guess that's the risk they run. More likely they'll just get a welt." She lifted her shirt to show him a mark on her stomach. "See? This is all it does."

All? An angry red mark marred the smooth skin of her stomach several inches to the right of her belly button. Although he hadn't seen her stomach in a long time, it didn't look much different than he remembered. He'd thought she might have a few stretch marks from her pregnancy, but there were none.

He should've known—nothing ever seemed to diminish her beauty. But, oddly enough, it wasn't her beauty that drew him to her. Not entirely. It was the vulnerability in those big blue eyes—and the way she was trying to show her love for Alexa, despite her difficulties. He couldn't help admiring a mom who was sitting out on her front porch with a paintball gun to protect her daughter and what was left of their belongings. "How'd you manage to shoot yourself with a *rifle?*"

"*I* didn't. I had Alexa do it, just so I'd know what it would feel like."

He slid a finger over the injury and felt a jolt of awareness. It wouldn't have surprised him, except that it was so strong. To cover his reaction, he gestured toward the door. "You shouldn't be outside, asking for trouble. There's no telling what might happen if they come back. If it's Chief Stacy, for instance, and you piss him off enough…he has a real gun."

"Nice. You think our chief of police might shoot me. Makes me feel really safe."

She pulled the blanket around her again. The house wasn't much warmer than outside. He guessed she'd turned off the heat to save on her utility bills. If the energy company had turned off her service, she wouldn't have any lights.

"No matter who it is…I'm not putting up with the punishment anymore," she said. "I've made my mistakes. You, of all people, know that. But since I married Skip, I've contributed to this community. I've put in hours and hours of volunteer service, even if no one wants to count the money we donated to so many causes."

"I know."

She seemed taken aback that he didn't defend the town, and her voice softened. "I understand that everyone's disappointed. But no one's more disappointed than I am."

"I know that, too." He held up the paintball gun. "But this isn't going to help."

"It'll show them I'm done being bullied."

"Or get someone mad enough to really hurt you."

"What's my other choice? *Call the police?*"

If he'd been in her situation, he wouldn't have called the police, either. There were three officers on the force besides Stacy, but they answered to him, and they were so cowed Ted couldn't imagine how getting them involved would do any good. "What about your in-laws?

Surely they'll help if they know people are targeting Alexa."

She looked around as if she wanted to sit down; other than a card table and two folding chairs in the kitchen, her house contained no furniture. The carpet in the living room would've been softer, but she slid down the wall and sat on the marble floor with her back against the front door. "Help in what way?"

"Let you stay there, get you out of this place." There certainly wasn't much left to move—or steal. "This house is such a visible symbol of…of everything people resented about you and Skip."

"What did they resent? You mean that we had money?"

"There wasn't just a slight disparity, Sophia. I won't pretend jealousy doesn't play a role."

"It doesn't matter *what* plays a role. It is what it is, and there's nothing I can do about it." She pulled her knees into her chest. "Anyway, I won't go to my in-laws for help. I'd rather die than live with them."

"Why?"

"Because they like me almost as much as your mother does. And now that they've been forced to accept the truth about their son, they're confused, hurt and grieving. That doesn't make them particularly concerned about us."

He leaned a shoulder against the wall. "Not even Alexa?"

"When they call, she tells them we're fine. If she told them the truth, they'd interfere, maybe try to take her away from me, and that would be worse than the way things are now." She rested her head against the door as her eyes surveyed the empty house. "Or…maybe

I *should* let Lex go to them. Maybe I'm being selfish keeping her here, when I can't even heat the house."

It had to be hard to take care of Alexa when she was struggling just to take care of herself. But Lex provided Sophia with a reason to get up each day. Ted understood that. Eve had told him what she'd been like a week ago. He didn't feel it would be wise for her to give up her daughter, even temporarily. "We'll think of something—after we've both had a chance to get some sleep."

She grasped the door handle to pull herself up. "You don't have to worry about it. We're not your problem. Go home and be grateful you didn't wind up with me. Eve's a great catch. Definitely one of the nicest people in town."

What Sophia said was absolutely true. So why did something rebel in him when she told him he should be happy with Eve? "Eve is nice," he said to conceal the fact that he wasn't more excited about being with her.

She gave him a tired smile as she turned toward the stairs.

"Wait. You said whoever was here left you a note. You were going to show it to me."

"Was I?" She shrugged. "I don't know why. Doesn't matter what it says."

"Maybe I can tell who wrote it."

"You can't. It was written with crayon in capital letters. Give me the gun in case I need it. The door will lock automatically when you let yourself out."

She reclaimed the gun and dragged the blanket behind her as she climbed the elegant, winding staircase. She seemed too weary to move. He felt so bad about what she was going through that he almost offered to help her up to bed, but after the jolt he'd felt when he touched her, he knew he had to keep his distance.

Eventually, she reached the top and disappeared from view.

"Damn you, Skip," he grumbled. "I wish you were alive so I could break your freakin' jaw." He'd never been in a fight, but for Skip he would've made an exception. No one deserved a leveling blow more than he did.

Cold air streamed in through the broken window. Ted rummaged around in the kitchen and garage until he found some tape and a piece of cardboard to cover the hole. Fixing it made him feel somewhat better. He told himself he should go home and climb into bed—his deadline was looming closer with each passing day. But then he realized that a rock the size of a baseball was sitting on the fireplace mantel. That had to be the one that was thrown through the window. It sat on a crumpled piece of typing paper that had obviously been wrapped around it.

With a final glance up the stairs to make sure Sophia wasn't coming back down, he crossed the living room and smoothed out the paper so he could read it.

Look at the beautiful Sophia DeBussi. Broke. Alone. Despised. I'm laughing. What does it feel like to fall so far? It couldn't have happened to a nicer person. But let me be the first to warn you. If you have our money hidden away somewhere, and you think you can lie low until the FBI quits paying attention, you'd better think again. Because if I ever find out you've been lying, I'll see that you live to regret it.

Ted's heart pounded as he reread those words. Was this an idle threat? Someone in town with a loud bark but no real bite? Or was it the opposite—someone who'd let his anger grow until he acted on it?

No wonder she'd been standing guard over her daughter and what was left of her house. She had to protect what she could. But a paintball gun wouldn't stop anyone with real intent.

Taking the stairs two at a time, he hurried to the second floor. He'd never been inside Sophia's home, but it wasn't difficult to find the master bedroom. A set of elaborate double doors at one end of the hall gave it away.

He knocked, just in case she wasn't dressed.

"Come in," she said.

He found her lying on the carpet, curled up on one side with a blanket and a pillow. The furniture had been removed from this room, too.

"Who the hell would write this?" he demanded, showing her the note he held in his hand.

She didn't bother to lift her head. "I have so many enemies these days you could take your pick. Maybe it was Chief Stacy."

"I doubt he'd be stupid enough to *threaten* you."

"I wouldn't bet on that. He feels he can get away with anything." She punched up her pillow. "Maybe he can."

"You can't stay here anymore. You realize that." She didn't even have a bed. Or heat. And it was only going to get colder....

She chuckled. "Oh, yeah? Where am I supposed to go?"

He thought of his guesthouse. No one was there at the moment. It was furnished. It had heat. She could easily get to work. And he could keep a protective eye on both her and Lex.

But then she'd essentially be living with him!

No, not living with him. It would be like having her as a…a neighbor. He could handle that, couldn't he?

"How long until the bank takes your car?" he asked.

"You think we should move into my car?"

"No. I want to know what we're dealing with."

"*We* aren't dealing with anything other than work-related matters."

"Answer the question."

She leaned on her elbow. "Why? There's nothing you can do."

"Just give me an idea."

"Not very long," she admitted. "A week?"

"You should have more time than that," he said. "They don't repossess until you've missed a few payments."

"Skip wasn't paying the bills *before* he jumped off the yacht."

Ted felt even more disheartened. "Why am I surprised?" he grumbled. "So…how far behind are you?"

"According to the bill collector who keeps calling me, it's been four months."

Had he *ever* known anyone in a worse situation?

No. Never.

"Is that true for the house, too?"

"I'm afraid so."

"How come you didn't get the notices?" She'd told him before that she hadn't known they were in financial trouble, so this must've been as unexpected as Skip's initial disappearance.

"Until he died, everything went to Skip's office."

Ted couldn't get over what Skip had done to his own wife and child. He shook his head. "Okay, back to your car. What will you do without transportation? Because the Mercedes will go first and, if you're four months behind, it'll be very soon."

"I'll walk."

"To *my* house? That's ten miles round trip. What about Alexa?"

"She'll have to ride her bike to school. And we'll have to ask Sharon to drive her out to your place every afternoon—at least until they move. After that? I can't plan so far into the future."

"You can't leave her vulnerable to the little monster who's been tormenting her at school."

Sophia pushed herself into a sitting position. "I don't know what you want me to say! That I'll buy another car with the piles of money I have sitting around? There *is* no money, Ted! I'm doing all I can to get through this, but I don't have a lot of options and no resources."

"You could've told me you don't even have heat!" he said.

"We have heat. We just can't pay for it. I'm trying to keep the bill down, so they won't turn it off before we get kicked out. Anyway, why would I complain to you? You're my employer. I don't want you to regret hiring me. My job's the one thing that might save me."

"I wouldn't fire you just because you need help."

"The problem isn't that I need help—it's that I need more help than anyone in their right mind would want to give me. I've crashed and burned in a very ugly and humiliating way. I don't blame everyone for wanting to get as far from me as possible. You should do the same thing."

"I don't mind giving you a hand. That's not the problem."

"Then what is?"

The fact that he still cared about her. That was what made this situation so impossible.

"We'll talk about it in the morning," he said and walked out. But just as he was opening the front door to leave, he noticed a pair of headlights coming toward him. The glare was so bright, he couldn't see who it was, couldn't tell the make and model of the vehicle. He ran out, but the driver spotted him immediately, threw the transmission into Reverse and burned rubber as he accelerated backward.

Ted jumped in his Lexus and tried to follow. Only one road led to and from the DeBussi mansion. He thought he could catch whoever it was, or at least get close enough to see if he recognized the car. But the vehicle seemed to disappear into thin air.

"Son of a bitch." Smacking the steering wheel, he headed back to Sophia's. It didn't matter that she was his ex-girlfriend. He couldn't leave her and her daughter alone, not under these circumstances.

19

"Mr. Dixon?" A hand jiggled his shoulder. "Mr. Dixon? Are you okay?"

Okay was a relative term. Ted had a crick in his neck. He knew that much.

Lifting his head, he squinted to bring Sophia's daughter into focus. The bruise on her face looked worse than yesterday. But the cut looked better. She was ready for school, all scrubbed and polished. With her hair pulled back, she was the spitting image of her mother—fortunate for her considering the wide disparity in Skip and Sophia's physical traits.

"I wanted to try sleeping at your kitchen table." He yawned as he stretched.

"That couldn't be comfortable." She frowned, obviously perplexed. "Why would anyone want to try it?"

He hadn't had many options. There were probably thirty rooms in the house, but thanks to Skip's investors trying to recoup whatever they could, there wasn't a mattress or an extra blanket in sight.

"I should've brought a sleeping bag," he muttered.

She started to say something else, but Sophia's voice

came down to them from upstairs, interrupting. "Lex, hurry up and grab some cereal. We have to go. I can't be late."

He made a face. "Or what? Sounds like she has a really mean boss."

That got a smile out of her. "I don't think she knows you're here."

"Neither do I, but she'll find out soon enough." He stood to ease the pain in his back and neck. "Can I scramble you some eggs for breakfast?"

"You could if we had a frying pan," she said. "We had a good one, but someone took it that night they came for the furniture."

"I see. So…what's for breakfast?"

She pulled a couple of cheap plastic bowls out of the cupboard. "We got these at the grocery store. They're not as pretty as what we had before, but they were only a dollar." Setting one in front of him, she took two plastic spoons and went to the pantry. "What's your favorite cereal?" she asked from inside.

"Wheaties, the breakfast of champions. I hope, if you had some to begin with, your father's investors didn't take it."

She laughed. "They took some of the meat out of the freezer, but they left the cold cereal. Thank goodness," she added, "because I was tired of eating soup.

"Sorry, no Wheaties," she said a moment later, holding out a box of Cap'n Crunch. "This is as close as I can get."

"Shouldn't we set a bowl for your mother?"

"No, she won't eat." She was carrying the milk to the table, but hesitated for a second. "I think she's trying to save most of the food for me."

"She really loves you."

"Believe me, now that I know what it's like to have a parent who doesn't, I'm a lot more grateful."

What she'd said was both sweet *and* sad. "Did you get your homework done last night?"

"Yeah."

"What topic did you choose for your English essay?"

"Bullying."

"Great choice. That's something you should feel passionate about, which always makes for an easier argument."

"I like the way it turned out. But—" she slumped into a chair and poured her cereal "—I still don't want to go to school."

He leaned down to catch her eye. "Good thing you're brave enough to do it anyway."

"Nice try, but that doesn't make me feel any better."

"Come on, a smart girl like you?" he said with a grin. "Nothing can keep you down for long."

She allowed him to pour the milk. "My mom said you're Eve's boyfriend."

He wondered what had brought that up. "We're... seeing each other."

"I like her." She scooped up her cereal. "She's nice, like you. And beautiful."

"Eve's special," he agreed.

She slanted him a shy look. "Do you *love* her?"

Fortunately, Sophia called down at that moment. "Lex?"

When Ted pressed a finger to his lips, indicating that she shouldn't give him away, she giggled.

"What?" she called back.

. "Remember that typing class you took at the library over the summer?"

"Yes?"

"Do you think they have that during the winter?"

They could hear Sophia coming down the stairs. "I don't know," Lex said. "Why?"

"I need to learn how to type. For my job."

Lexi covered her mouth as she laughed. "Or what? Mr. Dixon will fire you?"

Ted stopped chewing while he awaited Sophia's response.

"He might," she said. "He doesn't like me. I can tell you that."

The smile disappeared from Alexa's face. "Mom—" She was obviously going to explain that he could hear, but it was too late. Sophia entered the kitchen, saw him sitting at the table and froze.

"What are you doing here?" she asked.

He didn't answer the question. He asked one of his own. "Who said I don't like you?"

"It's a safe guess. Right now, no one does."

"I don't have many friends, either. Not anymore," Alexa chimed in, relaxing when she realized they weren't going to have a problem despite what he'd heard. "It's just the two of us."

"And me," he said.

She gave him a conspiratorial nudge. "And you. He slept slumped over on our kitchen table," she told her mom.

"For the record, it's as uncomfortable as it looks," he said with an exaggerated scowl.

Sophia came closer. "I don't understand why you didn't go home last night."

He didn't want to bring up the threatening note or the person he'd seen last night in front of Alexa, didn't see any point in frightening her. "I stayed because I wanted to help."

"By doing guard duty?"

"By getting you moved."

They both gaped at him. "Moved where?" Sophia asked.

"Into the guesthouse."

Confusion brought Alexa's eyebrows together. "What guesthouse? We don't have a guesthouse. My dad said my grandparents would want to move in if we built one."

Ever the loving son. Ted wanted to say that but, for Alexa's sake, he didn't. "The one behind my house."

Sophia marched across the kitchen and pulled her keys from her purse. "We are *not* moving into your guesthouse."

"Why not?"

"Because. Just…forget it."

"No one's living there," he said. "You might as well use it. Then you won't have to worry about—" he glanced at Lex and stated what he had to say as euphemistically as possible "—what might happen here."

"What if people start throwing rocks through *your* windows?" Sophia asked.

"They won't." He grinned. "They like *me*."

She glanced at the clock. "Lex, run up and put your backpack together, okay?"

Apparently, the risk of being late for school was enough to motivate her, because she jumped right up.

Once her daughter was gone, Sophia lowered her voice. "You know what people will say."

He played dumb. "No, what?"

"They'll think we're sleeping together!"

"Doesn't matter what they think."

"And *Eve?* She can't want me there! I may not be much competition for her now, but you and I...we have a history."

"I'll make sure she's okay with it." He dropped his voice to match hers in case Alexa came hurrying back. "What else are you going to do? Your days here are limited. You're already down to sleeping on the floor. My guesthouse is furnished and empty. It's not large, but at least you'll be safe and warm."

"I can't afford rent yet."

"Consider it part of your wages. It won't cost me anything to help you out until you can get back on your feet, except the utilities, of course, and I can afford to cover that."

Her skeptical expression said his offer had to be some sort of trap. "Why would you do this? There's nothing in it for you."

He checked to assure himself that Alexa wasn't returning yet. "Sophia, last night when I was leaving, I saw a car come down your street. I can't say that whoever it was meant you harm, but...they acted suspicious once they saw me."

She started digging at her cuticles. "In what way?"

"They hauled ass to get out of there."

"You couldn't see who it was?"

He stopped her before she could draw blood. "The glare of the headlights was too bright. I tried to catch them, but...no luck."

"Still, I'm not sure moving us into your guesthouse is the answer."

"Do you have a better idea?"

He knew he might regret having them so close, but there'd be a lot more to regret if he left them here and something terrible happened. "It's not like we'll be living together, Sophia. They're separate houses. What's wrong with that?"

Her expression grew earnest. "I don't want to be so vulnerable."

He couldn't prevent his eyes from lowering to her lips. "You'll be far more vulnerable here."

"Not in the same way," she said, but before he could respond, Alexa entered the kitchen.

"Did I miss it?" she asked breathlessly.

Sophia grabbed a granola bar and shoved it in her purse. "Miss what?"

Alexa hiked up her backpack. "Will we be moving to Ted's?"

"We'll talk about it after school," Sophia replied. "Go and get in the car."

Eager for a more definite answer, she glanced between the two of them, but Sophia motioned her toward the door and she did as she was told.

"Goodbye, Mr. Dixon," she called back.

"It's Ted from now on, okay? That Mr. Dixon stuff is making me feel old."

She tossed him a smile. "Okay. Goodbye, Ted."

"Hey," he called and she turned around.

"You'll get through it."

The gratitude in her eyes convinced him that he was doing the right thing in taking her and her mother in. But when he returned his attention to Sophia, he sensed that she was waiting to tell him something.

"We won't stay there long, Ted," she said when her

daughter was gone. "I promise." Her gaze was as intense as her words. "I'll get out of your life as soon as I can."

He remembered what Alexa had revealed in his kitchen yesterday. "Lex says you're planning to move away from Whiskey Creek."

"We are. As soon as I can save up the money. If you could just…tolerate us for three months, we should be okay. That might sound like an eternity to you right now, but…it'll go fast."

"I'm sure I can manage," he said, but could he manage without falling into the trap he'd just set for himself?

"Thanks." Her tone sounded as worried as it did relieved.

"Why don't you let me run Lex to school while you start packing?"

She bit her lip as she considered his words.

He knew he shouldn't, but he reached out to touch her arm. "You really don't have a better choice. I'll pick up some boxes on my way back."

With a nod, she handed him her keys.

"I've got my car," he said and hurried out.

20

"What's going on with you?" Cheyenne asked. "You've been flying high the past couple of days."

Eve glanced over at her friend. They were both in the small office at the back of the B and B. Eve was catching up on the accounting while Cheyenne placed some ads using a separate computer. Right after lunch was the quietest part of their day. The maids were busy cleaning the rooms that'd been vacated at checkout, breakfast had been served, the kitchen cleaned and they had no guests other than one couple who planned to stay for several days. "I have?" she said.

Chey sent her a pointed look. "Stop pretending you don't have a clue what I'm talking about. We've been friends for too long. I can see through the act." Giving up on her work for the moment, she swiveled around. "I've got it! You put your profile back up on that dating site, and this time you've met someone who's a real possibility."

"No. I don't trust that site. Not after my past experience."

"So you got a couple of weirdos. They can't *all* be dysfunctional."

"Maybe it's just my luck, but…remember the first guy I met? The one who told me he was self-employed?"

"Who turned out to live with his mother and was growing pot in her backyard?" Cheyenne said with a laugh. "How could I forget?"

"The next guy was a registered sex offender. You should've heard Chief Stacy give me a hard time when he confirmed *that* little tidbit. He thought it was hilarious that I almost dated him."

"You should've trusted that P.I. you hired."

In retrospect, Eve wished she had. "The guy seemed so normal. He knew exactly what I wanted to hear. And he was handsome as sin."

Cheyenne laughed even harder. "Then there was the one who was secretly married."

Eve shook her head. "I'm telling you, online dating is frightening. Expensive, too."

"Most people don't hire a P.I. to run a background check on every romantic possibility."

"Then most people could wind up dating those guys we just mentioned—or maybe an ax murderer."

"I'm not making fun of you for verifying facts. I'm *glad* you're cautious."

"I'm *more* than cautious, Chey. I'm done with online dating. It's too hard to get to know someone who lives out of the area, anyway. My family, my business, my friends are all here. I want a husband who's connected to this town, too."

Cheyenne narrowed her eyes. "So why are you smiling? If I remember right, you'd despaired of ever finding a guy like that."

Focusing on her computer screen, Eve acted as though she was too engrossed to answer.

"Eve…"

Smiling at the suspicion in Cheyenne's voice, she played innocent. "What?"

"What aren't you telling me? Are you seeing someone?"

Eve couldn't help it. She was too happy to hold back the truth, especially from Cheyenne. They'd been best friends almost since Cheyenne had come to town as a high school freshman, and they worked together. How was she supposed to keep anything *this* monumental a secret from her? "I am."

Cheyenne swung her chair around so they were practically nose to nose. *"Who?"*

"I can't tell yet," she said. "But you're gonna die!"

"Don't leave me in suspense! Why is it such a big secret?"

"Because…because we want to see how things go for a while before everyone else…reacts."

"Everyone else being…"

"Our family and friends."

"So he's local."

She nodded.

"And I know him?"

Pursing her lips, Eve folded her arms. "*Quite* well."

Cheyenne whistled. "It's not Joe.…"

There'd been a time when Eve had wanted to date Gail DeMarco-O'Neal's brother. He hadn't returned her interest, but she preferred to blame that on the fact that he'd been through such a painful divorce. "No, it's not Joe."

"Is this guy…marriage material?"

"Definitely. He's a good man, a smart man. Handsome, too."

"Divorced?"

"No. I told you it's not Joe."

Cheyenne propped her elbows on her armrests and laced her fingers together. "I can't think of anyone else you'd be this excited about. How old is he?"

"Our age," Eve said with a grin. "He went to school with us."

"Now you really have me stumped." She got up and began to pace—as much as the space would allow. "Who's our age that you'd be willing to date? All the *really* great guys are part of our group of friends."

When Eve covered her mouth, Cheyenne's eyes flew wide. "Don't tell me you're seeing Kyle. No, he's divorced. Riley, then. Or Ted. Ted!" she screamed. "I saw the way you stuck by his side on Halloween. You're seeing Ted!"

Eve rocked forward. "Can you believe it?"

"I can't. I mean, I've never sensed any…you know… *sizzle* between you two."

"Until Halloween, there wasn't any. But after everyone left…"

Cheyenne grabbed her by the shoulders. "You didn't sleep with him!"

Eve suddenly questioned her sanity in finishing what she'd started here. "I did."

Some of Cheyenne's excitement dimmed, and she let go of Eve. "Oh, no."

"What's wrong?" Eve sobered, too. "There isn't a better guy out there."

"I agree. I adore Ted. But…that doesn't mean he's right for you."

Disappointed by Chey's response, Eve sank back

into her seat. "Don't be such a killjoy! Why *wouldn't* he be right for me?"

Chey began to pace again, this time wringing her hands. "I don't know. Don't you think you would've felt something before now?"

"Not necessarily. A lot of people are friends before they fall in love."

"Whoa. You're saying you're in *love?*"

"We're not that far down the road yet, but we're both excited by the possibility of it."

Cheyenne pivoted toward her. "Yet you've slept together. That's a pretty big risk to take."

"Ted and I know what we're getting into." She wasn't willing to let Cheyenne destroy the hope she felt for this new relationship.

"I'd like to believe that," she responded. "Because Kyle and Callie got burned when they—"

"This is different," she broke in. "We're not just... hooking up."

"You're sure."

"Positive. This is Ted we're talking about, not Noah."

"Noah's married. What does he have to do with this? You didn't sleep with him, too...."

"No! Never! He was a playboy, that's all. Ted's never been free and easy. His approach to life is far more serious. He was raised by the principal of our elementary school, for crying out loud!"

She came to a stop. "So you're actually *seeing* each other."

"We are." Eve got out her iPhone to prove it. "Look, I took this picture of him when he came over last night. Cute, huh?"

Cheyenne pushed back her hair as though it was too

hot in the office, but it wasn't. "Ted's handsome. There's no denying that."

"So…why are you acting like this might be a mistake?"

"I'm shocked, I guess."

"Could you at least be 'happy' shocked?"

"I'm trying," she replied. "It just feels…odd."

"Because it'll change the dynamics of the group. But that doesn't have to be for the worse."

Cheyenne sat down again. "When will you tell the others?"

"Ted said we should give ourselves time to make the adjustment first."

"Probably good advice, but—" she pulled her chair closer "—wasn't it kind of…distasteful sleeping with him? I can't imagine having sex with him or Noah or any of the other guys we've hung out with for so long."

"I thought it might be," she admitted. "But it wasn't. Like I said, plenty of relationships are based on friendship."

"Could you see yourself marrying Ted someday?"

"Of course!"

Cheyenne sighed. "Wow."

"You're not even a little excited for me?"

"I am. I'm just worried that it might blow up in your face."

"Why would it?"

She wrinkled her nose. "The timing is off."

"No, it's not. We're getting older. We're both ready to have a family. We care about each other."

"But why is this happening after so many years? Why *now*?"

"I told you." Suddenly, she caught on. "Wait, you're thinking it might have to do with Sophia."

"Don't take this the wrong way, but she started working for Ted the same day he slept with you."

"So? I fully supported him giving her a job. I *still* support it. What else would she do?"

"Her return to his life doesn't concern you?"

"Why would it? We've talked about it. He says he's over her."

"Eve, he's been saying that for *years*."

"And?"

"No one believes him."

She understood what Cheyenne was getting at but didn't want to consider it. "Stop. Don't ruin this." Her phone rang, and she checked Caller ID. "It's him." She raised a finger to her lips before answering. "Don't tell him I told you. And don't tell anyone else about us. Not yet, okay? You promise?"

Cheyenne's smiled looked pained, putting even more of a damper on Eve's excitement. "I won't. I promise."

Trying to throw off the odd feeling she'd gotten since revealing her relationship with Ted, Eve answered the phone. "Hello?"

"Hey, what's up?" he asked.

"Not much." She stepped out of the office so she could talk without Cheyenne listening in. "Are you getting some pages written today?"

"Not too many. I've been busy with…other things."

This surprised her. He'd gone home early last night because he was under so much pressure to get the rest he needed so he could work. "What other things? You're on deadline, remember?"

"I'm afraid this couldn't be helped."

"What's 'this'?"

The resulting pause told her he was searching for the right words. "I had to move Sophia and Alexa into my guesthouse."

Her blood ran cold. She liked Sophia, felt sorry for her, but on the heels of what Cheyenne had just said…. *"What?"*

"Someone's been harassing them, vandalizing the house, even threatening them."

"Who?"

"I wish I knew. Maybe then I could put a stop to it without having to go this route."

"But…you're already helping her. Isn't there someone else who could come to her rescue?"

"Like…"

"If she's being harassed, the police would be a logical choice."

"Chief Stacy is no fan. Not anymore. I told you what he said when he came here on Monday."

But Sophia was still a citizen of Whiskey Creek, and the citizens of Whiskey Creek should be able to count on their chief of police to do his job. "That means she'll be around you almost 24/7."

"Not for long. She's planning to get out of town as soon as she can afford it."

"That could be months."

"I realize this isn't what either of us would wish for." He lowered his voice as if he was afraid someone—Sophia?—might overhear him. "But they couldn't stay where they were. They're not safe there. Not only that, but she can't afford to heat that big house."

Eve remembered her relief and excitement when he'd hired Sophia. She'd been so grateful to him. But now… jealousy bit deep. Was Sophia using her situation to get closer to Ted? Was she playing the martyr, preying on his sympathies?

It was even possible that Sophia's house hadn't been vandalized. Maybe she'd done it herself.

As much as Eve hated suspecting the worst, she couldn't forget who Sophia had been in high school. "Ted, she must be aware that you're…successful." *And still single.* "Maybe she hasn't changed as much as I thought. Maybe she's a…a parasite looking for a new host."

"I doubt it. If so, she's not looking to me. I saw the damage at her place with my own eyes."

How? Why? Had she called him? Asked him to come by?

Eve wasn't sure she wanted to know. "Either way, you won't make the mistake of getting back with her…."

"Of course not," he said. "You and I are together, aren't we?"

She drew a deep breath, but still felt shaky. "That was my understanding."

"It's true. You don't have anything to worry about. I won't let you down."

That was exactly what she wanted to hear, but the way he'd stated it left something to be desired. *She can't hold a candle to you.* Or *why would I want her when I've got you* would've been more flattering. More convincing, too. But their relationship was new. She couldn't expect him to be madly in love with her yet.

"I'll admit this has me concerned," she said.

"Eve, I made my decision about us on Monday."

In the hot tub. When he was drunk. That didn't bolster her confidence, but she knew she could rely on his integrity. And she was the one who'd championed Sophia. It wasn't as if she could get angry about his involvement in Sophia's life when she'd been so supportive of it.

"I know."

"Are you still interested in getting together tonight?"

"I am." *More than ever.* "Your place okay?"

She wished there hadn't been another pause, but there was.

"Sure."

"What time?"

"Seven? I'll have Sophia prepare extra for dinner."

It made her feel slightly better that he expected Sophia to cook for both of them. "I'll bring my swimsuit."

"Sounds good. See you later."

After he hung up, she remained in the hallway, thinking. She'd been as convinced as everyone else that Ted wasn't over Sophia. Was she only buying into it now because she wanted to?

"Everything okay?" Cheyenne stood in the doorway of their office, wearing a concerned expression.

"Of course. That was Ted." Hoping to seem more confident than she felt, she smiled. "He wants me to come over for dinner tonight."

Obviously relieved, Cheyenne returned her smile. "I'm happy for you. I really am."

Eve knew she should probably tell her friend that Sophia was moving into Ted's guesthouse, but that would only feed her skepticism, and Eve didn't need that. Fortunately, Sophia wouldn't be staying at his place for long, she told herself. Ted had said she'd be leaving Whiskey Creek.

Eve had to admit she'd be glad when that happened. She even wished she had some money to give her so she could go right now.

21

With a master bed and bath upstairs, and a bedroom with bath, a small kitchen, a living room, mudroom and laundry area downstairs, Ted's guesthouse was tiny compared to what Sophia was used to. It was no more than eight hundred square feet. But she was thrilled to have furniture—and heat—again.

Exhausted from so many sleepless nights, the stress of starting a new job, the worry over Alexa's situation at school and hauling box after box through Ted's side yard and into his guesthouse, Sophia dropped onto her new bed. He'd helped her by carrying in the heaviest boxes, but then he'd left her to finish on her own so he could work.

Now she was alone, and it felt like heaven to lie down somewhere that didn't remind her of Skip. Somewhere that felt safe. Somewhere no one would expect to find her. She had to walk over to Ted's house and get to work now. It wasn't fair to him that the move had taken up more than half their day. He'd already had to warm up the leftover soup for his lunch. But she needed a few minutes to rest.

She was *so* tired....

Settling beneath the goose-down comforter on the bed, she closed her eyes and breathed deeply. She wished she could hide out here forever. But before she could drift off, she made herself get up. She couldn't show her gratitude to Ted by falling asleep when she was supposed to be cleaning his house.

Dragging her tired body from the bed, she patted her cheeks to try to revive herself and hurried downstairs. She was going to like the cozy guesthouse. Sheltered from the road by Ted's much larger house—not that many people came out this way—it was new and smelled of the pine planks that'd been used for the ceilings. And the scenery! On one side she had a magnificent view of the river, on the other a more than decent view of his yard, pool and Jacuzzi.

Sophia entered his house via a small walkway of stone steps. That wasn't the main back door. The main back door led into the living room off an expansive deck one floor above. But this allowed her quick and easy access to the kitchen.

She could see that Ted had set his soup bowl in the sink, noticed he'd left out a bag of chips and felt her stomach growl. She needed to eat. She wasn't getting enough nourishment these days.

She made herself a sandwich and sat down to flip through the cookbook she'd used before, hoping to find a good recipe for pasta. Ted had said he wanted that for dinner today. She'd made spaghetti and fettuccine for Skip many times, but she felt like a completely different person now than she had a month ago and didn't want to return to the past, even to create a meal she was familiar with.

Noise in the hall caused her to glance up. Ted appeared, carrying his coffee cup. "I need another jolt of caffeine," he explained.

She put her sandwich on her plate and got to her feet. "I'll make it."

He waved her aside. "Eat. That's the first thing I've seen you put in your mouth since you started here. I don't want to interrupt."

"But I feel responsible for the fact that you're so tired, and it makes me feel bad when you've been so… kind to me."

He turned to look at her as if she'd surprised him somehow, and she wished she'd consulted a mirror before hurrying over to the main house. She'd seen the dark circles under her eyes this morning. Hopefully, they were less noticeable in this light.

"What?" she said, tucking her hair behind her ears.

"Nothing. It was my decision to stay last night. Don't worry about it."

"But you wouldn't have done it if you'd thought you could leave."

"I'll survive."

She went back to the table but was suddenly too nervous to eat her sandwich. She didn't want to be a burden on him, didn't want him to regret the kindness that had saddled him with an ex he'd rather not even see.

"How's the book coming?"

"Not so good."

He'd probably be getting more done if he didn't have so many distractions—like taking in a woman and child who might've been homeless without him. "I'll be careful not to interrupt you this afternoon."

He didn't say anything.

"While I have you here, what do you think of this for dinner?" She showed him a picture of bowtie pasta with prosciutto, onions and peas in a Parmesan cream sauce. "Does this look like an entrée you might like?"

His eyebrows slid up. "Definitely."

"I'll make that tonight, then."

Having started the coffeemaker, he turned around to face her. "I was going to talk to you about tonight."

The gravity in his voice put her on high alert. "You'd rather have something else?"

"No, that's fine. Could you make enough for Eve, too?"

She managed to maintain her smile. "Of course. Is this a—a date? Would you like me to do something special?"

"You don't have to go to too much trouble. Just add a bottle of wine, a salad and maybe some dessert."

She'd already been planning to serve a salad and bread with the main meal. "I can do that. I'll set it up in the dining room."

"That'd be great."

She pointed to the coffeemaker. "You don't have to wait. I'll bring you a cup when it's ready, if that'll help."

"I'd appreciate it." He walked away but turned back at the last second. "Why'd you do it?" he asked. "Why'd you sleep with Skip?"

This was the first time he'd ever given her the opportunity to explain. But now that he had, she didn't know where to begin. What did it matter, anyway? What could she hope to achieve? She could tell by his tone that, all these years later, he was still speaking out of condemnation and anger. And after the kindness Eve had shown her, Sophia wouldn't interfere in their relationship even if she had the chance. "I made a mistake."

"One you made worse by marrying him."

It wasn't easy to tolerate the accusation in his eyes, not without launching a few accusations of her own. She wasn't the only one who'd been egocentric at that age. He'd been so preoccupied with all his projects and classes that he hadn't paid much attention to what was happening—or not happening—in *her* world. He'd taken it for granted that when he finished setting the world on fire she'd be waiting for him in Whiskey Creek. "I was pregnant. I didn't have any other choice."

"Your parents would've helped you. They did *everything* for you."

Not after he went to college. And especially not in that last year when he'd been so busy they'd barely talked. Once her mother could no longer hang on to reality, her father hadn't been able to cope with the grief. He'd stepped down from his position as mayor and promptly fallen apart, and without any new money coming in, their savings had dwindled. They managed to get her mother into a facility where the state would pick up the bill, but almost as soon as they did that, her father received news of his own diagnosis. Although they'd been too proud to let anyone know the extent of their problems—it hurt to be humbled in one fell swoop—she couldn't have afforded the chemo or anything else, not without Skip. "I panicked."

"You mean Skip had the money you wanted."

The money she'd desperately *needed*. There was a difference. And Skip was the father of her child. Was Ted saying he would've accepted Alexa? She couldn't imagine that—couldn't imagine him forgiving her for what she'd done. "If that's how you want to look at it," she said.

"There isn't any other way," he retorted.

When the doorbell sounded signifying Eve's arrival, Ted wasn't sure where Sophia was. She didn't answer the door, so he assumed she'd left for the day. She was probably in the guesthouse, unpacking. The last time he'd seen her was when she'd slipped into his office, put a cup of coffee at his elbow, along with some sliced fruit, and slipped out.

It had been a quiet afternoon, which he'd needed to get some pages written. But as he passed the living room on his way to the door, he saw that she'd been busy. Every room in the house was immaculate. He could smell several delectable scents drifting from the kitchen, and she'd set a beautiful table. He paused when he saw it because he didn't recognize the pretty crystal vase that served as a centerpiece or the fresh flowers inside it. Neither had he ever seen the matching candleholders. And he knew for a fact that he didn't own those elegant dinner candles.

She'd gone to extra trouble to make this romantic—but he wasn't sure that made him happy. He had such mixed reactions when it came to her.

The doorbell sounded again.

"Coming," he called.

As soon as he opened the door, Eve gestured toward Sophia's black Mercedes. "Looks like your houseguest will be spending her first night here."

He wondered how things had gone for Alexa at school today. When Sophia picked her up, she must've had her go straight to the guesthouse to do her homework because he hadn't seen or heard her at all. "I can only hope that'll make it harder for the repo company to find her car."

"Right. Or she'll be using *your* car as well as enjoying everything else you have to offer."

He didn't say anything. He hadn't asked for Sophia to land in his lap—at least not in a long time. But there hadn't been any way to avoid helping her, not if he wanted to maintain his humanity. "Believe me, my mother isn't any happier about the situation than you are. She hung up on me the day she learned Sophia was working here, and I haven't spoken to her since."

"Aren't you going to call her?"

"I'm giving her some time to cool off." He held the door. "Come on in."

"Your mother's never liked Sophia," she said as she passed him.

"My mother likes *you*," he told her.

Her lips curved in a grudging smile. "That's an accomplishment. She's not easy to please."

"*That's* an understatement." He chuckled. "Are you hungry? I requested pasta."

"Smells delicious." She drew him to her for a kiss. He purposely deepened it, searching for that same fire in his belly he'd always felt for Sophia, wanted it to consume him to the point that he *had* to carry her up to his bedroom right this second, dinner be damned. But it wasn't there. He felt the same respect and affection he'd always felt—that was all.

Pulling away, he smiled to conceal his disappointment. "Come see what we've got," he said and took her hand as he led her to the kitchen.

On the counter, he found a note from Sophia.

Pasta is in the oven. Don't wait too long to serve it, or it will dry out. Warm the bread for 15 minutes first. Wine is chilling in the fridge with the salad. Homemade vinaigrette is in the small pitcher. The cheesecake can be served with or without berries on top.
S
P.S. Matches on table

For the candles. To add to the romantic atmosphere. He got that.

"She's gone to a lot of trouble to make it nice." Eve sounded slightly petulant, but she was the one who'd asked to come here. They could just as easily have had dinner out or at her place. Ted was fairly certain she'd wanted to scope out the situation, to stake her claim—not that he could blame her.

He was carrying the salad and wine into the dining room when the doorbell rang for the second time in fifteen minutes.

"I'll get it," Eve said and before he could return to the kitchen for the bread, his mother walked into the room.

Sophia had brought some of what she'd cooked home so she could have dinner with Alexa in the guesthouse. They'd eaten together. Now they were lying on her bed, staring at the shadows the lamp cast on the ceiling. They still had unpacking to do, but this quiet moment was the best she'd had all day. Alexa never used to rest her head on Sophia's shoulder when Skip was alive, not since she'd been a very small child.

"That was such a good dinner," Alexa said.

"I liked it, too," Sophia responded.

"I bet Ted thinks you're the best cook in the world. I bet he's glad he hired you."

Had Ted and Eve enjoyed it? They'd been in the back of her mind ever since she'd left the main house. But she refused to succumb to the jealousy that slithered beneath her skin. She'd spent her own money at the grocery store for the flowers and candles because she'd wanted, in her own small way, to thank them for all they'd done. She wanted Ted to be happy and knew a woman like Eve could do that for him.

So she had nothing to feel sad about, she told herself. She wanted Eve to be happy, too. Maybe *she* couldn't have the relationship she wanted—with either one of them—but she wished them well in spite of that and owed them both for their kindness.

"How come you've never made those noodles before?" Alexa asked, breaking the silence again.

"You mean the pasta? I didn't have that recipe."

"Don't lose it."

"I won't." She combed her fingers through her daughter's hair. "Do you think you'll like living here?"

"It'll be different, but…it's okay. What about you?"

"It has a lot going for it. It's nice and cozy and clean."

Alexa raised her head. "You're getting better at looking on the bright side."

Sophia laughed. She was afraid to look anywhere else. "You didn't say much about your day at school."

"I told you it was okay."

"I know. But…what does 'okay' mean?"

Her daughter shifted onto her stomach and propped herself up on her elbows. "That nothing's changed."

"What about detention?"

"Boring!"

"At least you got your homework done while you were there." As wrung out as Sophia was, she was grateful for that. "Connie didn't give you any trouble?"

Lex plucked at the comforter. "She kept glaring at me. And once, when she passed by to get a book from the back of the room, she whispered that she'd kick my *you know what* if she ever got me alone."

Sophia adjusted the pillow to make it higher. "What did you do?"

"I ignored her."

"Good for you!" She reached out to stroke her daughter's cheek. "What about Babette and the others?"

"I do my best to ignore them, too." Alexa suddenly gave her a shy smile. "There was *one* good thing that happened today."

"You got a C on your math quiz. I consider that good, since it's an improvement. Next time you'll get a B, right?"

"Right. But this is even better."

"Really? Then I can hardly wait to hear about it."

An endearing expression appeared on her pixie face. "Royce Beck walked me to my fifth-period class."

"Royce… I've heard that name before."

"Because he came to my birthday party last year."

"I hope his dad wasn't an SLD investor."

Alexa winced but laughed. "So do I! I don't think he was. At least, Royce didn't act mad, like everyone else."

"Sounds as if this boy is somehow special to you."

There was a slight pause as well as another blush.

Despite enjoying this time with Alexa, and the relief of seeing her daughter slowly returning to her former spirits, Sophia was *so* tired. Sleep seemed to be washing up around her ankles like a warm surf, pulling at her. But she didn't want to fade out on Alexa, so she fought the heaviness of her eyelids. "Well, if he has *any* taste, he'll like you back."

"Maybe not." Her smile grew pensive. "He might choose Babette now that…now that everyone thinks *she's* so hot."

That gave Sophia a shot of energy. "Don't tell me she likes him, too!"

"She *always* likes the same boys I do," Alexa said with a grimace.

That meant her daughter was still setting the standards. "Did she see him walk you to class?"

"Yes. She walked past us on the way."

"I doubt that'll help your friendship."

Alexa rolled her eyes. "What friendship?"

Feeling her exhaustion return, Sophia covered a yawn. "Where do you think we should move?"

"What about Los Angeles?"

"You want to live in a bustling city?"

She pursed her lips, considering. "It would be close to Disneyland."

Sophia smiled. They could use a trip to "the happiest place on earth." She took Lex's hand for a moment. "That's a plus, but L.A. is such a big place. Feels to me as if we might get lost."

"But doesn't getting lost sound kind of nice? At least no one would know Dad or what he did."

"True. That's a definite benefit. And there'd have to be more job opportunities…."

"Do you like the job you have now?"

Surprisingly, Sophia did. Although she missed the massages and spa treatments of her former life, the sense of accomplishment she got when she looked around Ted's house more than made up for the lack of pampering. She just didn't like feeling so indebted to Ted, hated that they couldn't be on an equal footing. And it had cost her Eve. Tonight was proof. She'd thought maybe Eve would come to the guesthouse and tell her she'd enjoyed dinner, at least acknowledge her proximity. She would've liked to know that Eve didn't resent her presence on Ted's property. But Sophia talked with Alexa for another hour before they went to bed, and there was no knock or call.

It's okay, she told herself. *She can't be glad I'm here. What woman would be?*

Why'd you sleep with Skip? The disgust in Ted's words chafed even in retrospect. *He* couldn't be glad she was here, either.

The wine cellar and the bottles of liquor he stored there came to mind. Alexa was in her own bed; they were in a safe place. Surely, she could have a drink *now.* She'd been so immersed in her troubles that she'd scarcely thought about booze for days. But the memory of the smooth burn of whiskey as it went down and the rush of euphoria that came after suddenly grabbed hold of her and nearly dragged her to the door.

One drink. She was alone, didn't need to drive, didn't need to answer to Skip, didn't need to do anything for her daughter.

It couldn't hurt to have a drink occasionally. Lots of people did that and it caused them no problems.

She got up and started down the stairs. She could cross the backyard, slip into the kitchen and sneak out a bottle in a matter of minutes. Ted and Eve would never be the wiser. She'd pay for it out of her first paycheck. She wasn't a thief like her husband had been.

But the memory of Skip's words brought her to a halt before she could even get out of the guesthouse. *You're nothing but a lazy drunk.*

"No, Skip, I'm a lot more than that," she whispered.

Talk was cheap, however. She had to prove it.

Even though her mouth was dry and her head ached—for some odd reason she felt as though she was going through withdrawal all over again—she went back to bed and forced herself to lie there.

She'd been so exhausted just minutes before. But the alcohol in Ted's cellar seemed to be calling out to her: *I'm right here. Come and get me!*

Why wouldn't the temptation release her so she could sleep?

You can do it. Stay put. You're building a new life, brick by brick. Having a drink will only set you back.

She needed to join AA, she decided. Skip wouldn't have allowed it if he were alive. He would've been too afraid someone would find out—or recognize her at the meeting. She certainly didn't need to give the people of Whiskey Creek any more reason to malign her. But wasn't what she turned out to be more important than what she used to be?

22

Sophia must've slept because the next time she was conscious of being awake it was three hours later—nearly midnight. She had to go to the bathroom so she peered out her window as she passed by and noticed that the lights were off at the main house. Eve had either gone home. Or she was staying over.

The thought of her staying over made Sophia crave a drink again. Somehow, for the past week or so, she'd been able to push her addiction into the background. But now that her other problems had receded just a little, her love affair with alcohol was shoving its way to the forefront.

Couldn't she have a single night of peace?

When she returned to bed, she tried to fall back asleep, but she kept imagining Ted with Eve.

"Whatever fulfills him," she murmured. He was with the right person; Eve had so much more to offer him. She wasn't down-and-out. She didn't have a drinking problem. And she'd never hurt him in the past, so they had nothing to overcome. Sophia didn't want to be like a drowning person flailing around, dragging under everyone who was trying to help.

That image brought home the reality of her situation. But it didn't bring the oblivion she desperately needed. She kept tossing and turning, wrestling with her envy.

At last, she got up, put on her swimsuit, grabbed a towel and went out to the Jacuzzi. She thought the hot water might help her relax.

It was doing just that—until she heard a door open and close and two sets of footsteps cross the deck. She tensed. With the lights off, she'd assumed Ted and Eve were in for the night!

What was she going to do? She didn't want them to catch her in the hot tub. She doubted Ted would care if she used it, but it would be horribly awkward to interrupt his private time with Eve.

Because he and Eve were talking, she hoped they couldn't hear the splash of the water as she scrambled out. Fortunately, she hadn't turned on the jets for fear they'd make too much noise. But there was no way she could get the cover on or creep back to the guesthouse without being seen, not beneath a full moon.

So she picked up her towel and darted under the deck instead, thinking she'd slip around the perimeter of the yard when she had the chance. She didn't dare move quite yet, afraid she'd draw their attention.

"I *still* can't believe your mother invited me to lunch." Eve sounded pleased, and Sophia could understand why. She'd probably pass out from shock if Mrs. Dixon ever extended such a friendly invitation to her.

"Why?" Ted asked. "My mother's always liked you."

"You've told me that before. But it can be hard to tell."

A bitter smile tugged at Sophia's lips when she heard

the wry note in Eve's voice. She could've told Eve what it was like when Mrs. Dixon *didn't* like you.

"She's...selective about the people she accepts into her life," Ted said. "But she has a positive impression of you from elementary school. So you had that going for you from the start."

"She sure knew how to police the yard at lunch. I was terrified of her—like most other kids," Eve said. But Sophia hadn't been afraid of Mrs. Dixon back then. She hadn't been afraid of anyone. She'd been sitting on top of the world.

Too bad she'd had to learn just how fast one could fall from such a lofty perch.

"My mom comes off as stern, but—" Ted stopped talking when they reached the hot tub—obviously he was reacting to finding the cover off. He glanced around as if he expected to see her or someone else, but she shrank farther into the shadows and behind one of the support beams, and his gaze passed over her without stopping. Since the guesthouse was dark, he probably thought she'd used the Jacuzzi earlier and forgotten to be polite about it.

She didn't like the idea of him thinking she was careless enough with his belongings to do that—letting the heat escape when it was so expensive to keep the water hot. But he didn't make a big deal about the cover to Eve. He didn't even mention it, and she didn't seem to notice. They just got in.

"She certainly wasn't too pleased to hear about Sophia living here." Eve's voice was barely audible above the gurgle of the jets. She was no doubt being careful so that her voice wouldn't travel to the guesthouse. Ted was careful, too, when he responded. But that didn't make as much of a difference as they thought—not when she was standing a mere ten feet away.

"She's never been one of Sophia's admirers," he admitted.

That came as no shock yet Sophia hated hearing it. She was too vulnerable to withstand much these days. And she felt even worse when Eve climbed into Ted's lap and slipped her arms around his shoulders. "It's nice out here."

"We're having a mild fall."

"That means winter will probably hit hard."

"It's supposed to rain this weekend."

When they kissed, Sophia attempted to look away. She didn't want to see it—but her gaze moved back as if drawn there by a high-powered magnet.

Fortunately, Ted broke off the kiss before it led to anything else and started talking about the book he was writing. Then Eve brought up Adelaide's baby, whom they'd just learned was a girl. After that they talked about the fact that both Kyle and Noah had invested with Skip, which Sophia hadn't known and was sad to hear.

Hoping they might finally be preoccupied enough not to notice, she began to creep over to the fence so she could swing wide and follow it to the guesthouse. Despite the towel she'd wrapped around her, the heat she'd absorbed from sitting in the hot tub had slowly dissipated, leaving her chilled to the bone. But with the reference to Skip, the conversation had already worked its way back to her, and that made her pause despite her discomfort.

"Did you tell Sophia she can't smoke in the guesthouse?" Eve asked.

"No, it never came up."

"You should've warned her, since you feel so strongly about it."

"I don't think she's smoking at all. At least, I haven't seen her. Haven't smelled it on her, either."

"That's good. It's *so* unhealthy."

He stretched out his arms along the sides of the Jacuzzi and leaned his head against the rim. "On the phone last Friday you said something that made me curious."

"What was it?" she asked.

"You said Sophia told you she was taking up smoking because she couldn't drink."

Sophia clapped her hand over her mouth so they wouldn't hear her gasp. Eve was aware of her drinking problem; they'd discussed it at length the night Eve brought Alexa home and made dinner. Sophia had been so despondent she hadn't held anything back. She'd needed friendship too badly to pretend she was anything other than what she was, knew it was either grab on and trust, or sink into the quicksand of her depression.

But she didn't feel quite the same need to be transparent now, didn't want Eve to tell Ted about her addiction. Her situation was pitiful enough. She preferred to leave town without him ever having to learn.

"That's what she said," Eve told him.

"So…what stopped her from drinking?"

Eve had no reason to keep Sophia's secrets, not from Ted. Sophia was mildly surprised she hadn't already told him—and was downright stunned when Eve covered for her instead of blurting out the truth.

"She was in a vulnerable place," she said. "She probably didn't want it to mess with her mind."

Relieved—and grateful—Sophia let her breath seep out.

"You're okay that she's living here, aren't you?" Ted asked.

At least, that was what Sophia thought he said. He was almost whispering now.

"I'm trying to be," she replied. "It'd be easier if she wasn't so damn beautiful," she added with an uncomfortable laugh.

Ted kissed her again. "You're beautiful, too," he said, and Sophia had to agree. Eve was even more beautiful on the inside.

Not long after that, Eve said she had to go; she had a big group coming to the B and B in the morning— several ladies from the Red Hat Society who were on an antiquing odyssey. Ted got out with her. Once he'd turned off the jets and they'd gone inside, Sophia had the perfect opportunity to return to the guesthouse. But she'd become so cold she couldn't stop shivering.

She waited to see if Ted would come back and put on the cover. But when the minutes lengthened and he didn't reappear, she assumed he'd forgotten, and decided to warm up before returning to bed.

After tossing her towel on a nearby chaise, she sank into the hot water all the way up to her neck. Blessed warmth! But before she could get comfortable, she heard the door open again. And this time she didn't make it out of the Jacuzzi before Ted saw her.

23

"I thought you were asleep," he said.

Sophia froze on the steps, where she'd started to climb out. "No."

"How long have you been out here?"

"For a while," she admitted. "I'm sorry. I should've said something, but I didn't want to upset Eve, didn't want to ruin your night."

He glanced around, as he had before. "Where were you?"

She gestured at the dark area under the deck. "I tried to make it back to the guesthouse unseen, but...there didn't seem to be a good opportunity. I'm sorry," she said again.

He seemed taken aback, as if he was embarrassed by what he and Eve had said—or should've been more careful when he saw the cover missing—but ultimately shrugged as if there was nothing he could do about it now.

"No worries." He waved her back into the water, turned on the jets and climbed in himself. "It's just... late. And the past few nights have been rough. Why aren't you sleeping?"

She slid around to the other side, putting as much distance between them as possible. "I napped for a little while. And then—" she shrugged "—I woke up and couldn't seem to relax. I thought this might help."

"Probably feels funny, being in a strange place, but you'll get used to it." He studied her through the steam. "How did Alexa do at school today?"

He acted like he really cared. "It seemed to go pretty well."

"No trouble with Connie?"

"Nothing more than a verbal threat."

"That girl had better not act on it." Leaning back, he gazed at the stars overhead. "How does Lex feel about moving here?"

"Seems okay with it. She knows we're lucky to have a comfortable place to live. She's grateful to you."

"She's a good kid."

Sophia smiled. In a way, it felt like she and her daughter were getting to know each other, *really* know each other, for the first time—and Sophia liked what she saw. "She is."

He shook his hair off his face. "I looked but I didn't see a receipt for the extra groceries and other stuff you bought today—the flowers and candles."

"That was my treat. I don't expect you to repay me."

"You wanted Eve and me to have flowers and candles?"

"I know it's not much. I just hoped to make your dinner extra nice. You've both been so generous to me."

He didn't say anything but his eyes never left her face.

"What?" she said, growing uncomfortable. Being out here alone with Ted like this, in the dark, made her have thoughts she *shouldn't* be having—especially after

Eve's kindness in not telling Ted about her alcoholism. She wouldn't do anything that might undermine Eve's happiness, wouldn't reveal the longing she felt now, and had felt for years.

"It was nice," he said. "Eve liked it."

She cleared her throat. "I'm glad." She wondered if *he'd* liked it, too. He didn't say, but she got the impression that he had.

When she found herself glancing at his bare shoulders, wishing things could be different, she stood up. "I'll let you have some time to yourself."

"Sophia?"

She looked at him as she passed.

"You seem to have changed a great deal."

"Well, it would have to be for the better, right? There was only one way to go." She laughed as if she wasn't quite serious, but she knew that he—and half of Whiskey Creek—would probably agree with that statement.

She stepped out and got her towel, but even then he didn't let her leave. "How's your mother?"

It'd been ages since anyone had asked about Elaine. Her mother had been gone from Whiskey Creek for so many years that the hole her absence had initially created in the community had filled in long ago. At least that seemed to be true for everyone else. Sophia found it ironic, considering that the town had once revolved around her parents.

"She was okay the last time I checked," she said. "I don't speak to her very often."

"Because..."

She wanted to blame Skip. He'd been so nasty whenever she planned to visit the hospital. "I don't see the point!" he'd growl, and he'd usually refuse to go with her. But she knew the real reason she avoided contact ran much deeper.

"She doesn't know me anymore," she said. She wasn't sure why she'd told him about her mother. That wasn't something she normally talked about. It had just…popped out, as if she couldn't keep something so painful inside anymore. But she regretted it the second the words left her lips and she saw the sympathy on his face. She didn't want him to think she was trying to make excuses for herself or manipulate his emotions. So she hurried to get behind closed doors where she couldn't say anything else. And where she'd no longer be tempted to tell him how much she'd always loved him.

Cheyenne and Dylan were at coffee the next morning. So were Riley, Callie, Levi, Kyle and Eve. Once again, Ted had thought about skipping the weekly ritual. He was falling so far behind on his book. He figured that provided the perfect excuse to avoid the ribbing he was going to get for helping Sophia after being so opinionated about her. But then Eve called to see if he'd pick her up, and he knew that with Sophia living in his guesthouse, he needed to do all he could to be available to Eve and help his girlfriend feel secure.

When they walked into Black Gold together, they weren't holding hands or doing anything else to announce that they were a couple—and yet Cheyenne's smile stretched so wide Ted could tell she knew. That meant Dylan did, too—and the others would inevitably find out. He wasn't ready for the added pressure. He and Eve would be the first official couple inside the group after all the years they'd been friends and that would generate more attention than he felt comfortable with. Especially now, when he had so much going on inside his head. But he couldn't expect to keep the relationship a secret for very long. They were both too close to their friends.

At least it would put any suspicions that he had plans to get back with Sophia to rest.

Noah was the first to start in. "Hey, Ted. I hear that Sophia got a job."

Everyone sitting at the table laughed and glanced at each other.

"I heard that, too." Kyle joined the fun. "Apparently she wasn't quite so mean in high school that you couldn't forgive her. So...tell me, what was all *that* talk about?"

"Shut up," Ted grumbled. "It's not as if any of you were stepping up to help."

"You were the one with the job," Noah said. "We're heading into the winter, which is my slowest time. I would've had to let someone go in order to hire her, and that didn't seem fair."

Ted spread his hands. "I felt sorry for her, okay? No big deal."

"What was it he said last week?" Riley asked. "'Actions have consequences'?"

Thank God no one seemed to know he'd let her move in with him, too....

Eve slipped her arm through his. "Come on, guys. Go easy. No matter what he says, Ted has a heart the size of Texas. That shouldn't come as any surprise."

Ted didn't want Eve sticking up for him. It made the change in their relationship too obvious—obvious enough that Kyle suddenly took note of the possessive way she was touching him. "What do *you* know about his heart?" he asked.

Eve let go of him and tried to shrug it off. "We've been friends for years."

"Are you *still* friends?" Riley asked, searching their faces.

Ted couldn't *deny* the truth. That would imply that he was embarrassed about their involvement. So when Eve seemed uncertain about how to respond, he came out with it. "We're seeing each other."

Adelaide's mouth dropped open. "Seeing each other as in...*dating?*"

"Isn't that what seeing each other is?" he asked.

"I wasn't sure, since you've been friends for so long and see each other all the time." Addy hadn't been part of the original group, hadn't even been around after high school. Noah had included her when she returned a year ago.

"Since when?" Callie asked.

"Halloween," Cheyenne chipped in with a knowing laugh.

"Whoa, apparently *some* people had more fun in the hot tub than others," Riley teased.

Eve blushed. "Do you have to make it so embarrassing? It's enough of a transition already."

Noah rubbed his chin. "You hired Sophia but you're dating Eve. Interesting reversal."

Ted sent him a look that told him to stuff it. "We'll skip the editorials, if you don't mind." Eager to get away from the group until the shock wore off, he turned to Eve. "Can I get you something? You want a yogurt?"

"Oh, my gosh!" Cheyenne cried. "How weird that Ted's going to be buying Eve's yogurt from now on!"

Kyle was the only one who didn't seem to think this development was funny. He hadn't said a word since the "big reveal"—and he got up and followed Ted to the line of people waiting to order at the register. "Hey, man, are you sure you know what you're doing?" He kept a smile on his face, for the sake of the others, but his eyes were serious.

Ted couldn't admit the truth, couldn't show any uncertainty. That wouldn't be fair to Eve. "Of course."

Putting his back to the group's table, Kyle tried again. "You remember how it went when Callie and I—"

"I remember," he broke in to save him from having to spell it out.

"You have to think long and hard before getting that intimate with one of these girls."

"I *have* thought about it."

Kyle gave him a skeptical look as they moved forward in line.

"What?" Ted snapped, irritated by the fact that Kyle was forcing him to examine his motives and decisions.

"It's just…so fast. One day you're friends, like always. And now you're lovers?"

"These things happen. You should know."

"Exactly. So…where's the heat between you two?"

"Maybe it's not that kind of relationship."

When the person ahead of them in line seemed to be listening, Kyle lowered his voice. "But it's supposed to be now, isn't it?"

"Eve and I don't base everything on sexual attraction. Not *everything*," he repeated when he realized that made it sound as if he didn't want to make love to her. "Listen…"

The guy ahead of them ordered, giving them more

space but less time than they probably needed to finish this conversation.

"I lost the one girl I was dying to have," Kyle went on.

Ted was surprised to hear him confess that, for him, there'd been no one who could compare to Olivia.

"It hasn't been the same with anyone since," he continued. "My marriage failed for a lot of reasons, but first and foremost it was because I didn't love Noelle to begin with. We should never have gotten together. The year I spent with her, and the year I spent recovering from the divorce, which is when I slept with Callie, were the two worst years of my life. Some days it's still hard dealing with the aftermath. Besides all the emotional bullshit, I have to pay Noelle a hefty amount of spousal maintenance each month. That means there's no way to cut her out of my life entirely."

Not only that, but he had to watch his stepbrother with the woman he really wanted—although Brandon and Olivia hadn't shown up today.

"Anyway," Kyle went on, "I don't want you or Eve to go through anything like I did."

The earnest emotion in his plea scared Ted. He'd been so decisive, so sure he could remain committed to Eve. But when he made love with her—like last night before they got into the Jacuzzi—it just wasn't as satisfying as he wanted it to be. He'd actually felt a little… hollow afterward.

Was he letting her down by trying to force this? Were they better off taking a step back and admitting that they felt pretty much the same way they'd always felt toward each other? Or were *his* emotions the only ones that weren't changing?

She seemed so happy. He didn't want to wreck that, didn't want to hurt her. He'd already promised himself he wouldn't. Besides, he wasn't sure he'd given it long enough to make a final decision. They used to tease Noah for his inability to commit. Ted had never messed around as much as Noah had, but he suspected *he* was the one with a commitment problem—and that came as a shock.

"Why did you decide to make a move on Eve?" Kyle asked.

It had seemed safe. Smart. But was that only because she wasn't Sophia? He had to admit he hadn't been thinking clearly on Halloween night, even though he'd assured himself that he was. Alcohol had a way of doing that to a person.

"Can I help you?"

The barista was ready to take their order, so Ted couldn't answer Kyle's question. There was no time. And he was grateful for that. He couldn't imagine what might come out of his mouth now that he felt so torn. He didn't want to say he'd been drinking. That would only convince Kyle that he had indeed made a huge mistake.

But something in his eyes must have revealed his uncertainty because Kyle took one look at him, shook his head and cursed.

Eve was busy that night. And she was going to be gone for the next week. It was her grandmother's eightieth birthday, so she was flying to Montana with her parents for a family reunion and party. That gave Ted some breathing room. He was relieved to have it, needed the time to write. But it wasn't as if he could slip into isolation like he used to. Although Sophia was supposed to be off on the weekends—that was what he'd originally intended when he'd advertised for a housekeeper—she was so grateful for the free rent and so determined to do all she could to repay him that she insisted on cooking for him regardless of the day. And it was tough to complain about that when she made such delicious meals, which were always right when he wanted them.

There were other benefits to having her around, as well. He wasn't sure he'd ever seen the house quite so clean. And if he listened carefully, he could hear laughter, which somehow made him smile. It was Alexa, who spent her time with her mother whenever she was out of school. He liked Sophia's daughter, he realized, despite her paternity.

It was Saturday night and the two of them were in the kitchen. Sophia was instructing her daughter on how to tell if a turkey potpie was done when he walked into the room.

"Can I get you something?" Sophia asked.

Alexa shot him a smile, and he returned it. "I'm beat," he said. "It's time for a glass of wine."

The smile disappeared from Alexa's face as her gaze shifted to her mother.

"Did I say something wrong?" he asked.

Sophia answered. "No, of course not. What kind would you like?"

"A nice Chablis." He sat at the table to talk to Alexa while Sophia went into the cellar, but Alexa seemed distracted. She kept turning around, looking for her mother.

He waved to attract her attention. "Everything okay?"

"Fine," she said. "Where's your corkscrew? I'll get it out so you can open the bottle."

He was fairly confident that Sophia could handle that, but he directed her to the right drawer and she got it for him. Then, as soon as Sophia emerged, Alexa took charge of the bottle and brought it over. "Here you go."

"Thanks." He popped the cork while Sophia brought him a glass. "Would you like some?" he asked her, raising the bottle.

It seemed as if she didn't even want to look at it. "No, thanks," she said and busied herself with finishing up their meal.

"How are things going with Connie, Babette and the others?" he asked Alexa as he sipped his wine.

"Okay. I don't talk to them anymore."

"They're not giving you any trouble?"

"Sometimes they make fun of me when they see me, but…it's okay."

When Sophia removed the potpie from the oven, Ted could tell it had been made from scratch. It looked as good as the ones from Just Like Mom's. "That smells *fantastic,*" he said.

Sophia glanced up at the appreciation in his voice. "I hope it tastes as good as it smells."

She hadn't gone wrong yet.

She put it on top of the stove. "I set a place for you in the dining room, but—" she gestured at the table where he was sitting "—if you'd rather eat in here, I can move your plate."

He remembered stipulating that they eat separately. Although that seemed silly now—to be on the same property and eating the same meal but purposely splitting up—he didn't ask them to join him. He needed to keep some separation between them, didn't want their relationship to drift in the wrong direction just because they were starting to feel comfortable with each other.

"The dining room is fine," he said, so she served him there. She even put out one of the candles she'd bought for his romantic dinner with Eve. The dancing flame added a nice touch in the gathering twilight. But as he sat in the silence of his big house, eating alone, he could see her crossing the backyard with her daughter. Both of them had their hands stuffed into pot holders and were carrying dishes as they walked and talked, and somehow the camaraderie he sensed between them made him feel left out.

Maybe that was why he decided to go over a little later to see if they wanted to come and watch a movie. Or maybe it was because Sophia wouldn't let him order cable for the guesthouse. She said she needed to save her money for other things, which was true. But with such limited funds, and no TV, he couldn't imagine what they'd do on a Saturday night. They wouldn't continue to unpack; they'd been doing that for days—and Alexa deserved to have *some* fun. Everything she used to have, including her friends, was gone.

So he convinced himself that by picking up ice cream and other treats and heading over to Redbox to rent a movie, he was just trying to do a nice deed for a kid who'd had a rough go of it lately.

But he knew in his heart that she wasn't the only one he was hoping to please.

24

Ted had never expected Sophia to turn him down. He figured a woman in her situation would be desperate enough to accept almost any invitation—just to get out of the house, if for no other reason. What fun had she had since her husband jumped off that damn yacht?

He couldn't believe she'd had *any*. But if not for Alexa, begging her to agree, Sophia would've sent him away. As it was, she came but kept to herself.

"Thanks for inviting us over." Alexa was almost enthusiastic enough to compensate for her mother. Almost, but not quite. Although she seemed to have none of the qualms Sophia did about sitting next to him, Sophia tried to coax her off the couch. Did she think Alexa might be crowding him? Or getting on his nerves? Or… worse?

He couldn't figure it out, so when Alexa asked him to pause the movie so she could go to the bathroom, he waited until she was out of the room and asked Sophia. "Why do you keep telling her she can't sit on the couch? Is it because I'm on the couch, too?"

"There are other chairs."

"But a couch is meant for more than one person, so what's the big deal? It's not… I would never do anything to hurt her. You know that, right? You don't think I'd ever act *inappropriately* with your daughter.…"

"God, no!" she said, dismissing his concern. "It's just…her father really let her down."

Ted didn't immediately see the connection. "What's that got to do with me?"

"Quite a bit. She likes you—a lot. I don't want her to latch on to another man who—whom she'll lose contact with when we move."

"You're trying to make sure she and I don't become friends even though you'll be living here for months?"

"We might not be here that long."

"It'll take time to save up the money you need to relocate."

"I just feel bad. I know Eve doesn't want us here, and that could change our situation. Why set my daughter up to be disappointed?"

Sophia had a point. Eve was a wonderful person, but she felt threatened, and he couldn't expect her to put up with that for long. Still, there was a part of him that believed he should have the right to befriend anyone he wanted to, especially a child who was lonely and needed him.

Unsure of how it would sound if he said that, he hesitated. Then Alexa came back, so he let it go and started the movie.

"Where's your girlfriend tonight?" Alexa asked during a slow part of the show.

Blinking, he drew himself out of his thoughts. "Eve?"

"Do you have more than one girlfriend?" she teased.

He pretended he'd needed clarification because he'd

been engrossed in the movie, but even after sleeping with Eve, it was difficult to think of her as his girlfriend. "She's out of town."

"I bet you miss her."

When he made a noise he hoped would pass for agreement, Alexa spoke in a conspiratorial manner. "Too bad you don't still like my mom."

"Lex!" Sophia nearly gasped her daughter's name. "Eve wouldn't be happy to hear you say that, would she?"

Chastened, she shook her head.

"That's in the past," Sophia said firmly.

But she'd finally told her daughter. Ted wondered why.

Lex turned back to him. "So…are you going to marry her?"

Sophia jumped in again. "Come on, honey, don't ask such personal questions. That's none of our business."

Feeling pensive for no particular reason, Ted shrugged it off. "No worries. I'd answer, but…our relationship is relatively new. No one can say what will happen." Especially since even *thinking* about marrying Eve felt odd. Shouldn't he be missing her? Shouldn't he be craving the touch and feel of her?

Maybe that wasn't happening because he'd just seen her this morning. There hadn't been enough time to miss her.…

Or maybe he was expecting too much from love. Chances were good that you didn't experience the same heady rush at thirty-four as you did at seventeen. Emotions often grew more subdued as a person aged.

But, God, he wasn't old yet. He kept coming to

the same conclusion: something was missing. He just hoped, with enough effort, that would change.

"Sorry," Lex said. "Didn't mean to be rude."

He smiled. "It's not a problem." It would've been even less of a problem if those questions had come from anyone other than Sophia's daughter. And if this evening in front of the TV was turning out to be as placid and relaxing as he'd intended. But he and Sophia were never meant to be friends. He was coming to the conclusion that, with her, it had to be all or nothing. There was so much tension between them he could hardly keep his knee from jiggling with nervous energy.

Fortunately, that tension eased as the minutes ticked away. At least for Sophia. She fell asleep about halfway through.

Alexa started to wake her, to tell her she was missing the movie, but Ted shook his head. "Let her sleep. She can watch it tomorrow if she's really interested," he said, but by the end of the movie they were all asleep. When Ted woke up, the TV was looping the intro music, and he had no idea how long it had been playing.

He got up and turned off the TV. Then he considered what he should do with his guests. He could throw a blanket over them, but he was sure they'd sleep much better in their own beds. So he opened the back door of his house and the front door of the guesthouse before carrying Alexa over. She didn't wake up, even as he placed her carefully on the downstairs bed. Then he came back for Sophia.

"I zonked out? I'm sorry," Sophia muttered, but she was so groggy that she didn't fight him when he lifted her into his arms.

"It's okay. I've got you." She didn't weigh much more

than her daughter, so it wasn't hard to carry her. But he hadn't bargained on the ten steps leading to the second story of the guesthouse, which he'd have to climb to get her to her room.

He was exhausted by the time they were halfway up, and that was when she began to rouse in earnest.

"What's going on?" she asked. "Where are we? Wait, I can walk. I'm sorry, I didn't—"

"Relax." He tightened his grip so her wriggling wouldn't send them both crashing down the stairs. "We're almost there."

"Put me down! I'm too heavy."

"And you're getting heavier by the minute," he joked. "But now that I've started this, you have to let me finish or it'll wound my male pride."

Surprisingly, she stopped fighting and laughed like she used to laugh when they were younger. She also made his job easier by slipping her arms around his neck, which helped him keep his balance.

"I may not be the athlete Noah is, but I can carry a girl to bed," he muttered. He didn't realize how bad that sounded until it was out of his mouth, but she pretended not to notice the double entendre. At least she didn't comment on it.

"This is so gallant of you," she teased. "Not many employers would be so kind."

"It'll be gallant if I get you there in one piece. I doubt it'll be seen that way if we both break our necks."

"I have absolute faith in you."

She sounded genuine when she said that, which he found oddly gratifying. But he was staggering so badly by the time they reached the top that they were both laughing.

"It's harder to carry someone up a flight of stairs than I thought it would be."

"And that's a long flight of stairs—not to mention that you had to cross the lawn first."

"I'll have to get more serious about my weight-lifting." He nudged her bedroom door open with his shoulder. "But we made it. Here you are, my lady."

He put her down on the bed, but before he could withdraw, her arms tightened around his neck.

For a moment, it felt like the warmest embrace—as if they'd never meant to be parted for all these years.

He almost allowed it, almost responded to the passion he sensed in her—which scared him. No way did he want to be the kind of man who would cheat. He knew how low he'd feel afterward.

His muscles tensed, but before he could break her hold, her mouth found his ear and she whispered, "I'm sorry, Ted. I'm *so* sorry."

The entreaty in her voice left no doubt that she wasn't making a move on him as he'd first thought. She was apologizing for the past. The fact that she immediately released him confirmed it. She didn't even look at him again. She rolled over and buried herself in the blankets as if she couldn't *bear* to look.

Ted wasn't sure how to react. The way she'd clung to him had nearly taken his legs out from under him— had flooded his system with so much testosterone he couldn't think straight.

He forgave her, didn't he? Of course he did. Or he wouldn't be helping her. But it wasn't what he wanted to *say* that held him fast; it was what he wanted to *do*. The desire to feel her under him once again—to claim

her mouth and her body as he had many times before—
was so powerful he felt himself go hard in an instant.

But what about Eve?

"Damn it!" He tore down the stairs before temptation
could get him in such a chokehold he no longer cared
about his integrity.

Ted seemed eager to avoid her after that. Although it
made Sophia sad to find the friendship that had started
between them suddenly gone, she was also relieved. It
wasn't easy to maintain a friendship when she wanted
more. Maybe she could've done it with someone else,
but not Ted, and their new boundaries helped keep her
hopes and thoughts in check. She hadn't been trying
to steal him from Eve when she'd clung to him long
enough to apologize. She'd just wanted him to *finally*
understand that she was sincerely sorry. Now that she'd
said her piece, he could go on with his life, and she
could, too—hopefully without the regret that had eaten
at her for so long.

"Do you think Ted's mad at us?" Alexa asked Sophia
one morning while they were having breakfast. Fortunately, she was doing better in school. Connie seemed
to have lost interest in fighting with her, Royce was
walking her to class almost every day, and the other
kids didn't want to take her on when she had Royce's
support. But this proved she was disappointed that Ted
no longer paid her much attention.

Sophia added some brown sugar to her oatmeal. "No.
He's busy trying to get his book done."

"He's *always* busy. I wish he had more time."

"I do, too," Sophia said, but she was just playing
along. Deep down she believed they couldn't be hurt if

they were careful not to get too close to him. They had to remember that they were merely putting in time in Whiskey Creek. They wouldn't be staying much longer, especially now that she was beginning to work through the worst of her financial problems. Thanks to Skip's many debts, she would have to file for bankruptcy as soon as she could afford it, but she was doing a "deed in lieu of foreclosure" on the house so it would be out of her hands soon. The Ferraris were already gone. She and Alexa had driven by one day after school to check on the house and found that someone had broken the side door on the garage and taken both cars. Sophia hoped it was the repo company and not someone else, but that was out of her hands, too.

She still had her Mercedes—but she was pretty sure that was only because the repossession people couldn't find it. The lienholder had been calling her more and more frequently, so she knew they were stepping up their search. No doubt someone in town would eventually point the repo man in the right direction, and then she'd no longer have transportation.

Knowing she was living on borrowed time, she held her breath every day she came out of the house to take Alexa to school, fearing *this* would be the morning her vehicle would be gone, but so far, so good.

Besides that one nagging worry, she was beginning to feel as if she was pulling her life together—and it was Ted who'd made that possible. What he'd done for her, and was still doing, made her love him even more. But she knew that if she was really thinking of him and not herself, she'd stay out of his personal life as much as possible.

So she cooked and cleaned and ran Ted's errands

with very little oversight or direction for the next two and a half weeks. During that time, he didn't ask her to do any clerical work. Maybe Eve was taking care of it for him. Sophia didn't know because she hadn't heard a word from Eve other than the few polite exchanges that occurred if they happened to bump into each other. Sophia hated that their friendship had stalled, but she couldn't blame that on Eve. Sophia hadn't called her, either. She couldn't bring herself to pretend they weren't in love with the same man.

Cheyenne had checked in a few times, which was nice. But Cheyenne was Eve and Ted's friend, and Sophia knew they wouldn't appreciate her joining the group, so she kept their conversations cordial but distant.

As the days passed, Ted and Eve seemed to be getting closer and closer. Eve came over quite often in the evenings. Occasionally Sophia would see her passing by a window, or she'd go out to run an errand and find Eve's car parked next to her own. Sometimes Ted went over to Eve's place instead; at least that was where Sophia assumed he went when he left at night.

It wasn't until Thanksgiving that he trudged out to the guesthouse to talk to her about something besides a menu choice, a grocery run or to ask where she'd put his shirt.

She'd managed to keep her phone service so he usually texted her if he needed anything. Because he hadn't visited since the night he'd invited them over to watch a movie, Sophia was surprised by the knock at the door and was obliged to answer it herself. Alexa wasn't up yet. She had the week off school and was sleeping in.

"Morning," he said when Sophia swung open the door.

He looked better than ever, but she tried not to notice. She'd just rolled out of bed and hadn't had a chance to put on any makeup. "Morning." She shaded her eyes from the sunlight streaming in around him. "I'm sorry, was I supposed to do something for you that I forgot? I thought you told me I have the day off."

"Relax. Of course you have the day off. It's Thanksgiving. I didn't come because…I needed something. I was just wondering what you had planned for today, if…if you had somewhere to go for dinner."

"Of course. We're going to Alexa's grandparents'," she said, but really it was only Alexa who'd be joining them. Sophia's relationship with the DeBussis had grown so strained that she didn't want to be around them. She'd spent a lot of time with Alexa since she'd been out of school, so she didn't begrudge her former in-laws Thanksgiving afternoon. But she preferred to stay home alone rather than sit at their table feeling unwanted and unaccepted. "And you're going to your mother's?"

"To Eve's parents' and then my mom's."

"Just a sec." She went into the kitchen and got one of the pumpkin cheesecake strudels she'd baked. It was a new recipe she hadn't tried before, but it looked and smelled delicious. "I was going to bring this over, but since you're here…"

His eyebrows jerked up. "This is really…nice, but not necessary. I didn't expect it."

"I thought you could take it to your mom's. I was making one for me and Lex, anyway—to share with the DeBussis—and decided I might as well make one for my boss. And his girlfriend," she added to fill the uncomfortable silence.

"Thank you. I appreciate it."

She nodded and was about to shut the door, but he didn't get off her stoop.

"Sophia?"

"Yes?"

"There *is* another reason I came over."

The concern in his voice worried her. Had he proposed to Eve? Would her job end sooner than she'd expected? "I hope it's not that you're letting me go."

"No, nothing like that."

She started digging at her cuticles again, which was stupid because they'd just about healed. "Then what?"

He shifted to his other foot. "I heard…some clanking noises a few minutes ago. So I looked out the window to see what was going on and—"

"My car!" She tried to slip past him, but he cut her off.

"It's too late. I tried to stop them. Asked if I could make up a few payments, thinking you could always pay me later, but…he wouldn't agree. I knew you wouldn't be able to keep such an expensive car for much longer anyway."

She'd known she'd lose the car—so why did this make her feel sick? "I wonder how they found it."

"I asked. They said they stopped by the police station."

"And Chief Stacy told them."

"He's a prick. We already know that."

She drew a deep breath. There was no reason to get upset. She'd worked things out so far; she'd get through this latest setback. But did it have to happen on Thanksgiving?

"Thanks for letting me know," she said.

He nodded. "So…can I give you and Lex a ride over to the DeBussis? Would that help?"

"It's okay," she said. "I'll have them pick us up. No need for us to impose on a holiday."

"I don't mind."

But Eve probably would, and she didn't want him to know she wasn't really going to the DuBussis'. "Really. We're fine," she said and closed the door.

"Who was that?" Lex asked, rubbing her sleepy eyes as she stumbled into the hallway.

"Ted."

"What'd he want?"

"You're going to have to ask your grandma to pick you up."

"You can't take me anymore?"

Sophia drew a deep breath. "The car's gone."

"Oh, no. That means you'll be here all day and you won't be able to go anywhere." She sighed as she used her fingers to comb through her tangled hair. "I won't go to Grandma and Grandpa's. I'd rather stay with you."

"Are you kidding? It's been weeks since you've seen them. And your uncle and cousins will be there. Go have fun. I'll be fine. I can spend the time catching up on my sleep."

She rolled her eyes. "That sounds about as much fun as saying, 'I'll spend the time throwing up with the flu.'"

Sophia laughed in spite of her repossessed car. "Sleep sounds wonderful to most adults. You'll under-stand when you grow up. Besides, I don't have a turkey to bake or anything else to feed you for dinner. What will you eat if you stay here?"

"I'll eat whatever you eat."

Now that her Mercedes was gone, Sophia had no idea what that would be. Although she hadn't told Alexa this, she'd been thinking about going to Sacramento to visit her mother. She figured that if she could marshal the resolve, they'd eat the special Thanksgiving feast prepared by the cafeteria—or she'd go out and bring something in, if her mother had a special request. And if it went well, if she felt encouraged, maybe she'd start taking Alexa over for regular visits. Skip hadn't been willing to expose his daughter to Elaine, but now… things were different.

It all depended on how her mother behaved. Sophia couldn't take Alexa back there if Elaine insisted on acting inappropriately, as she so often did since succumbing to her disease. "I'd rather you went, really."

Still unconvinced, Alexa shuffled over and gave Sophia a hug. "Are you *sure* you won't come with me?"

She'd rather stick a fork in her eye. "I'll have a better time here, promise."

"Okay…I'll call Grandma."

Sharon said she'd come, but asked if Alexa could stay the night. Because the cousins were also staying, and Sophia felt Alexa needed a night to just forget and have fun, she agreed. By two o'clock her daughter and Ted were both gone and Sophia had the whole place to herself.

She called her mother, hoping for a small glimmer of recognition—anything that might connect her with the positive memories she had of her childhood. But Elaine was so drugged she barely said anything. When she did talk it was to claim that she had spiders and snakes in her bed.

At her mother's insistence, Sophia spoke to a nurse,

just so she could convince Elaine that she'd done all she could to make sure there were no spiders or snakes—but she already knew there wouldn't be. Her mother had been having the same delusion for years.

25

When Ted ran home to get something he'd forgotten for Thanksgiving dinner and found a box of cold cereal sitting on his dining room table next to a bowl and a spoon, he knew something was up. He hadn't had cold cereal that morning—or any morning the previous week. And he certainly hadn't eaten it by candlelight. Yet the candle that Sophia had bought for his romantic dinner with Eve several weeks ago was on the table, as if whoever had eaten that cereal had tried to add a little celebration to it.

He walked over and turned the box toward him. Golden Crisp—recently opened.

The candle smelled as if it had just been extinguished and the wax was still warm. He doubted a burglar would break in to eat Sophia's favorite cereal over candlelight on Thanksgiving afternoon, which meant she'd probably done it. But why? Why wasn't she at the DeBussis'?

He heard the murmur of a female voice coming from the direction of the kitchen. Sophia was in the house, all right. She was talking to someone. Alexa? Their plans must've fallen through. Or maybe, like him, they'd forgotten something—some ingredient they knew he wouldn't mind their taking from his pantry—and somehow come back for it. He'd returned for a bottle of wine—a Napa Valley pinot grigio that was his mother's favorite, which he brought to Thanksgiving every year. He couldn't believe he'd driven off without it this morning, but he'd been distracted by the repossession of Sophia's car and trying to make sure he wouldn't be late when he picked up Eve. Then there was his dilemma over the pumpkin dessert Sophia had given him. He knew his mother wouldn't even try it, not if she guessed—and she would—that Sophia had baked it, so he couldn't take it to dinner. He couldn't leave it in the house where she might find it, either, or share it with Eve's family. So he'd eaten what he could in his car, dumped the rest in the garbage behind the liquor store and put the pan in his trunk before he reached his girlfriend's.

At least that dessert had been good—one of the best he'd ever tried. As far as he was concerned, his mother had lost out because of her attitude. Already, he regretted disposing of what he couldn't eat and wished he'd figured out a way to save it for later.

"Hello?" he called.

There was no answer, but as he headed down the stairs, he recognized Sophia's voice. She wasn't talking to Alexa. And she wasn't in the kitchen. She was sitting on the steps leading down to his wine cellar, talking on her cell phone. If Alexa was around, she didn't seem to be in *his* house.

He was pretty sure Sophia hadn't heard him call out and didn't know he was there. He was about to make her aware of his presence, to ask where Alexa was and why they both weren't at Thanksgiving dinner, when he heard the tears in her voice. She was trying to talk to her mother, but whatever was being said on the other end of the line was upsetting her. She kept saying, "Mom, listen to me. The nurses checked your bed." And then, "It's Sophia. Your daughter, remember? *Sophia?*"

Finally, she grew so frustrated she hung up and sat staring at the bottle of wine she had clasped in her other hand. "Hey, what's going on?"

She was so startled when he spoke that she nearly dropped the wine as she twisted around to face him. Then she scrambled to her feet. "Ted! I'm sorry! I—I didn't expect you back until late tonight."

Her face went so red he could tell she was mortified to be caught crying on the steps of his wine cellar. "It's no problem. But why aren't you at your in-laws'?"

"Oh…I—I decided not to go at the last minute."

Was that true? Or had she not been invited? Eve had once told him how badly the DeBussis treated her. He hadn't thought too much about that earlier—relationships within a family could go back and forth, and some did, quite often—but Eve's words stood out in his mind now. "And Alexa?"

"Sharon picked her up an hour ago."

"So you're here alone."

"Yeah." She smiled as if she didn't have tears in her eyes. "It's a nice break. I—I'm grateful for the solitude. As a mother, you never get much time to yourself."

She was trying too hard to sell it. He played along, but Thanksgiving generally wasn't a time people wanted to be alone. "It's always nice to have some peace and quiet," he said.

"Exactly." She lifted the wine bottle. "I was going

to pay you for this. I—I wasn't just going to take it. I hope you know that."

He trusted her. Since he'd started having her pay for his groceries with a credit card, he often found the receipts with two or three bucks and some change on his kitchen counter for whatever little thing she'd picked up for herself or Alexa. "Either way, it's fine. You're welcome to whatever food I have. I've told you that before."

"I appreciate it, but I don't want to take advantage. And…just so you know, I don't usually come into your house when you're gone. I merely wanted—" she lifted the wine again "—to get this."

He didn't mention the Golden Crisp on his dining room table. "It's no problem, like I said."

"Thanks." With a smile that was obviously intended to mask what she was *really* feeling, she hurried down the stairs to return the wine bottle to the rack.

"I thought you wanted that," he said when she walked back up.

"Oh, no. Not really. I was just…thinking about it. But I've changed my mind."

"Because I came home?"

"No, because I'd rather save my money."

"Consider it a Thanksgiving gift—a trade for that great dessert you gave me."

"You liked it?"

"You bet."

"Good. I'm putting together a book of your favorite recipes for your next housekeeper. I'll add that one."

The idea of her going away left him conflicted. No doubt it would be better for both of them not to spend so much time in the same house. It was a constant battle to keep his thoughts where they needed to be. Not that long ago, he'd wanted her gone, even if it meant foisting her off on someone else. But he didn't feel that way these days. His life was so much more comfortable now that she'd started taking care of the house and the cooking. Reluctant though he was to admit it, he'd miss her on a personal level, too. "That'd be great."

There was a slight pause. "Did your mother like it?"

He hated the hope in that question, the desire to please, because she was bound to be disappointed. His mother would never like anything she made. "She hasn't tried it," he said. "I got into it early. We haven't eaten dinner yet."

She rubbed her palms on her jeans. "So you're back because…"

He gestured at the racks. He could see row upon row of wine bottles above her head. She stood below him, and he was already quite a bit taller than she was. "I forgot the wine my mother was expecting."

"Oh. Which one? I'll grab it for you."

He told her which pinot grigio he wanted and she brought it to him. He wished he could invite her to dinner. He felt bad taking the wine and abandoning her here, alone, on a major holiday. She didn't even have her daughter—or a car so she could visit someone. Then there was that heartbreaking conversation with her mother.…

"What will you do?" he asked.

"Maybe I'll take a walk or get in the hot tub."

That would fill only so many hours. He knew he'd be thinking about her the whole time he was having dinner. "Okay. I hope you…have a nice day."

"You, too." She gave him an encouraging wave, one that said he should go and not worry about her. But

when he returned that night around eight, he guessed
she'd never made it out of the wine cellar. He found
her passed out on the stone floor, two empty bottles
beside her.

Someone was shaking her, but Sophia didn't want to
embrace consciousness. Then she'd have to face what
she'd done—and she knew it wasn't good.

Shit...

If only she'd made the AA meeting. She'd used the
laptop in Ted's office to find the closest location, but
there wasn't a meeting within fifteen miles of Whiskey
Creek. Without a sponsor, she didn't even have anyone
she could call.

She'd thought of joining AA since moving to Ted's,
but she'd talked herself out of it. She was afraid he'd dis-
cover where she was going with such regularity; she'd
also been reluctant to leave Alexa home alone at night.
And, if she was honest, she'd admit that she'd started
to believe she could handle the temptation on her own.

She'd obviously been wrong.

Squinting into the light shed by the single bulb dan-
gling overhead, she peered around her, saw the two
empty bottles and groaned. "I screwed up, didn't I?"
she said, her voice deadpan.

"You've had a hard day. It wasn't wise to leave you
by yourself. I feel bad about that."

Ted. Great. Just who she wanted to find her. She saw
him looming above her and tried to push away, to get
up. She didn't want to humiliate herself, especially in
front of *him*. But who was she kidding? It was too late
to pretend she wasn't drunk. A sober person didn't fall
asleep on the floor of a wine cellar.

"I tried," she told him. "I *really* tried. I hope you believe me. But…the AA meeting was too far away. I couldn't walk there."

"AA meeting?" He frowned as if he was…what? Angry? Disappointed? Maybe even disgusted?

She couldn't be sure but assumed the worst. She deserved the worst for succumbing.

"Are you an alcoholic, Sophia?"

She couldn't trust her own mouth at the moment. She needed to get away from him as soon as possible.

She lunged for the stairs but staggered and would've fallen if he hadn't caught her.

"Whoa, let me help. You're moving a bit too fast," he said, but he did more than steady her. He picked her up in his arms and carried her out of the wine cellar.

"Please don't tell Alexa," she mumbled as he put her on the couch. "I don't want her to know that I… that I messed up. She's relying on me. And now I've let her down."

He checked his watch, looking concerned. "When will she be home?"

"Tomorrow."

"That makes it easier." He let his breath go in a whistle. "You'll be sober by then."

"I can't believe I did this. I'm *so* mad at myself." She tried to stand so she could go out to the guesthouse. Then she wouldn't have to worry about what she might say or do, but he held her back.

"I'll put on some coffee. Stay right there."

"I haven't had a drink in three months," she told him. "Not one. I made it for ninety-four days. Why'd I blow it?"

"I think the answer to that is pretty clear."

"It is?"

"You didn't have any support."

"But I made it this far."

He knelt down beside her. "Listen, Sophia. You've suffered a setback. That doesn't mean you're going to give up the battle. Now that I know what you're up against, I'll make sure you have a way to get to the meetings. And see your mom."

She shook her head. "I can't see my mom."

"Why not?"

"Like I told you, she doesn't even remember me. Having her treat me like a stranger is one of my triggers. In rehab, they told me it's the loss and disappointment that sets me off. But it's Thanksgiving. What was I supposed to do—not check on my own mother?"

He smoothed her hair off her forehead as if she were a child. "You did the right thing."

Now that he was close and she had the opportunity to really study him, she admired the laugh lines at the sides of his eyes. Those lines hadn't been nearly as marked when they were younger, of course, but she liked them. They added character to his face. "Do you think I'm going to turn out like her?" she asked.

"I don't see any reason why you would."

"Skip told me I would. He said that someday I'd be in a padded cell."

Ted's expression hardened. "Nice of him to ease your fears like that."

She smiled at his sarcasm. It felt like they were friends, that he was her *only* friend.

"What else did he tell you?" he asked.

"The truth."

"And that is…"

"That I'm a no-good, lazy drunk."

He grimaced. "Don't say that! You made it three months, didn't you? You won't break down again."

"I hope not."

Ted took her hand and toyed with her fingers. "Did he hit you, Sophia?"

Part of her knew this was information she didn't want him to have, but she could no longer remember why. Skip was gone. She could tell the world; there was nothing he could do about it. And after finding her like this…what more did she have to hide from Ted? "Doesn't matter. He can't hurt me now."

"So he did."

"All the time." She showed him her front tooth. "See this? It's not real. He knocked my real one out. I didn't even know he was mad! We got home, and he accused me of coming on to his cousin. I didn't like the guy, and I tried telling Skip that. But it didn't matter because his cousin had pulled out a chair for me, and that somehow signified…something. So, out of nowhere, *bam!*"

"He punched you."

"Right in the mouth. It felt like he'd used a brick or… or a pipe, something more than his fist. The next thing I knew, I was on the ground with blood pouring from my mouth. He had to lock Alexa out of our bedroom so she wouldn't see. But we finally told her I fell and hit my mouth and let her in so she could help us find the tooth. It had flown clear across the room." She laughed because, when she was drinking, she could. Somehow it all seemed fantastical and not quite real, as if she'd been living in a dream world. "I looked so terrible with that big gap. Skip was horrified. Who'd think he was lucky to have me if I looked like an old hag?"

When Ted didn't laugh with her, she felt her smile wilt.

"That time you came to coffee with a bruise on your cheek—"

"Oh, that's when he broke my cheekbone." She indicated her left eye. "But it was almost healed. I covered it with makeup, didn't think anyone would notice."

"It was faint, but we noticed."

"Anyway, that was nothing. It hurt, but not as much as the tooth."

A muscle twitched in his cheek. "Why didn't you get help?"

"I tried to once. But—" she shook her head "—that was a mistake. By the time he was finished with me, I couldn't come out of the house for three weeks."

He stood up, shoved his hands in his pockets and began to pace. "I still don't understand why you didn't get away from him."

"It was complicated."

"How?"

"Because I felt like I deserved it."

"For marrying him in the first place?"

"For everything I'd ever done wrong." She struggled to articulate because she knew she was slurring her words. "Causing Scott Harris to get into that—" she winced "—that crash when we were in high school. Acting so spoiled and selfish all the time. Disappointing you by...by getting with Skip."

"So you were letting him punish you."

"Not only that, I *couldn't* leave. I was afraid that if he ever got...got hold of me, I wouldn't survive it. He said that if I told anyone or tried to leave him, I could kiss Alexa goodbye." Just the thought of losing Alexa made her so sad, tears trickled down her cheeks. "So even if I did get away, I'd lose my daughter."

When Ted swore under his breath, she rested an arm over her eyes so she wouldn't have to look at him. She couldn't tell if he was angry with her for not getting away, or for turning to alcohol. Or if he was angry with Skip. "At least he was gone most of the time."

She'd already started to drift off when Ted spoke. "I brought you some turkey and other leftovers from dinner. Any chance I can talk you into eating?"

"Not right now, but thanks. I had cereal." She lifted her arm to peer up at him. "Did you have a nice Thanksgiving?"

He hesitated.

"Did something go wrong?" she asked.

"No, it was fine."

"And Eve? Did she like it?"

"I think so."

"She's a nice person. She knew about my drinking when you asked her that night in the Jacuzzi, but she didn't tell you. I'll always be grateful to her for that. She's someone special. You're lucky to have her."

Pivoting, he came back toward her. "Since she's so much better than you, you mean?"

Squinting, she struggled to bring him into focus. "Well, she does have her life in order while mine's a complete mess, so..." She giggled, which wasn't appropriate. On some level she knew that, so she forced herself to stop and when he didn't respond, she rolled over onto her side. "Are you sorry you hired me?"

"No," he said. "I'm not sorry."

"Someone else would've been less hassle—and wouldn't have passed out in your wine cellar."

"Someone else wouldn't have been facing your challenges. I know you're doing the best you can, that you're trying."

"I'll try again tomorrow," she promised, and this somehow evoked a smile from him.

"I'm sure you will."

"Did your mom like the pumpkin dessert?"

He cleared his throat. "You asked me that."

She blinked at him, trying to remember his answer. "Did you tell me?"

He pinched the bridge of his nose. "In case I didn't, she loved it. Ate two pieces."

That made her happy. It was the first thing today that had. "I'm glad," she said. "That's nice. I was thinking I'd take a piece to my mom, but…you know what happened to the car."

"I know."

"Principal Dixon really ate *two* pieces?"

"Go to sleep," he told her and, she couldn't be sure—maybe she just imagined it—but she thought he bent and kissed her forehead.

26

"Why didn't you tell me she has a drinking problem?" Ted asked.

There was a brief silence on the other end of the line before Eve answered. "How'd you find out?"

"How do you think? She was here alone all day, on Thanksgiving. Her car was just repossessed and she was trying to cope with her psychotic mother. That doesn't sound like a recipe for disaster to you?"

"Oh, no. I hope she's okay...."

He remembered the moment he'd found her lying on the floor. He'd felt such a jolt of panic when he thought she might be injured—or worse. Suicide had crossed his mind, which was why he hadn't been all that upset when he'd realized it was only alcohol. "She's fine. She's sleeping it off. But...I wish I'd known so I could've been more prepared."

"And how would you have prepared?"

"By locking the wine cellar so it wouldn't turn out to be a booby trap for her!"

"Ted, if she wanted to drink badly enough, she would've found a way to get some booze."

"Without a car? I live five miles out of town. She would've had to want it pretty badly."

"What else did she have to do today? You said she was home alone. She could've walked that far." The tenor of her voice changed. "She might not have made it back, depending on whether she drank on the way home, but…"

He didn't care to imagine it. At least she was safe. "You still haven't answered my question."

"There were a lot of reasons I didn't tell you."

"Like…"

"I'd promised her I wouldn't tell anyone. I didn't feel it would be fair to break that confidence just because you and I started seeing each other."

He remembered Alexa's reaction not too long ago when he'd gone down to the kitchen for a glass of wine—and finally understood it. "We're not talking about spreading random gossip. She's my housekeeper! You don't think I had a right to know that my wine cellar might cause her some serious problems?"

"Last I heard, alcohol addiction isn't something people are required to reveal on a job application. I figured it didn't matter as long as it wasn't affecting her work. She's had it hard enough since Skip died without me going around blabbing about her personal problems—especially to her employer who didn't really want to hire her in the first place. From what she told me, alcohol was her only escape. Skip controlled *every* aspect of her life, wouldn't even let her have a job. So I wasn't feeling particularly judgmental. And you can be a very exacting person."

He sat up. "What's that supposed to mean? *I'm* judgmental?"

"You're capable of so much, and you expect others to live up to your standards."

"I don't understand what Sophia's addiction has to do with that."

"Besides the job issue, and whether or not you'd be willing to hire her, I thought that learning she was an alcoholic might change the way you look at her—and at me. I didn't want that to be the deciding factor in our relationship, didn't want you to choose me over her just because I've never been to rehab. I hoped you'd fall head over heels in love with me just like you once did with her. We all know how you used to feel about her, Ted. How much she meant to you and how long it took you to get over her. If you were going to date me, I wanted it to be because of who *I* am instead of what *she* isn't. Does that make sense?"

"Not entirely," he grumbled, but it did. He was just hesitant to acknowledge the legitimacy of her concerns. He wasn't sure that, in the past four weeks, he'd been able to come very close to the target she'd painted for him.

Was he falling in love with her? It didn't feel like it. He kept telling himself that he had to give their relationship more time, try harder, be more dedicated, stop thinking of Sophia. But he couldn't order his heart to love one person instead of another. Despite the hurt she'd caused him, it was still Sophia who took his breath away.

"When it comes to me, to us, I don't want you to rely on some…checklist that has more to do with your head than your heart," Eve explained. "No girl wants to be a consolation prize."

"I appreciate what you're saying," he told her, but he feared her expectations were set too high. If she hoped to own his heart the way Sophia once had—he couldn't deliver that.

"You *appreciate* it?" she said. "That's your response?"

She'd given him an opportunity to reassure her, and he'd blown it. They'd been sleeping together for a month. He could see how, after that much time, she might be curious as to where he stood on the relationship. But how could he convince her they were heading toward marriage when he felt no closer to it today than the morning after they'd first made love? Just a few minutes ago, it had been all he could do not to carry *Sophia* to his bed. If she hadn't been drunk, there was even a chance he might have succumbed.... "I care about you—"

"You cared about me a month ago, Ted." She paused and he waited, tense, for her to continue. "Is that all you've got?"

Think how easy your life will be if you stick with Eve. Don't be Rhett Butler! "I don't know what to say." He scratched his head, hard, as if that would somehow set his brain straight. "I *want* to feel the way you want me to."

"But it's not there. That's the rest of the sentence, isn't it?"

Shit. He could hear the disappointment in her voice. He was hurting her even though he'd promised himself he'd never do that. "Maybe not yet, but...that doesn't mean what we have can't develop into whatever we want it to be. I won't give up. Not as long as you're interested in trying."

"How flattering. You're asking me to rely on the power of your will. Your *determination*."

He'd said the wrong thing, been too honest. "It's not just determination. It's knowing that you're…that you're everything I should want in a wife."

"So I get a better score on your checklist."

"I don't have a checklist!"

"Never mind. I think a month of giving it all we've got is enough, don't you?"

"A month isn't that long, Eve. We've barely gotten started. And we have a…a good relationship. We never fight. We enjoy each other. We *trust* each other."

"There we go. That's it. You trust me, but you don't trust Sophia."

Could anyone trust Sophia? Maybe she wouldn't be able to beat her addiction. Maybe what she'd been through had scarred her too deeply. Or maybe she'd get back on her feet but move away. "Look, there's nothing wrong with basing a relationship on trust, nothing wrong with what we've got."

"Except that we're trying to make it into something it's not!"

He said nothing, could say nothing.

She was the one who eventually broke the silence. "That night in the hot tub…"

He fell back on his pillows. Remembering that night should've brought him pleasure. But it didn't, not any more than the encounters he'd had with various other women along the way. Only Sophia stood out. "What about it?"

"*Why* did you make it sexual?"

"I couldn't see why we shouldn't be together. I thought it would fulfill both our needs."

"I'm glad you didn't say it was because you were drunk."

"Come on, we've discussed this."

"Except that there's more to it than what you've admitted. You wanted to protect yourself from getting back with Sophia, right? You needed to insert someone between you and her to feel safe."

This conversation was moving into dangerous territory, but he had no clue how to turn it around. "If you know that now, you knew it then. So why'd you go along with it?"

"Because I wanted to believe. I wanted to delude myself as much as you did."

At least she was taking some responsibility for the situation.

He closed his eyes. "I'm sorry, Eve. My brain has never functioned properly when it comes to her."

She laughed without mirth. "Hello! Then stop pretending you don't know what love is!"

"I feel sorry for her and, yes, I'm attracted to her. I'm not sure that's love," he said. "Anyway, love doesn't necessarily make a relationship successful."

"No, but it gives you a hell of a lot more to fight for—and it makes life far more rewarding when you win. In any case, I'm stepping out of the picture. That means you'll have to figure out what you feel for her and deal with it one way or another," she said and hung up.

Ted stayed on his bed for…he didn't know how long. He just lay there, wrestling with himself and staring at the ceiling. He wanted to give Sophia a chance. She seemed to have changed in all the important areas. But her life was in shambles. After coming out of such a bad marriage, after going through what she'd endured for fourteen years, was she even in a position to know what she wanted?

And what if she couldn't overcome her addiction?

As soon as she heard Cheyenne's voice, Eve almost hung up—but it was too late. It didn't matter that she hadn't spoken yet; she'd placed the call so her name would've come up on Chey's screen.

"Happy Thanksgiving!" Cheyenne said cheerfully.

That confirmed it. There was recognition in that greeting. "Happy Thanksgiving to you, too."

Normally, Eve loved this time of year. They were heading into December, which was her favorite month. It was a tradition that she and Cheyenne decorate the B and B for Christmas the day after Thanksgiving. Once they came back from coffee, they'd drag the wreaths and garlands out of the attic and, by Sunday night, Little Mary's would look like the subject of a Norman Rockwell painting, with a fire burning in the hearth and the old-fashioned Victorian Christmas tree in front of the window. The competing B and B at the other end of town spent a lot of money when they re-modeled a couple of years ago, but Eve didn't think they came close to the quaint charm of her place—not dur-ing the holidays. Even the cemetery next door, with its lovely iron filigree fence and century-old tombstones, added to the ambience. And if they were lucky, there'd be snow....

But after her last conversation with Ted, decorating the inn didn't sound half as appealing as it had before. She'd thought that for the first time in a long while she'd have someone special, someone besides her family, to share Christmas with. And now it would be awkward at coffee on Fridays, too, especially once everyone learned that they'd already ended the relationship.

"Did you spend the day at Ted's mother's place?" Eve asked.

"The last part of it. The first part we spent with my parents. What about you? Did you have the Amos boys over like you were planning?"

"They had dinner with us, but…it was a little uncomfortable."

Eve slid beneath the covers of her bed. "Why's that?"

"Presley told me she'd be with her boyfriend, but they got into a fight and she ended up calling me. She was lonely and wanted to come over, but…I had Aaron here."

"They can't get along well enough to have a Thanksgiving meal together?"

"She wants no contact with him. And…it's not just that." Eve heard a door open and close, then Cheyenne's voice dropped. "There's something else going on, something even more difficult."

Cheyenne's behavior pulled Eve out of her own sadness for the moment. "What is it?"

"I've never told you this. I've guarded the secret carefully because…because I haven't even told Dylan. I *can't* tell him—"

"You're keeping a secret from your *husband?* The man you love more than anything in the world?" She sat up. "About what?"

"You have to promise me—*swear* to me—that you'll never breathe a word of this to anyone."

"Of course! Surely, we've been friends long enough for you to trust me."

"I trust you with *my* secrets. But this isn't my secret, and I haven't told a living soul."

Eve had no idea what to make of this. The two of them had been through a lot of ups and downs ever since Cheyenne's mother had dragged her and Presley to town in that beat-up old car they'd been living in twenty years ago. Not only that, but Eve and Chey worked together five days a week. How could there be a secret Cheyenne hadn't shared—with her *or* Dylan? "Whose secret is it? Presley's?"

"Yes."

"And it involves..."

"Wyatt."

"Why would you have any reason to keep a secret about Presley's son from—" Suddenly, Eve realized what had been right in front of her all along. "Oh, shit! Aaron's Wyatt's father!"

She'd asked if that was a possibility before. Most of the town knew that Presley had been sleeping with Aaron around the time—or not long before—Presley got pregnant. But they'd never been an item. And Presley had insisted that a man she met in Phoenix after she left Whiskey Creek was the father of her child.

"Wait. Aaron knows Wyatt exists—" she started but Cheyenne interrupted.

"He knows Presley has a child. But he thinks the father is from Arizona, like everyone else. They always used birth control."

"It just didn't work."

"Apparently."

"Isn't she ever going to tell him?"

"I've asked her that repeatedly. She says she probably will—one day. But she keeps putting it off. She's terrified Aaron will ruin her happiness and maybe Wyatt's, too. But it's getting harder and harder for me to be 'family' to both sides. I feel disloyal to my husband because this is his brother we're talking about. I feel disloyal to Aaron, too—as his sister-in-law. And yet…I understand *exactly* where Presley is coming from. Aaron's never been stable. He wasn't ready for a child when she got pregnant. He wouldn't have been interested, anyway—so she did him a favor by letting him off the hook."

"I sure hope he looks at it that way when he finds out," Eve breathed. "Dylan, too."

"I'm afraid they won't see it that way at all. And I can't blame them. Part of me believes Aaron has the right to know, especially now that he's changing, growing up. He still has his moments. He may deal with anger and resentment his whole life. But I'm seeing *some* maturity there. And I love him. It's almost impossible *not* to love him."

"You love your sister, too."

"Exactly. I tell myself she's never had anything. That she deserves Wyatt. You know how we grew up, what happened with our mother."

"But Aaron's led a hard life, too."

"And what if Wyatt could make a positive impact on him—get him to change his priorities and settle down?"

"You think he might try to get custody or cause problems for her?"

"Maybe. It's common knowledge that he's something of a loose cannon. If I told him, and he did wind up making her life hell—or demanded even partial custody—she'd never forgive me. I'm so torn, I don't know what to do!"

"God, you've been carrying this secret for what—two *years?*"

"Wyatt's fourteen months old so...yeah, two years, including the pregnancy. I'm telling you, it's harder every day. As Wyatt gets older, he's looking more and more like his father. I'm scared that Dylan will eventually see the resemblance, and that no matter what I say, I won't be able to refute what's staring him in the face. It's not as if he hasn't asked me if I thought there was any chance Wyatt could be Aaron's."

Eve tightened her grip on the phone. "When he asked, you told him *no?*"

"I had to! He'd tell his brother. I have no doubt of that. Maybe they don't always get along, but he raised Aaron."

"You're caught in the middle, all right."

"And the pressure is mounting. This was just Thanksgiving. What will Christmas be like? Again, Dylan and I will have to work out a way to see Presley separate from Aaron, which'll leave one or the other alone."

"Surely Presley understands. She can't expect you to always accommodate her."

"She does understand. She tells me all the time that she'll be the one to bow out. But she needs my support so badly. She's hardly making ends meet working at that thrift shop while she's going to massage school. And now she's hooked up with a guy who's worse than Aaron ever was. I live in fear that she'll slip back into her old habits."

"Gee. Now I feel better about my own problems."

"*What* problems?" Cheyenne asked. "We're going into the Christmas season, which we both love. And you're dating one of the most eligible bachelors in Whiskey Creek."

"*Was* dating," she clarified.

The phone went silent. Then Chey said, "You just told me you went to his mother's for Thanksgiving."

"That's true. But afterward, we had a talk and decided that...that it's not working," she said, coming out with it.

"What part of it isn't working? What went wrong?"

"You can't guess?"

Cheyenne sighed. "I doubt you really want me to. It'll sound too much like 'I told you so.'"

"I think he's still in love with Sophia."

"I'm sorry, Eve. I really am. Maybe I wasn't all that excited when I first heard about you and Ted, but I wanted it to work out. I mean, what could be better than having two of my best friends get married and start a life together?"

"Ted and I should've listened to you and everyone else. If it was meant to be, it would've happened long before now."

"Not necessarily. I could see why you gave it a chance."

Now Chey was downplaying her initial concern so Sophia wouldn't feel like an idiot. That was nice, but a bit too obvious to be effective. "So...you said Aaron's showing signs of maturing. Maybe you could set me up with him."

"There's no way I want you dating my brother-in-law—my nephew's father!" Cheyenne cried. "That situation is complicated enough."

"It was a joke!" she said, and this time it was true. "I just don't seem to be having any luck picking 'good guys.' Maybe I should try the odd 'bad boy' for a change."

"You'll find the right person to love."

"Maybe I should settle for Martin Ferris."

"Martin Ferris! Where did *that* come from?"

"You know him, don't you?"

"Of course I know him. He's our bread vendor—and he hits on you whenever he makes a delivery."

"That's my point. He likes *me*—not you or Sophia or anyone else."

"He also has the IQ of a rock."

"Beggars can't be choosers. With luck, *my* genes will prevail if we have a child."

Cheyenne laughed. "I'm glad you haven't lost your sense of humor."

"Deep down I think I knew that Ted wasn't over Sophia. I was just…hoping we were all wrong."

"Ted's a great person. It was worth a try. But tell me that you're not mad at him."

"I *want* to be mad at him. We could've had a good thing."

"And Sophia will probably break his heart. I doubt she's in any position to get into another relationship—not after what she's been through."

"I've considered that. But…he deserves the chance to go after what he's always wanted."

"Wow, you're taking this well. I'm proud of you. Does that mean you're coming to coffee tomorrow?"

"No. I'm not taking it *that* well!" she said. "I'm not ready to see him again so soon. And I definitely don't want to tell the others."

"Fine, we'll let them have coffee without us."

"If he shows up *he'll* need to tell them. There's no avoiding that."

"No, but at least we won't be there to hear everyone's reaction."

We. That was the earmark of a true friend. Although it was *her* stupid mistake, one Chey had warned her against, Chey was in her corner.

"That's tempting." She cringed as she remembered some of her more intimate moments with Ted, moments when she thought their relationship might last. She'd slept with him last night, for crying out loud—and now he was suddenly nothing more than her friend?

Yes, she should skip coffee tomorrow. The switch was too sudden. She needed some time. "I was really starting to fall for him, Chey."

"I was getting that feeling—and I was *so* hopeful for you. It's not like Ted to be wishy-washy. What did he say?"

"*He* didn't break it off. I realized he wasn't necessarily interested in *me,* he was just running from *her.* So I threw him back into her arms."

"It's better to face the truth, but…I'm sorry you had to do it."

"I'll survive. I survived Joe picking *you* two years ago, didn't I?" she teased.

"You took that well, too."

She rolled her eyes. "I'm getting good at being rejected."

"It only takes one Prince Charming and, like I said, you'll find him. Meanwhile, I'll come over first thing in the morning and we'll start decorating."

"No, I don't want everyone to think I'm dividing

the group. You and Dylan should go to Black Gold, like always."

"You sure?"

"Positive." It was a long shot, but maybe Ted would miss her. Maybe if he got together with Sophia, he'd realize he wasn't missing anything after all.

Thinking that way was sort of mean. But Eve hadn't been lying when she told Cheyenne that she'd fallen for him.

27

Ted decided he wasn't going to pursue Sophia right away. He'd been with Eve too recently, felt he owed her some discretion as a gesture of respect if nothing else. So he'd take it slow, and he wouldn't get physical until he was absolutely certain that they had a chance of being successful this time around. Sophia had a child, a child who'd recently been through hell. Alexa was flailing around, searching for some stability; he didn't want her to latch on to him, thinking he might become her new daddy, if Sophia couldn't convince him that she was capable of the kind of love he wanted—and could remain sober.

So he stayed in his own bed. He didn't even go back downstairs where he'd left Sophia sleeping on the couch. But it wasn't as if he could drift off like she had. He'd fantasized about her for so many years, his body felt as though it had waited too long already. It didn't help that Alexa was at her grandparents', which meant he and Sophia were alone in the house.

He thought about last night's conversation with Eve. Would they have made it if not for Sophia?

No. He'd honestly *tried* to sway his heart; it just hadn't worked. He felt too much relief that it was over to believe they were as compatible as he'd first hoped.

His mother would be disappointed. She'd fawned over Eve for hours at dinner yesterday, no doubt planning the day when Eve would become her daughter-in-law. But all he'd been able to think about was the woman who'd made him the pumpkin dessert he'd scarfed down in the car.

Sophia woke up with a hangover—and she knew she deserved every ache and pain. What she'd done last night had been such a huge mistake. Giving into her addiction undermined her confidence and sense of well-being when she could least afford it.

"Stupid…" she muttered as she threw off the blanket and looked around Ted's living room. Fortunately, he wasn't there. Although he'd taken care of her last night—she could see that he'd put new bandages on her fingers to protect her cuticles and set out two pain tablets and a glass of water—he'd left her to recover on her own. Thank God. Maybe she could slink off and try to forget that last night ever happened.

Sometimes people needed a second chance.

Sometimes they needed more than that.

How many chances had she burned through?

Too many. But this was her first screw-up since Skip had disappeared from her life. Without him, she was actually happier and *more* in control, despite her other problems. So why would she succumb and wreck her perfect ninety-four-day record? For *this*?

She pressed her fingers to her throbbing head and

told herself she had to remember what drinking was like once the euphoria had worn off.

A creak from above brought her head up despite the pounding inside it. Was Ted getting out of bed? He usually went to coffee on Fridays. She guessed he was walking to the shower.

Staggering to her feet, she used the walls to steady herself as she made her way to the deck, down the stairs and across the yard to the guesthouse.

Only once she was safely home with the door locked behind her could she breathe easier. She didn't have to work today. Because of the holiday, she had Friday and the weekend off. Hopefully during the next three days they'd both be able to forget that she'd raided the wine cellar.

Chief Stacy was in the grocery store. Sophia saw him from behind and quickly steered her cart one aisle over. She didn't want him to see her; nor did she want to talk to him. Her headache had subsided and she felt much improved since she'd doctored her hangover. But she was in a hurry to purchase the things she needed so she could get out of there. Once she'd worked up the nerve to see Ted again, she'd offered to make dinner despite having the day off if he'd allow her to use his car, and he'd pulled away from his computer to get the keys out of his pocket. He'd tossed them over as if it was no big deal, but she couldn't imagine Eve would be too thrilled to see her driving around town in his Lexus.

She thought she'd escaped Stacy's notice. She'd already gone through the checkout line, loaded her groceries in the backseat and started the car when he came out of the store pushing his cart. But just as she was backing out, he thumped the side of the vehicle to let her know he was coming up alongside and motioned for her to roll down her window.

Sophia considered ignoring him. She hadn't done anything wrong. As far as she was concerned, he had no right to detain her. But he was the chief of police. The power he held frightened her enough that she didn't dare defy him.

"Is there something I can do for you?" she asked.

He glared down at her, making her glad she'd put on sunglasses. It wasn't warm enough for shades. The clouds rolling across the sun promised rain—maybe snow later on if the temperature dropped. But her eyes were red from last night's bender, so she'd taken the precaution of covering them. She'd learned, from her years with Skip, how to camouflage just about anything.

"I see you're not going down without a fight," he said, gesturing at the car.

"You must be sad that I still have some way to get around, since you were so eager to see me lose my own transportation."

He spat on the blacktop. "Wasn't my fault you lost that shiny Mercedes. You weren't keeping up with the payments," he added with a facetious *tsk*.

She glanced in the rearview mirror. There was nothing behind her. She wanted to go, but if Chief Stacy tried to stop her, his cart could scratch Ted's car. She couldn't let anything happen to the Lexus while it was in her possession. "What is it you want?"

"Besides what you owe me?"

"I don't have any money. You know that."

"You could get five grand for selling one of your eggs to a fertility clinic."

She felt her mouth drop open. "One of my...*eggs?*"

"That's right. A lot of women do it. It wouldn't even take much time, wouldn't interfere with your *important* position cleaning up after the big suspense writer. And think how happy you might make some young couple who can't have a baby on their own."

"I could make you happy, too, by giving up the money. Is that it?"

"Why not? Fair is fair. Then we could be better friends."

"You're crazy," she said. "Get out of my way."

"What's crazy about doing whatever you can to make things right after squandering other people's hard-earned money? *I've* never lived in the biggest mansion in town. *I've* never driven the fancy cars you and Skip drove. It's time to pay the piper, Sophia."

She clenched the steering wheel that much harder. "No fertility clinic would take one of my eggs."

"Of course they would. Look at you. You were once the envy of Whiskey Creek. You've got great genes!"

"Do I? My mother has a mental illness, and my father died of cancer. I doubt my genes will be worth as much as you think."

"Don't give up before you try."

She narrowed her eyes. "Are you the person who threw that rock through my window? Who vandalized my house?"

He conjured up an expression of mock innocence. "I don't know what you're talking about."

"I'm talking about *harassment*. You're harassing me—and if you don't stop, there'll be trouble."

"Oh, yeah?" He quit pretending. "What can you do

about it, huh? Who are you going to tell? No one will believe you over me."

"You make me sick."

"The feeling is mutual. Anyone who can walk away from the carnage your husband caused doesn't have a conscience."

"You're a bully, no different from Connie Ruesch."

"Connie who?"

"Never mind. This is the important part—I won't put up with what you're doing to me."

"You have no choice. You pick a fight with me, you'll lose." Suddenly, he smiled and took a bottle of wine from his cart, then handed it to her through the window. She didn't want it, but if she hadn't taken it, she was fairly certain he would've dropped it in her lap.

"A token of my goodwill," he said. "I know you'll want to guzzle it the second I turn my back, but I wouldn't advise it. DUIs are expensive."

Laughing softly as if he was the cleverest man on earth, he wheeled his cart around and headed in the other direction, but not before calling back to her, "Look at the beautiful Sophia DeBussi. Broke. Alone. Despised."

A chill rolled down Sophia's spine. Those were the exact words on the note attached to the rock that had broken her window! Stunned that he had the nerve to admit that *he* was the one who'd vandalized her house, Sophia sat gaping at the wine he'd handed her. Obviously, on top of everything else, he was aware of her drinking problem. Word of that could've come from her in-laws, who'd told Agent Freeman. Or maybe Agent Freeman had mentioned it himself. He would've had no idea he couldn't trust local law enforcement with that information.

"Stacy, you bastard." She shifted her gaze to watch him in her side mirror—and it was all she could do to stop herself from getting out and throwing that bottle at his head.

Ted had a lot to do. He shouldn't have been so focused on the fact that he'd missed coffee this morning, but he kept wondering if Eve had told everyone that they were no longer seeing each other. That they'd failed when they'd been so certain—or at least hopeful—had to be embarrassing for her. It was embarrassing for *him*. But what could he do? The further he got from last night's conversation, and the commitment he'd made to the relationship before that, the freer he felt. They weren't meant for each other. It would've been a huge mistake to keep forcing it. As illogical as it seemed, picking a mate based on character traits alone didn't seem to be any more foolproof than letting his heart run amok. A certain amount of chemistry had to be present.

When someone knocked on the door, he assumed it was FedEx with the check he'd been expecting from his publisher. It required a signature, so he hurried down from his office. But there was no courier; instead, Kyle stood on his front porch.

"Hey, man, what's up?" Ted greeted him.

Kyle looked him over. "You okay?"

He knew about Eve. Ted could tell. He'd expected to hear from someone. It wasn't as if Eve could go to coffee without being asked where he was—which would lead to the inevitable "we're no longer together" conversation. Maybe that was why he hadn't been able to get his mind off his friends.

At least Kyle was the first to approach him. Kyle had tried to warn him not to get involved with Eve but, because he'd made a similar mistake with Callie, he'd also be more understanding.

"I'm fine." Ted stretched his neck. "Between you and me, I'm better than I should be. It's Eve I'm worried about. I hope—I hope I didn't make her feel bad."

"Well, you damn sure didn't make her feel *good*," he said wryly. "That's what I was hoping to help you avoid in the first place."

"I know. How'd she act this morning?"

"Wasn't there."

So neither of them had shown up. "Then how—"

"Cheyenne announced it."

It made sense that Cheyenne would be the first to hear, since she and Eve were so close.

He waved Kyle into the house. "Come in."

They went to the game room and lounged on either end of the leather sofa. "How'd Cheyenne break the news?" Ted asked.

"Just came right out with it. She also said she didn't want any of us asking about you when we see Eve again. And we're not allowed to tease her."

Ted feared that might be too tempting for some of the guys to resist. But he'd probably get ribbed about it more than she would—thank God. "So…could you tell how she was taking it?"

"Chey said she'd be fine. She said you'd both be fine…given time."

"But you came over anyway."

"I wanted to see how much time you're going to need."

Ted grinned sardonically. "Your sensitivity overwhelms me."

"Okay. I came to rub your nose in your mistake. So let's hear you say it."

"Say what?"

"'Kyle, I humbly apologize for not listening. You were absolutely right in trying to warn me away from one of our close friends.'"

Ted gave him a playful kick. "Screw you."

Chuckling, Kyle got up and started racking balls on the pool table. "At least tell me what happened."

Ted walked over and selected a cue stick. Kyle didn't have to ask; he wanted a game or he wouldn't be racking the balls. "I'm not discussing it with you or anyone else. I doubt she'd appreciate me running my mouth."

"Uh, huh. Okay. Good answer." He seemed intent and supportive, but then he grinned. "So what happened?"

"I just told you—"

"So?"

Ted scowled. "Quit it!"

Kyle chucked him on the chin. "It wasn't there, am I right?"

The fact that Kyle had guessed without any effort at all made Ted feel like even more of an ass. "Okay, I should've listened to you. Happy now?"

"I am," he said. "At least I'm no longer the only one who's ventured into no-man's-land."

"You're making me feel *a lot* better."

The smile curving Kyle's lips stretched wider. "No problem."

Ted watched him select a cue stick now that he had the balls in place. "You want to go first?"

"After you."

He took the shot and watched the balls scatter. Two striped ones found their way into a pocket, giving him a nice start. He circled the table looking for his next shot.

Kyle waited off to one side. "When are you going to start dating Sophia?" he asked.

Ted glanced up. "Who said anything about Sophia?"

"Come on!"

"She's not ready for a relationship." He used a dismissive tone, hoping that would be enough to get Kyle off his back, but Kyle wasn't so easily discouraged.

"Does that mean you're *not* going to date her?"

"Why are you so set on finding out?"

"Because Riley and I have both considered asking her out."

Ted had just bent over to take another shot but, at this, he buried the white ball along with the one he'd been aiming for.

Kyle slapped him on the back. "That's what I thought."

"No, go ahead." Ted spoke as if it was nothing.

It was Kyle's turn to miss his shot. *"What?"*

"You heard me." Ted didn't want Sophia to "settle," didn't want her back just because she felt she had no one else. Giving her other options and letting her choose—that was the only way he'd ever be sure.

Sophia was in the hot tub when Ted came out of the house; she was alone because she'd agreed to let Alexa stay over another night.

"It's cold this evening," he said.

She tilted her head up. He was standing on the deck, but she couldn't see him clearly. It'd been raining, so dark clouds obscured the moon.

Sadly, her mood was as dark and unsettled as the weather. Since her encounter with Chief Stacy, she'd been examining her budget, trying to get some idea how long it might take her to save up enough to leave Whiskey Creek. But it all seemed so far off because she was starting with nothing. She didn't even have a car. "The water's perfect."

When he came down, she saw that he was wearing swim trunks and realized he planned to get in with her. He'd spent the day in his office, trying to catch up on his book. At least that was where he'd been when she made dinner. He'd been so engrossed when she carried up his tray that he'd barely acknowledged her.

"There's a bottle of wine sitting on my kitchen counter," he said.

She sank lower in the water to avoid the cold air. "That's for you. I'm hoping it'll make up for one of the bottles I drank. I'll pay for the other one, of course— for both if you don't care for that brand."

"The brand's fine. I'll take it off your hands, but after how bad you felt last night I'm not sure you should be cruising the liquor aisle."

"*I* didn't buy it. Chief Stacy did."

At the mention of Whiskey Creek's chief of police, he studied her more closely. "Come again?"

"It's a long story," she said.

"Looks to me like we've got all night."

Not really. She had to get some sleep. She'd come to the conclusion that she had to make better use of her off hours, had to gain some skills and figure out other ways of making money or she'd be trapped in Whiskey Creek indefinitely and that meant leading a disciplined life. But she took a few minutes as he settled across from her to explain what had happened at the grocery store. It gave them something to talk about other than the debacle she'd created last night.

"Hard to believe someone in his position would T.P. your house," he said. "What is he...twelve?"

"That happened a few days before and was probably kids. But he was behind the vandalism and the rock that broke the window."

"Are you *sure* it was him?"

"Positive. He quoted the first part of the note wrapped around that rock."

Ted stared at her. "That's ballsy, to give himself away like that."

"He couldn't resist. He's too proud of what he's done."

"That's out of line for *anyone,* but especially for him," Ted said, his words clipped. "I'm going to talk to Noah's dad and see if there isn't something that can be done."

Sophia felt his feet brush against hers and jerked back. "Don't waste your time. Chief Stacy's been tight with the mayor ever since he was elected." She swished some of the bubbles away. "I just have to get out of Whiskey Creek. There's too much bias here. I'll never have a chance to start over."

"But leaving means you'd need a job. And what will you do without a car?"

"Depending on where I go, I might be able to take public transit. Or ride a bike."

"What kinds of jobs will you apply for?"

"Maybe I could get on as a hostess at a restaurant or a receptionist at a day spa. Or I could do in-home daycare."

"You have to be licensed for daycare."

"I could get licensed."

He didn't say it, but she could tell he didn't think she'd make enough to survive. "Where's Lex?" he asked. "Wasn't she coming home tonight?"

"She was, but her cousins wanted her to stay with them. I don't normally let her sleep over at Colby's. I don't trust Skip's brother to stick around and supervise, but...she hasn't had much of a social life since everything happened, and I couldn't bring myself to say no."

"That's understandable."

"I hope everything's okay."

"The decision's been made. Worrying won't help." As he rested his arms on the edge of the Jacuzzi, she couldn't help admiring his biceps. But she loved his hands most. She'd always loved his hands.

"I was thinking of getting a tree tomorrow," he said, changing the subject.

Her headache was back and rising to new proportions. She rubbed her temples in an effort to ease the pain. "For the garden? What kind of tree?"

He gave her an expression that said, *Are you really asking that question?* "There's a little thing called Christmas coming up."

"Oh. Of course." Thanksgiving had been hard for her. She wasn't looking forward to Christmas.

"I thought maybe you'd like to go with me," he said.

She knew better than to think Eve would be pleased if she accepted. "No, thanks. I've got other plans."

Her response seemed to surprise him. "Like what?"

"I'm walking over to the library in the morning."

"For..."

"They're offering that typing class Alexa took last summer."

"Sounds like a good idea." He squinted through the steam. "I'm willing to wait until afternoon, if that's more convenient."

Wasn't *Eve* going with him?

Either way, being around Ted would only confuse her, make her want things she couldn't have. For once, she was going to protect herself. She was going to get out of the mess she was in and figure out how to stand on her own two feet, even if it killed her.

And sometimes she thought it would. When she woke up this morning and realized what she'd done, she'd been ready to give up. Booze would beat her even if she overcame everything else. So why try?

Then she'd remembered the night Eve had appeared in her room and dragged her out of bed to eat the first *real* meal she'd had in days. Maybe, because of their current circumstances, they couldn't be friends, but that moment had left an indelible impression on Sophia. She needed to honor the spark Eve had given her, as well as the promise she'd made that night to keep fighting, regardless of how bad it got.

"I'm afraid I don't have time for stuff like that this year," she said. "After the library, I've got to get on-line and see if I can find an inexpensive car. There are places advertising that they'll finance anyone. 'Good credit. Bad credit...' You've heard the ad."

"You have a busy day planned."

"I need to take advantage of my off-hours. I've got to become independent." She spoke with the determination she felt, but a small part of her still feared that the odds against her were too high.

"Can you make time for an AA meeting tomorrow night?" he asked.

"I have no way to get there," she said. "That's why I'm hoping to buy a car as soon as possible."

"I'll take you until you can arrange your own transportation."

She raised a hand. "That's okay. I'd feel too guilty dragging you to something like that. You don't deserve the humiliation or the tedium of hearing everyone's story."

"What's *your* story?"

"You don't want to hear that, either," she said. "Anyway, I know Eve wouldn't like it if I dragged you off."

He started to speak, then changed his mind. "Eve's very supportive of you. She was really excited when I hired you."

She gave him a sad smile as she climbed out of the Jacuzzi. "That was *before,*" she said.

28

Before he'd started sleeping with Eve.

Ted understood what she meant. Essentially, he'd cost Sophia her only friend. Although he hadn't recognized that until tonight—hadn't even thought about it that way—she was right. Before Halloween, Eve had been all about helping Sophia. After he took Eve to bed, that changed. Eve hadn't been *unfriendly.* She hadn't even said anything bad about Sophia. But she'd stopped reaching out to her.

"Damn," he said with a sigh. As much as Eve and his other friends teased him for being ambitious and organized and having his shit together, he'd taken a wrong turn last month. The only thing he'd succeeded in doing was making life harder, for himself and both women. He still had to face his feelings for Sophia. The past four weeks with Eve had done nothing to change that.

And getting together with Eve hadn't been his only mistake. He remembered saying, when Skip's body washed up on the shores of Brazil, that Sophia would solve her problems by hooking up with another guy who had the money to bail her out of the mess she was in.

But he'd seen no evidence of that. She hadn't been out partying. She hadn't brought anyone home. She didn't have access to the internet in the guesthouse, so she wasn't cruising the dating sites.

He *liked* what he saw in her, despite her problems. She'd proven herself to be a loving mother. She did her best to earn what he paid her, even if it meant staying late. And she never took advantage of what he was willing to do for her. He was impressed whenever he found a receipt with $3.58 on the counter or some other odd amount that showed him how hard she was trying to be honest. Those were traits anyone should be able to admire.

Ted didn't tell her he and Eve had broken up, but Sophia soon figured it out. It was sort of obvious when Eve didn't come over for the next three weeks. It became even more obvious when he had Sophia and Alexa decorate his Christmas tree, do the Christmas shopping for his business contacts and eat dinner with him instead of carrying their meals out to the guesthouse.

Even if all of that hadn't given it away, she would've realized they were no longer seeing each other on the eighteenth, when she overheard him arguing with his mother. Mrs. Dixon must've told him he was making a big mistake letting Eve go because he responded with comments like, "I love her, too. Just not in that way." And, "It's my life. I have to trust my own judgment."

As conspicuous as Eve's sudden absence was, Sophia never mentioned it, and she told Alexa not to say anything, either. She thought that if he wanted to talk about his love life, he'd bring it up—but he didn't, so she focused on her job, taking care of her daughter, practicing her typing and handling as many errands as possible so Ted could finish his book.

He was working hard, spending long days at the computer, but he found time to drive her to an AA meeting every other night. He also helped her negotiate with a bankruptcy attorney, whom she put on retainer with the small amount she managed to save so far, which stopped Skip's creditors from hounding her. And because she hadn't been able to find a car, the weekend before Christmas he took her to Sacramento to shop for one. Alexa had been planning to come with them but she'd made friends with a whole new group of girls and stayed behind when she got the opportunity to go on a two-day snowmobile trip.

"How come you haven't asked me about Eve?" Ted wanted to know as they drove.

Sophia shifted in the confines of her seat belt. "I figured it wasn't my place."

"I see."

"Is she okay, though? With how things turned out?" She'd considered calling but was afraid Eve would misinterpret the gesture. Sophia didn't want her to think she was secretly celebrating—or had been rooting against her from the beginning.

Sophia did, however, feel a certain amount of relief....

"Eve's a great person," he said. "She'll be fine."

"And the rest of the gang? What do they have to say about it?"

"Fortunately, not too much. It's a bit...uncomfortable when we go to coffee. She's not really speaking to me yet, which is hard. But we're trying not to let what happened ruin our friendship or the chemistry of the group."

"Are you sure you won't regret breaking up with her? I mean...who wouldn't want a girlfriend like Eve?" As far as Sophia was concerned, Eve had it all—looks, personality and character.

"What makes you think *I* broke it off?"

She was territorial enough to have kept a close watch. But she couldn't admit that. "I saw the way she looked at you."

He glanced over at her. "I feel bad enough, okay?"

She pulled her own gaze back to the road before he could realize that she looked at him the same way. "Just being honest."

"It was a mistake to try to make more of our relationship. I shouldn't have started it to begin with."

If Eve couldn't win Ted's heart, who could? Certainly *she* had no chance, which was why she'd been careful to keep their conversations and interaction so impersonal the past few weeks. She couldn't afford to get her hopes up just because Eve was out of the picture. Who'd want the town pariah?

Her alcoholism would scare Ted away before he even had a chance to worry about the rest of her problems. How could someone who made so few mistakes ever sympathize with someone who made so many?

He turned down the volume on the radio. "Kyle said he gave you a call this week."

She pretended to be absorbed in the scenery flying past her window. "He did."

"And?"

"And what?"

"He said he invited you to his company Christmas

party last Thursday. He thought it might be nice for you to get out and enjoy yourself, enjoy the season."

"I couldn't go," she said. "Alexa had a math test the next day. I was helping her study."

"Is that the one she aced?"

The memory of that fat red A at the top of her daughter's paper brought Sophia a great deal of relief and pleasure. Alexa's schoolwork required a lot more effort than it used to, probably because neither one of them had any emotional reserves. But the effort was paying off. Her daughter was doing much better. If she kept it up, there'd be no danger of her flunking seventh grade. "That's the one."

Ted had been so pleased when she showed it to him that he'd insisted on taking them out for ice cream and posting her test on his fridge.

"Okay, that explains why you refused Kyle," he said. "What about Riley?"

"He told you he called me, too?"

"He mentioned it in passing." He turned to glance at her. "He also mentioned that you said you had to work. He thought I was being an ogre."

"He wanted to go to the Victorian Christmas Celebration tonight."

"And you didn't?"

"It's not that, it's just…it makes no sense to ask me to something so…public. Why would anyone want to be seen with me?"

"I'm sure he knew your situation before he asked, Sophia."

"He only understands part of my situation."

"What's that supposed to mean?"

"He doesn't know about my drinking problem. And

I don't want to tell him. I'd rather your friends think highly of me—well, as highly as they can, considering that most of my shortcomings are common knowledge."

"You're saying you're not going to date *anybody?*"

"Not in Whiskey Creek."

"Other alcoholics date and marry."

"I wouldn't risk letting someone fall in love with me if they didn't know, and what's the point of telling if I'll be leaving soon?" Even if she wasn't planning to leave, she wouldn't date the guys Ted hung out with. She found Riley more handsome than Kyle, but she knew there were women who'd claim the opposite. Handsome didn't matter. And it didn't matter that they were nice. A relationship with either one wouldn't end well, because she was in love with someone else. That was the mistake she'd made when she'd gone out with Skip— she'd gotten involved with a man who, in her mind and in her heart, couldn't compare to Ted.

She'd been trapped for nearly *fourteen years* thanks to that poor choice.

"All you do is hang around the house when you're off," he said. "You might want to get out and have some fun once in a while."

"It wouldn't be fair to waste their time or money." She'd been so engrossed in the conversation that she hadn't been paying attention to where they were going. When Ted had exited the freeway, she assumed he was heading to Fulton Avenue and all the car dealerships along that street. But this didn't look like…

Wait a minute! They were right by the hospital where her mother was institutionalized….

"Where are we going?" she asked.

At the alarm in her voice, he said, "It's okay. I

thought we could stop by and check on your mother, maybe drop off a little gift. And if you're feeling up to it, we can visit her for a few minutes. But only if you're feeling up to it."

Sophia's heart began to pound. It was difficult to come here, to see her mother in this setting. Elaine was so far from the woman she'd once been. To make matters worse, Sophia feared the same type of mental illness could overtake *her* and she'd be facing a similar future. The memories of how disjointed and upsetting their conversation on Thanksgiving had been made her anxiety that much more intense.

But when she looked at Ted, he said, "I'll be right there beside you," and somehow that gave her the courage to buy a poinsettia and some chocolates and carry them through those doors.

The visit with Sophia's mother proved every bit as painful as Ted had feared. While they were there, she had almost *no* lucid moments. She didn't seem to care that she had visitors, probably because she didn't recognize them. She rambled incessantly about all kinds of things, including her underwear, which embarrassed Sophia and filled Ted's mind with images he didn't want to see. She tried to eat the poinsettia and ignored the chocolates, despite the fact that she was obsessed with the vending machine, specifically the candy bars it held. Sophia kept giving her dollar bills so she could slide them into the "magic slot," as she called it. She ate four of the same kind of candy bar inside twenty minutes.

Before long, Ted was kicking himself for bringing Sophia to the hospital. When the idea first occurred to him, he'd been hoping for *one* special moment, one glimmer of reassurance or love from mother to daughter. He knew what it would mean to a woman who'd lost as much as Sophia. But now he thought they'd to have to leave without that—especially as Elaine's behavior became increasingly erratic and the nurses checked in every few minutes, as if they were concerned about where it might lead.

"She can become violent," one gently warned. "It doesn't happen often, but you should be prepared."

When Sophia had to use the restroom and left Ted alone with Elaine, he couldn't quit squirming in his seat. He'd assumed he could handle this, that his calm would help Sophia cope. But he was pretty sure he found Elaine's condition as upsetting as Sophia did. He tried to talk to her, to tell her what Skip had done and how badly her daughter needed some kind word, but she wasn't paying attention. She kept rocking back and forth and babbling nonsense. Then she got up, returned to the vending machine and started shaking it.

She seemed to forget he was even there, but he cleared his throat, reminding her, and she came back to the table.

"Money!" she demanded.

Ted didn't mind giving her a few bucks, but he worried about letting her eat so much candy at one time. He was afraid it would make her sick. What if she discovered that the chocolates they'd brought were just as delicious as the candy she was getting out of that machine? She'd eat the whole pound on top of what she'd already had.

"Tell you what," he said. "If, when Sophia comes back, you'll give her a hug and tell her you love her,

I'll leave enough money that you can buy a treat every day for a long time."

"Money!" she demanded, as if he hadn't just stated his terms.

"Did you hear me?" he said. "Will you do it? I know you can do it." He actually *didn't* know that, but he was hoping to encourage her. Of all the things he could give Sophia, for Christmas or otherwise, he thought this would mean the most.

Her dark eyes studied him as if he was a creature she'd never encountered before. "Who are you?"

"Ted Dixon."

"Are you here to kill me?" she asked.

"Definitely not."

"You look mean."

"Sorry about that."

"Why are you here?"

"I came with your daughter. We used to date. You don't remember?"

"I don't have a daughter," she said as if she was tired of hearing otherwise and didn't want one, regardless.

He had to wonder if she'd convinced herself that Sophia didn't exist because it eased the pain of those moments when she came back to "herself" and remembered everything she'd lost. Or if she really believed, consistently, that she was childless. Maybe it would be just as difficult for Sophia, possibly more difficult, if Elaine remembered and begged to be released from the facility. He winced when he considered how helpless he'd feel if it was *his* mother in here.

"You do," he insisted. "Her name is Sophia."

"I like that name," she said.

The door opened as Sophia returned, and he shoved

the See's Candies toward Elaine to distract her. He didn't want her to say anything else about not having a daughter—or that she liked Sophia's name as if she'd never heard it before. "Maybe you'd enjoy one of these."

She knocked the box aside—almost onto the floor—and cast a longing glance at the vending machine. That was when Ted decided it was time to give up. He'd done what he could. This was heartbreaking to watch; he couldn't imagine what it was doing to Sophia. He'd meant to help, but he was afraid he'd done the opposite. He hoped it wouldn't send her back into a tailspin.

"We'd better get going or we'll run out of time to find you a car," he told her.

He was planning to take her to an AA meeting before they went home, but when he put a hand at her back to propel her from the room, her mother stood up and said, "Don't go!"

The panic in her voice took them both by surprise.

"Mom?" Sophia's eyes were wide and wary.

Nervous as to how Elaine might answer, Ted caught and held his breath. He held on to Sophia, too.

"I love you," Elaine said, then she looked to him for approval. It wasn't a perfect rendition of what he'd requested. There'd been less emotion in "I love you" than there'd been in "Don't go," and no hug, but Ted guessed Sophia hadn't heard those three words from her mother in a long, long time.

"I love you, too," she whispered.

Fortunately, the moment Sophia choked up, Elaine seemed to understand that the correct reaction to tears would be tenderness. Her expression softened and a vague smile claimed her lips. It was just normal-looking enough to encourage Sophia to step forward and embrace her.

Elaine didn't do much to respond, but she didn't try to break Sophia's hold, either. She seemed confused.

Taking Sophia's hand, Ted led her out of the room, and he was glad he had. As they left, he could hear Elaine yelling for money, but Sophia was so overcome with what'd just happened that she didn't seem to put two and two together. He walked her to the car before saying he thought he'd dropped his keys and headed back.

Elaine was so upset, the nurses were having to restrain her, but the second he walked back in and held up the money he'd promised, she calmed down.

"Thank you," he told her and put the hundred in her hand. "See that she gets a candy bar of her choosing every day for as long as this lasts, okay? And let her get it out of the vending machine herself."

"It'll rot her teeth," one of the nurses said, but what else did she have to enjoy in life?

"She earned it," he said. "Merry Christmas, Elaine. You did a wonderful thing a second ago. I appreciate it."

"I love you," she shouted after him as if that might bring more money, and he had to chuckle.

29

Sophia didn't think she'd ever had a better afternoon. It was cold outside and rainy, but the car dealerships were decorated with garlands and ornaments and there was Christmas music playing every time they ducked in out of the wet. More than once they had a salesman bring them hot chocolate or hot cider. They weren't having much luck finding a car she could afford, but just being with Ted made Sophia happy. They talked and laughed as they explored various possibilities and, during quiet moments when Ted was in discussion with a salesman or hurrying across the lot to see if the car he'd spotted in the distance might be worth investigating, Sophia reflected on what it had been like to hug her mother after so long.

Good, she decided, a miracle for the brokenhearted. She wasn't sure she could maintain the confidence she was suddenly experiencing, but it was so wonderful to feel even remotely capable of becoming what she wanted to be that she couldn't stop smiling. Ted seemed to like that; at one point he caught her hand and pulled her close to him as if he'd kiss her. He didn't, but he stared down at her and said, "You are *so* beautiful."

A salesman interrupted before either of them could say anything else, but she tucked that memory away, too, to savor like the warmth of the sun finally hitting her face after a long, cold winter.

She was just going over it again, wondering what he might've said or done next, when he nudged her. "What do you think?"

They were looking at a 2002 Hyundai Elantra with 139,000 miles for $4,500. It was silver and not bad-looking on the outside, but the inside was pretty worn.

The reality of her impoverished circumstances really sank in as she got behind the wheel and smelled the mildew the air freshener couldn't quite conceal. Was the engine in any better shape?

She had no way to tell, and Ted wasn't much of a mechanic.

"I'm worried it might need repairs," she told him. "It has so many miles. But…maybe it would last a year or so."

The salesman reassured her it was in great shape, but Sophia knew better than to trust *him*.

"Should we go home and think about it?" she asked.

"I doubt you'll find anything better," Ted replied, and that convinced her to give it a shot. This was the best option they'd come across. But when they went in to the office to see if she could get financed, they received bad news. Despite the ad Sophia had heard claiming this dealership could help anyone, the manager told her she hadn't held a job long enough to compensate for her bad credit. Before they gave up, Ted had offered to lend her the money, but she'd refused. He'd done enough for her already.

"I'm sorry to have wasted your whole day," Sophia said as they left. It was now dark and the lots were closing. "You should've been at home, writing."

"I needed the time off." He slanted her a meaningful look. "Shall we catch an AA meeting before we head back? Now that you have a sponsor, she'll be expecting you."

Her sponsor's name was Madge. She'd texted Sophia earlier, to check in. "You're not too tired? You don't want to sit through yet another one of those, do you?" He'd already been to several. Sometimes he stayed in his car answering email on his phone. But there were times when he came in with her, too.

"They're important. And I'm willing."

"I've had such a good day. I'd rather not cap it off with that. But...I don't want to screw up, either. So I guess we should."

"Maybe since you're feeling strong, we could put it off until tomorrow and go over to the mall instead."

She hadn't done any Christmas shopping yet. Of course, she didn't have the money to do much, especially after putting that attorney on retainer. But she needed to buy Alexa a few things. "That would be fun. I'll text Madge to let her know," she added.

He took her hand once they reached the mall, and it felt like the most natural thing in the world. Sophia had no idea where their relationship was going; she was afraid to even consider that. So she told herself she wouldn't. She'd take this day as a gift and leave it at that.

They closed down the mall, too. Sophia bought several small gifts for Alexa. It had taken her forever to choose each one, since she was trying so hard to make her money last, but she was certain that what she'd bought would please her daughter.

Ted had left her to herself for a while after they ate at the food court and returned with a few packages of his own. But he hadn't told her what was in them, and she didn't ask. She'd done his business shopping, but he was taking care of the gifts for family and friends.

"Will you be going to your mother's for Christmas dinner this year?" she asked.

He was holding her hand again. She pretended it was no big deal—nothing more than what any employer would do with his housekeeper. But the warmth of his palm against hers, and the memories of what it had been like all those years ago, made her feel love-drunk.

"I don't know," he said.

"If you'd like to save her the trouble of cooking, I'll make a feast for both of you before Alexa and I go to the DeBussis'."

He gave her a skeptical look. "Are you *really* going to the DeBussis'?"

She pretended to be preoccupied with navigating the traffic to get to his car. "Probably." At any rate, she wanted to put him on notice that he didn't have to worry about her, that she didn't expect to figure into his plans. She wanted him to feel free to go and have a nice time.

"I'm not sure what my plans are yet," he said.

"Okay. Just let me know. I've clipped some recipes, in case."

When he smiled at her, she felt her heart leap into her throat. Something was happening, something as wonderful as it was terrifying—but she dared not examine it too closely for fear she'd find it was only wishful thinking.

As they drove home, they talked for at least half the journey. About Alexa and what she was getting for Christmas. About the score Sophia had achieved on her latest typing test—nearly 60 words per minute. About Royce and Alexa officially "talking." About his book and how he planned to save his protagonist from certain death at the end. They even talked about the possibility of using some of what Skip had done in a future book. But after a while, Sophia couldn't stay awake.

"This has been one of the best days of my life," she told him and let her eyes slide shut.

He laughed softly. "You didn't even get a car."

"That's okay," she said and drifted off.

Ted woke Sophia when they pulled into his garage. He would've preferred to sit and watch her sleep, but that was a little too stalkerlike. He'd certainly never had that compulsion with any other woman. "Hey, unless you want me to try to carry you up those stairs again, you'd better start moving on your own."

Opening her eyes, she offered him a sleepy smile— one he also found incredibly sexy. "Can you make it look easy this time?"

He brought a hand to his chest. "Of course, being so strong. It's just that I've got a lot of shopping bags tonight."

Her laughter sounded more carefree than it had since she'd come back into his life. "I'll help."

Once they were inside, he suggested they wrap their gifts so there'd be something under the tree when Alexa came home. He looked forward to surprising Sophia's daughter and to spreading some holiday cheer. But Sophia seemed to think it would be too presumptuous to use his tree.

"We don't need to crowd in on your Christmas," she said. "I can stack Alexa's presents on my dresser. I know that doesn't seem very traditional, but she understands this year will be different."

"It doesn't have to be *that* different. Not when I've got a perfectly good tree."

"You sure you don't mind sharing?"

That would put them together on Christmas morning. He understood why she was hesitating. But he couldn't believe she had other plans, and he wanted her with him at Christmas. Alexa, too. "Of course not. I got it for all of us to enjoy."

"Okay." She flashed him a smile before pulling out some wrapping essentials. "I bought some pretty paper and ribbon. You're welcome to use it."

She seemed to think that wrapping was important, but he didn't usually go to much effort. "I've got some paper from last year, don't I?"

"Oh, right." She rose to her feet. "It's in the front closet. I'll grab it since we may not have enough here."

He went to his office for tape and scissors and they spread out on the living room floor across from each other with the lights of the tree twinkling in the corner.

"What'd you buy today?" she asked as he began to empty out his bags.

He'd bought a pretty jewelry box for Alexa, but he didn't want to make a big deal of that. He left it in the sack and held up a brown suede Calvin Klein coat. "This, for my mother."

She examined it. "Nice. I bet she'll love it."

"I doubt it. She's impossible to please. But I keep trying. And I bought this." He pulled out a Giants cap for Noah. "I get him a new cap every year, and he gets me a pen. It's sort of a standing joke between us."

"I envy you your friends," she said.

Hearing that wistful note in her voice made Ted feel like a real ass about how he'd behaved over the past few years. "I'm sorry I wasn't friendlier about letting you join us for coffee," he said. "I had no idea just how bad it was at home, how a little…camaraderie might've helped."

"I don't blame you."

"Still. I wish I hadn't been so involved in what *I* was feeling."

"Stop. I was busy getting what I deserved," she said, doing her best to make a joke out of it. "Anyway, I shouldn't have been so forward. I knew no one really wanted me there. It was just…"

"What?"

She squeezed her eyes shut. "God, I missed you so much!"

When she looked up again, she seemed as surprised as he was that those words had come out of her mouth, and immediately started backpedaling. "But of course I was married and you'd moved on. And it'd been so long. I was stupid to think we could ever be friends." She caught herself again. "I mean…I hope we're friends *now.* But…I'm talking about before."

"You seem nervous," he said with a grin. "Did you, by chance, reveal too much?"

"Maybe." She scowled at him. "But it's not funny. I wanted your forgiveness, okay? Are you happy now you've forced me to admit that?"

"I'm feeling pretty good about it, yeah."

She rolled her eyes at the cocky tone he'd used. "Can't you cut me some slack? I'm in an awkward situation here, working for someone who's hated me for years."

He grew serious. "I'm not sure *hate*'s the right word."

"Then what is?" She started fiddling with the Band-Aids protecting her cuticles as if she wanted to get them off, and he moved close enough to stop her.

"Maybe it's time I was honest, too."

She pulled her hands away. "That's okay. I've had more honesty than I can handle for one year. I know what you thought of me."

"You might not know this." He clasped her chin and tilted up her face. "I didn't want you at coffee because…" When she stiffened as though bracing for a litany of her past sins, he slipped his hand around to the back of her head. "I was afraid I *would* forgive you."

Her big blue eyes, so unsure of whom to trust these days, were riveted on his. "Would that have been so terrible?"

She'd been drowning in misery. Coming to Black Gold on Fridays was her way of searching for a lifeline, and he hadn't thrown her one. But if he'd opened his heart at all…

"It would only have made me want you back," he said and lowered his head to kiss her for the first time in nearly fourteen years.

Sophia knew better than to let that kiss go anywhere. She was too fragile to withstand the ups and downs of getting involved on such an intimate level, especially with Ted. He meant too much to her. Maybe once she got back on her feet, and recovered her emotional strength, she could handle something this powerful, this overwhelming. But not now. She had no hope of maintaining the relationship. What did she have to offer?

Nothing. Her confidence had been beaten to an all-time low, and she had so much work ahead to put her life back together. It was inevitable that she'd lose him again. But there was nothing tentative about what took hold of them the second they touched, no way to deny the raw desire that welled up and imbued that kiss with an urgency she'd never experienced before. Within seconds, they were clinging to each other as if that was the only way to weather the storm of sensation ripping through both of them.

"*This* is what I'm supposed to feel," Ted breathed against her mouth.

She couldn't say anything. She wasn't even sure what he was talking about. Her thoughts were too jumbled. She had his hands on her body again at last, and they felt even better than she'd imagined through all the years with Skip. Ted's touch, the familiarity of his taste and smell, made her feel like a weary traveler *finally* returning home.

"I've been trying to wait," he said, pressing his forehead against hers with a groan. "I don't want to push you. I know you've been through hell and you're not out of it yet, but thinking of you out there in your bed alone has had me walking the floor at night."

She'd had the same problem. But that didn't change her situation. She was about to say that maybe his first instinct had been a good one, that maybe they *should* slow down and be cautious. She couldn't handle a breakup in her current state, and any disruptions in her life would adversely affect Lex. She had to protect her daughter, which meant she was better off avoiding any path that might be too rocky.

But he managed to release her bra at that moment and the thudding of her heart drowned out the voice of reason. "I can't hold back no matter what I think," she whispered.

"Thank God." He pulled off her sweater and the already unfastened bra, and tossed them aside.

The intensity of his expression and the single-minded purpose of his movements put goose bumps on Sophia's flesh. She couldn't believe it, but after all this time, Ted wasn't angry with her anymore. She'd never thought she'd see this day but here it was—the day he wanted her again.

Or maybe she was dreaming. She'd dreamed of this so often....

"I've missed you, Sophia," he murmured as his mouth moved down her neck. "I've wanted you for years."

"Because I'm beautiful?"

He'd said something about her beauty while they were at the dealership, but compliments didn't flatter her like they used to. She preferred to hear him say something about her personality. He didn't.

"You *are* beautiful," he said.

Perhaps there still wasn't much else to admire. She'd been trying for years to become a better person, but trying wasn't enough....

She couldn't think about her faults right now, however. She couldn't think of anything except Ted's hands curling around her bottom and drawing her up against his arousal.

When she moved those hands to her bare breasts, his breathing grew ragged, his kisses more demanding. She didn't expect him to pull back, but he did.

"Are you okay?" he asked, his voice as hoarse as it was imploring. "Is this okay?"

It wasn't okay. It left her as naked emotionally as she would soon be physically, and that terrified her. She was in love with him, had never stopped loving him. That was the reason she should say no. No one had the power to hurt her like he did. But it was the strength of those emotions that made "no" so hard.

"It's fine," she murmured and managed a smile, afraid he'd let her go and walk away and she'd never even have the memory.

"Look what you do to me," he said, holding out one hand.

He was shaking. That reassured her—to know she wasn't the only one who felt as if she'd just stepped off a cliff. Maybe this would be okay; maybe they were in it together.

Or maybe she'd bitterly regret it. Regardless, seeing the effect she had on him made her want to press the throttle to the floor—to push him to the very edge of control.

"I want you even more now than I did when we were younger," she told him, and it was true. Back then she'd taken it for granted that there'd always be another encounter, and another after that. But now…she'd had to go without his touch for so long that she knew what a gift these moments were.

"That never changed for me," he admitted.

There was a fierceness, a possessiveness, in Ted's lovemaking that created such excitement. The muscles of his back and shoulders bunched as he lifted her in his arms and placed her on the rug. She felt the heat of his gaze like a hot flame licking over her body as he stripped off the rest of her clothes.

"Should we go upstairs?" he asked, glancing at the tree as if he'd only now realized where they were.

Sophia couldn't help it. She thought of Eve coming out of his room the morning after Halloween and shook her head. She couldn't hold that relationship against him, not after what she'd done with Skip, but she wanted to be in a different place, her *own* place.

"No. Let's do it here," she said. "I like that the Christmas lights are on and our shopping bags and wrapping paper are scattered all around. This is the perfect ending to the best day I've had in years."

He looked concerned. "I'm afraid you'll be uncomfortable."

"I'll be far from uncomfortable," she said with a laugh. She had so many hormones flowing through her they could probably make love on a bed of nails and she wouldn't feel the pain. "But...do you have any birth control?" She'd stopped taking the pill when Skip died; there hadn't been any point.

"In my wallet."

"Good." She unfastened his pants and pulled them down over his hips. "You might want to find it," she said, her voice husky as her eyes lowered to what she'd revealed. It wasn't December 25 yet, but this was her Christmas gift to herself—and she was going to let herself enjoy every minute. Even if it turned out to be a mistake.

30

Making love to Sophia was every bit as fulfilling as Ted had expected it to be. He knew in his heart that he should've waited, given her more time before getting physical. Their relationship had been progressing nicely, especially today. He would've been wise to nurture that a little longer. But it had been getting harder and harder to keep his hands to himself, especially because, as much as he hated to admit it, she'd been the one he really wanted when he'd slept with Eve.

"Everything okay?" he murmured when she stirred. They'd been dozing on the floor, lying naked in each other's arms.

"Fine," she mumbled and snuggled closer.

"You're getting cold." He rubbed a hand along the smooth skin of her side. "Let's go up to bed."

He wasn't sure she'd agree to spend the rest of the night with him.

She never got the chance to say one way or the other, because the doorbell interrupted.

"Shit," he groaned. "Do you think we can pretend we're not home?"

She hid a yawn with one hand as she sat up. "I doubt it. You didn't put the garage door down when we drove in, did you? And the lights are on."

"Good point."

He didn't want to bother answering, wasn't happy that Sophia had pulled away and was starting to put on her clothes. This was an intrusion he wouldn't have welcomed no matter who was at the door. But then he heard his mother's voice calling to him, and realized she'd let herself in through the garage.

"Holy hell!" he snapped and jumped up.

Sophia went white as a sheet and began to scramble, too.

As he yanked on his jeans, he wondered if he should yell out for his mother to stay put. But that would give them away for sure. He thought they still might have time to dress, but he was just reaching for Sophia's sweater so he could help her get it on when his mother walked into the room. She was carrying a stack of presents—which she dropped when she saw him standing there bare-chested and barefoot. He hadn't even taken the time to put on his boxers or fasten his pants.

"You can't wait for me to answer the door?" he asked, thrusting Sophia behind him to shield her.

"I wouldn't expect to find my son having sex in the living room!" she retorted. "Especially when he doesn't even have a girlfriend."

"Can you please go out and give us a chance to dress?"

He didn't have to ask twice. No doubt she was as embarrassed as they were. Leaving the presents where they'd fallen, she pivoted abruptly and headed down to the kitchen.

He turned to Sophia. "It's okay. No big deal. You don't need to worry about this."

"I'm sorry," she said as if it was somehow her fault. "I should've known better. I *did* know better."

"Better than what?"

She was so upset she was shaking, which made it difficult for her to get her sweater on. He saw that it was on wrong side out and stopped her to change it around.

"Relax," he soothed. "This isn't the end of the world. She's the one who walked in. She shouldn't have done that."

"But it was my fault we were in the living room." She started toward the door leading out to the deck, but he grabbed her hand.

"Stay. Don't scurry off like we were doing something wrong."

"According to your mom, we *were* doing something wrong. She's not happy she found you naked with *me*. Eve can have sex with you because she's a good person, someone she'd deem worthy of being her daughter-in-law. But me? *Never.*"

She pulled away but he went after her. "Sophia, stop! We've got to go in there together, or she'll continue to treat you the way she's always treated you."

She cast a longing glance at the door. "Dealing with your mother is a no-win situation for me. She'll never believe I'm not the terrible person she thinks I am. How could I convince her, anyway? With the embarrassing scene she just witnessed? I can guarantee she's *not* impressed."

"Maybe she can't be convinced, but she'd damn well better respect my choices!"

"That's between you and her. It has nothing to do with me."

"It has everything to do with you," he insisted.

When she started to dig at her cuticles, he stopped her.

"Fine. I'll go in there if you want me to," she said. "But...don't get into a fight with her, okay? I don't want to feel responsible for that, don't want to ruin your Christmas."

Christmas was the last thing he was worried about.

"Whether or not we get into an argument will be up to her," he muttered and walked downstairs to the kitchen, gently tugging Sophia behind him.

The second they walked in, his mother glanced pointedly at their clasped hands, and Ted didn't have to look at Sophia to know that her color had returned—with a vengeance.

"Well, wasn't that a lovely surprise!" his mother said.

He shrugged off her sarcasm. "I'm not the one who walked into your house uninvited."

"I apologize. When you told me you weren't sleeping with your housekeeper, I made the mistake of believing you."

"Why didn't you wait until I answered the door?"

"I assumed you'd be writing. Last I heard, you had a deadline looming. I thought I'd slip a few gifts under the tree, since I'd gone to the trouble of hauling them over here."

The fact that she'd been bringing gifts reminded him how much she loved him and helped keep his temper in check. "Mom, I appreciate what you do for me, what you've always done. And when I said I wasn't sleeping with my housekeeper, I wasn't. But…things change. At least, they did tonight."

Her lip curled. "As I'm sure she's been hoping all along."

Sophia tried to release his hand, but he tightened his grip, stubbornly believing that he could achieve some sort of truce. "If she was hoping for that, all she had to do was come to my bed," he said.

"She would've been there long before now if she'd known that," his mother said. "My God, Ted. You're not some randy teenager anymore. Can't you see what's happening?"

"Whatever it is, it's none of your business."

"It's none of my business that she's using you?"

"You don't even know her, not anymore!"

Rayma came to her feet, and her voice rose an octave at the same time. "What's to know? Can't you be objective enough to see the truth? Of course she's going to cling to you, and put out for you and do whatever you want. How else will she survive? There isn't another person in this entire town who gives a damn about her!"

Shocked silence followed this outburst. Even his mother seemed to realize she'd gone too far. He opened his mouth to tell her just how out of line she was, but before he could say a word, Sophia interrupted.

"You're right," she said. "You've revealed my whole diabolical plot. I'm the worst person ever born, and I wanted to sleep with your son so I could manipulate him into…what? Giving me money? Is that what you're afraid of?"

He'd offered her a loan for that car just tonight and she'd refused. Although he wanted her to say that, she didn't. Maybe she feared that it would only make his mother angrier at him.

Rayma started to answer, but Sophia cut her off.

"It doesn't matter. I take full responsibility for what happened tonight, so there's no need to be mad at him. But before you panic, I'm not trying to twist his arm into marrying me. I won't be staying here long enough for that. My typing's improved. I'll have other options soon."

When she walked out, Ted let her go. He regretted dragging her in here to be lambasted by his mother. Damn it! He'd known how fragile she was, how much she'd endured, but this encounter hadn't turned out as he'd expected. For one thing, he'd thought it might do Sophia good to see that he felt enough loyalty to her to tell his mother that she needed to butt out.

Now he realized how stupid he'd been to put her through more of the same kind of bullshit she'd been contending with since her husband betrayed her....

The door leading to the deck slammed as Sophia left the house. "Happy now?" he murmured in the wake of her departure.

Taken aback that Sophia had given him up that easily, his mother blinked. "Is it true?" she asked.

"Is what true? She didn't seduce me, if that's what you're asking. She's lost so much and been put down by so many people that she has a problem with trust. It's a miracle she let me touch her." He waved Rayma off when she started to interrupt. "I've been watching for my opportunity to take her to bed, but it wasn't there until tonight."

His mother sank into a chair. "That's more than a mother wants to hear."

"What you saw is more than a son wants his mother to see, but here we are."

"We've never let anything come between us," she said, her tone conciliatory, as if she was beginning to understand that she was the one who'd be excluded from his life if she continued her behavior. "All these years, it's been you and me against the world."

"Then don't let that change!"

She frowned. "I have to do what I can. She's no good for you."

"Then let me learn the hard way. Is that too much to ask? If you're right, you'll be able to say 'I told you so' later."

"That won't heal your broken heart."

"If I lose her, my heart's going to be broken anyway."

"She said she's leaving."

"She's planning to. As soon as she gets a car and earns enough money, she wants to put this place in her rearview mirror, and I can't blame her—"

"*She* hasn't been perfect, Ted."

"And she knows that. But how much longer do you think she should suffer for the mistakes she made when she was a teenager? *Another* decade and a half? Would that be enough?"

"She was suffering when she had everything money could buy?"

"With the way Skip treated her? Yes!"

"That's hard to believe. She was so cold and remote, always acting better than everyone else."

"It was a defense mechanism, a way to cover for the fact that she was miserable and hanging on the best she could."

His mother folded her arms. "So you're hoping to convince her to stay."

"I am. And I'm hoping you'll accept her, for as long as she's part of my life."

"How can she be happy here? With the way so many people in town feel toward her."

"If she has me and you and my friends and Alexa, she won't need anyone else."

"There's a lot stacked against you."

"Mom, do you need to hear me say it? *I'm in love with her.*"

With a sigh, she propped her chin on her fist. "I guess I'd better add her to my gift list, then."

That broke the tension enough that he almost laughed. "Now you're talking." It wasn't exactly an apology, but coming from his mother it was darn close. He walked over to massage her shoulders. "Having someone else to care for can't be so bad, can it? Think of this—she comes with a ready-made granddaughter."

She perked up immediately. "That's true…."

"And before you ask, she's the sweetest thing ever."

"I know Alexa. She went to my elementary school."

"There you go."

"We didn't have much interaction, but she seemed like a nice girl. A pretty one, too."

He could tell she was sifting through all the possibilities. "She's both," he agreed.

"But…if Sophia doesn't have any money, Alexa can't be getting much for Christmas."

Ted purposely didn't mention that he intended to take care of that. His mother needed to be needed, and he was glad to let her focus on someone else for a change, someone who would enjoy the attention far more. "That's true. And there's not much time. Christmas is only four days away."

"I'll go back to the mall tomorrow," she said, suddenly energized as she collected her purse. "What kinds of things does she like?"

Chuckling, he dropped a kiss on her cheek. "You're leaving?"

"I know when I'm beat." She managed a wry smile. "Go after your girl."

"You're not going to apologize to her?"

"I'll have to work up to that," she said.

When headlights crested the hill behind her, Sophia ducked into the weeds at the side of the road, so whoever was driving wouldn't see her. It was cold out—windy and dark, too—but she needed to get off by herself so she could think. And since she hadn't been able to buy a car earlier, she had no choice except to walk.

Ted's mother passed her once. Ted passed her twice. She recognized the Lexus. He'd tried phoning her several times, too.

When his calls and texts came in, she'd stare down at her cell phone, think about what they'd shared in his living room tonight and wish her life was less complicated. But she wasn't ready to talk to him. His last text said he was worried about her, so she texted him back that she was fine. Then she shoved the phone in her pocket and kept trudging toward town.

When she spotted the Gas-N-Go, with its Christmas lights and plastic sleigh on the roof, complete with waving Santa, she thought of the liquor store only a block away, but she didn't turn in that direction. She circled wide to avoid even getting close and trudged up the hill to her old house.

It'd taken over an hour to walk this far, but the solitude helped her focus. She had to come to grips with all the sudden reversals in her life. During the past few weeks, she'd felt like a phoenix, rising out of the ashes. She'd begun to feel stronger, to feel some pride in her accomplishments and some hope for the future, which was why she was so afraid of what she'd done tonight. Getting involved with Ted might just destroy her again.

Once she reached the top, she kicked a pebble as she walked. Even from a distance, the house looked empty, soulless. She'd never particularly appreciated Skip's taste in architecture or furnishings. He'd insisted on overdoing everything, making it too big or lavish or ornate. She preferred design that was classic, understated. But seeing the state of the house made her sad all the same. Since she'd moved out, the yard had become overrun by weeds, several more windows had been broken and graffiti covered the porch.

"Look what you caused," she muttered to Skip. She was still angry with him, didn't know how long it would take to get over that. Maybe she never would. He'd stolen so much from her—fourteen years of her life, her sense of security, her self-esteem, even her front tooth.

But he was gone now. Their daughter was hers alone. And the future could be anything she had the courage to create.

So what did she want it to be? What risks was she willing to take?

Was Ted one of them?

She wanted him to be. Just looking at him made her happy. She couldn't imagine loving any man more than she loved him. But that meant putting her heart on the line and risking her daughter's heart, too. It also meant facing down the people of Whiskey Creek *and* his mother, easily the sternest school administrator she'd ever encountered. Could she do all of that while she was trying so hard just to survive?

Wouldn't she be crazy to make the attempt?

Restless, she wandered around the property. She didn't want to go inside. The utilities had been turned off, so she wouldn't be able to see anything, and she didn't know what she might find. The bank hadn't taken it back yet. That process took several months, leaving the house vulnerable while it sat empty. Some homeless person might've moved in. At least if she stayed outside, she could run if she needed to.

She meandered down the drive, kicking that pebble again, and opened the mailbox as she had so many times over the years. She hadn't really expected to find anything inside, but there was a stack of mail. The dates indicated that these letters had arrived after Skip's business had been "frozen" by the government and before she'd moved to Ted's. When they packed up, she hadn't even thought to check the box. All she got were bills anyway and she didn't have the money to pay them.

Sure enough. These were bills, too. And turn-off notices. There was a letter from the IRS that looked ominous. No telling what Skip had done with his income taxes. She didn't dare open it. Making a mental note to bring it to her bankruptcy attorney, she continued to sort through the envelopes. She was about to stuff all of it in her purse when she came across a letter that seemed different. According to the return address, it came from S. Hoover Fine Jewelry in Sacramento.

"What's this?"

She opened it and as she read, she felt her jaw sag.

Dear Mr. DeBussi,
Enclosed, please find the appraisal of your ring.
The diamond is nearly flawless, one of the most
perfect I've ever examined, especially for a stone
its size.
As you requested, I have been in touch with sev-
eral of my contacts and have found someone who
is interested in purchasing it. They are coming in
with an offer $30,000 below appraisal, but you
mentioned you were in a hurry and they have
cash.
Please let me know if you would like to pick up
the ring or proceed with the sale.
Sincerely,
Sam Hoover

Numb with shock, Sophia stumbled back to the porch and sank down on the step. Her wedding ring. Skip hadn't absconded with the money. She had no doubt he would have, given the opportunity, but this letter suggested he hadn't been able to liquidate it fast enough.

Had Sam Hoover, the man who'd signed this letter, seen the news and recognized Skip's name? Did he know about the probe? Had he contacted the FBI?

Or did he still have the ring—*and* the buyer?

31

Ted was relieved when he found Sophia. She looked like a lost little girl sitting on the front steps of her old home. The jagged edges of the broken windows winked in the moonlight, the yard was filled with weeds and frost-covered grass, and the word *Bitch* was spray-painted behind her. The picture she made spoke volumes about the destruction Skip had wrought.

It was tragic—but as far as Ted was concerned, Skip had done him a favor. If things had gone any differently, if Skip and Sophia had merely divorced, maybe he and Sophia wouldn't have discovered each other again. Sophia's desperate circumstances were what had brought her back into his life, stripped away her pretenses and erased his resentment. Now he liked her even more than when they'd dated in the past. There was a humility born of struggle about her. The excitement she showed over her improved typing speed, for instance, made him smile every time he thought of it—especially when he remembered how badly she'd bombed on her first test. She'd used her improvement on a keyboard to prove her value to his mother, which showed that she was taking real pride in it. He was proud of her for trying and for planning to continue her progress.

Simply put, he loved her. Probably too much. He was willing to dive back into the relationship despite what lay ahead. He just hoped he wasn't making his move too soon. Things were happening fast, but he didn't know how to slow them down. It didn't feel as if they were starting over; it felt as if they were picking up where they'd left off.

As he drove down the street, he saw her drop something in her purse. Then she got up and walked out to the car, as though she'd been waiting for him to pick her up.

"What was that?" he asked.

"What was what?" she replied.

"That paper you stuck in your purse. A notice posted by the bank?"

"No, just some mail that was left in the box. More bills, of course."

"Don't tell me you walked all the way over here to get the mail."

"No, I needed time to myself, needed to meditate on some things."

He slung his arm over the steering wheel and bent lower, so that it was easier to see her. "Before you meditate too much, I'm sorry about what happened at the house."

"It was your mother, not you."

"Still, I feel like I set you up."

"You did *sort of* set me up," she agreed, but she was smiling when she said it. He knew she was teasing.

"But I didn't mean to! That's the part you have to remember. Anyway, she's going to apologize."

"What'd you threaten her with?"

"Just the fact that I'll never speak to her again if she doesn't."

"You pulled out the big guns, huh?"

He shrugged. "I was willing to use whatever I had to. I wasn't going to lose that fight. Shall we drive over to her place now—drag her out of bed? Would that be sufficient revenge?"

"No way," she said. "We're not even going over there during the day. She doesn't need to apologize. That would be as agonizing for me as it would be for her."

"Then what else can she do to get back in your good graces? Because I'm insisting she do something."

"We can forget it ever happened."

"You're sure?"

"Positive."

"She'll be grateful for that option. By the way, it was nice of you to text and let me know you're okay. Most people who are really upset don't bother to do that."

"I didn't want to be rude."

There was more of that humility. He chuckled at her response. Even when she had the right to be angry, she was trying to be nice.

"What?" She'd been sincere in her response, hadn't expected him to laugh.

"Nothing," he said. "I'm just glad to find you here and not at the bar."

"I considered going to the liquor store."

"What made you decide not to do it?"

"I don't *ever* want to feel the way I felt about myself on Thanksgiving. Never again."

That strengthened his confidence in her ability to avoid alcohol in the future. "Good answer. I'm sure

Madge and your AA group would be proud. I know I am. But I'm also tired. And I'm dying to curl up in bed with you. Please tell me you're ready to come home."

"My bed or yours?"

"I'm not picky. You choose."

"Okay. Count me in."

After she got her seat belt buckled, he reached over to examine her hands. She'd been digging at her cuticles again.

"Are you ever going to stop this?" he asked.

She held them out as if she hadn't even looked at them in a while. "I didn't drink tonight. How much more do you want?"

"I plan to tell you as soon as we get back." The second he slipped his fingers through hers, the knot of tension in his stomach eased. He could buy some more Band-Aids to protect her cuticles; she was going to be okay.

This time Sophia was different when they made love. Ted couldn't explain exactly what was missing, but she seemed a bit…disengaged. Or maybe she was just tired. It had been a long night.

"You're not still upset about my mother, are you?" he asked in the quiet aftermath.

"What?"

He pressed his lips to her neck. "That run-in with my mother. You're not letting it bother you…."

"I'm embarrassed that she walked in on us, but I'm not dwelling on it. I knew she didn't like me."

He kissed her neck. "Do you have to be so frank?"

She laughed. "The truth is the truth."

"Well, I'm glad you're not the type to hold a grudge."

She rolled over to face him. "That's *your* department. And you can hold one for a really long time."

She was referring to what he'd felt about her before she'd started to work for him.

"What did you want me to do, carry you off in the middle of the night? You were another man's wife." He had to admit it had been hard to forgive her for marrying Skip. He'd wanted her every day for so many years.

"That would've been nice," she said, running her fingers through his hair. "We could've run away together. Except…you'd never want to leave Whiskey Creek."

He was drifting off to sleep, so he didn't answer until she prodded him.

"Am I right?"

"About what?"

"Would you ever be willing to leave this town?"

"It's home. And I just got my house the way I like it. So…I wouldn't be thrilled about leaving. I want you to stay here with me."

She didn't respond. She was probably falling asleep, too, so he was content to leave that discussion for another night. It would take her quite a while to save the money she needed, he told himself, so he had nothing to worry about.

Sophia borrowed Ted's car under the guise of going Christmas shopping while he finished his book. She promised she'd only be gone for the morning and would work late to make up for it, but he didn't seem to care one way or the other. He said she'd already worked plenty of extra hours, that it was Christmastime and she could take the whole day if she wanted.

She was grateful for his generosity, because if she'd

had to wait until quitting time to drive clear over to Sacramento, S. Hoover Fine Jewelry would likely be closed. And if she waited until tomorrow, Alexa would be home.

Just in case Mr. Hoover still had possession of her ring and could conceivably give it back—or finish the sale and provide her with the money—she took Skip's death certificate, as well as a copy of his will and her ID. Then she dressed up in a Versace dress with matching coat, Jimmy Choo pumps and a Gucci handbag. She wasn't the one who'd dropped off the ring, so she needed to look like a woman who might own such an expensive piece of jewelry. No doubt Mr. Hoover had to be extra careful about handing over something so valuable.

She put a picture of herself wearing the ring, taken the night Skip had given it to her, in her purse for good measure. Then she walked through the side yard instead of going through the house so Ted wouldn't see her and wonder why she'd gotten dressed up for a visit to the mall.

Her nerves were getting the best of her an hour and a half later when she pulled into the parking lot at the jeweler's. Two hundred thousand dollars was a lot of money. It would release her from the terrible panic she felt when she went over her finances. It would also enable her to get a car, cover the security deposit plus first and last month's rent on a nice condo somewhere. She and Alexa could move just about anywhere they wanted to go. She'd finally have the means to escape Whiskey Creek and would no longer have to face the people Skip had cheated, including Chief Stacy.

But it meant she'd have to leave Ted. That thought

made her sick—and yet how could she miss this opportunity? Nothing like it would ever come again.

And what if Ted's interest in her lasted only a few weeks, like it had with Eve? He could decide that she wasn't what he wanted, after all, especially with his mother trying so hard to pry them apart. So she'd be foolish to depend on him. This was her chance to leave the past behind and start over.

The bell jingled over the door as she walked in. The store was small and carried only high-end jewelry. She could tell that from a glance at the cases as she approached the saleswoman who'd looked up when she walked in and now asked if she needed any help.

"I'm Sophia DeBussi," she said. "I'm here to pick up my wedding ring."

The woman threaded her fingers together, showing off her lacquered nails and a gorgeous tennis bracelet and opal ring. "Do you have the claim check?"

"I'm afraid not. My husband dropped it off for an appraisal at least four months ago—" she lowered her voice as if this was painful to get out "—and then he passed away."

"I'm so sorry." If she recognized Sophia's name, she was too polite to let on.

Sophia managed a grateful smile. Anxiety tempted her to speak too fast, to push too hard, but she had to ease into this, act the part. "Thank you. Anyway, I didn't know where he'd sent my ring, so I thought I'd lost that, too. Imagine my surprise and excitement when I came across this letter in a pile of discarded mail." She showed the young woman what Mr. Hoover had sent her.

"Oh," she murmured after reading it. "We've been

wondering about this piece." So she *hadn't* recognized Sophia's name, but the letter had reminded her. "Just a moment."

Taking the letter with her, she went into the far corner where a man who seemed to be about sixty was working with a loupe. After she murmured in his ear, he lifted the loupe and looked over. Then he got out of his chair to come and speak with her.

"I'm Sam Hoover," he said. "And you are…"

"Sophia DeBussi."

"I'm sorry about your husband, Mrs. DeBussi. I remember hearing about what happened on the news. I'm sure it was tragic for you and your daughter, and it probably hasn't gotten any easier since."

"Truer words were never spoken."

"To be honest, I thought I might be hearing from the FBI. But…they haven't called. Maybe it's because this is your wedding ring."

Sophia was willing to bet they just hadn't known where to find it. How would they if *she* didn't?

"I'll admit I have no knowledge of how a probe works," he added.

"Neither do I, really," she said. "Except they froze all my credit cards and bank accounts and took every other asset my husband and I owned. It's been difficult to get by."

"I bet."

"Is my ring here?" she asked.

"Indeed."

She let her breath seep out. "Then I'd like to claim it."

"Of course. But…your husband wanted to sell it. I don't suppose you have any interest in that."

She cleared her throat. No doubt Mr. Hoover would

receive a handsome commission for brokering the deal, which was probably why he hadn't called the FBI. If he'd seen the news, it was odd that he'd sent a letter addressed to Skip. The one she'd received was dated two weeks after his death. But she didn't mention that. Perhaps he'd been hoping to reach *her*—as, in fact, he had.

"Actually, I *would* be interested," she said. "Like I told you, I'm in a very precarious situation."

"Desperate times call for desperate measures. I understand. I'll contact my buyer, let him know the deal's back on."

"Can you tell me how long that might take?"

"A day, two at the most, provided I can reach him during the holidays."

"So I might hear from you before Friday—Christmas Day?"

"It's possible."

"That would be wonderful since it would allow me to get a few gifts for my daughter."

"I'll call you as soon as I've received the funds, and you can come in and pick up a certified check. Meanwhile, you might want to open a bank account—" he lowered his voice "—in someone else's name, just so you don't send up any red flags."

In other words, he thought the FBI might still be watching her. And maybe they were. She hadn't heard from Agent Freeman since he'd left Whiskey Creek, but she didn't know any more about how a probe worked than Sam Hoover did.

"Right. I'll take that under advisement. Thank you," she said. But the thought of having to go to such lengths to hide the money troubled her. She'd come here feeling she deserved to get *something* for what she'd been through with Skip. She'd been a loyal wife—even if she was unhappy. She'd seen that letter as the universe's way of making life a little more fair. Nearly a quarter of a million dollars would give her safety, security, independence. All the things she'd lacked since Skip ran out on them; all the things she craved.

But setting up an account under a different name felt so...underhanded and sneaky, not all that different from what her late husband had done.

Did she really want to sink to his level?

Since Alexa was home that evening, Sophia didn't spend the night with Ted. The three of them had dinner together, and Alexa admired the presents Sophia had wrapped and arranged under the tree. But at bedtime, they said goodnight and went their separate ways, like they had in the past. Then Sophia spent the next two hours with her daughter in the guesthouse, talking about all the fun Alexa'd had on the snowmobile trip, what she hoped was in those Christmas presents and what she might get for Royce. Alexa fell asleep around eleven and Sophia had been lying awake ever since— for an additional two hours—staring at the window that looked out on Ted's house.

She missed him, wanted to feel his warm body beside her. Now that she knew their time was so limited, she hated the thought of wasting it and that left her too unsettled to sleep.

She considered calling Madge, her sponsor, a matronly and sympathetic woman. But she wasn't particularly tempted by liquor. She just needed a distraction. Otherwise, she might give in and text or call Ted, who was proving to be a far more powerful addiction. Part of her insisted it wouldn't hurt anything. The other part didn't want him to know she couldn't get through a single night without craving his touch. It made her fear that even if she took the money and ran, she'd never be happy without him.

"Go to sleep!" she ordered herself. But after another hour, she broke down and texted him.

I want you, she wrote.

His answer popped up almost immediately. Thought you'd never ask.

Relieved that he seemed be having just as much difficulty as she was, she smiled.

Is it safe to leave Alexa here alone?

If you lock up, she should be fine. I've never had any trouble out here. I'd come to you, but it might be awkward if she gets up during the night.

He was right; it had been humiliating when his mother walked in on them. I'll be there in a minute.

He met her on the deck wearing nothing but a pair of jeans. "I thought I'd have to go all night without seeing you," he said as he drew her into his arms.

"I was on my way in. You didn't have to brave the cold."

"I came to make sure you didn't change your mind."

She chuckled. "You have to be freezing!"

"I'm feeling pretty warm, if you want the truth. Somehow I always feel warm when I'm with you."

Slipping her arms around his neck, she hugged him as tightly as she'd always wanted to. "God, I love you," she whispered.

He pulled back to look into her face.

"Did I really say that out loud?" she said with a laugh.

"You did."

"Well, so much for pretending you don't really mean that much to me."

His teeth flashed as he smiled. "I just want to know one thing."

"What's that?"

"Since when?"

Sophia could feel her pulse all the way to her fingertips. But what did she have to lose? This was potentially goodbye. "Since forever," she admitted.

He ran a finger down the side of one cheek and over her lips before bending his head to give her the softest, sweetest kiss. "Good. One down, one to go."

She felt like she was floating on air when she opened her eyes to look up at him. "One to go?"

"Now I just need to convince Alexa," he said with a wink and led her into his house.

32

An hour later, Sophia knew what she had to do, but she was terrified to follow through with it, especially since she had a child depending on her. Alexa figured into every attempt she made to justify keeping the money. For one thing, Sophia would lose her job if she and Ted broke up, and that could happen well before she was capable of getting anything else.

But even then her conscience wouldn't allow her to do what Chief Stacy had feared and suspected she might. She was *finally* in the driver's seat of her own life, no longer had to kowtow to Skip's wishes and demands. She had the opportunity to build her future on the basis of her own talent and ambition, not other people's money, and she wanted to do that.

She shifted in the bed so she could see Ted's sleeping face. To be honest, she couldn't bear the thought of leaving him, not for any amount of money. This time around she was going to hold out for love—and trust in his love—so that maybe they could spend the rest of their lives together. If that meant she had to take on everyone in Whiskey Creek whenever she left the house, so be it. She would stand her ground and fight.

"Why are you so restless tonight?" Ted asked sleepily.

"I have a lot on my mind."

"You're not thinking about my wine cellar...."

She laughed. "No."

"Your mother or my mother?"

"No. And I'm not thinking about Skip, either, since we're going down the list. Except to be glad he's gone."

"Then these are happy thoughts that are keeping you up?"

"How can a girl be anything but happy after what you just did to me?" she teased.

His hand curved around her breast. "There's more where that came from."

She rose up on one elbow. "If you broke up with me, would you fire me?"

"So you *are* worrying," he said, amusement in his voice. "Let me see your fingers."

"I haven't been digging at them. I'm not worrying, exactly. Just planning. I've decided that when I save up enough money, I want to go to college."

He pecked her lips. "I like that idea much better than hearing you talk about moving away from me."

"Do you think I could get in?"

"You could start at a community college. If you do well there, you could probably get into a university. What would you like to major in?"

"Business. I want to own a dessert shop someday. I'm good at desserts, don't you think?"

"I think you're good at lots of things."

"Like..."

"Like screaming my name when I make you come. And I love it because then I get to feel like a big stud."

"Stop! I'm being serious."

"Fine." He pecked her lips. "You could be anything.

And that's the truth. But whatever you choose, I hope it includes having my baby."

She squinted through the darkness. "Isn't that a pretty big leap of faith? We just got back together."

"We won't do it until you have a year of sobriety under your belt, to make absolutely sure that you're on stable ground. But…we're not like your average couple. It's been fifteen years or more since I wanted to marry you the first time. I think I've waited long enough."

"I hate to tarnish the excitement, but…what about your mother?"

"She'll come around."

"She's going to be mad."

"Not if grandchildren are involved and, fortunately for us, we already have one of those to give her."

"She'd better be a lot nicer to Lex than she is to me," she muttered.

"I'll make sure of it. I promise."

She rested her chin on his chest and toyed with his nipple. "And I want one more thing."

"You name it."

"I want to sign a prenup."

"What?"

"You heard me. Then no one can accuse me of marrying you for your money. I'll make my own money. With my dessert shop."

His fingers ran up and down her side. "In the end, you'll probably be richer than me."

"Then maybe *you* should sign a prenup, too."

"I'll sign whatever you want me to, as long as you're finally mine." He kissed her. Then he got up and started to put on his clothes.

"What are you doing?"

"I'm getting ready to walk you back to the guesthouse. I don't want to leave Lex alone for more than a couple of hours, just in case."

She considered asking him if he could love her daughter like his own. That was important to her. But she didn't even need to ask. She knew him well enough to trust that he would. They'd been more or less living together for two months; she'd seen how he treated Lex. "Before we go, there's something I need to tell you," she said.

He put his leg down instead of pulling on his jeans. "Is it bad news?"

She heard the caution in his voice. "Depends on your perspective."

"You definitely have my attention."

"Remember when you said I should tell you if I stumble across a pot of gold lying around the house so you can spread the word?"

"Yes...."

"Well, I haven't found a pot of gold *exactly*, but...I have come across $200,000."

"Holy shit, Sophia!" He returned to the bed. "Where did you find *that* kind of money?"

"Remember when I went to the house last night?"

"Of course."

She told him about the letter and her trip to the jeweler.

"This could've been your ticket out of town," he said.

"I realize that."

He studied his feet for a few seconds before raising his head. "Why didn't you take it?"

"Because you're worth a lot more than money."

He didn't speak for a moment. Then he said, "Even when you've lost practically everything?"

She was nervous about letting go of the security the

money could've provided; she had to admit that. But she knew she was doing the right thing. "Even then."

He sat down beside her and took her hand. "*Are* you going to turn it over to Chief Stacy?"

She wrinkled her nose. "I don't think I can bring myself to do that. But I *am* willing to call Agent Freeman."

"Giving up that much money after…after what you've been through. That's hard, babe."

She put her head on his shoulder. "I can make it on my own."

He slid an arm around her and kissed her temple. "You won't have to."

Straightening so she could look him in the eye, she said, "But I want to. I need to. For me."

Agent Freeman wasn't in. Sophia had to leave a message. Then she and Alexa started baking for Christmas. Alexa wanted to decorate sugar cookies for Royce, and Sophia wanted to try a new fudge recipe.

The call she'd been waiting for came when she was covered in flour, but she left Alexa to finish rolling out the dough—she figured it would be good practice for her, anyway—and washed her hands.

By the time she was able to answer, she was afraid she'd missed Agent Freeman, but that wasn't the case. As soon as she managed to slide the bar that answered her phone, she heard his distinctive, deep voice respond to her hello.

"Mrs. DeBussi?"

She didn't want Alexa to hear what she was about to say, so she carried her phone outside. "Thanks for calling me back," she said as she closed the door behind her.

"What can I do for you?" he asked.

He was all business again. Sophia smiled at that. He

came off as a hard-ass, but she knew he was more tenderhearted than he let on. "I have some exciting news for you and for Skip's investors."

"You do?"

She could hear the surprise in his voice. "Yes. Are you ready?"

"I'm ready." His tone suggested he wasn't used to having anyone act coy with him.

"I found my wedding ring."

There was a slight pause. "And you're calling me because…"

"It's worth $200,000, remember? Get this, Skip was trying to liquidate it but, for whatever reason, that didn't happen before our trip. Last night I came across a letter from a jeweler who has it. He even has a buyer lined up."

Silence.

"Aren't you excited?" she said.

"Mrs. DeBussi, I'm impressed that you made this call."

Sophia wasn't sure she'd ever felt so good inside. "Thanks."

"And that's exactly why I'm going to pretend I never received it."

"What?"

"You heard me. I told you, if you weren't in on the fraud you were the biggest victim of all, and I still feel that way. I know you've had one hell of a time. Now maybe you'll be able to get by and care for your daughter. That's more important than spreading that money out among hundreds of people so it really does no one any good."

"You didn't seem to feel I deserved anything before."

"I was doing my job. But as far as I'm concerned, this case is closed. Merry Christmas," he said and hung up.

Ted stepped out of the kitchen before she could fully absorb what had just happened. He'd joined her and Lex several times already. He said it was impossible to concentrate on his book when he'd rather be with them. "Was that the FBI agent—what's his name, Freeman?"

"It was."

"What'd he say?"

"He said the money's mine."

"No...."

"I swear. He said he was going to forget I ever even made the call."

"Wow." He stood behind her and slid his arms around her waist in an effort to warm her. Neither of them had bothered to put on a coat. "I'm sort of bummed about that," he said.

"Why?"

"I like you better when you're poor. Then I know you won't be going anywhere," he joked.

She glanced beyond him to see Alexa watching them through the window. When Sophia caught her eye, she blushed and ducked her head, but not before the sweetest smile Sophia had ever seen appeared on her face.

"I think my daughter's figuring out that her mother has a boyfriend."

Ted twisted around as Alexa looked up again, and her smile stretched from ear to ear. "Good," he said. "Because I was planning to wait a few months before asking you to marry me, but that's beginning to feel like a really long time."

She let him turn her in his arms so they were facing each other. "We have to wait until spring," she said. "We can make it that long, can't we?"

"Why?"

"Because I want to type 80 words per minute by the time I get married."

He started to laugh. "Seriously?"

"Stop! Yes. I have goals!"

"But now that you're rich all on your own, neither one of us will have to sign a prenup." He bent his head and whispered in her ear, "And if we get married right away, we won't have to keep sleeping in separate beds."

"Ah, now I see what you're *really* after."

"What can I say?" He nuzzled her neck. "Just looking at you drives me crazy."

It felt so good to be loved and admired the way Ted loved and admired her. It was completely different from what she'd experienced with Skip. Ted didn't hold her down; he buoyed her up. "There's just one problem."

"What's that?"

"I'm not keeping the money."

He straightened. "What will you do with it?"

"I'm not sure." She rose on tiptoe to rub her cold nose against his. "But I have some ideas."

"So you'll be broke again? I was joking when I said I'd rather you be poor." He was joking *now;* he didn't seem to care about her financial situation.

"Yes, but don't worry, I'll still be good in bed."

"At least you know what's important," he said and drew her inside, where it was warm.

The money from the ring came in on Thursday. Even though it was Christmas Eve, Sophia spent the afternoon going down the list she'd asked Kelly to send, making out checks. After that, she was so excited it was hard to get through dinner. Since she wasn't handing the money over to the FBI, she'd decided to tell Alexa about the situation. She thought her daughter should know why she was doing what she was doing, and she had been surprised by how well Lex had taken the news. She hadn't complained, hadn't asked if they could keep some or all of it; she agreed with what Sophia had planned and was eager to participate.

Fortunately, Ted was on board, as well. He'd finished his book, so he was in a great mood and ready to take some time off for the holidays.

"You all set?" he asked when he walked into the living room to see her putting on her coat. "We'll be intruding on everyone's holiday, so we don't want to show up too late."

She gestured at the Christmas cards stacked on the coffee table. "Considering what's inside those, I think people will want to see us, no matter what time we come, but I'm ready." She removed a scarf from her pocket, and tied it around her neck. They weren't having a white Christmas this year—but it was cold, and she'd be getting in and out of the car for the next two hours.

Grabbing the ends of her scarf, he pulled her to him. "You're such an inspiration. You know that?"

"It's nice to hear I have *one* convert." She smiled as she remembered him telling her how beautiful she was, and how much she'd wanted him to say something more meaningful.

"I can't help it if I'm smarter than everyone else."

Alexa came hurrying in. "Okay, my cookies are in the car and I told Royce we'd drop them by."

Sophia gathered up the stack of cards. Two hundred thousand dollars wasn't nearly enough to be able to return everyone's money, so she'd been forced to limit her payments to investors who lived in Whiskey Creek. Even then, she'd had to lay down some rules. Those who hadn't taken anything from the house received twenty percent of what they'd lost. That meant Kyle would get $20,000, Noah would get $10,000, and ten other investors would each get $5,000. Those who'd come to the house and removed furniture and other goods would get five or ten percent, depending on the value of what they took—Reverend Flores, Eric Groscost, and eight others. Chief Stacy wouldn't get a dime.

At first, Sophia hadn't wanted to give anything to his girlfriend, either. She was afraid he'd benefit. But then she realized it wasn't fair to hold Pam Swank responsible for her partner's actions—that was exactly what had happened to her with Skip. So Pam was getting $15,000, which was half the remaining balance. The DeBussis would get the other half. That hadn't been an easy decision, either, but they were Alexa's grandparents.

"We're not driving over to Jackson to deliver Pam Swank's, are we?" Ted asked when he saw her name on the top card.

"No, I'll mail that one." She knew they might run out of time and would mail quite a few others, as well. Skip had had a lot of investors, even here in Whiskey Creek. But she wanted to hand-deliver as many as possible. It would be worth the effort to see the shock and excitement on the recipients' faces. She was pretty sure she'd never feel more like Santa Claus.

Which reminded her...

"Don't forget that Santa hat you wanted to wear," she told Alexa, who ran to retrieve it from the kitchen.

"Shall we start with Noah?" she asked, thumbing through the cards while they waited.

Ted nodded. "That'll be fun," he said, and he was right. Noah and Adelaide were so surprised and grateful. Everyone else was, too. By the end of the night, Sophia knew that no Christmas would *ever* be as memorable as this one.

It was noon on Christmas Day, and the next few minutes were going to be awkward. Ted wasn't looking forward to seeing Eve. Not after having such an incredible Christmas Eve and Christmas morning with Sophia and Alexa. Sophia had given him a digital scrapbook she'd created on the computer containing all the old photographs she'd saved from when they'd dated as teenagers; he'd given her the promise ring she'd returned when she married Skip. Their gifts hadn't been expensive, but they'd been thoughtful and sentimental. He hadn't wanted to give her so much that she couldn't feel proud of her own gifts and, although he'd gotten her a few other things, he felt he'd managed that. They'd both spent most of their money on Alexa, who'd had a wonderful Christmas.

Ted hated to ruin an otherwise perfect day. But taking a homemade pie to Eve was so important to Sophia that he couldn't say no. Besides, she was right. Now was the time to reach out to Eve, before she could build up too much resentment. He'd tried to wait a respectable amount of time after breaking up with her to start a relationship with Sophia, but…the laws of attraction had been working against him.

Eve took a while to answer the door. When she did, and saw them standing on her stoop, he could tell that she wasn't too pleased, despite their peace offering. Her eyes shifted from Sophia to him and back again. Fortunately, Alexa wasn't with them. They'd dropped her off at the DeBussis so she could spend a few hours with her grandparents.

"I'm afraid you caught me at a bad time," she said. "I was about to head over to my parents'."

Sophia spoke before he could. "We won't hold you up. We just...we wanted to bring you this. And mostly we wanted to say that...of all the people we know, you're one of our favorites. We both feel that way."

Eve smiled politely and took the pie. "Thank you. I hope you have a merry Christmas."

She started to go in and shut the door, but Sophia wasn't satisfied. "Eve?"

Eve turned, eyebrows raised. "Yes?"

"We don't want to lose your friendship. It's a lot to ask that you forgive and forget, but...we—*I*—admire you so much."

Ted sensed that Eve wanted to say something trite just to get rid of them but the naked emotion in Sophia's voice, the absolute honesty, wouldn't allow it. She hesitated, glanced at him again, and then tears filled her eyes.

"Can't I be mad for a few weeks at least?" she asked with a watery laugh.

"As long as it doesn't last any longer than that," Sophia said. "Because I'm sorry if you've been hurt or disappointed or embarrassed. I don't know what I would've done if you hadn't dragged me out of bed that night you came home with Alexa. You—your support at that critical moment—saved my life. So, believe me, if I could've stopped loving Ted, I would have. I tried. But I've been trying for fourteen years and it never works."

"What happened was my fault," Ted said. "Not hers. When you and I were together, she was so careful to stay out of the way. I'm the only one you should be mad at." He offered her a sheepish grin. "But I'm sorry, too."

Eve put the pie on a side table so she could wipe her

cheeks. "We'll get past it," she promised, and this time her smile seemed genuine. "I know you two are meant to be together. There's no need to feel bad about that."

Sophia pulled her into an embrace. "I'm happy you feel that way. I would love for you to be a bigger part of my life."

"I'd like that, too," she said.

Ted hugged her next. "I'm sorry," he whispered again and felt her squeeze him a little harder in return.

Sophia was tired but happy when they left Eve's. She wanted an afternoon nap with Ted before they were supposed to pick up Alexa and go to Ted's mother's. Although Principal Dixon had been unusually pleasant when she called to invite them to dinner—she had invited Sophia and Alexa personally—Sophia was still a little nervous about spending the evening with her. It'd been hard enough to handle the chill when she and Ted dropped Alexa off at Skip's parents' house. They wanted to make it clear, despite the $15,000, that they didn't approve of how quickly she was moving on.

Sophia didn't care what they thought. But she did care about winning over Ted's mother. For his sake, that was important.

"Damn it," Ted suddenly muttered.

Surprised that he could be upset at anything today, Sophia twisted around to see what he was looking at in the rearview mirror. Chief Stacy was behind them in his cruiser—and he had his lights on.

"Were you speeding?" she asked nervously.

"Nope."

"Then what do you think he wants?"

"To give us a hard time. What else?"

The police chief approached the car wearing his uniform and carrying his pad, as if he planned to write them a ticket.

Ted was busy with his phone until Stacy got close, but then he rolled down his window. "I do something wrong, Chief?"

Stacy didn't answer. He leaned down and looked in at her. "Guess you came across some money after all, eh?"

She kept her hands clasped in her lap. She wasn't nearly as frightened of him when Ted was with her, but she didn't want to force Ted to come to her rescue, either. "I did."

He hooked his thumbs in his belt. "I'm hearing about everybody getting a payment. It's the talk of the town. 'Isn't that Sophia DeBussi wonderful?'" He gave her a hard stare. "So where's *my* money?"

"Your girlfriend will be receiving $15,000 very shortly. That should make you happy."

"Hardly. We're not seeing each other anymore," he said. "So you'd better just split that payment in two."

Ted jumped in. "Sorry, Chief. That's not going to happen. You got your money's worth when you walked away with her jewelry. And if you push this, half this town will be up in arms against you. I think it's fair to say that Sophia's popularity has returned. Now…is there a reason you stopped me?"

When he straightened, Sophia could no longer see his face, but she could hear the taunt in his voice. "The fact remains that she's going to want to play fair with me."

"Or what?"

"Or I'll make her life pretty damn miserable if she doesn't. And she knows I can do that."

Ted shook his head. "Come on, Chief. This is Christmas. You don't really want to start trouble today."

"It's my job to look out for public safety no matter

what day it is, *Mr.* Dixon. And I do believe you were driving way too fast as you sailed through town."

"Bullshit. You know I wasn't speeding."

"Who's to say otherwise?" he said. "Driver's license and registration, please."

Ted didn't bother reaching for the glove box. "Are you sure you're committed to this? Because if you write me a ticket, I'm just going to take it over to Mayor Rackham and file another complaint."

Chief Stacy spat on the road. "I heard you'd been down to city hall."

"It's true. Levi, Dylan and Aaron have been there, too. We're not making a secret of it. We're tired of seeing you abuse your power. And I don't mind telling you that Mayor Rackham isn't too pleased, either. The complaints are stacking up. Apparently, your ex-wife knows quite a bit about how you operate and has shared that information. She claims you've been harassing her since the divorce. So…you might want to consider yourself lucky that you've gotten away with your behavior so far and get back in your cruiser. Otherwise, you could lose your job."

Sophia felt the desire to dig at her cuticles but curled her fingernails into her palms instead. She hadn't realized Ted had taken action against Stacy, even though he'd once said he was going to.

Stacy sneered as if he wasn't scared at all. "Don't get carried away. You're not half as tough as you pretend to be. There's nothing you can do to me."

"I won't have to do anything. You've made enough enemies over the years to sink yourself."

Suddenly, Stacy's tone changed. "Let me tell you something, you little smartass prick. You go after my job, and you'll never know peace in this town again."

"That sounds like a threat to me, Chief," Ted said.

"That's a promise." Shoving his ticket book in his pocket, he strode back to his car.

"He's crazy," Sophia murmured. "Let's get out of here."

But Ted wasn't ready to go. He waved at Chief Stacy as if their exchange had been pleasant. "Thank you, sir. Merry Christmas!"

Obviously unhappy that he hadn't made more of an impact, Stacy pulled his cruiser up alongside the Lexus and glared in at them before punching the gas pedal and spraying gravel against Ted's door.

"He scares me," Sophia said.

Ted stared after him. "Don't worry. He won't be around much longer."

"How do you know?"

He held up his cell phone to show her that he'd recorded the whole encounter, then immediately sent the file to Mayor Rackham, Dylan, Aaron and Levi.

It was another two months before the city took action but by March, Whiskey Creek had a new chief of police.

Ted took Sophia out to celebrate when he heard the news—and that was when he proposed.

* * * * *

#1 *New York Times* Bestselling Author
SUSAN WIGGS

Single father Logan O'Donnell is determined to create the perfect Christmas for his son, Charlie. The entire O'Donnell clan arrives to spend the holidays in Avalon, a postcard-pretty town on the shores of Willow Lake.

One of the guests is a newcomer—Darcy Fitzgerald. Sharp-witted, independent and intent on guarding her heart, she's the last person Logan can see himself falling for. And Darcy is convinced that a relationship is the last thing she needs this Christmas.

Yet between the snowy silence of the winter woods and the toasty moments by a crackling fire, their two lonely hearts collide. The magic of the season brings them each a gift neither ever expected—a love to last a lifetime.

Available wherever books are sold.

HARLEQUIN®

super romance

More Story...More Romance

Save $1.00 on the purchase of

A TEXAS CHILD

by **Linda Warren**,

available December 3, 2013,
or on any other
Harlequin® Superromance® book.

Available wherever books are sold, including most bookstores,
supermarkets, drugstores and discount stores.

Save
$1.00

on the purchase of
A TEXAS CHILD by Linda Warren,
available December 3, 2013,
or on any other Harlequin® Superromance® book.

Coupon valid until March 4, 2014. Redeemable at participating retail outlets
in the U.S. and Canada only. Limit one coupon per customer.

Canadian Retailers: Harlequin Enterprises Limited will pay the face value of this coupon plus 10.25¢ if submitted by customer for this product only. Any other use constitutes fraud. Coupon is nonassignable. Void if taxed, prohibited or restricted by law. Consumer must pay any government taxes. Void if copied. Nielsen Clearing House ("NCH") customers submit coupons and proof of sales to Harlequin Enterprises Limited, P.O. Box 3000, Saint John, NB E2L 4L3, Canada. Non-NCH retailer—for reimbursement submit coupons and proof of sales directly to Harlequin Enterprises Limited, Retail Marketing Department, 225 Duncan Mill Rd., Don Mills, ON M3B 3K9, Canada.

U.S. Retailers: Harlequin Enterprises Limited will pay the face value of this coupon plus 8¢ if submitted by customer for this product only. Any other use constitutes fraud. Coupon is nonassignable. Void if taxed, prohibited or restricted by law. Consumer must pay any government taxes. Void if copied. For reimbursement submit coupons and proof of sales directly to Harlequin Enterprises Limited, P.O. Box 880478, El Paso, TX 88588-0478, U.S.A. Cash value 1/100 cents.

® and TM are trademarks owned and used by the trademark owner and/or its licensee.
© 2013 Harlequin Enterprises Limited

HSR1113COUP

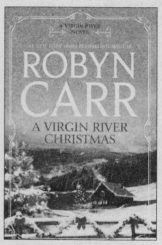

REQUEST YOUR
FREE BOOKS!

2 FREE NOVELS
FROM THE ROMANCE COLLECTION
PLUS 2 FREE GIFTS!

YES! Please send me 2 FREE novels from the Romance Collection and my 2 FREE gifts (gifts are worth about $10). After receiving them, if I don't wish to receive any more books, I can return the shipping statement marked "cancel." If I don't cancel, I will receive 4 brand-new novels every month and be billed just $6.24 per book in the U.S. or $6.74 per book in Canada. That's a savings of at least 22% off the cover price. It's quite a bargain! Shipping and handling is just 50¢ per book in the U.S. and 75¢ per book in Canada.* I understand that accepting the 2 free books and gifts places me under no obligation to buy anything. I can always return a shipment and cancel at any time. Even if I never buy another book, the two free books and gifts are mine to keep forever.

194/394 MDN F4XY

Name _____ (PLEASE PRINT) _____

Address _____ Apt. # _____

City _____ State/Prov. _____ Zip/Postal Code _____

Signature (if under 18, a parent or guardian must sign) _____

Mail to the **Harlequin® Reader Service:**
IN U.S.A.: P.O. Box 1867, Buffalo, NY 14240-1867
IN CANADA: P.O. Box 609, Fort Erie, Ontario L2A 5X3

Want to try two free books from another line?
Call 1-800-873-8635 or visit www.ReaderService.com.

* Terms and prices subject to change without notice. Prices do not include applicable taxes. Sales tax applicable in N.Y. Canadian residents will be charged applicable taxes. Offer not valid in Quebec. This offer is limited to one order per household. Not valid for current subscribers to the Romance Collection or the Romance/Suspense Collection. All orders subject to credit approval. Credit or debit balances in a customer's account(s) may be offset by any other outstanding balance owed by or to the customer. Please allow 4 to 6 weeks for delivery. Offer available while quantities last.

Your Privacy—The Harlequin® Reader Service is committed to protecting your privacy. Our Privacy Policy is available online at www.ReaderService.com or upon request from the Harlequin Reader Service.

We make a portion of our mailing list available to reputable third parties that offer products we believe may interest you. If you prefer that we not exchange your name with third parties, or if you wish to clarify or modify your communication preferences, please visit us at www.ReaderService.com/consumerschoice or write to us at Harlequin Reader Service Preference Service, P.O. Box 9062, Buffalo, NY 14269. Include your complete name and address.

ROM13R

BRENDA NOVAK

32993	INSIDE	___ $7.99 U.S.	___ $9.99 CAN.
32904	WATCH ME	___ $7.99 U.S.	___ $9.99 CAN.
32902	DEAD RIGHT	___ $7.99 U.S.	___ $9.99 CAN.
32886	DEAD GIVEAWAY	___ $7.99 U.S.	___ $9.99 CAN.
32831	KILLER HEAT	___ $7.99 U.S.	___ $9.99 CAN.
32803	BODY HEAT	___ $7.99 U.S.	___ $9.99 CAN.
32725	THE PERFECT MURDER	___ $7.99 U.S.	___ $8.99 CAN.
32724	THE PERFECT LIAR	___ $7.99 U.S.	___ $8.99 CAN.
32667	THE PERFECT COUPLE	___ $7.99 U.S.	___ $8.99 CAN.
31545	HOME TO WHISKEY CREEK	___ $7.99 U.S.	___ $8.99 CAN.
31423	WHEN SUMMER COMES	___ $7.99 U.S.	___ $9.99 CAN.
31351	WHEN LIGHTNING STRIKES	___ $7.99 U.S.	___ $9.99 CAN.
28858	DEAD SILENCE	___ $7.99 U.S.	___ $9.99 CAN.

(limited quantities available)

TOTAL AMOUNT	$ _____
POSTAGE & HANDLING	$ _____
($1.00 for 1 book, 50¢ for each additional)	
APPLICABLE TAXES*	$ _____
TOTAL PAYABLE	$ _____

(check or money order—please do not send cash)

To order, complete this form and send it, along with a check or money order for the total above, payable to Harlequin MIRA, to: **In the U.S.:** 3010 Walden Avenue, P.O. Box 9077, Buffalo, NY 14269-9077; **In Canada:** P.O. Box 636, Fort Erie, Ontario, L2A 5X3.

Name: _____

Address: _____ City: _____

State/Prov.: _____ Zip/Postal Code: _____

Account Number (if applicable): _____

075 CSAS

*New York residents remit applicable sales taxes.
*Canadian residents remit applicable GST and provincial taxes.

HARLEQUIN® MIRA®
www.Harlequin.com

MBN1113BL